BLUEGRASS BACHELORS

THREE-IN-ONE COLLECTION

D0107626

JENNIFER JOHNSON

BARBOUR
PUBLISHING

Published by Barbour Publishing, Inc., P.O. Box 719, Uhrichsville, Ohio 44683, www.barbourbooks.com

Our mission is to publish and distribute inspirational products offering exceptional value and biblical encouragement to the masses.

ecpa Member of the
Evangelical Christian
Publishers Association

Printed in the United States of America.

Dear Readers,

Welcome to the Bluegrass state, y'all! Grab yourself a glass of sweet tea, settle back in a comfy rocking chair, and kick off your shoes. Let them tootsies breathe. You're in for a real treat as you join me on an adventure through my beloved state.

Have you ever been to Kentucky? It's been my home for over thirty years. Met my husband here. Raised all three of my girls here. It's blessed land. Truly. Rolling hills of green. Gorgeous lakes and ponds. Fish and deer a'plenty. Farmhouses alongside rows of corn and tobacco. Cattle grazing in fields. Thoroughbreds racing through pastures. You can't step into the Bluegrass state and not come to the realization there is Someone far greater than us who created this beautiful land.

You may not know this, but Kentucky is also the birthplace of Abraham Lincoln—President of the Union—and Jefferson Davis—President of the Confederacy. They were born only a year and less than a hundred miles apart. The Hatfields and McCoys also found their roots here. Hmm. . .our state motto is "united we stand, divided we fall."

Which brings me to the book, *Bluegrass Bachelors*. A bit of dissension might run through our state's bones, but in the end we stand together. We're loyal. We're true. We love completely, which is what you'll see in the heroes of these stories. They were friends, practically brothers since birth. But they thrived on competition. So they made a bet. A bet that would prove quite challenging to win, and each of them would find he wasn't sure he wanted to come out the victor.

God is so good!
Jennifer Johnson

MAID TO LOVE

Dedication

This book is dedicated to my best friend in the whole wide world, Robin Ratliff. . . . Well, my honey is also my best friend, but Robin is my best girlfriend. Robin is a friend who holds me accountable even when I don't want her to. She encourages me in everything and always has my back. Nobody can even think about talking bad about Jennifer when Robin's around. She's a wonderful Christian woman. Her friendship is more precious than gems or gold. I love ya, Robin!

Prologue

Look at Bobby. Only twenty-two like me and standing at the altar. The man is plumb whipped. Whipped like a boy who's brought a garter snake in the house to scare his little sister."

Nick Martin grinned at one of his best friends in the world, Drew Wilson. He knew by the slow smile that formed on Drew's face he was remembering the time he and Nick had scared Drew's little sister, Addy, nearly half to death with a good-sized snake when they were in middle school. She'd run home and tattled, and the both of them received some consequence for their prank.

Drew's smile dropped to a scowl. "Henpecked is what Bobby is. Just two years older than me and already linked to a ball and chain."

"I sure don't want no part in it," Nick's youngest friend, Wyatt Spencer, added.

"Me neither," said Mike McCauley.

Nick huffed at the two younger friends. Mike and Wyatt were fresh out of high school. Of course, they didn't want any girls tying them down. Having bought a good chunk of land from his dad, Nick had been out on his own for four years now. Four hundred acres and a herd of cattle was a lot to handle at times. Still, the last thing he wanted was a wife, whining and nagging at him to do this and help her with that.

Drew turned toward them. "Let's form a pact."

Nick scrunched his nose. "A pact?"

"No wives."

Mike furrowed his brows. "What do you mean, no wives?"

Drew scratched his jaw. "No. Not a pact. Let's make a bet. Let's see who can wait the longest to get married. The loser has to. . ." He bit his bottom lip, obviously trying to figure out what to wager.

"I'm not betting money," said Wyatt. "I don't mind a bit of competition, but I'm not aiming to gamble."

Drew scowled. "I wouldn't gamble either, and you know it."

"How 'bout farmwork," Nick said. "The loser has to do the winners' chores every Saturday. . ."

"But I don't have a farm," Wyatt interrupted. "When I win, what will y'all do for me?"

"When you win?" Mike chuckled. "Wyatt Spencer, you ain't gonna win. You're as crazy over girls as my rooster is over his hens."

Nick snapped his fingers. "I got it. There can only be one winner. Whoever is the last to get married is the winner, right? Well, the three losers"—Nick pointed to each of his friends—"has to help plan and pay for the winner's wedding when he finally does decide to settle down."

Drew scrunched his nose. "Ugh. Who wants to do that?"

"That sounds awful," Wyatt added.

Mike frowned. "I wouldn't even know what to do. I don't want to pay for no silly wedding."

Nick grinned as he folded his arms across his chest and leaned against the chair. "Exactly why it's the perfect wager."

The guys seemed to think for a moment until Wyatt extended his hand. "I'm in."

Placing his hand on top of Wyatt's, Mike added, "Me, too."

Drew chuckled as he smacked his hand on top. "When I beat you all, I'm going to make you wear pink shirts."

Nick narrowed his eyes as he placed his hand on Drew's. "We'll see about that." Nick pushed the guys' hands down. "Deal?"

"Deal!" His friends responded in unison as they lifted their hands in the air.

Drew smirked. "Come on, guys. You know I always win."

Nick grunted but didn't respond. Drew had a knack for winning at absolutely everything the four of them competed at. But not this. Nick would be the last of them to get hitched. No matter what.

Chapter 1

Addy Wilson tore at the envelope like a child ripping open a birthday present. Her heart pounded in her chest. She'd been on three interviews—one rejection straight out, one rejection after a second interview. . .and this was her third job opportunity. The one she'd wanted the most.

She pressed the letter against her chest, closed her eyes, and envisioned her office at Dynamic Designs Unlimited in Lexington, Kentucky. She'd paint the walls a deep sage, accenting with cream and taupe. Of course, she'd have to add a splash of raspberry, as it was her favorite color, but only a splash, so as not to dissuade any male clients who might not care for the pinkish-purple color.

Inhaling a deep breath, she could already smell the light lavender-scented candle she'd warm in the office. Lavender, a fragrance she'd learned aids the mind in concentration. *God, I can hardly wait to get started. Please, let this letter be a yes. I'm going crazy working at the food court.*

The minimum-wage job had been perfect through college. Flexible hours. Flexible manager. Fairly easy, mindless work. Take orders. Fill soft drinks. Take money. Pass tray. Easy enough. Since she'd graduated five months ago in mid-December, Addy thought she would lose her mind if she didn't find a position doing her heart's desire.

Pulling the folded letter away from her chest, she exhaled a long breath. Her nerves tingled with the possibility of an acceptance letter. Her heart pounded with the fear of rejection. She'd never been so wrapped up in the want, the yearning as she was for this position. Even the stinging words of her ex-boyfriend, Trevor, when he dumped her two weeks ago hadn't incited such emotion. *I really want this job.*

Procrastinating no further, she unfolded the letter.

Dear Ms. Wilson,
  It is with great regret that I inform you. . .

"No." She shook her head as the words blurred beneath her tear-filled eyes. Her shoulders slumped as she fell backward onto the couch. "No."

She looked around her already furnished apartment, the only one she could afford. The drab colors always threatened to wrap themselves around her and strangle the very breath from her body, but now they seemed to swirl together in a jumbled frenzy, suffocating her while making her long to throw up. Her friend and roommate, Val, would be home soon. She would speak words of encouragement to Addy. Words she didn't want to hear.

After forcing herself to stand, she sulked her way to the bathroom and undressed. She turned on the shower as hot as she could stand it and stood beneath the pelting water. *God, I wanted that job so badly. I had such confidence, such peace about the interview. I thought for sure. . .*

It seemed as if only moments had passed when the water started to turn cold. Addy stepped out of the shower and wrapped herself in the oversize, fuzzy, hot pink robe her grandmother had bought her for Christmas. Normally she relished the soft fabric, nestling herself into it. Today she tightened the belt, padded to her bedroom, then slipped under the covers of her bed. She wanted Val to think she was asleep when she arrived home.

Renewed tears welled in her eyes as self-pity rose in her chest. Trevor's rejection of her after five months of dating tore afresh at her heart. Three job opportunities. Three rejections. She'd graduated top of her class in interior design. Sure, she'd had to take six weeks off from job searching when she had her appendix removed, but something else must be wrong with her. She began to doubt her interviewing ability, or maybe it was the clothing she chose to wear, or maybe they didn't like her designs. She'd always believed she had an eye for design, that she could feel and find the right materials to enhance any space, but possibly she was wrong.

One doubt rippled into another until her mind and tears were spent. She glanced at the clock on her nightstand. To her relief, Val was over an hour late getting home. Addy's stomach ached from having skipped lunch, and now it was well past dinner. *I might as well get up and grab a bite to eat.*

She pushed off the covers and sat up. Her cell phone sprang to life, dancing and singing "How Great Is Our God" from the dresser. Addy grabbed it and read the screen. It was her mom. Could she handle talking to her without breaking down? For a moment, she contemplated ignoring the rings, but she couldn't stand it. Pushing the TALK button, she said, "Hey, Mom."

"Addy, I'm so glad you answered. We need your help."

Addy's eyebrows furrowed at the urgent sound in her mother's voice. She hoped everything was all right, that no one had been hurt or… "What's wrong?"

"It's your aunt Becky."

Addy thought of her sixty-year-old aunt who'd moved in with Addy's parents when the woman's husband passed away two years ago. The gray-haired, fun-loving aunt had been a tremendous help and encouragement to her mom. "What about Aunt Becky?"

"She fell off the front porch. Accidentally stepped on one of the cats' tails, and when the thing screamed, it scared poor Becky to death, and she fell and broke her wrist."

"Mom, that's awful. I'm so sorry. Is she in a lot of pain?"

"The medicine is helping with that, but she has to have surgery tomorrow morning, and she won't be able to do anything with her wrist for six weeks minimum."

"Ugh." Addy shook her head. "That will be tough. I know Aunt Becky doesn't like to be tied down, but at least she's not working…."

"Well, that's what I want to talk to you about."

Addy scrunched her nose. "What?"

"Actually, your aunt does have a few jobs. She cleans houses. You already knew she cleaned Nick's house."

The mention of Nick Martin's name sent a shot of disdain through Addy's veins.

Her mom continued. "She's also cleaning for the Morgans and the Watkinses, and she doesn't want to give them up, plus she helps me and your daddy around the house so much."

A sinking feeling pushed down on Addy's stomach. "What are you asking me, Mom?"

"Would you consider coming home for a while…taking over Becky's jobs?"

"Mom—"

"Come on, Addy." Her mom's words sped up. "You haven't gotten an interior design job yet. You hate the food court, and we all miss you. It would be such a help. You could still look for a job from here in River Run. We're not that far from the city."

"Mom, I can't just leave Val without a roommate. We share the rent, and even though I hate my job, I'd have to give notice."

"Maybe not. You said they'd just hired three more girls and were trying to take some of your hours."

"What about Val?" Not to mention the fact that Addy didn't want to move back in with her parents, and she particularly didn't want to clean Nick Martin's house ever again.

"Your aunt's calling for me. Please pray about it. I'll call you back in a bit."

Before Addy could respond, her mom disconnected. *Isn't that just wonderful. I didn't get my job. I don't have a boyfriend. And now Mom wants me to move back in with her—oh, AND clean a bunch of houses for my aunt, including Nick Martin's house.* She looked up at the ceiling. "God, is this some kind of sick joke?"

The door opened. Addy walked into the living area. Now she was ready to talk with Val. Her friend's somber expression stopped Addy. "What's wrong, Val?"

"I don't know how you're going to feel about this."

Addy furrowed her brows. She didn't think she could handle any more bad news. "What?"

Val seemed to study the floor. "I've invited a girl I work with to come and live with us." She looked at Addy. "She's a new Christian who no longer wants to live with her boyfriend. She wants to live for the Lord, but she has nowhere to go, and something in my heart just told me to tell her she could move in. We'll just have to figure out the room arrangements. It will be crowded, but I know it will be fine. . . ."

Addy fell onto the couch. Her stomach seemed to sense its opportunity to add to the commotion of her heart and mind, as it growled loudly. Ever since she had opened the mailbox and retrieved the letter, her entire world had turned upside down. *God, this has got to be some warped dream that I'll soon wake up from.*

⁂

I cannot believe I am lugging this stuff into my old bedroom. Addy released the handle of the suitcase and allowed the overweighted container to fall over with a thud. Sighing, she flopped onto her bed. The mattress squeaked in protest, as it did every time she visited when she was in from college and all the while she had it through high school. She scrunched her nose at the inevitable loss of sleep she'd endure over the next few months. *I should have told Mom I wouldn't come back without them buying me a new mattress. You never know, she might have gone for it.*

She stared up at the stucco ceiling. "Just a few months," she whispered. "I can make it that long." Reality weighed on her as she realized her time at home was indefinite. Val had tried to hide her thrill when Addy shared that her mom wanted her to move back to River Run. In her heart, Addy knew Val wasn't trying to get rid of her as a roommate; Val was just excited to help out the girl from work. And yet Addy couldn't quite lick the feelings of betrayal that hovered over her that her college friend would be willing to let Addy move out so easily. *And so quickly.* Addy huffed, lifted herself to a sitting position, then crossed her arms in front of her chest. "Val was even eager to help me pack."

Trying to clear her thoughts of the pity party that was forming in her mind, Addy gazed around the room she'd spent the first eighteen years of her life growing up in. The walls were the same light purple that she'd painted them at the age of fourteen. A dead corsage still hung behind a picture of her double date with the high school's basketball star and her best friend, Gracie, and her boyfriend for junior prom. The left side of her mouth twitched in merriment as she remembered spilling half of her soft drink in her date's lap. *He never asked me out again. Not that I cared. I was too wrapped up in my crush on. . .*

She shook the thought away and shifted her gaze to the dresser. She drank in her teddy bear knickknacks and the various movie ticket stubs that she'd taped to her mirror. Her gaze moved to the deep pink curtains then the bookshelf filled with furnishing and design magazines. Aside from the antique, hand-sewn wedding ring quilt her grandmother had made that still rested on her bed, Addy was fully appalled at her interior taste during her teen years. But she couldn't deny the nostalgia the room incited. *If I can find time, I'll make this room my first project.*

"Addy, when you get settled in, will you come down here so I can talk with you?" Aunt Becky's voice sounded from downstairs.

Addy stared at the oversize suitcase. She wasn't in the mood to tackle unpacking. Pushing herself off the bed, she called, "I'm coming now, Aunt Becky."

Addy made her way down the steps and into the family room. Her mother had a bit of a fetish for turtles and angels. An odd combination, Addy had to admit, and yet, porcelain, ceramic, wooden, stuffed, even plastic objects of the two nearly took over the family room. Her classmates from college would collapse in shock and despair if they saw her parents' house, but Addy couldn't deny a certain comfort, a kind of coming-homeness from the tacky decor.

Wishing she'd grabbed a pair of socks before traipsing across the wood floors, Addy scooped an angel afghan off her dad's oversize black leather recliner, sat on the couch, then wrapped the blanket around her cold feet. "So, whatcha need?"

Her aunt looked at her and smirked. "I'm glad I wasn't going to ask you to get me a drink or anything."

"Oh." Addy pushed the blanket off and started to stand.

Her aunt held out her hand to stop her. "I'm only teasing you. I wanted to go over my cleaning schedule with you."

Addy settled back onto the couch, holding back a tentative moan. She wasn't the biggest fan of cleaning. Sure, she liked things when they were clean, but the actual process. . . Yuck. And the thought of having to clean Nick's house again—it sent shivers up and down her spine. She had hardly laid eyes on the man since she was a senior in high school, and that had taken some pretty serious finagling on her part. Especially since the guy was one of her brother's best friends and had attended the same hometown church since her birth.

Grabbing a pad of paper and pen from the basket beside the couch, Addy looked at her aunt. Despite the gray hair, the woman looked quite young for her age. Few wrinkles. Bright blue eyes. Addy hoped she looked as fit as her aunt Becky when she was sixty. If it weren't for the cast on her right arm, there would be absolutely no reason for Addy to be here. But she was here, and since she was needed, she needed to stop daydreaming and focus. "Okay, Aunt Becky, hit me with the schedule."

Her aunt chuckled. "I don't want to hit you with it, but I'll be happy to tell you. But since you insist on my hitting you"—her aunt tossed a throw pillow in Addy's direction—"how's this?"

Addy ducked before the pillow could hit her then pursed her lips at her aunt's teasing. "You knew what I meant, Aunt Becky. If it weren't for your wrist, this would be war."

Addy leaned back into the couch as Becky cackled and waved her left hand. "That was fun, but on to the business at hand. I go to the Morgans on Mondays, but you need to know they have a dog that isn't partial to strangers. You'll have to take a stick of beef jerky with you the first time. After that, he'll be your best friend. Now, after I finish at their house on Mondays, I always go to the store for your mother. I'll still want to go, so I'll want you to pick me up after you finish at the Morgans'. I go to Nick Martin's house on Tuesdays. . . ."

The shivers returned. A wave of memories wrapped themselves around her as she remembered baking a batch of homemade chocolate chip cookies for the man. It had taken her numerous tries to get the recipe right. He'd eaten them up, but without a single word of thanks.

She'd starting cleaning for Nick when she was fourteen. By the time she was sixteen, she'd fallen head over heels in love with the then twenty-one-year-old. What teenage girl wouldn't have? He was tall, dark, handsome. . . He was strong and independent, had already bought his family's farmhouse and land when his dad retired. Nick was even a Christian. Addy had begged God to allow him to notice her, but he barely paid any attention at all.

Until she fixed up his living room. Addy's cheeks burned with the embarrassing memory of his response. He'd thrown a fit, scolding her like a child. She bit back a giggle that threatened to surface. *I suppose I probably should have asked before I decided to paint an accent wall in baby blue.*

"Addy, are you listening?"

She shook away the remembrance and focused on her aunt. "Sorry, Aunt Becky. I missed the last part."

"I said I fix lunch for Nick every Tuesday. I usually eat with him, and you can if you want, but you don't have to. I haven't told him that you'll be coming in my place. Well, of course he knows about my wrist, and he knows I've taken care of getting someone over there, but I haven't gotten in touch with him to tell him it will be you. I'm sure he won't mind. . . ."

Addy bit the inside of her lip. *Why, God? Why does today have to be a Monday? I don't want to go to Nick's tomorrow.*

❦

Nick wiped his hands on his pants. The morning had gone well. He'd checked every task off his mental to-do list, with the last being to hammer a couple pieces of wood to a broken part of the fence at the far east end of his property. The sun, warmer than usual for May, seemed to smile down on his work. After several days of rain and muck, although he praised God for the rain and muck, the kiss of sunshine to his cheeks felt just right.

Making his way to the house, he noted a different car in the driveway. It was a newer, smaller car than the one Becky drove. He smacked his lips. "I forgot Becky wouldn't be coming today. I don't even know who's in my house."

Uneasiness crept up his spine as he lengthened his stride. He knew Becky wouldn't let just any ol' gal clean his home, but a guy had a right to know who the person was. The car looked familiar. He knew that much, but he couldn't quite place in his mind whose it was.

Aggravation welled within his gut. Becky should have called him. He didn't appreciate this. He knew he'd been busy, and he'd been spending a lot of time on the farm. And he knew that he didn't get cell phone service in a lot of places. Besides the fact he forgot to carry his cell phone most of the time. And he knew he needed to purchase an answering machine as his dad had suggested numerous times, but he just hadn't gotten around to it. None of that mattered. He still didn't like some stranger being in his house.

"There better not be a single thing out of order," Nick growled as he stepped onto the front porch, "and nothing better be missing."

He swung open the front door. A slight, blond-haired figure jumped nearly a foot off the ground when it slammed back against the jamb. She turned around, and Nick thought he'd swallow his tongue.

"Nick Martin!"

The woman had no trouble finding hers, as she placed a hand against her chest. Nick brushed his tongue against the top of his mouth to ensure it was still there. Satisfied, he swallowed the knot in his throat.

Long blond hair fell in waves across and down her shoulders. A white T-shirt and blue jean shorts, though modest enough, couldn't hide how the teen he knew had become a woman. He looked into her deep green eyes. Green as the grass in spring. He'd never realized they were green. She had full pink lips and a slight cleft in her chin. Had she always had that? "Drew Wilson's kid sister?"

The woman sighed. She bit the bottom of her lip. Something he'd seen a younger version do so many times before.

He stepped toward her. She was a sight for sore eyes—gorgeous, beautiful, a vision. The kid was gone, morphed from her caterpillar shell to an amazing butterfly. "Addy?"

"Yes, Nick, it's Addy."

A most primal urge to grab her in his arms washed over him, surprising him, making him take a step back. For a moment, softness etched Addy's features, and he thought maybe she would flirt with him as she had years before. Unlike when she was a kid, the idea sounded good, and Nick determined to take a step toward her.

Her features hardened, and she pointed toward the kitchen. "I made you a turkey sandwich. I put lettuce and tomato on it. Toasted the bread. I didn't put the mustard on it, in case you don't eat it that way anymore."

In two shakes of a sheep's tail, she scooped the cash he'd left to pay for the cleaning off the cabinet. "See ya later." Then she was gone.

Stunned, Nick walked toward the kitchen window and watched as the woman made her way to her car. Her hair shone and blew like mature wheat in the breeze. She slipped into her car then looked back at the house.

Her gaze met his. His chest seemed to be celebrating the Fourth of July when he caught a glimpse of a slight blush as she turned away, started her car, and pulled out of the drive.

That was not the Addy Wilson he knew.

The Addy Wilson he knew was skinny and freckly and just a kid. She was helpful and good at cleaning but a bit annoying and immature. And the crush. Nick rolled his eyes and puffed out a long breath just thinking about it. A man could get worn to death from the girl's incessant flirting. If it hadn't been for his love for God and for her family, Nick would have let the girl know in no uncertain terms just how annoying and aggravating she was.

He remembered the last time he'd seen her. The girl had actually painted a wall in his living room a baby blue color. Called it an accent wall. The only blue he ever wanted to see was the color of the University of Kentucky Wildcats shooting hoops through his television, but definitely not on his walls. He'd lit into her like a flame to charcoal. And she'd deserved it. He'd felt a bit bad for letting her have it so much that she'd left blubbering and sniffling, but the girl needed to leave his stuff alone, to leave him alone.

He looked back at the dust clouds from the car's disappearance down the dirt road. And she had.

Chapter 2

Addy looked at herself in the restaurant's ladies' room mirror. She could not stop thinking about Nick Martin. The years had been good to him. He still had the darkest hair she'd ever seen, rivaling only the deep, mysterious color of his eyes. Still tall and muscular, he seemed to have grown in girth in all the places he should. Strong arms and shoulders. Even his jaw set in strength and authority.

He'd barreled into the house, ready to fight whoever had trespassed on his property. A thrill raced up her spine as she remembered the look of shock then interest that draped his face when he saw her.

"Drew Wilson's kid sister?" Nick's question replayed itself in her mind. She would always and forever be Drew Wilson's kid sister. The little blond, ponytailed, freckly twig that she'd always been. The comment grated on her nerves. She'd tired years ago of chasing after Nick Martin.

After pulling a tube of peach lipstick from her purse, she painted her lips then smacked them together. "What do I care what he thinks?"

She tossed the tube back in her purse, pushing the desire for Nick's approval as far from her mind as she could. She walked out of the restroom and looked around the restaurant.

The Family Diner hadn't changed much since she was a girl. It still sported booths along the walls, tables in the center. Country crafts, most of them made by the church's senior ladies' group, hung and sat in every nook and cranny. The scent of country cooking overwhelmed her senses, making her stomach growl. The place felt like home, and much to her surprise, she was glad to be here.

Her phone vibrated, and Addy pulled it out of her pocket and answered it. "Hey, Gracie, where are you?"

"Looking at you."

Addy looked toward the front door and saw the best friend a girl could ever have waving at her. She raced toward her and wrapped her arms around her. "I'm so glad to see you. I've already got a booth. I just had to run to the girls' room."

18

The two walked to the booth, sat down, then clasped hands across the table. "I've been dying to talk to you," Gracie said.

"Me, too. This summer will be wonderful. We'll hang out, go to the movies. . .of course, whenever you can." Addy winked. "Now that you're a married woman."

It still seemed impossible to Addy that her best friend since birth was married. And married to Wyatt Spencer, one of the goofiest guys in their graduating class. Not that he wasn't a wonderful man now. Owner of River Run's hardware store. Hardworking. Doted over Gracie. Addy was truly happy for her friend. It just seemed so surreal. When they were teens, she'd never have pictured Gracie with Wyatt. Not in a million years. And she still couldn't imagine her friend married.

The fact that Addy missed the wedding because she was in the hospital having an emergency appendectomy made the marriage even more unbelievable. Addy was happy for her friend, but when she looked at Gracie, she thought of letterman jackets and pom-poms, pizza and bubble gum. Not marriage and—

"Addy, I'm pregnant."

Babies. Addy's jaw dropped. "You're—"

"Pregnant."

Addy could tell Gracie could barely keep her squeals at bay. It was obvious she wanted Addy to be happy for her. "But you've only been married—"

"Three months." She clasped her hands together. "Wyatt and I decided to let God choose when our babies would come." She touched her cheek. "We never expected it would be this soon."

The waitress took their drink orders, giving Addy time to digest the information. *Gracie is having a baby.* It seemed impossible. They were only twenty-three, which Addy knew wasn't too young, but still they were— Addy's thoughts jumped. *My best friend is married and having a baby, and I don't even have a boyfriend.*

Nick Martin flooded her mind, and Addy pushed the thought away. *Why didn't I think of Trevor? We were dating just last month.* She shook her head. She didn't want to think of him either. They'd dated just over five months, but she'd been only minimally upset with the breakup, only when she dwelt on it and the rejection. That was proof enough that her feelings for Trevor didn't run deep.

Gracie's married and having a baby, and I don't even have a job. Self-pity wended itself back into her mind. *God, help me not to do this. I know You have a plan for me. . .plans to give me hope and a future. Help me be happy for Gracie. To not focus on myself.*

"Aren't you happy for me?"

Addy snapped from her thoughts and looked across the booth at her friend's sad expression. She reached over and squeezed Gracie's hand. "Of course I'm happy for you. You're going to have the most precious little bundle this town has ever seen. And I'm going to give you the most fabulous baby shower. Oh—" Addy perked up. "And I'm going to decorate your nursery for free."

Gracie clapped. "That's a great idea. I know it will be wonderful. I can hardly wait. But there's more I want to talk to you about."

Addy smiled when Gracie asked her to help lead music for the church's annual vacation Bible school. With trying to complete school and then find a job, it had been almost a year since she'd visited her hometown church. She missed the people so much. She thought of sweet Mr. Bartlett, ninety-plus years old. He'd always had peppermints stashed in his pockets to pass out to the children. Though he could hardly see or hear, he told her he could recognize her anywhere because of her laugh. She focused on her friend again. "Of course I'd love to help."

Gracie laughed. "Remember the year the theme was about the ocean?"

Addy bobbed her head and pushed her arms one after the other in front of her, pretending to swim, then grabbed her nose with one hand, lifted the other, and pretended to sink down into the seat. She giggled once she'd finished. "How could I forget?"

"Hey, girls. Am I interrupting something?"

Addy looked up into the blue-green eyes of Mike McCauley. Having practically played in the playpen with him, he'd been almost as good a longtime friend as Gracie. In high school he'd grown closer to Addy's brother and Nick. By the time they graduated, the family teased that Nick, Drew, and Mike were the three musketeers or the three stooges, depending on who was talking. Despite moving away to go to college, Addy had heard Wyatt had joined their group of friends as well.

"Mike!" Addy jumped out of the booth and wrapped her arms around him. He smelled so good, like a mixture of nature and rugged cologne. He was as strong as a mule, though not quite as big as her brother and definitely not built like Nick; he was quick with a smile, and his hugs were honest and tight. Addy felt like she'd come home with his arms wrapped around her.

He squeezed her once more then lifted her off her feet. She squealed until he set her back down and released her. "It seems like forever since I've seen you."

Addy frowned. "I know."

"I hear you're back for the summer anyway."

"Yep." She smacked at the top of his ball cap, and he poked her in the ribs. Addy laughed. This definitely felt like home. Teasing with Mike and eating a burger in the diner with Gracie.

"Mike, are we going to sit down or not?"

Addy jumped at the familiar voice. She flinched as Nick walked up, scowling at both of them. His reprimand six years before resurfaced, and Addy found herself wanting to hide beneath the booth like a misbehaving pup. Shaking the thought away, she grabbed Mike in one more hug. "See ya soon."

Without a glance toward Nick, she slid back into the booth. Gracie furrowed her eyebrows as she looked from Nick back to Addy. "What's eating Nick?"

Addy shrugged. "I don't know."

But she did know. *It's me. Something about me rubs Nick Martin the wrong way.*

⸎

Nick growled as he sat at the table. Why did Addy have to be in a booth directly in his line of sight and sitting on the side that faced him? For that matter, why did she have to be here to begin with?

He hadn't stopped thinking about Addy Wilson since the moment she left his house three days ago. She haunted his nights and traipsed the farm with him in his mind through the days. Each time he walked into the kitchen, he saw her handing him a plate of cookies as she had years ago. This time she wasn't the teen but the beautiful woman she'd morphed into. When he walked into the mudroom, he remembered her slipping on her boots. When he walked toward the barn, he saw her petting his horses. When he walked toward the fence, he saw her sitting atop it. No matter what he did or where he went, he saw her.

He grabbed the menu and opened it, attempting to read what the restaurant offered.

"You want your usual?"

Nick looked up to see Lacy Abrams making goo-goo eyes at Mike. Nick smirked. Leaning forward, he placed his elbow on the table then scratched his scruffy chin. "Yeah, Mike. You want the usual?"

Mike's ears blazed red. Nick knew the younger man had a crush on the waitress. The gal would say yes to a date quicker than hay catches fire if only Mike would ask her. With a piercing stare, Nick dared him to ask her.

Mike cleared his throat and nodded without so much as looking up at Lacy.

Nick shrugged as he yanked the menu out of Mike's hand then handed his and Mike's up to Lacy. "I suppose we'll both have the usual."

Lacy glared at Nick. It was obvious she didn't like him. Not that Nick cared so much. Sure, he wanted to be a Christian witness, but if people didn't like him when he was just being himself—well, what could he do about that?

Mike crossed his arms and leaned back in the chair. "What's the matter with you?"

Nick cocked one eyebrow. "Nothing." The aggravation he felt at Addy's return to town bubbled up inside him. Needing something else to think about, he stared at his young friend and smirked. "Something wrong with you? You about to lose a bet?" He nodded toward Lacy.

"That bet is just about the stupidest thing we've ever done. Look at Wyatt. He and Gracie are as happy as can be. The bet sounded fine five years ago, but don't you think it's getting a little old now? Wouldn't it be nice to have someone to care for, someone who cared for us?"

Nick huffed, crossed his arms in front of his chest, and leaned back in the chair. He nodded his head slowly. "If you want to lose the bet, go ahead. No sweat off my back. I'll call Lacy over here for you." He lifted his hand and waved the waitress back.

Lacy made her way back to them and smiled down at Mike. "You need something?"

Mike glared at Nick. "No, Lacy. I'm sorry. We don't."

Nick chuckled when the woman's shoulders dropped and she walked away dejected. It would just be a matter of time before Mike couldn't stand it anymore and asked the woman out. He'd be the second to lose the no-women bet they'd made five years before.

The day they'd witnessed Bobby Fields succumb to the death of his bachelorhood, Nick, Drew, Mike, and Wyatt had vowed not to marry, to not even date. Bobby was tied down with a wife and two babies. The man worked his fingers to the bone on his farm and never had time to do anything he wanted to do. But the bet had been five years ago, and Wyatt had already given in. It was obvious Mike was getting a bit tired of it. It made no matter; Mike would end up losing, just like always.

Now, Drew. That man would be a hard one to beat. He was a natural competitor, winning more bets than losing. He remembered how Drew had beat him at horseshoes the week before, shot the larger buck last fall, even raised the biggest Angus steer last summer. But Nick was determined to come out on top this year with his prize Angus. Neither Drew nor Mike had an animal as nice as his, and Nick would relish the victory.

"I've said it once. I'm going to say it again. What is the matter with you, Nick?"

Nick snapped from his thoughts and looked at his friend. Mike's hardened expression was proof that Nick had nudged a nerve. Feeling defensive, he frowned. "Nothing's wrong with me."

"Something is. You've always been a bit gruff, but today you've been mean to me and cruel to Lacy. And you seem to be enjoying it." Mike folded his hands together on top of the table. "That's not like you."

Nick chewed on Mike's words. He rubbed his face with his hand. He was being a jerk. Grumpier than usual. And he was being mean. But he was tired. He hadn't slept well, and he couldn't seem to clear his mind. *God, I don't want to be unkind to Mike and Lacy. I've got this pent-up anger or frustration or something ever since I saw Addy. I don't know what it is, why she bothers me so much.*

Before he could respond, Addy walked to their table. She pulled Mike's hat down over his eyes. "See ya later, friend." Without looking at or speaking to Nick, she walked out the door and down the street.

Nick felt as if he'd been punched in the gut. He squared his shoulders and lifted his chin. How dare she come over to their table!

Mike's eyebrows rose, and he grinned. "I think I see the problem."

"What?"

"You got a thing for Addy?"

Nick howled. "You think I have a thing for skinny, freckle-faced Addy!"

"She ain't so skinny or freckle-faced anymore."

Boy, didn't Nick know it. He couldn't stop thinking about it. Couldn't stop arguing with himself for thinking about it.

"Maybe you'll be the one to lose the bet first."

Mike's mocking tone sent shots of fire through Nick's veins. "No, Mike, I don't think so."

"I don't know. You seem a little jealous to me."

Nick fumed. "Jealous? We'll see who's jealous when my Angus steer stomps yours into the ground in the judge's eyes at the fair."

Mike shrugged. "I guess we'll just have to wait and see."

Nick's retort was on the tip of his tongue when Lacy stopped at their table with their lunches. Grabbing the ketchup bottle, he unscrewed the top and tried not to think about how adorable Addy looked when she pounded the bottom of her ketchup container.

Chapter 3

*B*less these résumés. May they end up in the right hands. Addy opened her eyes and pushed the envelopes into the mail slot. She'd applied for a position at every company she knew of that was within an hour of River Run. She didn't *have* to live in her hometown, didn't even plan on it. But she wanted to be close enough to her family that she could visit often.

If she landed a job with one of the companies she'd just sent résumés to, she would be able to commute. For a while anyway. Besides, she was ready to settle into a job. She was twenty-three, finished with school, and it was time. She thought of Gracie, married and preparing for the birth of a baby. *It's time, God. I want to be settled, at least in my occupation.*

As a girl, she'd envisioned herself married and working from home. Her old dream resurfaced in her mind. She'd wake up and fix a nice breakfast for Nick. In her dreams, it had always been Nick. He'd eat it up, mumbling about what a wonderful cook she was. Once finished, he'd take his plate to the sink then wrap his arms around her, sending shivers up and down her spine. He'd kiss her lips, murmuring about how beautiful she was. As he walked out the door to his day's work, she would clean up the kitchen then pull out her work. She'd be busy all morning, working on designs for her various customers.

Snapping from her reverie, she chuckled to herself as she walked to her car. *No one can claim I'm not a dreamer.* But now wasn't the time for dreaming. She started to the car. She'd agreed to redecorate the church's Sunday school rooms. The pastor loved her idea of a Noah's ark theme and set up a church-wide workday in three weeks. Now she just had to pick up Gracie, and the two of them would find the items she needed for the church; hopefully they'd find a few things for Gracie's nursery as well.

They were meeting Nick for lunch, which made Addy as nervous as a cat traipsing through a dog pound. But it had been set at the pastor's suggestion, since Nick was in charge of the workday, and Addy was in charge of the design. *At least Gracie will be with me.*

She pulled into her friend's driveway. Before Addy had a chance to call

Gracie to let her know she'd arrived, her friend opened the door and walked toward the car. She looked a little paler than usual, but she still attempted a weak smile as she slipped into the passenger's seat.

Addy frowned at her friend. "Not feeling too good today, huh?"

Gracie shook her head. She leaned back against the seat. "The doctor gave me some medicine for nausea. I'm hoping it will kick in soon."

Addy's heart beat so strong it nearly burst from her chest as she thought of meeting Nick alone for lunch, but she cared about her friend too much to ask her to go with her when she obviously felt so poorly. "You don't have to go, Gracie. If you need to stay home—"

"I'll be fine."

Addy placed her hand on her friend's hand. "You don't look like you'll be fine. You look like you need to stay home."

"I know." Gracie looked at Addy and let out a long sigh. "I've been cooped up in the house for a week. It just seemed to hit me all of a sudden. Smells make me sick. Sights make me sick. Movement makes me sick. But I'm so tired of being stuck at home. You know I'm a doer." She attempted a faint smile.

Addy chuckled as she thought of all the times Gracie had dragged her out of the house to go on one adventure after another. "Yes. I know you like to go, go, go."

"Then let me try to go with you. I took the medicine an hour ago. Surely it will kick in."

"Okay. We'll go nice and slow and easy."

Gracie smiled. "Thanks, Addy."

Though Addy had planned to drive to Lexington for more selection, she decided to stay closer to home. They were able to make it through a few stores, and Addy was surprised she'd found almost every template, color, and supply she needed for the church in her own hometown. They hadn't found much for the nursery, but with lunchtime approaching, Gracie's color was growing pale again.

"I don't think I can make it to lunch," Gracie said. She leaned her head back against the seat and closed her eyes.

"I know." Addy turned toward Gracie's street. "I was already heading to your house."

"I'm sorry." A tear trickled down Gracie's cheek. "I know you didn't want to meet Nick alone for lunch."

Addy pulled into the driveway, turned off the car, and turned toward her friend. She touched Gracie's arm. "Why are you crying? I'm a big girl. I can eat lunch with Nick."

Gracie huffed and smacked her hands against her lap. "I cry all the time. I'm a sick, emotional wreck."

Addy grinned as she leaned across the seat and hugged her friend. "Do you need me to help you inside the house?"

"No." She opened the car door. "I'm going to try to down some saltine crackers and lemon-lime soda." She snarled as her tone became more sarcastic. "It's become my favorite meal. If I can handle adding some chicken noodle soup, that will be a real treat."

"Before long, you'll feel better, and you'll eat everything in sight."

Gracie gagged. "The very idea makes my stomach turn."

Addy laughed.

Gracie turned toward her and grew somber. "I'll pray the meeting goes well."

Addy lifted one shoulder and swatted the air. "Piece of cake. Why wouldn't it?"

"Because you've had a crush on the man more years than you haven't."

Addy's heartbeat skipped as she forced a smile to her lips. "I'm past all that."

She waited until Gracie made it into the house before she pulled out of the driveway. *I am past all that, right, Lord?*

<hr />

Nick walked into the diner. He scanned the place to see if Lacy was working. She worked the lunch shift almost every day, but sometimes. . . He spied her and sucked in a breath as he made his way toward her. He cleared his throat. "Lacy, I need to talk to you."

She gave him a wary look. "Yeah?"

"I'm sorry for being so grumpy with you last week. Will you accept my apology?" He extended his hand. "Friends?"

Lacy grinned. She pushed her glasses higher on the bridge of her nose. Her blue eyes softened, and Nick inwardly admitted she was an attractive girl with a kind heart. She'd probably be good for Mike. "God's been workin' on you, huh?"

Nick shuffled his feet. He felt like a newly broken filly. "Yeah. I already apologized to Mike. I was just out of sorts the other day."

"Every dog has a few fleas. Even you, Nick Martin." She reached out and gave him a quick hug. "All's forgiven. You eating lunch?"

"Yeah. I'm meeting Addy Wilson and Gracie Spencer. We're going to talk about the workday scheduled at church—"

Lacy nodded toward a booth at the far side of the room. "Gracie's not here, but Addy is."

Nick turned around and saw Addy look quickly from him to her hands. She started to pick at one of her fingernails with such intensity that he felt she would draw blood. Even so, her long, blond hair hung in perfect waves down her shoulders. Her profile was too pretty for words. *Lord, when did Addy Wilson become so beautiful?*

She's always been beautiful.

"But now she's so grown-up," he murmured under his breath.

Lacy giggled, and Nick snapped from his thoughts. He felt heat climb up his neck when he saw Lacy's all-too-knowing expression. She nudged his arm with her elbow and winked. "Go on over there. I'll come get your orders in a minute."

Nick made his way to the booth and slid in across from Addy. Begging God to keep him from making a fool of himself, he cleared his throat as he clasped his hands together then rested them on the table. "Gracie couldn't make it?"

Addy shook her head. "She's not feeling well." Her gaze traveled around the room until she spotted Lacy. "If you want, Lacy could join us. I'm sure she'll get a lunch break sometime, and she'll be helping with the rooms as well."

Though he knew she tried to mask it, Nick heard the edge of jealousy in her voice. *She does still have a bit of a crush on me.* Confidence swelled within him, and he sat up straighter. "I think we'd be waiting for quite a while if we did that."

A memory of being a senior in high school, having just bought his first work truck, and making plans to get a loan to buy part of his dad's land filtered into his mind. Little Addy Wilson, probably no older than seventh grade, marched up to him one Sunday after church.

Her face was painted with far too much makeup, and she'd knotted her extralong blond hair in some weird fashion. She bit her bottom lip as her fingers played with the coat's zipper. "I'll come help you on your farm, Nick. Anytime you need."

"Don't worry 'bout it." He'd brushed her off, barely acknowledged her. He'd been too busy waiting for the pastor's oldest daughter to venture into the parking lot.

"This is what I want to do."

Nick snapped back to the present at Addy's authoritative tone. The woman before him had changed quite a bit since that day. He still couldn't quite come to grips with the memories he had of her as a little girl and teen and what he could see in her now as a woman.

Lacy came to their table and took their orders. While they waited for their meals, he listened as Addy described her vision. He liked it. When she showed him her drawings, all planned to the nth degree with measurements, supplies, and expected expenses written into them, Nick had to admit he was impressed.

"These are really good, Addy. Very detailed."

"You like them?"

The glimmer in her eye—the desire for his approval—tugged at his heart. "Very much."

Lacy arrived with their food, and Nick reached across the table and took Addy's hands in his as he said a quick blessing. His heartbeat quickened with the feel of her soft palms in his hands. It took all his energy to focus on the prayer. He looked up at her, noting the slightly red tint to her cheeks.

Purposely focusing on his food, he picked up his burger and took a bite. Swallowing it down, his mind played around with the Noah's ark theme she'd shown him. He wiped his mouth with the napkin. "You know what would be great to go with your idea?"

Addy cocked her head to one side. "What?"

"An ark for the playground. It could be like an open fort of sorts. The kids could pretend to be Noah. There could be a couple of slides coming off the sides of the ark. Maybe some monkey bars in the center."

Addy's eyes brightened. "You could do that?"

Nick shrugged. "I don't think it would be too much of a problem. It would just be a matter of getting the materials, and I could donate those."

Addy chuckled as she cupped her hands on her cheeks in obvious excitement. "I think it's a wonderful idea. I can just see the kids playing on it now. They'll have a blast."

Nick shoved another bite of hamburger in his mouth as he felt heat speed up his neck again. He was surprised at the pleasure he felt at her approval, and he definitely didn't want her to see it. The silly no-women bet seemed more ridiculous with each bite. Maybe it was one he'd be willing to lose.

⁂

Addy reflected on her lunch with Nick as she walked up Gracie's sidewalk. She wanted to make sure her friend was feeling better before she made her way back to the house. As a girl, she'd had such a strong crush on Nick because he was so good-looking—the epitome of the cowboy-riding-a-white-horse of her dreams. But she'd also admired his strong character and integrity. Today she'd seen a softer side to the man that drew her with a stronger force than she'd expected.

She'd listened, fully engrossed in the excitement of his tone and the glistening of his eyes. He could see the kids playing on his mental creation, and Addy found herself pulled into his anticipation. A smile tugged at her lips as she pushed the doorbell.

Gracie opened the door, not quite as pale as she'd been two hours ago. She motioned Addy inside. "How are you feeling?"

Gracie gave her a quick hug. "A little better actually. I was able to hold down some chicken noodle soup, and I took a nap."

"I'm glad." Addy looked around the room. "Do you need me to help you with anything?" She walked toward the kitchen, noting a sink full of dishes. She dropped her purse on the counter and started the water.

"You're not doing my dishes for me, Addy!" Gracie wailed and turned off the water.

"Yes, I am." She pointed to the breakfast nook. "You sit."

"Addy!"

"If I were pregnant and not feeling well, would you help me?"

With a look of defeat, Gracie nodded and sat down. "I suppose I would. So, how was lunch?"

Addy stared at the pile of dishes in the sink as her stomach knotted with thrill at the memory. "It was fine."

"Just fine?"

"Well, he was very supportive of my designs, even came up with an idea to make an ark for the playground." Addy rinsed a plate then slid it into the dishwasher. She knew Gracie wanted more information than that, but Addy couldn't quite get her mind wrapped around the renewed feelings she had for Nick.

"And?"

Addy shrugged. "And the workday is in three weeks. He's going to take care of the supplies we didn't find, and—"

"That's not what I mean, and you know it."

Addy stared at the dishes. She couldn't look at her friend. If she did, Gracie would see the confusion she was sure covered her face. She tried to sound nonchalant. "What do you mean then?"

"I mean—you used to keep me up nights talking about your wedding with Nick Martin. You had planned when you would have kids, how many, even what you'd name them."

Addy closed her eyes for a moment. She remembered planning two kids, a boy and a girl, Amanda Renee and Nicholas Bryan. Names taken from both of their families. She bit her bottom lip to keep from laughing at what a silly girl she'd been. She shook her head, still not able to look over at her friend, and mumbled, "That was years ago."

"True, but sometimes a girl has a hard time forgetting."

Addy shoved the last dish into the dishwasher. She needed to finish these dishes and head home. She needed time to think through the feelings she was having, to ask God to guide her heart and mind. *The problem isn't forgetting. It's the remembering.*

Chapter 4

Addy sat at the kitchen table blowing the steam away from her morning cup of coffee. It had been three weeks since her lunch with Nick. Aunt Becky's wrist seemed to be healing well. Only two more weeks and Becky wouldn't need Addy's help with the cleaning jobs. The time had passed quicker than she'd expected, and Addy found herself wanting to spend more time in her hometown. *I could stay for a while. It's not like I have a roommate waiting on me for rent money, and I still don't have a job.*

She sighed when she thought of the résumés she'd sent and messages she'd left with no response. She felt out of sorts, like a colossal lowlife living with her parents without a job at her age. She knew her parents enjoyed having her and that she'd been a huge help to Becky, but with her aunt's recovery time coming to an end, Addy wanted to know her independent life would soon begin.

She thought of the scripture she'd read that morning during her quiet time. She'd memorized the verse as a girl, but the reminder this morning had come at just the right time. She whispered, " 'Those who hope in the Lord will renew their strength. They will soar on wings like eagles; they will run and not grow weary, they will walk and not be faint.' "

She needed to cling to God and what He desired and not what she thought would be best for her. *God, I seek You daily. I long to always be in Your will. I trust You with my job search.*

She thought of Peter and how he was able to walk on water as long as he kept his eyes on Jesus; and the father who'd begged Jesus to heal his son, but when Jesus told him to believe, the man responded by asking Christ to help his unbelief. She bit her bottom lip and closed her eyes. *Help me trust You even when I get anxious and start not trusting You.*

She opened her eyes and looked at the kitchen clock. Her family would be awake in a matter of minutes. At already half past five in the morning, Addy was surprised her dad and Drew weren't already rummaging around in the kitchen. Val would be here in only a few hours as well. Addy looked forward to visiting with her past roommate, but she hated they'd be at the church for the workday the entire morning and most of the afternoon. But Val had insisted she would enjoy helping.

"You're up early, aren't you?"

Addy turned at the sound of her brother's voice. "Yep. You ready for the workday?"

Drew stretched his arms over his head then scratched his mop of blond hair. "I suppose I better be. It's all Nick's talked about for weeks."

Addy's insides warmed at the mention of Nick's name. Cleaning his house had been easier than she'd expected the last few weeks. She found herself learning more about the man he'd become, like that he was faithful to separate his laundry when he took off his clothes in the evening and that he kept the pantry stocked with bottled water and various cans of stew.

But what she loved the most that she'd learned was that either in the morning or the evening he spent time with the Lord. The proof was in the checkmarks on a read-the-Bible-in-a-year pamphlet that sat beside his worn Bible on the bedroom nightstand. Though tempted, she never read the notes he'd written around the checkmarks, but the knowledge that they were there encouraged Addy's attraction for the man.

"Addy?"

Realizing she'd ignored her brother's response, Addy blinked and looked at him. "I'm pretty excited myself. We have all the materials we need, and I think the kids will really love it."

"Mmm-hmm."

Addy felt her cheeks and ears warm as her brother cocked his head and studied her. She punched his arm. "What's that look for?"

He squinted at her. "You can't possibly still have a thing for Nick Martin."

"What?" She huffed and swatted the air. "I think I've grown quite past the years of crushes, thank you very much."

Drew scratched the stubble on his chin. "Hmm. That might be why Nick's been so fired up about this project." He looked her up and down. Addy wanted to punch him in the face when he squinted and scowled. "You know you're not the pipsqueak you used to be."

She needed to stay calm. Drew would know if she threw a fit. Anger had always been a telltale sign that he'd gotten her in the right spot. She rolled her eyes and purposely pushed down the thrill she felt that Drew thought Nick might have grown to have feelings for her. "Drew—"

"He better not be thinking of you like that, because I will pummel him if he thinks about hurting my sister. He may be my friend, but. . ."

Addy stared at her brother. Anger etched his face in the most Neanderthal form she'd ever seen. Like he had a say about who liked her and whom she liked. She'd spent her life having to listen to Drew try to tell her what to do. Since he was older and bigger and won at absolutely everything, she was always stuck doing whatever it was Drew wanted.

Feeling frustrated and aggravated and a need to just—just scream for her daddy to make Drew stop being such a bully, she punched him in the arm again. "Cut it out, Drew. You're being ridiculous. I'm going upstairs to get a shower."

Addy turned away from her brother and practically raced up the stairs. Drew had a way of making her feel like such a baby, and she hated it. Besides, the very idea that Nick Martin would start to have feelings for her wreaked havoc on her heart and mind. *God, I'm too old for all these silly teenage feelings and wonderings. Help me not to worry about Nick.* And yet, in the back of her mind, she couldn't help but hope he might be starting to care for her.

Nick was done with the foolishness. Today was the church's workday. As soon as they finished, they'd have a potluck dinner. At that time, he was going to ask Addy on a date. He'd pondered it and prayed about it. He was attracted to Addy for many reasons. She was pretty. She was kind. She was giving. And most importantly, she loved the Lord. She had everything he'd want in a woman, even if he'd never really thought about what he would want.

The only thing that's stopped me from asking her is that ridiculous bet. Though competitive to his core, Nick had decided he was willing to lose. If it meant having the opportunity to get to know Addy as a woman, he would happily be the second of the four to give in.

Having already taken most of the supplies to the church, he tossed a couple of twenty-four-packs of water bottles into the bed of his truck. He knew the ladies took care of the food and drinks, but a man could at least bring some water to help out. After checking once more to ensure he had everything he needed, Nick hopped into the truck and headed toward the church.

The morning was especially warm for early June, but the land seemed to bask in the sun's warmth. With his window down, Nick was able to drink in the fresh smell of late spring. After several days of rain in May, nature was in full bloom with hills covered with grass that waved in the breeze. Trees were adorned in their full foliage. Birds flew on and off the branches, singing their songs of praise. "A farmer can't help but look at all this and know You exist, Lord."

He passed over the creek they used to play in when they were all kids. Nick remembered how he and Drew used to run as fast as they could through the creek to get away from Addy. Now he'd run after her. It was funny how things changed.

After pulling into the church's parking lot, Nick searched the buildings for Addy. He wanted to show her the four- and five-year-olds' classroom.

"Hey man, you ready to work?"

Nick turned at the sound of Mike's voice. He shook hands with his friend. "Of course. Are you?"

He patted the hammer that hung from his belt. "Ready as I'll ever be. Drew was looking for you."

"Nick, we need to talk." Drew's voice sounded from his left.

"Sure thing." Nick looked at him. "What's up?"

"Do you have a thing for my sister?"

Nick gawked at his friend, who seemed quite agitated. He peeked at Mike, who'd puckered his lips and lifted his hands in surrender. Nick looked back at Drew and squinted. "What is that supposed to mean?"

"That means you better not be playing games with my sister." Drew crossed his arms in front of his chest. "We may be friends, but she's my sister, and I won't have you—"

Nick widened his stance, crossing his own arms in front of his chest. "Won't what?"

"Nick, Drew, I need your help for a minute." Addy waved to them from the top of the two-level parking lot.

Nick glared at Drew. "We'll talk about this later."

"Yes, we will," Drew said as he walked toward his sister.

Nick followed Drew, matching him stride for stride. *I don't know who Drew thinks he is, accusing me, acting like I'd do anything to hurt Addy.* The notion infuriated and hurt him. As long as they'd been friends, Drew should know Nick would never lead Addy on. He'd never encouraged her crush years ago.

Reaching her car, he and Drew carried the supplies she needed help with into the church. Nick hadn't even considered Drew not *approving* of him dating Addy. The very idea grated him. They'd been friends since they were knee-high. *Surely Drew thinks more of me. I'd never hurt anyone in his family.*

Drew's reaction, when he hadn't even told anyone he was interested in dating Addy, made him wonder what his parents would think. What her parents would think. Their moms had been best friends for more years than they'd been married to their dads. When he, Addy, and Drew were kids, they'd ventured to each other's houses for one get-together or another. In truth, he hadn't dreamed either family would be opposed.

Before Nick could say anything else, Drew marched back down to the lower parking lot, as Addy walked up beside him. "Thanks, Nick." She pointed to a tall, dark-haired girl he'd never seen before. "Nick, this is my roommate from college, Val."

He nodded and extended his hand. "Nice to meet you."

"Wow. You are awfully handsome."

"Val!" Addy swatted her friend's arm, and Nick noted a tinge of pink rising up her neck.

Her friend winked. "Just telling it like I see it."

Nick looked at Addy, wondering if the blush meant she'd told Val she thought Nick was good-looking or if she was just embarrassed her friend would say that. Admittedly Nick hoped it was the former. He grabbed Addy's arm and led her toward the four- and five-year-olds' room. "I need to show you something."

"Okay."

He opened the door and watched as Addy took in his handiwork.

She smiled. "It's already painted. Green on the bottom half. Blue on the top. Just as I wanted."

His heart swelled at the sound of approval in her voice. "I stayed after on Wednesday and painted it. I knew you wouldn't be able to start on the mural today with wet paint. I thought I'd give you a room to start in."

Addy wrapped her arms around him, and Nick felt his knees go weak. A sweet, soft scent from her hair rushed into his nostrils, making him lightheaded. She let him go, and he felt empty. He wanted to hold her longer. "Thanks so much, Nick." She grabbed her friend's hand. "Let's go get my paint."

⁂

Addy stepped away from the wall to inspect her design. A large ark rested in a grassy area. The ark's door was open, with pairs of animals exiting it. She'd drawn a pair of elephants, giraffes, monkeys, tigers, horses, and more. Several kinds of birds, including two doves, sat atop the ark. Noah and his wife stood in front of the ark, holding hands and smiling. The sun and a rainbow shone above them, and Addy still planned to stencil the scripture "I have set my rainbow in the clouds, and it will be the sign of the covenant between me and the earth" in the sky.

She turned toward Val. "So, what do you think?"

"It's amazing."

"More than amazing."

Addy twisted around at the sound of Gracie's voice. "Gracie." She wrapped her in a hug. "I didn't think you were going to be able to make it today."

"I didn't either."

Addy released her friend. Gracie's coloring was still pale, and deep bags hung beneath her eyes. She touched Gracie's hand, trying to believe the doctor's words that many women spend only the first trimester of pregnancy quite ill. "You didn't have to come."

Gracie smiled. "Yes, I did." She looked at Val. "It's nice to see you again, Val. I know Addy's glad you came."

"I'm glad to be here. Watching Addy create a mural has been a lot of fun."

Addy wiped her hands on an old towel. "You've been a lot of help." She turned back to Gracie. "But you don't need to make yourself any sicker."

"I'm going crazy sitting at home, alternating between hugging the toilet and racing to the wastebasket. I needed some sunshine and fellowship." She covered her nose and mouth with her hand. "But I don't think I'll last long with these paint fumes."

"We need a break anyway." Addy motioned for them to follow her out the door. "Let's go check to see how they're doing with the playground."

"Yeah. I think that's a great idea. Maybe that absolutely adorable Nick Martin will be down there." Val winked at Addy and Gracie.

Gracie frowned. "Addy's always liked Nick Martin. You shouldn't—"

Val patted Gracie's shoulder. "I know about her lifelong Nick Martin crush. I'm only teasing her."

Addy shushed her friends as she looked down the hall to ensure no one was listening to their conversation. "He is not *my* Nick Martin, and that crush ended several years ago."

"Mmm-hmm." Val nudged Gracie's arm. "Wait till you see the way he looks at her."

Gracie giggled. "Oh, I've seen it. And she keeps saying she doesn't still care for Nick, but I've known her all my life and—"

"I'm leaving you two." Addy walked down the hall and out the door. She admitted, only to herself, she did want to see Nick. She wanted to see his progress with the playground. She wanted to see him. And she wanted to believe what her friends said. That he wanted to see her, too.

God, what am I thinking? I'm just emotionally vulnerable right now. I'm graduated with no job prospects. Trevor and I broke up a little under two months ago. And I'm back at home, under my parents' roof, and I'm simply reverting to my teenage years. That's all this is, isn't it?

Addy sighed as she walked down the concrete stairs that led to the playground area. Val and Gracie laughed at something one of them said, and Addy hoped the twosome had decided to talk about something besides her and her love life. She stopped at the bottom of the steps and turned to wait for them.

A smile tugged at her lips as she drank in the side view of the sanctuary she'd grown up in. Resting at the top of a hill, the small brick building with its dark green roof still looked much the same as it did when she was a girl. However, since her childhood, the church had grown so much they'd had to add a Sunday school building and a fellowship hall. She loved the design, how the buildings seemed to walk down the left side of the sanctuary. The playground sat at the bottom of the hill, just outside the fellowship hall, a perfect setup for various activities involving food and games.

"Are you two coming?" Addy called up to her friends.

"I forgot my dishes in the car," Val responded. "Gracie and I are going to go get them then bring them down to the kitchen. You go ahead."

"Okay." Addy turned and walked around the building to the playground area. Nick and Mike held one of the slides against the ark while Drew bolted it into place. Within moments, the slide was attached, and Nick was thanking Drew and Mike for their help.

Her heartbeat quickened as he instructed them about how to connect additional pieces. The excitement in his tone at the near completion of his project warmed her heart. Who Nick was as a person hadn't changed in the years since she'd left River Run, but he'd matured and possibly softened a bit. And the knowledge of it attracted her to him more than ever before.

⁂

Nick couldn't stop taking peeks at Addy sitting on one of the picnic tables beside the playground. Every few moments she and her friends would lean back in laughter. Her eyes seem to sparkle when she smiled. Her whole face lit up, drew a fellow in, making him smile without meaning to.

She shooed a fly or bug of some kind away from her plate then picked up a brownie and bit into it. She nodded her approval and pulled off pieces for Val and Gracie. He couldn't hear her, but he watched as she shared her approval with Ms. Cooper, one of the oldest and dearest members of their church and the maker of the brownies. Ms. Cooper beamed with pride. Nick found himself even more drawn to Addy when she scooted over on the bench to make room for the woman to join them.

"You up for a game of cornhole?"

Nick turned at the sound of Drew's voice. Drew tossed the corn-filled beanbag in the air and caught it in his right hand. He hadn't mentioned their earlier discussion, and Nick wasn't sure how to broach the subject with his friend. The truth was, he didn't know what to say. He was attracted to Addy, and the truth of it surprised and confused him, and yet he couldn't stop thinking about her. He wanted to pursue a possible relationship. At least he thought he did. But what would happen if that didn't work out? *Who's to say she'd want to go out with me anyway? Maybe I need to think about this some more. With my head and not my eyeballs. Just 'cause she comes home looking prettier than a spring sunrise doesn't mean I need to go chasing after her.*

"Well?"

He looked at Drew. "Of course I wanna play."

"All right then. I'm gonna give you and Mike a break since I'm always whooping up on the two of ya. You and Mike against me and Joe."

Nick sucked in his breath and squinted at his friend. "If I remember right, Joe beat you at cornhole last week, even though he is only twelve years old. So, I don't think you taking Joe as a partner is going to make things easier for me and Mike."

Drew crossed his arms in front of his chest. "Fine. You take Joe, and I'll take Mike."

"You know, guys, I am standing right here. I don't like y'all talking about me like I'm not even here."

Nick turned. Mike was standing beside them, and Nick hadn't even noticed. Poor Mike. He was a great buddy, but he did tend to lose every single bet the three of them ever made, and he was the worst cornhole player of the bunch, including his little brother. When Wyatt hung out with them more, at least Mike had a constant companion to lose with, but now that Wyatt had Gracie to take care of—well, Mike did a great deal of losing.

Nick patted Mike's shoulder, keeping his gaze locked with Drew. "No way, Drew. You can't have Mike. He and I are going to show you how it's done."

Before Drew could respond, Nick and Mike walked toward the two game platforms. Each one had a six-inch hole nine inches from the elevated end—just enough room to fit the corn-filled beanbags. Because they loved to play the game so much, Nick's dad had built the game to the exact measurements—a two-foot-wide by four-foot-long piece of plywood made up each platform, elevated twelve inches at the far end and two inches at the near end. The platforms sat twenty-seven feet apart, exactly thirty-three feet from hole to hole. His mom had sewn the beanbags in patriotic colors, blue and white stars for one team, red and white stripes for the other.

Nick scooped up all eight bags in his hands. He handed the stripes to Drew and the stars to Mike. As Drew walked toward the pitcher's box, an area four feet by three feet, one on each side of the platform, Nick turned to Mike. "You wanna go first?"

Mike nodded. "Yeah, I should. You may have to make up for any I miss in the end."

"I'll try not to show you up too bad, big brother," Joe said.

Mike grabbed his little brother in a headlock and messed up his hair. Nick shook his head as he walked toward Drew at the other end. Mike was often too hard on himself. If Nick didn't know any better, he'd think Mike didn't like all the good-natured competitions he and Drew always came up with.

"You going against me?" Drew pointed to his chest.

Nick blew out a breath. "Of course."

Joe threw a bag first. It zipped straight through the hole. Three points. Mike threw a bag. It landed on top of the platform. One point.

"Great job, Mike." Drew pumped his fist through the air. "I knew you couldn't cancel out my toss."

Nick encouraged Mike. "It's okay. You'll get the next one."

The brothers continued to take turns through the first round until Mike had made seven points with two bags through the hole and one landing on the platform, and Joe had made nine points with three bags through the hole.

Drew bent down and picked up the stripes while Nick picked up the stars. "You're going down now, Nick."

"We'll have to wait and see."

Drew threw first and hit the hole perfectly; the bag didn't even sweep the sides. He turned to Nick, lifted his eyebrows, and shrugged. Nick threw and hit the hole as well. The next throw Drew missed, but Nick hit again.

They continued to play, brother against brother, friend against friend, until the score was 19 to 18. Joe and Drew were ahead by one, and it was Nick's and Drew's turns to throw.

Drew threw first and hit the platform—20 to 18, unless Nick hit the platform and canceled out his throw.

Nick threw. Miss.

Drew threw. Miss.

Nick threw and hit the platform—20 to 19.

"Good job, buddy." Drew patted Nick's shoulder. "But as soon as I hit this one, the game is over. I mean, all I have to do is hit the box." He chuckled then grew serious as he released the bag toward the hole. He missed again.

Nick bit his lip. He wanted to say some kind of smart remark to his friend. It was all in good fun, but Nick hated losing. He hated it. He threw the bag and hit the side—20 to 20.

Drew growled. He juggled the bag in his hand for a moment, studying the platform. He threw the bag, and it landed right next to the hole. It would be almost impossible for Nick to throw his bag, make the hole, and not knock Drew's in as well.

And Drew knew it. He clapped his hands. "See if you can make that now, Nick."

Nick aimed for just left of the hole. If he threw it just right, he'd be able to slip his in—barely. He threw and hit. Drew's bag didn't even move.

"Yes!" Nick pumped his fist through the air.

Drew chuckled and patted Nick's back. "Good job, Nick. That was an excellent throw."

Nick extended his hand to Drew. "Thanks, man. It sure feels good to beat you."

Drew laughed out loud. "Don't get used to it. That was a lucky shot, and you know it." He clapped his hands together. "But hey, everybody deserves a turn to win."

Nick scowled. Drew had grown more competitive with each game, each fair, everything they did. Nick wanted to knock Drew off his high horse once and for all. The man needed a good dose of humility.

He glanced at Addy then looked away. Now was not the time to be losing any bets to Drew Wilson. His feelings for Addy would just have to wait—at least until Nick had the opportunity to teach his young friend a thing or two.

Chapter 5

Addy scrubbed the inside of Nick's commode with the toilet bowl brush. The discontentment she'd felt over the past several months seemed to deepen each day she spent in River Run. *This is not what I planned to be doing at twenty-three.* She placed the brush back into its container then flushed the toilet. She watched the soapy water spiral down the drain then turned toward the soap-ringed tub and snarled.

Bathrooms had always been her least favorite room to clean, and five weeks ago she'd never have imagined cleaning this one again. Admittedly the whole job had been much easier than she'd expected. She and Nick had both matured since she cleaned his house years before, and their new relationship had been more than amicable. She'd found herself thinking of him often. Too often. At times, she thought she felt him drawing closer to her as well. Then he'd back off again, for whatever reason. She certainly couldn't figure him out.

But her unsettled feelings weren't just about Nick. They were more than that. They were spiritual, and she knew it. Once finished with the tub, she walked into the laundry room and retrieved the mop. Her thoughts jumbled together as she mopped both bathrooms, the kitchen, the pantry, the laundry room, and finally the mud room.

She stepped outside the back door with the mop in her hand and looked around her. "What was I thinking?" she mumbled. Normally she mopped herself into the living area, where she could watch a game show until the floors dried and she could head into the kitchen to fix lunch. Today she'd mopped herself right out the back door.

She peered out at Nick's land. Soaking in the warmth of the early morning June air, the lush green grass, full trees, and rolling hills that were Nick's backyard drew her. She placed the mop beside the door. She needed some time alone with her Maker.

Thankful she'd worn tennis shoes, she made her way past the barn and onto an old trail the boys used to run around on when they were kids. A slow grin formed on her lips as she thought of the many times she'd tagged along behind them.

How she'd wished for a girl playmate back in those days! Sure, Gracie was her dearest friend, but Gracie's house wasn't within walking distance like Nick's farm to the left of their property and Mike's farm to the left of Nick's. The boys were always meeting at Nick's for one excursion or another. Not wanting to be left out and yet never invited, Addy would always try to scamper along behind them.

As the trail thickened with trees on either side, Addy picked up a good-sized stick, the size of a walking cane. She hadn't seen any copperhead snakes this year, but it was the right time to see them. Without a gun, a stick would be her best defense. She knew they would want to stay away from her every bit as much as she wanted to stay away from them. Still, this was an old trail, and she knew some might be coiled up or hidden somewhere on the path. She patted her jean shorts' pocket. Her cell phone was there in case she needed help. *If I have bars.* She pulled it out of her pocket, and sure enough she did.

Knowing she'd reach a clearing soon, Addy pressed forward. She remembered a small creek at the end of this path. A large rock sat beside the creek. She loved to climb on top of the rock, soaking in the warmth of the sun atop it and watching the water run gently and freely along its path. One time, to her surprise and wonder, a doe and her fawn had walked right up to that creek and gotten a drink. Even with Addy sitting right there.

It had been a place of contentment to her, a place of peace, her absolute favorite spot to talk with God. When she was a girl, she always thought it looked like God had picked up the boulder, only a pebble in His hand, and placed it right in that spot just for her. Just so they could spend time there together.

God, I really need some time with You. Some quiet time. Some listening time. She continued her trek, enjoying the squirrels that raced up and down the trees and the birds as they chirped their conversations at one another. This was something she had missed living in the city. God's creation.

The trees cleared, and she spied her favorite rock beside the creek. Her heartbeat quickened as she stepped up on the smooth surface and sat down. Closing her eyes, she took a deep breath, inhaling the fragrance of her Lord. At least she'd always imagined He smelled as pure and perfect and earthy as this very spot.

She opened her eyes and leaned back, placing her palms against the sun-warmed surface. This spot was breathtaking. Thick trees wrapped themselves around her from the back and each side, but nature seemed to open up in front of her just past the creek to display some of Kentucky's most beautiful rolling hills. She couldn't conceive of a more glorious sight in any other place in the world.

"God," she began, lifting her eyes toward the clear blue sky, "I'm not content. I want to be. Your Word tells me to be, but the truth is I'm not."

She pulled her knees to her chest and wrapped her arms around her calves. "I thought I had everything all planned out. I thought I was following Your plan. I graduated in December, and I still don't have a job. Now I don't even have an apartment. I'm living with my parents."

She peered into the creek's flowing water. "How lame is that? I feel like a complete failure. I want to live for You. I've always wanted to use the talents You've given me for You, to be a light to my colleagues and customers, to donate my time and talents to help others—but look at me. I'm cleaning a couple of houses and living at home. God, I want to—"

Her thoughts jumbled together again. What did she want? She was saying she wanted to live for the Lord. She heard those very words coming out of her mouth, but what did that mean?

She looked up at the heavens. "God, I want to—"

She paused again. She thought of Paul from scripture saying he'd learned to be content in every situation. Suddenly a vision of him in prison slipped into her mind. Surely he felt he was making little to no impact for God as he sat in a prison cell, hungry and filthy, and wrote letters to the churches he loved. Did he know that those words of encouragement and concern would become God's tool to teach others, for years and years to come, how to live for the Lord?

Paul had been educated for other things, to be a Pharisee, to be a man among a certain select circle of men. He was a Roman citizen with rights many wished to have. But God used him differently.

"Are You telling me I'm not going to be an interior decorator?" Her heart seemed to weigh heavy in her chest. "Do You want me to live with my parents and clean houses? That's what You have for me?"

For now.

The two words formed so strongly in her heart that Addy knew the Spirit spoke them within her. God called her to be content in every situation, even the ones she didn't understand. She'd always known the scripture. She quoted Paul's words in Philippians that she'd repeated time and time again as a girl. " 'I have learned to be content whatever the circumstances.' "

Never before had God asked her to stick it out in a situation she didn't want to be in. She didn't want to live with her mom and dad. She didn't want to not have a job in the field she'd trained four years for. She didn't want to be where she was.

But God placed her in River Run, Kentucky, at this moment for some reason.

She sighed as she looked back up at the heavens. " 'I know the plans I have for you,' declares the Lord, 'plans to prosper you,' " she quoted part of a scripture from Jeremiah up to her heavenly Father. "You know what You're doing with me, God. My head knows that. My head chooses to be content with where You have placed me. Help my heart to be, as well."

She closed her eyes again, allowing God's peace to fill her heart. She knew she'd have to surrender her will to Him again, especially if He kept her in a place of uncertainty for a while, but she knew that no matter what, God was doing with her what He wanted to do. His will always had her best in mind. She would trust Him.

⌖

Nick wondered where Addy was. Her car was still in the driveway, but she was nowhere to be found. It would be lunchtime in an hour, and though he'd told himself over and over again he didn't want to date her, he just couldn't get the notion of taking her up to his pond out of his mind.

Remembrance seeped into his mind, and he grinned in the direction of the old trail. He knew where she was. At the rock. Hoping she wouldn't come back before he could get everything together, Nick fixed a couple of ham sandwiches and threw a bag of chips and some bottles of water in a basket. He jumped on the four-wheeler and sped toward the cabin he'd built himself.

Within a half hour, he'd returned from the spot he'd built and parked the four-wheeler just to the side of the clearing of the trail. He wanted to surprise her. Hopefully she'd go with him. He'd never shown anyone the spot, not even his buddies. Of course, he'd only finished it last fall, but because it held a special place in his heart, he wanted to share it with Addy.

He shook his head, trying not to think too hard on why he felt so anxious to show her. He hadn't invited the stampeding of emotions the woman had incited in his heart and mind, but he couldn't lasso them in either. No matter what Drew thought, no matter if he lost the bet, he couldn't stop thinking about Addy Wilson.

He heard branches snapping just a ways down the trail. She was coming out. He bit his lip, determined to surprise her silly. He watched as she made her way toward him. She was so cute with her face free of makeup and her blond hair all pulled up in a ponytail. Her blue jean shorts and old high school T-shirt had seen better days, but they were perfect for cleaning and perfect for what he had planned. He placed two fingers in his mouth, ready to whistle once she was just a few feet closer.

"Don't even think about trying to scare me, Nick Martin," Addy said without so much as looking over at him.

He smacked his thigh. "How'd you know I was here?"

Addy turned toward him, crossing her arms in front of her chest. "You, Mike, and Drew took great pleasure in trying to scare the life out of me all the time. You don't think I know to listen and smell for you now?"

"Smell for me?" Nick sniffed under his armpits.

"Don't go getting your feathers ruffled. You've always smelled good." Her faced reddened, and she looked away. "I mean. . ."

Nick puffed up at the idea that she knew his smell—and liked it. "I'd like to have lunch with you."

Addy pulled her phone out of her pocket. "Sorry, I'm a little late making it. I just needed a little time alone, and—"

Nick patted the back of the four-wheeler. "I've got it all ready, but you have to go with me to get it."

Addy squinted at him. "What?"

"I have something I want you to see. We'll have lunch there." He straddled the four-wheeler. "Come on. Hop on back."

Addy stood still, working the inside of her lip with her teeth.

"Come on, Addy. It's not like you haven't been on a four-wheeler before."

"Yeah, but I remember how you drive."

He pinned her with his gaze. "I was just a crazy kid back then. I won't scare you. I promise."

She cocked her head. "Like you weren't going to scare me a minute ago?"

Nick laughed. "That was different. I hadn't made any promises about not scaring you then."

She still didn't move.

He patted the seat behind him. "Come on. We'll have fun."

Though obviously reluctant, Addy slipped onto the four-wheeler behind him. His skin tingled as she wrapped her arms around his waist. He started the vehicle, and she pressed herself against his back. He must have scared her pretty good when they were younger.

Taking care to drive at a slower speed, Nick felt her start to relax, and she sat up. He drove up a hill, through one of the more wooded areas of his land. The clearing was just ahead, and his blood seemed to race through his veins with anticipation.

The cabin and the pond came into sight, and he felt, more than heard, her gasp. Pride filled him when he stopped the engine, jumped off the four-wheeler, then helped her off.

"This hasn't always been here." He watched her gaze span the pond and the cabin.

"No. Only about six months. I built it all. The pond. The cabin. The pond was done over a year ago. I stocked it with bluegill and bass. I just finished the cabin about six months ago." He pointed toward the small building set in a thicket of trees. The shade helped to keep it cool during the hot summer months. "Come on. I'll show you."

Without thinking, he grabbed her hand and guided her toward the cabin. He realized he held her hand, but when she didn't pull away, he couldn't bring himself to either. It felt good to hold Addy's hand. It felt nice. Natural.

He opened the door and watched as she took in the room. An old, nearly broken-down bed with a plain maroon comforter sat to the left. A small table and a chair sat in the middle of the floor. He'd put in a small fireplace on the right, as well as a few cabinets to hold some utensils and some basic food supplies, like cornmeal and salt and pepper.

He didn't have any electricity or running water, but he'd stocked it with several bottles of water for drinking and cleaning dishes. He'd built a small fire pit for any cooking he wanted to do. In fact, he'd already spent a few days up here, fishing for his dinner, cooking it up, then bedding down for the night. It was peaceful, and he found he could really think and talk to God about the things that were bothering him.

"Nick, this is amazing."

Addy's genuine praise warmed his heart. "Thanks."

She looked up at him. "You did this all yourself?"

He nodded. "You're the first person I've shown."

She shook her head. "Not even Drew. Or Mike. Or Wyatt."

"Nope."

"Why me?"

Nick gazed down at the woman he'd spent more than three-fourths of his life trying to avoid because she was the pesky fly that wouldn't leave his side. Now he wanted nothing more than to claim her pink lips with his. He wanted to run his fingers through that blond ponytail to see if it was as soft as it looked. He wanted to wrap his overgrown, calloused hand around her small one again.

He cleared his throat. Why did he show her? He didn't know himself. He shrugged. "I don't know."

She swallowed and lifted her hand. For a moment, Nick thought she would reach up and touch his cheek with her palm. He wouldn't stop her. He wanted her to, but instead she lowered her hand and smiled. "Thank you for showing me."

"You're welcome." Any man could tell she would welcome his kiss. He only needed to make a move. She'd kiss him back. He could tell she would. But he wasn't any man.

He wanted to do right by Addy. He respected her. He respected her family and his God too much. He wouldn't kiss her or lead her on until he could decide if he was ready to care for Addy in that way. He cleared his throat. "I've brought us some lunch. It won't be anywhere near as good as what you make, but afterward I thought we'd fish—"

Addy giggled. "I haven't fished in years."

"Well, it's a little late in the day. They may not bite too well."

Addy shook her head, excitement filling her face. "Doesn't matter. It will be fun just the same."

If she didn't stop looking so cute all the time, Nick was about to become any man and scoop her up and give her a big ol' kiss.

⁂

Addy lifted a red worm out of the plastic container and pushed it onto the hook. With a flick of her wrist, she cast the fishing line. She smiled as the bobber popped up in the exact spot she was aiming for. "Like riding a bike."

"Sure looks like it." Nick cast his line. "Tell you what. If we catch anything, I'll freeze it, and we'll come up one evening and fry it up for dinner."

Addy nudged Nick's shoulder. "Are you asking me on a date, Nick Martin?"

Nick's face flamed red, and he stood to his feet and took a couple of steps away from her. "I wasn't trying to—I mean, I didn't mean to make you think—"

Addy's heart plummeted to her gut. She didn't exactly want Nick to ask her on a date, but she didn't exactly not want him to, either. She'd thought about him almost constantly since she'd returned home, but she was determined not to fall back into those teenage-crush years. And she'd just spent a good deal of time having a heart-to-heart with God. She wanted Him to lead her life, wherever that led. She patted the folding chair he'd been sitting in. "Sit down. I was just kidding you."

He didn't move toward the chair. Instead, he looked away from her. "I don't want to lead you on, Addy."

"You're not. Believe me, I've known for years you're not."

"No, Addy. . ."

He turned toward her, and the intensity of his gaze quickened her pulse. She swallowed and looked away from him. "Please, Nick. I was kidding. Let's just have—"

Her pole jerked, and Addy focused her attention back to the water. Her bobber pounced up and then back down into the water. She hopped out of the chair, pulled back to secure the hook in the fish's mouth, then started reeling in her line. She struggled for a moment against the strength of the fish.

"Come on, Addy. You got him."

Addy yanked again then reeled some more. Finally, the bass made an appearance out of the water. She grabbed it by the mouth and held it out for Nick to see. The approximately two-pound fish flapped its tail. "Not too bad for my first catch in years."

Nick patted her back. "Not bad at all. You want me to string him, or do you want to do it?"

She pulled the hook out of the fish's mouth and handed it to Nick. "I'll let you do it. How's tomorrow night for a fish fry?"

"Addy, I didn't mean—"

"As friends. For fun."

He slowly nodded, but Addy felt more rejected by his nod than she had by her breakup with Trevor and her job rejections combined. She'd left River Run vowing to never care again what Nick Martin thought of her. Now that she'd returned, once again she was caught on the man's line. *What is it about him, God? It's like I'm that poor bass. He's got me strung on his string.*

Chapter 6

Addy pushed open the large glass doors of Designs and Such. The interview she'd just finished had gone well. She'd said the right things and shown off some of her best work, but she still didn't have a good feeling about it.

Hefting her purse strap higher on her shoulder, she made her way toward the parking garage. It had been a few months since she'd worn two-inch heels. She was surprised how much her feet ached walking around Lexington's downtown. The noise and congestion of the city grated on her nerves.

She spied one of her favorite coffee shops all through college just a little ways across the street. Smiling at the memories of late-night cram sessions the place conjured, she made her way to a crosswalk and pushed the button to cross.

At almost lunchtime, people crowded around her to cross as well. A sense of claustrophobia overwhelmed her, and she remembered how it took a full semester of college before she'd adjusted to the crowdedness of city life. *It's funny how quickly I've readjusted to living in the country.*

She grinned as she thought of riding behind Nick on his four-wheeler. *Guess I'll always be a country girl at heart.*

The light changed, and Addy walked with the group across the street. Her toes felt even more scrunched as she walked another thirty yards to the coffee shop. After opening the door, a waft of the fresh brew washed over her. She inhaled the heavenly smell and looked toward the counter. A girl she didn't recognize was taking orders. She was a young girl, probably in her first year of school. Addy's heart sank a little. *I don't know why I expected to see someone I knew anyway.*

Addy thought of walking into the diner back in River Run. Lacy'd been working there since they were in high school. Rick had been the owner and head cook since before Addy was born. Addy loved that. She loved the feeling of home she got in River Run. The feeling of everybody knowing everybody and looking out for everybody. Even though there were times in her life when she'd have given anything to simply be left alone. Her town had her back, so to speak, and Addy liked that feeling more than being able to be left alone.

She ordered her favorite meal—small pieces of country ham on biscuits with a side of fresh fruit and a large white chocolate mocha. Once her food was ready, she sat at a small table in the corner. She closed her eyes and took a sip of the coffee. *Mmm. It's so good.* She hadn't missed the city, but she had missed this.

Opening her eyes, she took a bite of her sandwich. It was still as yummy as it had ever been. She scanned the room. In the fall, the place would be packed with college students. Some in groups with books scattered across the table. Some sitting alone with a book and a laptop. With everyone on summer break, she only saw businessmen and businesswomen. It just didn't seem the same.

She finished her lunch and walked out of the shop. As she approached her car, a terrific thought came to mind. *I'm going to run by the apartment and visit Val.* She looked at her watch. Val usually went home for lunch, so if Addy hurried, she'd be able to stop by for a quick visit.

Addy walked through the parking garage, found her car, clicked open the lock, and slipped inside. Within minutes, she'd driven the few miles to her old apartment. She walked up the steps and knocked on the door. Val's new roommate opened it. Addy smiled and extended her hand. "Jessica, right?"

The dark-haired woman smiled and motioned Addy inside. "Yep. You're Addy if I remember correctly."

Addy walked into the apartment. "You remember right." Addy had to blink twice at how much the place had changed. Val and Jessica had painted the living room a light yellow color. *They must have asked the owner about updating the place.* It didn't look bad, but it wasn't the best for a living area. Artificial flowers and plants seemed to take over every open space in the room. Overkill didn't quite describe it, but Addy remembered Val always liked a spring look; obviously Jessica did as well.

"Who's here?"

Addy turned at the sound of Val's voice from the kitchen. Val squealed as she raced toward Addy and wrapped her arms around her. Addy squeezed her friend in a bear hug then released her. "I had a job interview today."

"Yeah? How'd it go?" Val looked at Jessica. "Ugh. Where are my manners? Do you two remember each other?"

Jessica nodded. "We do. We already said hello." She grabbed her purse off a floral-patterned wingback chair that sat near the door. "I've got to head back to work." She turned toward Addy. "It's nice to see you again."

Before Addy could respond with more than a wave, Jessica turned and walked out the door.

Val grabbed Addy's hand. "Come on. Have a seat. I still have a half hour. Tell me how everything is going."

Addy sat on the deep mauve love seat across from the television. "You changed the room a bit."

Val laughed as she sat in the wingback. "Just a bit." She motioned around the room. "Jessica's taste is a bit much, even for me." She looked back at Addy. "But she's been wonderful. Her faith in the Lord has grown by leaps and bounds since she moved in here. We have a group of single ladies from the church over every Thursday night for Bible study. And even though her boyfriend has pleaded with her to move back in with him, she's held firm." Val leaned forward in her seat. "He's even shown up at church a few times. I'm so proud of her."

"That is wonderful. I'm so glad you asked her to move in here."

Val picked at a piece of lint on her pants. "Yeah, but I didn't mean for you to leave. How are things going? I know your aunt's got to be close to healed. If you want to move back in, we'll figure out—"

Addy lifted her hand. "No. Actually, my aunt has decided that she wants to take a ten-day cruise. She leaves in two weeks. She's asked me to keep her jobs just a bit longer."

Val snarled.

Addy laughed. She knew how much her roommate hated cleaning. "Actually, I'm fine with it. I'm enjoying living back in River Run." She scooped a throw pillow off the love seat and felt its texture, a habit she'd developed over the last few years. "To be honest, I haven't much enjoyed my visit back to Lexington today. Weird, huh?"

"Not weird at all. And I'm not surprised. When I saw you in River Run, you were glowing. The country is your element. It suits you. You have an amazing eye for design, but your heart is in the country."

"I don't know about that. Maybe my heart just isn't in Lexington. Maybe another city—"

Val looked at her watch. "I only have a few more minutes. Tell me about Nick."

Addy's heart sped, but she determined to look nonchalant. She shrugged.

"What about him?"

Val squinted at her. "Don't give me that. It's obvious the two of you have the hots for each other."

Addy burst into laughter. "The hots, huh? No. I don't think we have the hots for each other."

Val nodded. "Oh yes, you do. You're not looking me in the eye. I was your roommate for four years. I think I know when—"

Addy lifted her hands in surrender. "Okay. Okay." She bit her bottom lip as she gripped the throw pillow tighter. "He did kinda steal me away for a surprise lunch at a cabin he built and hasn't told anyone else about. We went fishing, and I caught a two-pound bass. We fried up what we caught for dinner—"

Val scrunched her nose. "Ew. Gross. You're definitely a country girl at heart. There's no way you'd catch me touching a live fish." She looked back at her watch. "Oh no. I gotta go." She jumped up and grabbed Addy in another bear hug. "I'm so glad you stopped by."

Addy smiled. "Me, too." She headed toward the door. "Have a good rest of the day at work. I'm going to go get ready to teach music at vacation Bible school."

They walked outside. Addy made her way to her car. She watched as Val scurried down the street toward her job just a few blocks away. Val's words resurfaced in her mind. *Is the country my element, Lord? I've promised to trust You with whatever Your will is for me, but why would I go to school for four years for interior design to then go back home and stay there? I really thought I was following You then, just as I long to follow You now.*

She started the car and turned toward the interstate heading back to River Run. She couldn't think about all that right now. She slipped in a CD of the vacation Bible school songs. The animated voices of children singing echoed through the car. Right now she needed to focus her mind and heart on showing Jesus to children.

❧

Nick placed two tubs filled with water and two buckets at one end of the fellowship hall parking lot. Then he set the two empty tubs about thirty feet away from the filled ones. He couldn't wait for the vacation Bible school kiddos to have recreation time. Every year he and Drew headed up recreation. With an ocean theme again this year, they'd decided to have all water games.

Tonight the kids would line up in two teams in the space between the filled and empty tubs. On their mark, the person closest to the filled tub would fill the bucket with water then hand the bucket to the person in front of them. The trick was, the first kid would have to hand the bucket underneath the legs of the person in front of them, then that person would switch and hand the bucket over the head of the person in front of them, then switch again.

It was a game he and Drew had learned years ago when they were in Bible school. Since it was sure to be wet and messy, it had always been one of his favorites. He grinned at the filled tub. *It's a good thing we warned the parents ahead of time to have the kids wear old clothes and bring towels.*

With the temperatures higher than usual for the last week of June, he knew the kids would welcome the chance to get a little wet. He looked at his watch. The first batch of kids, the first and second graders, would be making their way from Bible study time to recreation at any moment. Drew called and said he'd be late, but Nick had hoped his buddy would get there before the kids.

The fellowship hall's door opened, and fifteen-plus six- and seven-year-olds burst through like a group of ants fighting their way out of their mound.

"Woo-hoo!" yelled Samuel, the pastor's youngest son, as he raced toward Nick.

The first grader's hair flamed fire-engine red under the sun's bright rays. The kid was the epitome of the redhead stereotype. He was as ornery as the day is long, as Nick's grandmother used to say. A person had to keep an eye on the boy. You never knew what he was going to do—jump off the top of the slide, pull a garter snake from his pocket, or punch another fellow in the eye. The kid was just plain ornery. Samuel stopped just short of knocking into Nick.

He grinned, exposing two missing front teeth. "What're we gonna play, Nick?"

Nick patted the boy's head. He guided him to one of the empty tubs, a place where he knew the boy would get drenched. Samuel would love it. "You stand right here."

After explaining the rules to the children, he placed the ones who seemed the most hesitant as close as he could to the already filled tub. They had a better chance of getting out of the game dry. The wilder ones, like Samuel, he put in places he thought they might have the best chance to get wet. He looked at both teams and raised his hand. "Okay. When I say go, fill up the buckets." He lowered his hand. "Go."

The kids squealed as splashes of water spilled from the edges of the small bucket as they moved it over shoulders and between legs from the filled tub to the empty one. By the time Samuel's bucket reached him, the little stinker jumped into the empty tub and poured it over his head and into the tub.

"Samuel!" His mother, who was also his class leader, rolled her eyes and shook her head. She looked at Nick and grinned. "He's going to be on fire for the Lord like no one you've ever seen. The boy has so much zeal. That's what his daddy and I are praying anyway."

Nick laughed as he cheered the kids to keep going until the empty tubs had been filled to their goal line. Samuel's team lost since most of their water was stuck to his body instead of in their tub, but no one would have been able to tell by the giggles spilling out from the boy. He was thrilled to be soaked from head to toe.

The pastor's wife grabbed her son's hand. "I brought extra clothes for him."

"You came prepared."

"I know my son." She pointed toward the other children. Most of them had only splashes of water on their clothes and were already wiped dry with towels. "Will you take them to their music rotation? I'll be there in just a minute."

"Sure." Nick guided the children up the grassy mound that led to the sanctuary, where Addy and Gracie were leading the music. He walked inside, taking in the various shades of blue paper waves that covered the stage. Brightly colored cardboard fish of all sizes and shapes seemed to swim through the water with an enormous gray whale made to appear as if it were coming toward them with a toothy grin and bubble spewing from its blowhole. They'd placed a lifeguard's chair at the right of the stage with a mannequin decked out in beachwear sitting on it. The Bible school music boomed through the auditorium while a video of animated fish swimming through water played from the overhead screen.

Half of the sanctuary's padded chairs had been removed, leaving a large space for the children to sing and dance to the music. Addy appeared from the sound booth and raced up the stairs.

He smiled as he took in the long blond ponytails that trailed down both her shoulders and the beach hat atop her head. Barefoot, she wore beach shorts and T-shirt and a lifeguard's whistle around her neck and had sunscreen patches beneath her eyes. She looked absolutely adorable.

Realizing he had a break this rotation, Nick sat with a few parents on the side of the sanctuary that still had chairs set up. A man he didn't recognize leaned over to him. "Watch this girl. She's really good with the kids."

Nick shook the man's hand. "I'm Nick Martin. I don't think I've seen you before. It's nice to have you here."

"Phil Balton. We're new to the community. I sell real estate in Lexington. It's an hour's commute, but I wanted to get my family out of the city." He pointed to a blond-haired boy who stood close to a now-dry Samuel. "That's my son, Clark."

Nick nodded then watched as Addy made her way to the stage. The kids were mesmerized as she explained in animated tones and gestures that they were going to learn some songs and motions to perform for their parents on family night. She nodded to whoever was in the sound booth.

The music started, and Addy transformed. Her passion for the lively music covered her expressions and flowed through her body. She seemed to be having an absolute blast, and the kids were drawn into her good time. She belted her love for Jesus when the tune turned to the chorus. The children mimicked her again, and Nick couldn't help but think it was one of the most reverent, God-honoring displays he'd ever seen. *From the mouths of children. And Addy is leading them in childlike faith, just as Jesus tells us to.*

Nick continued to watch, finding himself more drawn to Addy than he'd been in the last few weeks. He hadn't wanted a girl, hadn't been seeking one out, but Addy drew him like cattle to a tree during a thunderstorm. *Maybe she'll agree to get an ice cream with me after Bible school.*

Someone tapped his shoulder. "Come on, man. The fourth and fifth graders are getting ready to show up for recreation."

Nick looked up at Drew. A sour expression covered his friend's face. Nick nodded to Phil then walked outside with Drew. "Everything okay?"

"No. Everything is not okay. I'm late 'cause I had to fix a flat tire on my truck. I get here and my *friend* is making goo-goo eyes at my sister."

Nick stopped. "Now wait a minute, Drew."

Drew whipped around toward Nick and pointed at him. "I told you you better not be playing games with my sister."

"I am not—"

Drew crossed his arms in front of his chest. "Nick, you haven't given two bits about a single woman in this county. You love living alone. My sister, who had a crush on you for more years than I can recall, is not going to be hurt by you."

"When have I ever hurt your sister? Name one time."

Drew exhaled. "Her entire middle school and high school life, Nick. She was head over heels for you. Don't you get it? Of all the women you'll ever meet, Addy is the one you cannot lead on."

Before Nick could respond, Drew turned and walked down the hill to the recreation area. The fellowship doors opened, and the fourth and fifth grade students peeled out. Anger filled Nick's gut at Drew's insinuations. He would never mess around with Addy's feelings, but he also didn't feel like he needed to pledge marriage just to go on a date with the woman.

She'd been a teenager when she had that crush. She was a woman now. She'd grown. She'd matured. Drew acted like Nick needed to exchange vows with her if he even wanted to say a word to Addy. The notion was ridiculous, and it really grated on Nick's nerves that Drew would treat him like he was some kind of fiend toward Addy. He'd been as close to Drew's family as he'd been to his own. He cared about the Wilsons, cared about them to the core of his being.

Still fuming, Nick stormed toward the tubs and buckets, the kids and his friend, his mind still in a storm of its own. Drew had already separated the kids into teams. He pointed to the row of kids closest to him. "Fourth graders, what do you say we show Nick and those fifth graders how to play this game?"

The fourth graders whooped, while Nick's fifth graders howled that they'd beat Drew's team blindfolded. Except for one kid who said, "Man, I wish Drew was leading us. He wins at everything."

With his nerves riled, Nick snorted. "Not today. Today we're going to beat them." He lifted his hand. "On my mark." The kids nearest the filled tub leaned over, ready to pick up the bucket and fill it with water. Nick dropped his hand. "Go."

The kids raced. They filled the buckets then lifted them over, then under, over, then under. Drew smiled as he encouraged the fourth graders. Nick didn't feel so generous. He tried to sound lighthearted as he encouraged his team, but they had to win. He was tired of always being known for coming in second place to Drew Wilson. "Come on, fifth graders!" Nick hollered as the bucket made its way back to the kid who had to fill it up again.

Nick and Drew continued to cheer as both tubs almost reached the marked line. The fifth grade seemed to be marginally ahead. The buckets traveled over and under, over and under. The kids dumped the water. The fifth graders had done it. Nick's team had won.

"Woo-hoo!" Nick pumped his fist in the air. He high-fived each one of the fifth-grade students. "Good job, y'all. You worked hard for that one." He turned toward Drew and his team. While Drew congratulated the fifth graders, Nick patted the fourth graders' backs. "You all did great."

Ribbing each other as they went, the kids raced up the hill toward the music rotation. Drew patted Nick's back and smiled, but Nick could tell it didn't quite reach his eyes. "Well, you beat me again, but I reckon I'll have you on the no-women bet."

Nick clenched his jaw. He wouldn't be asking Addy for ice cream tonight. He wasn't about to lead her on as Drew suggested, and he wasn't ready to lose to Drew Wilson yet either.

Chapter 7

Addy, make sure you grab the mustard out of the refrigerator!" her mother called from just outside the back door. "Other than that, I think I've got everything."

"I've already put it in the bag!" Addy yelled back. She exhaled a breath, trying to calm her nerves. Family night for vacation Bible school was that evening. The church would provide dinner for the children and their families. Every year the Wilsons and Martins fixed several pounds of homemade potato salad and coleslaw. Normally Aunt Becky helped Nick's and Addy's mothers make the side dishes, but since she'd left for her cruise two days before, the job fell to Addy.

Not that she minded the work. She was quite nervous about the program that night, with it being the first time she'd ever been in charge of the music, and she needed to keep her hands and her mind busy. It was going over to Nick's parents' house that had butterflies flittering in her stomach. She hadn't visited Renee and Roy's house since high school. At that time, she'd spent most of her conversations with Renee talking about Nick.

Addy's cheeks burned at the remembrance of constant confessions of feelings for Nick to the woman who was very much like an aunt to her. Renee had always been so good to Addy, letting her help out in the kitchen. It was Renee who'd taught her to can vegetables, as Renee had the nicest garden of anyone in River Run.

Roy had been just as sweet, treating her like one of his own children. She remembered how many kids were afraid of the mountain of a man, what with his scruffy dark brown beard, thick eyebrows and hair, but not Addy. She loved Roy, even when he fussed at her for doing something she wasn't supposed to be doing.

An ache pierced her heart. She missed them. She'd spent precious little time with them since Nick embarrassed her, hurt her pride, all those years ago. Now that she was older, she knew she'd driven the man crazy with her flirting. She'd been such a silly teenager. But she wished she hadn't walked out on all of River Run just because Nick hurt her feelings. *God, I had so much growing up to do.*

"Are you coming, Addy?" her mother's voice sounded from outside the door.

Addy hefted two bags of food in one hand and her purse and two Tupperware bowls in the other. "I'm heading out the door now, Mom."

She walked out the back door, placed her things behind the seat, then hopped into the truck cab beside her mom. Her mom patted her leg after starting the engine. "This will be a lot of fun. We haven't cooked together like this in years."

Addy nodded and looked out the window as her mother drove down the blacktopped country road. She missed this life, more than she ever realized while she was in college. She missed the smell of grazing cattle, though most people scrunched their noses at it. She missed the comfort of crickets chirping and coyotes howling while she lay snuggled in her quilt at night. She missed River Run.

And she had missed Nick Martin. Even though she hadn't realized it.

Her cheeks warmed again. She didn't need to start this crush all over again. She didn't want to. She was older now, more mature. She'd grown in her faith. She longed to live her life for God, not to get caught up in an old teenage crush.

She closed her eyes. *At least he won't be there today. Drew is helping Mike mend his fence so the cattle won't get out. The three of them have to do everything together. I'm sure Nick will be with them. He probably wouldn't be at his parents' house anyway.*

Her mom drove up Renee's lane and parked the truck behind Roy's. Addy let out a breath when she saw Nick's truck parked beside the barn. She bit the inside of her lip as she grabbed the bags and bowls out of the backseat of the truck. *I can do this. I can spend an afternoon with Nick's parents and Nick. Just because I was fawning all over the guy the last time I spent time with Renee and Roy doesn't mean I'll do it again today.* Addy groaned as she followed her mom toward the back door.

Please, God, let Roy and Nick be traipsing out on the farm somewhere. Please, Lord. Addy walked into the kitchen, and Renee grabbed the stuff out of her hands, placed it on the counter, then wrapped Addy in a hug. "I've missed you so much, sweetheart." She released her from the hug but held tight to Addy's arms. "Don't you ever wait this long to come visit with me again."

Every concern Addy felt drifted away as she peered into Renee's eyes.

The woman loved her. Renee had missed her every bit as much as Addy had missed her. "I won't."

"Dad," Nick's voice pealed from the family room, "what do you do? Practice all week long so you can show me up on Sundays?"

Roy responded, "Of course."

Addy furrowed her eyebrows as she pointed toward the living area. "What are they doing in there?"

Renee laughed. "Playing tennis on the Wii. It's become a Sunday afternoon tradition in the Martin house."

Addy felt her jaw drop. "A Wii? Roy plays a Wii?"

"Yep. It's good exercise for him. He needs exercise for his high blood pressure." Renee grabbed Addy's hand and started toward the family room. "Come on. I'll show you."

Addy shook her head and pulled back. "Oh no. I've seen a Wii before." She looked at the kitchen clock. "It's almost two o'clock. We need to start working on the potato salad and coleslaw."

Renee frowned. "Nonsense. Roy will want to see you."

"Go on, Addy," her mother shooed her. "At least go and say hi to them." Renee grabbed her hand again. "Roy, look who's here."

Addy's heart raced as Renee practically dragged her out of the kitchen. She wanted to see Roy. She wanted to see Nick, wanted so desperately to see Nick, but she wanted to see him as a woman, not as someone reliving a teenage crush. And she just couldn't quite distinguish between the two.

Roy turned and saw her in the door. "Addy!" he howled as he grabbed her in the second bear hug she'd received in the last five minutes.

"Hey, Roy." Addy wrapped her arms around the older man. He smelled just as he always did, like a mixture of Old Spice and wintergreen. Nostalgia raced through her, and she couldn't hold back the giggle.

Roy held her at arm's length and inspected her. "What a beauty you are!" He turned to Nick and clicked his tongue. "I always told you she would be."

Addy felt her cheeks and neck burn. Peeking at Nick, she noticed his cheeks had deepened a shade as well.

Roy smacked his hands together. "Have you ever played tennis on the Wii?"

Addy shook her head.

"It's the funnest thing." Roy pointed at Nick. "Son, why don't you show her how to play the game?"

A cold sweat washed over Addy. "Oh no. I've got to help Mom and Renee fix food for tonight. Besides, you two sounded like you were having such fun."

"Nonsense. I need a break." He looked at his watch. "I'm fifteen minutes past my Sunday naptime. Nick probably wants to play someone he might be able to beat."

"Thanks, Dad." Nick looked at Addy. "It's a lot of fun, if you want to try it."

Renee added, "What a great idea. Your mom and I don't need any help just yet."

"No, I—"

"I insist." Renee took the controller from Roy and handed it to Addy. "Nick will be bored stiff if you don't."

Roy waved as he made his way down the hall, while Renee headed back into the kitchen. Addy turned the controller around. She looked at Nick. "I have no idea how to play."

Nick grinned. "I think you'll like it."

"Can you believe that?" Renee's hushed voice sounded from the kitchen. "Not too many years ago Addy would have been begging Nick to play, and Nick would have been avoiding her."

"Funny how things change, isn't it?" her mom responded.

Addy wanted to sink into the floor. She couldn't remember when she'd been so embarrassed, when she'd felt so young.

"Things have changed."

Addy gasped when she felt more than heard Nick's voice so close to her. He stood mere inches from her, and she tipped back her head to look into his eyes. Though he seemed hesitant, he reached up and touched one of her ponytails. She sucked in her breath as he allowed the full length to fall through his fingertips. "Things have changed a lot."

❦

Every fiber in Nick's body longed for him to lean down and kiss her slightly parted lips. Her hair was soft, so soft, and he knew if he moved his hand just the slightest bit, he would be able to feel the soft, warm skin of her cheek and jaw.

How had this happened? When had this happened? Well, he knew when it had happened. When he walked into the sanctuary and watched her sing and dance with the children for vacation Bible school. Love and happiness, a true sense of joy simply radiated from her, and he knew she had claimed his heart. Not as his friend's little sister who he'd protect in time of trouble or tease in time of play, but as a woman, a woman he wanted to know on a more personal level.

She peered up at him, her gaze mimicking that of a scared deer who'd spotted its hunter. She didn't moon over him as she had a few years back. Now he wasn't as sure if she felt what he was feeling. He pulled his hand away from her hair and heard her exhale. A smile welled in his spirit. If she was holding her breath, maybe she did still feel something.

Nick showed her how to play the game. She was awful. Nick had to practically close his eyes and stop swinging to allow her to beat him. He found it harder to lose against Addy than it was to win against his dad.

Addy looked at him and stuck out her bottom lip in the cutest pout he'd ever seen. "I'm not very good at this."

"You're doing fine."

"I know you're letting me win."

Trying to act offended, he placed his hand on his chest. "What?"

Addy grinned. "I saw you close your eyes during the last match."

Nick laughed out loud. He dropped the remote onto the couch and raised his hands in surrender. "You caught me." He took the remote from her hand and threw it beside his. "Let's go take a walk."

Addy's eyebrows rose, and she glanced toward the kitchen. "I really should help our moms with the food."

He touched her arm. He desperately wanted her to say yes. He needed to spend time with her, just her and him, talking, getting to know each other. "You know they're fine. Come on. I'd like to take a walk. Just kinda get to know each other again. We haven't really talked in a long time."

She squinted and crossed her arms in front of her chest. "Since when do you want to talk with me?"

Nick peered at her, resisting the urge to scoop her up and fold her over his shoulder. "I told you things have changed."

For a brief moment, he thought he saw a flicker of hope mixed with excitement flash across her expression. She sighed and looked away from him. "Okay. I'll take a walk with you."

Nick placed his hand in the small of her back and guided her toward the front door. He hollered, "Mom, we'll be back. We're taking a walk."

"Okay!" his mom yelled, but before they got out of the house, he could hear their mothers snickering and whispering that they'd always known Nick and Addy would be a couple. He knew Addy heard what they said, but he pretended ignorance as he shut the front door behind them.

They stepped off the porch and walked through the grass until they reached the blacktop road. Addy walked a little ways ahead of him. Nick reached out and touched her arm. He smiled at her when she looked back at him. "Slow down. It's not a race."

She grinned, and Nick couldn't help but notice how beautiful her smile was with her straight, white teeth. He remembered the silver braces that covered them the first few years she'd started cleaning his house for him. He'd been barely eighteen, newly graduated. She'd been about to start her eighth grade year of middle school. "Sorry 'bout that."

She slowed her pace, and Nick walked beside her. His mind raced for things to say to her. He wasn't ready to tell her how he felt. The feelings he had, the thoughts he thought, they still seemed so new to him, and he wanted to be sure of God's leading in them before he said anything to Addy.

"I love it here." Addy's words interrupted his racing thoughts. She continued, "I didn't realize how much until I came back six weeks ago." She looked up at him with a steady confidence he'd never known in Addy. "I missed you, Nick, and I didn't even realize it."

"I missed you, too, Addy." He fought for his thoughts to unjumble. He wanted to say the right words to her, to tell her that he couldn't stop thinking about her. Day, night, on the farm, in the house. No matter where he was or what he was doing, he thought of her and what she was doing.

She plucked a piece of wild asparagus from the side of the road. "I felt so sure God was calling me into interior design, and I still love it. I'm still sending out résumés, still looking for opportunities to do what I love—"

Nick wanted to interrupt her, to tell her that he didn't want her to send résumés to places where he wouldn't be able to see her, to places where she would have to move away.

"But I've felt such peace since I moved back here. The community, the church"—she spread her arm out—"the beauty of this place. I truly want to stay here, and that surprises me."

Nick opened his mouth. He should tell her he wanted her to stay as well.

She continued, "But is that what God wants for me? I was so sure of His guidance to go into interior design. It was a passion I felt came from Him. But how could I possibly find a job close enough to River Run to be able to do my passion and live here?"

I'll ask her to redecorate my house. I'll pay her for it. Nick started to mention the idea when a prick stabbed at his heart. He could hire her, but it wouldn't be a permanent job. He thought of the church and all the decorating she'd done for it. God had truly given her talent, a natural eye for making things beautiful. He couldn't step in the way of what God had planned for her, especially when he couldn't decide if his thoughts and feelings were from the Lord.

God, give me the right words. Guide my thoughts and feelings.

Nothing came. Knowing he didn't want to say the wrong thing, he walked beside her in silence as she shared her heart's ponderings with him. As he listened, Nick knew his adoration for the woman grew. She longed to be in the center of God's will, no matter where that was, no matter what she was doing. He needed to make that daily commitment to God as well, especially as his heart seemed more and more drawn to her. He couldn't confess his feelings until he knew they were in God's plan for his life and hers.

They walked back to the house. Nick looked up and saw his dad sitting in a rocking chair on the front porch. His mom leaned out the front door and motioned for Nick and Addy. "Come on, you two. Help us get the dishes in Amanda's truck. Y'all gotta get to scootin'."

Nick looked at his watch. Church would start in just over an hour.

"Oh my," Addy squealed as she looked at her watch. "We've been walking forever." She raced up the porch stairs, barely waving at his dad as she went inside.

He followed behind her, grabbed a couple of the bowls of potato salad, and took them to the truck. Within moments, Addy and Amanda had left. Needing a moment to simply sit, Nick walked to the front porch and sat in the rocking chair at the opposite end of his dad's.

For several moments, his mind swarmed with all Addy had said. The only sounds he heard were the creaks of the rocking chairs, the calls of birds, and the distant lows of cattle.

His dad's voice broke his train of thought. "What's on your mind, son?"

"Nothing."

"Nothing?" His dad laughed. "I'd say there's something on your mind."

Nick shrugged. He really didn't want to talk about his feelings for Addy. He wanted to wait for God to show him.

"I'd say Addy's on your mind. If my guess is right, she's been on your mind for quite a few weeks now."

Nick glanced at his dad. The older man's piercing gaze seemed to threaten to take him behind the woodshed and whip his tail if he even considered fibbing to him. Nick sighed in defeat. "I'd say you're right."

His dad started rocking again. "What's the problem?"

"The problem is, I'm starting to care about her."

"Why is that a problem?"

Nick stood and walked to the edge of the porch, looking away from his dad. "The problem is she kinda wants to work in the city, and yet she kinda wants to stay here. I don't want to tell her how I feel—" Nick smacked his leg. "The girl had a crush on me for half of forever. I don't want to lead her on, in case—"

"In case you don't really care about her? Well, that's about the silliest thing I've ever heard. You either care about her or you don't. And if you're honest with her about what you're feeling, you're not playing games with her. Son, what do you want? Where do you want your feelings for her to go?"

He turned back toward his dad. "That's just it. I haven't thought about this. Drew and Mike and Wyatt and I had a bet we wouldn't let any woman take over our lives, and Wyatt's already lost, and—"

"What?" His dad hopped out of his chair. "You'd let a sweet, kind, beautiful, Christian woman get away because of a bet?"

"No, Dad. I just need to know what God's will is." As the words slipped through his lips, he thought of beating Drew at cornhole or his kiddos beating Drew's at Bible school. Drew had been particularly grumpy lately, and Nick had thoroughly enjoyed his victories.

"I think God is being pretty obvious. You're just thickheaded and full of pride." His dad walked into the house, allowing the screen door to smack against the jamb.

Nick stared at the door. A fist seemed to twist his gut as his dad's words washed through him. Was it his own pride, his unwillingness to lose that had his thoughts and mind in a jumble?

Chapter 8

The very next morning, Addy's exhilaration at the Bible school children's presentation plummeted. She hung up the phone and rubbed sleep out of her eyes. Peering at the clock above the kitchen stove, she trailed her fingertips through her sleep-matted hair. It was barely past eight. The company had called her first thing in the morning to let her know they'd selected a different designer. She hadn't gotten the job.

She trudged to the kitchen sink, gripped the cool metal against her hands, and peered out the window. Staring at God's creative design that had been her backyard as a girl, a peaceful calm rushed through her. God had a plan for her life. *And it wasn't working for that company.*

She walked to the refrigerator and pulled out the container of orange juice. After pouring herself a glass, she took a long drink, thankful she'd told Nick the night before that she wouldn't be cleaning his house until after lunch. At church, Gracie had introduced Addy to a woman who owned a hotel on the outskirts of Lexington and who needed some advice about design. Addy had agreed to meet the woman that morning at Gracie's house.

She placed the glass in the sink. *I might as well get my shower and get ready to head over there.* She scaled the stairs and got ready for the meeting. Unsure of what she would need to take with her, Addy packed most of her samples in her bag and headed out the door.

Despite the heat of the mid-June weather, the drive to town seemed more beautiful each day. Contemporary Christian music pealed out of the speakers, and Addy couldn't help but lift her voice in praise to her heavenly Father. *I seem to be running out of options for a job near River Run,* her heart seemed to cry out to God, *and yet I don't care. I trust You. You have a plan for me. I'm more sure of it every day.*

She thought of the disciples, leaving the jobs they'd known most if not all of their lives, who followed Jesus wherever He led. And Jesus took care of them. *He even provided His and Peter's tax from the very lips of a fish. He knows what He has for me. He will provide what I need when I need it.*

With her heart refreshed and revived, Addy pulled into Gracie's driveway. An unfamiliar car was already parked in front of the house, and Addy assumed it was Sarah Abell's, the hotel owner's car. Addy slipped out of her car, grabbing her bag and hefting it over her shoulder. She made her way up the sidewalk then rang Gracie's doorbell.

Her friend opened the door. "Hey, Addy."

Gracie lifted her arms to wrap her in a big hug, and Addy noticed the slight pooch of her friend's belly. Addy giggled, and she singsonged, "I see the slightest proof of a baby."

Gracie's face flushed. "I know." She patted her belly. "Wyatt won't leave me alone about it."

Addy's mouth dropped open, and she furrowed her brows. "He better not—"

"No." Gracie placed her hand on Addy's. "He loves it. I'm just over three months along, and the man already talks to my belly every chance he gets."

Addy's defensive feelings settled, and she grabbed her friend's hand as a twinge of jealousy wrapped around Addy's heart. A vision of Nick making over their baby popped into her mind, and she brushed it away. Nick hadn't said the first word that would make her think he was interested in her. Sure, there'd been moments she was almost certain she could see it in his eyes, but he'd never actually said anything. Focusing back on her friend, Addy smiled. "I'm glad he's so excited."

Gracie waved Addy farther into the room. "Well, come on in here. Sarah can't wait to hear your ideas."

Addy followed Gracie into the dining room, where Sarah had several papers sprawled across the table. Addy hadn't expected the woman to have so much information with her. She thought she was only giving a few ideas, maybe a few tips. The older woman extended her hand to Addy. "Hello, Addy. It's so good to see you again."

Addy nodded. "It's good to see you as well." She placed her bag on one of the chairs. "I see you have your blueprints and some pictures of the rooms."

"Yes. I know you haven't had time to prepare anything, but I wanted to hear any first thoughts you had."

"She has the most amazing eye," Gracie said in a proud-as-a-mama-bird-whose-babies-just-flew-for-the-first-time tone.

Butterflies started to swarm in Addy's stomach. She really hadn't expected all this. She thought she might talk about a few colors that worked well together, maybe look a little bit at how the rooms' space was being used, but not the entire layout of the hotel. She picked up one of the papers. "Well, let's see. . ."

Ideas seemed to flood her mind all at once. She pulled out palettes and colors and textures from her bag. She grabbed her sketchpad and scratched out an idea to help the front desk have a better flow and more appealing design. She gazed at the clock on the wall. Two hours had passed in what seemed like only moments. Addy sucked in her breath. "Oh my. I've got to go. I'm supposed to be at someone's house in half an hour."

Gracie rolled her eyes. "I don't think Nick will mind if you're a little late coming to clean his house."

Addy studied her fingernails. "I know he wouldn't, but I told him I'd be there by eleven thirty, and I like to stand by my word."

Addy felt Sarah studying her. She couldn't decipher if the woman was angry that she needed to leave. Addy started to collect her samples and slip them into the bag. She'd had a blast sharing ideas for the hotel with Sarah. It renewed her desire for the opportunity to design.

"Would you be willing to take on this job?" Sarah's voice came out low and laced with confidence.

Addy thought she must have had plugs stuck in her ears. She thought the woman just asked her, a woman who hadn't "officially" designed any businesses, to take on her fifty-four-room, four-star hotel. Addy looked at Sarah. "Excuse me?"

The woman leaned back in her chair. "Of course, I would want you to bring a couple of ideas to my office for me to choose from, but. . ." She clasped her hands and rested them on the table. "Well, I'm good friends with Henry Isaacs. I believe he was one of your professors."

Addy nodded. She couldn't believe what she was hearing.

"Yes, well, he has only the most wonderful things to say about you. And after hearing all your ideas right now, I think you might be the right choice for me. This is what I can offer you."

Speechless, Addy listened to the woman's offer. Never in her wildest imaginings would she have thought this would happen. *Isn't that just like God?* Her spirit seemed to smile within her; more than smile—it seemed to jump for joy within her. God had a plan. He always had a plan.

With the agreement verbally set, Addy shook Sarah's hand and said she'd be by her office the following morning to sign an official contract. Gracie followed her to the door. Addy turned toward her friend. "Did you know that was going to happen?"

Gracie's face lit up as she shook her head. "I didn't. But I have to admit I had a feeling. God wants you here right now. Here in River Run."

Addy felt her heart might burst from her chest in excitement and praise. She loved when God worked in ways she'd never even dreamed of. "I believe you're right."

⚜

Nick walked up the hill toward his house a little later than usual. He'd spent a good part of the day asking God for His leading about Addy. There was just too much to worry about in terms of that woman. The fact that she'd had such a long crush on him made him not want to make her think he liked her if it wasn't more than him being infatuated with her growing up into such a beautiful woman. *There's no way I'd hurt her family. I'm as close to them as I am my own.*

But the truth of the matter was that it did nag at the back of his mind that he didn't want to lose the bet, especially not to Drew. The man had been so cantankerous since Addy'd been home, at least when it came to Nick, that Nick didn't have the foggiest idea what had gotten into him. His constant grumpiness just made Nick want to beat him even more.

He looked at the driveway, noting Addy's car still sat there. He hadn't expected that. Usually she finished with his house in about three, maybe four hours. It was well after five o'clock and she hadn't left. He blew out a long sigh. "God, I've been talking to You all day, and You haven't told me anything. Now I have to talk to the woman who's causing me to lose sleep at night?"

Even in Nick's frustration, God seemed to be quiet. Nick knew his attitude wasn't right, wasn't God-honoring. Remorse flooded him. *I'm sorry, God. I know sometimes You want us to wait. I'm tired of waiting, but I know You're the boss, and I want You to be the boss. Everything works better when You're in charge.*

Shaking off his bad attitude, Nick pushed through the back door. He walked into the dining room, and Addy nearly jumped a foot off the ground.

She placed her hand on her chest then looked up at the clock. "Oh, Nick. I'm sorry. Time got away from me."

He looked at the scattering of papers and slips of colored papers and fabrics spread across his dining room table. "What are you doing?"

Excitement filled her features as she pointed to all the stuff. "I've been hired to redecorate Sarah Abell's hotel, the one just off the interstate."

Nick nodded. He knew which hotel was Sarah's. "That's a pretty big job."

She slid into a chair, her gaze resting on the materials before her. "I know. I feel so overwhelmed." She looked back up at him, her eyes filled with thrill and joy. "But I know God gave me this job. Just yesterday I was telling you I wanted to stay in River Run. Well, this morning I got a call about the job I'd interviewed for, and they decided not to hire me."

A strong wave of relief washed over Nick.

Addy continued, "Then I went to Gracie's house to talk with Sarah about some ideas." She placed her hand on her chest. "I thought we were just going to talk about a few color schemes, maybe a new way to arrange some furniture, but she asked me to do all this." She waved her hand over the table. "I just can't believe it."

Nick's heart felt as if it melted straight through to the bottom of his belly. It made his day to see the excitement on her face, to hear the humility and joy in her voice. Coming home to this every evening would make him a better man, a better Christian.

He thought of the happiness he'd witnessed in Wyatt since he and Gracie tied the knot. Sure, Wyatt had moments when Gracie got him all riled up, but mostly Nick had noticed a change for the good in Wyatt. He seemed more conscious of what his customers needed, and Gracie's smiling face, when she was there, made it kinda nice to go in the store. It just seemed she made Wyatt better. To Nick's surprise, Wyatt himself hadn't changed all that much. He was still the same guy, just better.

I think I might like that, Lord.

"Why don't you stay for dinner?" The invitation slipped through his lips before he realized what he was saying.

"Well, I—" Addy started to straighten the papers on the table. "I didn't mean—"

With the idea out, Nick realized how much he would like for her to stay. He touched the top of her hand, wishing he could just trace his fingertips around and take her whole hand in his grasp. "I'm serious. I have two steaks set out in the refrigerator, all ready to grill. We can wash up a few potatoes. I'm pretty sure there's a pack of rolls in the pantry."

Addy looked at his hand atop hers. He couldn't seem to make himself move it. For what seemed an eternity, she didn't pull away either, simply stared at his hand. Finally, she looked up at him and nodded. "Okay."

Nick released her hand. "All right then." He swallowed the knot in his throat, willing his desire to wrap his arms around her to wash down as well. He didn't want to make a fool of himself or scare the life out of her. What would she think if he wrapped his arms around her? A vision of her slapping his face swept through his mind, followed by a vision of her wrapping her arms around him, welcoming his kiss. He had to shake the second vision away. He didn't need to think like that. Not yet. He knew how he felt, and he was beginning to think God would approve of him telling her how he felt; he wasn't ready, though, to just put himself out there until he could tell a little better how she felt about him.

He walked into his pantry and pulled out two good-sized potatoes and the bag of rolls. "If you wouldn't mind. . ." He turned around abruptly, thinking Addy was still in the dining room. She stood mere inches from him, her eyes big and wide as she hadn't expected him to turn around so quickly. A flash of desire to bend down and kiss her lips overwhelmed him, and he leaned toward her.

Addy blinked and grabbed the food from his hands. She looked away. "I'll start this if you'll grill the steaks."

"Sure." Nick felt heat race up his neck and cheeks as he turned to the refrigerator and got out the steaks. Without a backward glance, he headed out the back door. *Well, maybe that's how she feels about me.*

Or maybe she doesn't want me kissing her when I haven't even told her how I feel.

Renewed embarrassment washed over him as he placed the meat on the grill. He would never in his lifetime take advantage of a woman. Never lead a woman on. Addy should know that. He'd made his feelings clear to her the night he'd come home and found a wall painted and all his furniture moved around, the night she'd stopped cleaning for him five years ago.

His mind replayed the words he'd said to her.

"Addy, I will never think of you in that way. Never. You are not my girlfriend and will never be my girlfriend. So stop trying to pretend that you are."

He remembered pointing his finger at her.

"You clean for me. That's it. Nothing more."

His mind replayed the expression that covered her young face. She'd thought she'd done something nice for him, and her smile had been so big; then it seemed to crumble off her face. The biggest tears he'd ever seen welled in her eyes but didn't slip down her cheeks. She whispered an apology, said it would never happen again, then slipped out of his house. He'd only seen glimpses of her since that day. Even when she came home to visit, she managed to sit in the church's balcony and slip out of the sanctuary before he had a chance to see her. But then he'd never been worried about seeing her anyway.

He'd been meaner than a copperhead watching over her nest that day, and he'd never thought a thing about it. Until now.

No wonder she wouldn't take a kiss from him. She wouldn't want one. He flipped the steaks then sprinkled salt and pepper on top of them. He owed her an apology. He wasn't very good at giving them, never had been, but he knew he owed her one just the same.

Once the steaks were finished, he placed them on a plate and took them in the house. Having microwaved the potatoes, Addy already had them in a bowl on the kitchen table. Butter and sour cream containers sat beside them.

She didn't look at him but said, "The rolls should be done in about three minutes."

Nick placed the steaks beside the potatoes. He opened the refrigerator and pulled out some steak sauce and a couple bottles of water. "I need to talk to you, Addy."

Addy busied herself at his sink, rinsing off a couple dishes she'd used in the last few minutes. She stuck them in the dishwasher and didn't turn toward him. "Of course." She opened the oven door. "I think the rolls are done enough." She grabbed a pot holder off the counter and lifted the rolls out of the oven. She still wouldn't look at him as she placed them in a bowl and then set them on the table. "Can we say grace first?"

Nick nodded as Addy slipped into one of the chairs. With a sigh, he sat across from her and extended his hands. She didn't place her hands in his. Instead, he knew she pretended not to notice and closed her eyes. Saying a quick prayer, Nick opened his eyes and watched as Addy hurried through making her potato and cutting her steak. As soon as she could swallow her food, she was gonna run.

"Addy, I need to apologize."

Addy shoved a piece of roll in her mouth and swallowed. "For what?"

"Well, not for what you think." He reached across and touched her hand, attempting to get her to look up at him. It worked. She peered at him, but Nick almost faltered at the uncertainty that reflected in her gaze.

Willing himself to have strength, he said, "I almost kissed you."

She lifted her chin and to her credit continued to look into his eyes. "I know."

"I'm not sorry for that."

Confusion seemed to etch her features.

"I'm sorry for the way I treated you all those years ago. For the things I said. I was wrong."

Addy looked down at her plate. "I was a silly girl. I wasn't exactly innocent. I know my crush made things hard for you, especially since I was so vocal about it."

"But I shouldn't have been mean." He reached over and cupped her chin with his thumb and index finger until he could peer into her eyes again. He wanted her to see the truth in his words. He needed her to know he meant them. "Those words aren't true, not anymore, and I'm sorry."

"Look, Nick. That's in the past. It doesn't matter—"

"It does matter," Nick interrupted her. "My feelings have changed, and to be honest, I don't know how to think or feel or what is right, and God doesn't seem to be as vocal with me as He has been with you."

A slow smile tugged at the corners of her lips.

"But I want to be honest. And I want you to know I'm sorry."

Addy bit her bottom lip, a habit she'd had in a moment of nervousness since she was a small girl. Her expression softened, and she smiled fully at him, nearly taking his breath away. "Okay."

"And I want to know if you'll go to the fair with me this weekend. I'm showing my Angus steer as I do every year." His confidence started to wane, and he lowered his voice. "And I'd like you to go with me."

"Okay."

Nick nodded. "Okay."

He looked down at his food, pierced a large piece of steak, then shoved it into his mouth. He glanced up at Addy, who still smiled at him. She chuckled lightly then shook her head before she took a bite of her potato.

He reckoned that meant they had a date. His last bantering with Drew slipped into his mind. A guy didn't lose the bet until he actually tied the knot. He'd just have to find a girl for Drew—then everything would be perfect.

Chapter 9

A wave of concern had washed through Addy when Val showed up on her doorstep for a surprise visit the night of her and Nick's fair date. Thankfully Drew had been all too happy to go with them, making them a group of four instead of three. Addy feared Nick would be upset that they wouldn't be alone, but he had been thrilled with the idea of Drew and Val joining them.

"Oh! I haven't been on a Ferris wheel in forever!" Val exclaimed pointing to the huge circular ride as they walked through the entrance.

"Well then, let's head over there." Nick took Addy's hand in his. She noted the scowl on Drew's face as Nick guided her away.

Why was her brother angry? He and Nick had been friends for, well, for all her life. Trying not to think about it, Addy focused on enjoying the sights and smells of the fair. Her stomach growled as they passed a funnel cake booth. Due to some kind of conditioned programming in her head from childhood visits with her mom, she simply could not leave the fair without purchasing one.

They passed several game booths. One required a person to flip a ring around the top of a milk jug. Another had the player throwing darts at balloons. The prizes were all very cheap trinkets and stuffed animals. As a child, she remembered begging her parents to help her win a coveted teddy bear that held a bowl of honey in its grip. Before the fair moved on, Drew had won her the bear, which lasted about a week before their dog got ahold of it and ripped it to shreds.

She held tight to Nick's hand as they approached the Ferris wheel. It was actually one of her least favorite rides. First, the carnival workers erected the enormous contraption in less than a day's time. Second, it appeared, as it always appeared, that the ride had seen better days—many better days ago. Third, the monster took you high up in the air in a slow circular motion while you sat suspended in little more than a bucket made for two. The Ferris wheel was definitely one of her least favorite rides.

Nick turned and looked behind them. "Here we are."

Val laughed as she pushed her head back to take in the monstrosity. "Wow! These things are always bigger than I remember."

Addy tried to disguise her discomfort. "I always remember how big they are."

"Don't worry," Nick said to Val. "Drew will hold on to you if you're scared."

Addy watched as her brother clenched his jaw. He shoved his fists in his front pockets, and Addy knew he was about to pummel Nick. Addy looked at her date. What was wrong with him? The entire evening he'd seemed more concerned about Val and Drew than he was about her.

She'd felt so sure he cared about her after their dinner at his house the other night. Tonight he was acting like a teenager who was just trying to help his buddy get a girlfriend. And it was obvious his buddy didn't want a girlfriend.

Trying to ignore her frustrated thoughts as their turn came up, Addy climbed into the Ferris wheel seat. Nick slipped in beside her. Feeling a moment of panic, she grabbed hold of his hand. He smiled at her, and for a moment, she thought he might lean over and place a quick kiss on her lips.

The ride moved up a few feet and stopped to allow Val and Drew to get on. "Don't be afraid, Val! Drew will take care of you!" Nick hollered down to them.

Addy couldn't take it anymore. She glared at Nick. "What is wrong with you?"

Nick furrowed his eyebrows. "Nothing's wrong with me."

"Why are you so worried about Drew and Val? I thought you wanted to go with me to the fair."

Their seat suddenly lunged forward as the operator started the ride in a full circle. Addy squealed and dug her fingernails into Nick's arm. Nick wrapped his arm around her, and she tucked her face into his shoulder. "I did want to go with you."

His arm tightened around her, and she felt his lips press gently against the top of her head. "Don't be scared, Addy. I'm here for you."

She felt tears well up in her eyes. She really, really hated the Ferris wheel. She should have just told them that. Val and Drew could have ridden it. Nick could have even ridden it. She didn't have to do this.

A few tears slipped from her eyes, wetting Nick's shirt. He probably thought she was a total nut, crying on the Ferris wheel. His hand cradled her chin as he lifted her face toward his. His gaze shone with the concern he felt at her fear. He tightened his grip around her shoulder then released her chin and wiped her tears with his index finger. "I'll always be here for you."

He's going to kiss me. I'm sure of it. And she wanted him to. She loved

Nick Martin. She had since she was a little girl. She'd dreamed of marrying him, taking care of him, having children with him for as long as she could remember. Even after five years away, seeing him again was like wiping the dust off an antique item that still held its value. Her love for Nick remained, even more valuable than a schoolgirl crush. Priceless.

She parted her lips ever so slightly and leaned close to him. The seat swung backward as the operator stopped the ride. Terrified, she clutched his shirt and buried her face once again into his shoulder. Nick chuckled. "It's almost over, Addy. It's almost over."

The operator finally stopped her seat at the bottom, and she was able to get off. Standing on solid ground, Addy exhaled a deep breath. "I lived."

Nick laughed as he wrapped his arm around her shoulder and squeezed. "Yes, you did."

"Now I'm ready for funnel cake."

"What? You don't think that will make you sick?"

Addy shook her head. "Oh no. That will make everything all better."

Nick grabbed her hand in his and turned toward Drew and Val. "If you two don't mind, I'm going to take Addy to get some funnel cake."

Val smiled. "We don't mind. Drew and I are going to ride the pendulum."

Addy looked at the ride that had a single arm reaching way too high in the sky with two covered bucketlike seats on each side. She watched it swing the buckets up and down. Addy shook her head. "I'm definitely not going on that ride."

Addy looked at her brother, who still stared at Nick as if he wanted to punch him in the face. She couldn't figure out what was going on with the two of them. They'd acted a little funny when she first moved back in with her parents. They'd always been over-the-top competitive with each other, but lately they seemed to be out for vengeance.

"Let's go get your funnel cake."

Nick guided her toward the booth they'd passed earlier. As they stood in line, Addy watched a man dump the batter into a vat of hot grease. He lifted it out and shook powdered sugar on top. Just the smell of the pastry sent Addy's stomach to growling again.

Nick paid for the treat and soft drinks. They headed to an open table in the pavilion and sat down. Addy pulled a piece off and slipped it into her mouth. The warm, sugary doughnut tasted wonderful, just as it did every time she ate it. "Mmm."

Nick grinned as he wiped the left side of her chin with his index finger. "You've got sugar on you."

Addy felt her face heat up. She'd spent many a night dreaming of a first date with Nick. Now that it was finally happening, she felt like a teenager again. She took a sip of her Coke, trying to think of something to talk about. She looked at him. "How do you think your Angus will score tomorrow?"

Nick's face lit up in animation. "Pretty good. My biggest competition is your brother, and normally he beats me. But this year I think I have a really good chance."

"That's great." She pulled off another piece of funnel cake. "I'll be here to cheer you on." She popped it into her mouth, chewed, and swallowed. " 'Course I have to cheer Drew on as well."

He leaned forward. His deep brown eyes seemed to pierce through hers. "But you're gonna cheer a little more for me, right?"

Addy felt dizzy at the smell of his cologne, at the closeness of his face. Her heart still sped up and stopped at varying times when she was around him. Now it felt as if it would beat through her skin. Unable to resist, she touched the slight cleft in his chin with her index finger. "Of course."

A stunned Nick stared at the oversize blue ribbon and the certificate that named him the winner of the category. He could hardly believe it. His Angus took first place. Drew's took second. It was the first time Nick had experienced the victory. The first time Drew had to buy him a steak dinner instead of the other way around. And winning felt good.

"You finally got me." Drew walked up to him, his hand extended.

Nick grabbed hold of his hand and shook it. "It's about time."

"One of these days I'm going to beat you both," Mike put in as he walked up beside Drew.

Nick and Drew looked at each other and laughed. Poor Mike—he never won at anything they wagered on. Not that Mike wasn't a great guy and a terrific friend. He just didn't seem to come out on top in their contests.

Nick rubbed his belly. "I'm going to order myself the biggest steak on the menu."

Drew grinned. "That's what I always do—and will do again next year."

Mike piped up. "I'm telling you two. Next year is my turn."

"Nick!" Addy's voice sounded from behind him. He started to turn around when long, soft arms wrapped around his neck. A whiff of her floral shampoo washed across his nostrils. He wrapped his arms around her, welcoming her hug. All too soon she released him. "Congratulations. You finally beat my brother."

He looked at Drew. His friend squinted. If he'd been able to, he'd have shot fiery arrows at his sister and him from his gaze.

"Look. I gotta go." She flitted her hand in the air. "Val's running around here somewhere, but I told Gracie I'd meet her at the front."

She turned toward Drew and Mike. "Bye, y'all. See you in a bit."

Once Addy was out of earshot, Nick crossed his arms and widened his stance. "What is the matter with you, Drew?"

Drew gripped the metal fence gate for the animals. "I told you that you better not lead my sister on."

"I'm not leading her on." Nick unlaced his arms. "The truth is, I'm really starting to care for Addy."

"Oh, really." Drew nodded his head. He looked at Mike then back at Nick. "So, you're gonna lose our bet?"

Nick snorted. "Well, I don't know. You seemed awful cozy with Val last night."

"I was not cozy with Val. You were trying to push her on me. I suppose so you won't lose the bet. Is that right?"

Mike shook his head. "That ain't cool, Nick."

"I was not trying to push Val on you." Conviction weighed Nick's gut. That was exactly what he was trying to do. He didn't give one whit about Drew finding a girl. And after last night, Nick felt even more confident about his feelings for Addy.

He glared at his friends as his feelings and his guilt mixed together. "I don't care if you get yourself a girl or not. I don't care about that ridiculous bet."

Drew cocked his head. "So you're willing to lose?"

Nick hesitated. It had been awesome beating Drew at cornhole, during Bible school, and now with his Angus. He'd beaten Drew at times before, and of course he always beat Mike, but lately he'd been winning every good-natured competition they had. "Well, I—"

"This is what I'm talking about. You're hesitating." Drew took a step forward and pointed at Nick's chest. "You and I have been the best of friends since I was born, but I won't let you hurt my sister. I won't let you play games with her. She is not to be a part of any bet."

Anger rose within Nick's chest. "Of course she would never be a part of a bet."

"Oh, yeah." Drew spread his arms wide. "You're dragging her into it by not being honest with her. Either you care about her and you stand beside it, or you don't. You don't go around trying to hook me up with someone just so you can have my sister and win our bet. I thought you were more of a friend than that." Drew turned away from him. "I thought you were more of a man than that."

Everything in Nick wanted to grab Drew by the neck and wring some sense into him. But the truth of his words pounded at his chest like a hammer to a nail.

Mike's voice sounded lower than Drew's when he added, "He's right, Nick." Then he turned and walked away.

Nick stared at the certificate and the ribbon in his hand. His gut knotted until he felt he would be sick. Walking away from the stalls, he wandered toward his truck. Opening the door, he hopped inside and rested his hands on top of the steering wheel.

He stared at the fair. Dozens of people meandered in and out, venturing to booths and games and rides. He watched couples walk hand in hand and parents holler after their children to slow down. Addy was somewhere in there. With Val and Gracie. Wyatt would be in there as well. Tagging along with his wife and their unborn baby.

Nick wanted that with Addy. He wanted what Wyatt had. His mind cleared of all the doubts and concerns. It was his own foolishness and pride that had his mind all wadded up in knots.

Closing his eyes, he leaned back against the seat. "God, I've been a complete fool. These bets between Drew and Mike and me, Lord, they were supposed to simply be in good-natured fun, but I've made it something ugly."

He leaned up and tapped the steering wheel with the side of his fist. "Actually, the bets couldn't be done in good fun. We're all too competitive. None of us want to lose."

He exhaled a long breath. His heart nearly overflowed with the feelings he felt for Addy. A few months ago he'd not even considered making a woman his wife. Now each day he longed to do just that.

He closed his eyes again. "Forgive me, Lord. I have to tell Addy the truth. I have to tell her why I've been so hesitant. I'd always thought she was such an immature little pest who wouldn't leave me alone, and yet I'm the one who's acted like a little spoiled boy. Forgive me, Lord."

A weight lifted off Nick's chest, and he knew he needed to find Addy.

He needed to find Drew and Mike. Apologizing did not come easy for him normally, but when it was the right thing to do, he had to do it.

Just ahead of him, he watched a middle-aged couple walk into the fair, hand in hand. The man turned to the woman and gave her a quick kiss on the lips. They walked closer together toward a booth. That was what he wanted with Addy. He wanted to grow old together.

He opened the truck door and hopped out. First he'd find Drew and Mike and apologize to them. He'd tell them the bet was off. All bets were off. He was done with them. They weren't worth putting so much strain on their friendship.

Then he'd find Addy. He sucked in a deep breath as he thought of his blond, long-haired beauty. The fresh apple scent of her hair had driven him to distraction when she wrapped her arms around him and burrowed into his chest. He could get lost in her deep green eyes. And her lips. How he longed to touch her soft lips to his.

He had to find his friends before he found her, because once he found Addy, he wouldn't leave her side. He'd confess his feelings for her, and she would admit she still cared for him. At least he hoped she would.

He believed she did. He thought of her tight grip against his arm and chest on the Ferris wheel. He remembered the faraway look that glazed her eyes when he almost kissed her. She had parted her lips. She would have allowed his kiss. *She has to still have feelings for me. She just has to.*

"Lord, no more foolishness. No more pride. I'm giving myself over to You. Wholly and completely. Thank You for bringing Addy back to River Run."

Nick strode back toward the fairgrounds a new man. He'd find his friends and Addy, and he'd start a new life. Everything was just perfect.

Chapter 10

Fury welled up inside Addy as she listened to Val. It took a lot, a whole lot, to make her mad. And she was mad. Really mad.

Val shook her head as she continued. "I heard it myself, Addy. I knew you were heading over to congratulate Nick, and I know I'd said I'd wait for you at the table, but I thought I might congratulate him as well."

Addy squinted. "Tell me again. What did he say?"

"He and Drew were having a fight about some bet. Drew was accusing Nick of trying to get me and Drew together so that Nick could get you and still win some bet." Val shrugged. "I didn't quite understand it."

"Oh, I understand it." Addy clutched the strap of her purse so tight she feared she would rip the thing in half. "Those two have been making bets against each other since before Nick was old enough to go to kindergarten and Drew was barely out of diapers. They must have some foolish bet about who'd get all wet behind the ears for a girl first, and Nick's been trying to make sure it's Drew."

Addy clenched her jaw and looked up to the sky. "It all makes sense now."

"What makes sense?"

"The way both of them were acting last night when we were all together. I couldn't figure out why Nick was pushing Drew at you, and why Drew looked so mad at Nick." In frustration, she smacked her hip. "At least my brother was defending me."

Gracie walked up to them smiling. "Ugh. One of the roughest things about this pregnancy is having to go to the bathroom every five seconds." She looked at Addy and frowned. "What's the matter? What did I miss?"

"Apparently my brother and Nick have a bet about women going."

Gracie rolled her eyes. "I thought they dropped that stupid bet when Wyatt and I got married."

Addy gawked at her friend. "What?"

"Yeah. It was all four of them. Wyatt, Nick, Drew, and Mike. They'd made some silly wager when they were like nineteen or something that whoever was the last of them to get married, since none of them had any intention of getting hitched, that the other three would have to pay for the wedding. They gave Wyatt all kinds of grief when he and I said our vows."

Addy's blood boiled beneath her skin. She'd been so sure Nick cared about her in the way a man should care for his wife. They hadn't officially dated, but they'd spent a lifetime, all but the last five years, at each other's doorsteps for one reason or another. If she hadn't been so immature and vocal about her crush on him as a teenager, he might have even begun to notice her on his own as she grew into adulthood. *Apparently I'm not the immature one now.*

Still, she couldn't deny her feelings for him. She loved that he grew so excited about the church redesign and came up with and paid for new playground equipment for the kids. She loved that he spent every Sunday with his parents and played Wii with his dad. She loved that when he was only eighteen he'd bought land from his parents and had been so frugal with his finances that in only nine years he'd paid them back completely. And she knew he loved the Lord.

But those ridiculous bets.

She looked at her friends. "You know what? I'm not playing games with Nick Martin. I'm going to find him and tell him exactly how I feel."

She turned on her heel and headed toward the parking lot. Her brother had started to load up his second-place Angus, and she assumed Nick was doing the same. She searched several places, but she couldn't find him. Spying her brother, she walked up to him. "Have you seen Nick?"

"No." Drew growled the single syllable, and it took every ounce of strength within her not to put her brother in a headlock as she'd done when they were little, even if he always did weasel his way around and end up scrubbing her head with his knuckles.

Trying to control herself, Addy widened her stance and crossed her arms in front of her chest. "I heard about your bet."

Drew looked over his shoulder at her.

"I wish I could have been the one to tell you." Nick's voice sounded from behind her, and Addy twirled around to face him.

"Really?" Addy uncrossed her arms and waved her hands out in front of her. "Well, I would have rather you'd just dropped the bet completely."

His expression seemed devoid of all emotion, which sent Addy's emotions into a spiraling gyro. She'd tucked her wounds deep down in her heart the last time he'd hurt her, but this time she had grown up. She was a woman.

A woman who didn't mince words or play games or pretend things that weren't true.

"Addy—"

"Don't you talk." She walked toward him, pointing her finger until she jabbed it into his chest. "I don't play games."

She dropped her hands to her sides, making fists so tight she could feel her fingernails biting into her skin. "I care about you, Nick. I've always cared about you. In fact, I'm absolutely crazy about you. Always have been."

Something seemed to snap within her brain, and she found herself wrapping her arms around him, gripping the back of his neck in her palms until her fingertips touched the base of his hair. She pressed her lips against his, sending sparks through her veins until she thought fireworks would pop from her fingers and toes.

He seemed surprised at first; then he wrapped his arms around her waist and pulled her closer to him. For a moment, Addy forgot that she was angry, forgot that he had acted like such a jerk. Then she remembered.

She opened her eyes and pushed away from him. "Like I said, I don't play games, Nick. I love you, but you're not the man I thought you were."

Nick started to open his mouth to say something, but Addy didn't want to hear it. She couldn't hear anything he said right now. Her emotions were raw and coarse, and she was absolutely infuriated with herself for having been so gullible.

Once she found Val and Gracie, the anger had simmered to a gut-wrenching sadness. Tears welled in her eyes, and though she tried to swipe them away, they fell too fast. Gracie pulled a tissue out of her purse. "Come on, Addy. Let's go."

Addy nodded and followed her friends to the parking lot.

Val touched Addy's arm. "Why don't you stay with me tonight? Jessica is gone visiting her family this weekend."

Gracie nodded. "I think that's a good idea. Get a change of scenery, at least for tonight."

"Okay." Addy wiped her nose with the tissue Gracie had given her. "I don't think I can face Drew tonight either."

They drove in silence to Addy's house. Thankfully her mom and dad still hadn't gotten home from the fair. She grabbed a few belongings and wrote a note to her parents, telling them she was spending the night with Val. She spied her design bag and several samples of fabrics and color swatches she'd been working with for the hotel spread across the dining room table. She shoved her favorite paisley patterns for the furniture and wood samples and design layouts into her bag then walked out the door. They had to drive back to the fairgrounds to take Gracie to her car. Gracie turned to Addy. "Call me if you need anything."

Addy nodded. "I will."

Gracie slipped out and shut the door. Addy watched as she got into her car and drove off. She looked at Val, who seemed to be chewing the inside of her lip.

Addy sighed. She knew that look. "Go ahead. Tell me what you have to say."

"I think he loves you."

Addy stared out the windshield at a long row of cars. "I think he does, too, but he didn't want to lose that bet." She looked back at Val and squinted. "What does that say?"

"That says he made a foolish choice."

"Definitely foolish." Addy leaned back in the seat. "It also says he doesn't have his priorities straight. God's worked on my heart so much since I've moved back to River Run. I can't get wrapped up with a man who lets a bet come before a God-honoring relationship." She blew out a long breath. "And I was so sure God was bringing us together."

"He may be."

Addy shook her head. "Not if the bet is more important."

⁂

Nick looked at Drew. "I messed things up."

Drew scowled and turned toward his trailer. "Yes, you did."

Nick grabbed hold of the metal lock on Drew's trailer and pulled on it, helping Drew inspect that the Angus was properly locked inside. "I was coming over here to apologize. I wanted to find you and Mike first; then I was gonna go find Addy."

Drew didn't respond.

"Look, I give up. I lose. I'm in love with Addy."

Nick waited for Drew to say something. Instead, his friend kept his focus on the metal bars. He took a handkerchief out of his back pocket and wiped the sweat from his brow then turned and looked at Nick. "All those years we teased and picked on her. I knew you loved her every bit as much as I did." He shoved the fabric back in his pocket. "I guess once we grew up that love switched a little bit for you."

Nick grinned. Drew wasn't mad at him anymore. He pinched his finger and thumb together. "Just a little bit."

Drew walked to the front of the truck, and Nick followed him. "She's madder than those bees were when we knocked down their hive."

Nick remembered the time when he was about nine that he, Drew, Mike, and Wyatt had knocked down a beehive from the side of Mike's folks' old barn, hoping to get a taste of fresh honey. Of course, Mike and Wyatt, being the same age as Addy, had begged him and Drew not to do it. But he and Drew were young bucks, determined to prove their power over the insects. They'd armed themselves with flyswatters to ward off the swarm, but when the bees got the better of the four of them, they were stung all over with no less than ten bee stings apiece. Wyatt's bee stings blew up so big his mom had to take him to the hospital to get a shot. That was the last time they talked Wyatt into anything. "I suppose you're right, but I'm going to talk to her."

Mike walked up from several trucks over. "Did I just see what I think I saw?"

Drew jabbed his thumb toward Nick. "You mean my sister kissing on this guy?"

Mike's eyebrows rose. "So, I wasn't just seeing things."

Nick shook his head. "No. You weren't seeing things, but she heard about our bet. And she's pretty riled up at me."

"So, she gives you a big ol' kiss?"

Drew scratched his jaw. "I know. My sister's crazy."

"No." Nick pulled his truck keys out of his front pocket and gripped them in his hand. "No. Your sister is trustworthy and honest and right." He faced Mike. "I just got through telling Drew that I came over here to apologize. I'm sorry for the way I acted, and the bet's off for me. I lose. Hopefully Addy will forgive me, and I'll be hitched long before either one of you. I'll pay for one of your weddings myself if that woman will just give me a chance."

Drew patted Nick's shoulder. "Now that's the kind of guy I'm willing to let date my sister."

Mike motioned Nick to head toward his truck. "What are you waiting for? Go find her."

"Don't worry about your Angus." Drew adjusted the flap of his cap. "Mike and I will take him back to the farm."

"No—" Nick started to protest.

"Go find my sister."

Nick didn't need any more encouragement. He practically raced to his truck, hopped into the cab, and headed toward Gracie and Wyatt's house. If Nick's guess was right, she'd be hanging out with her for a while.

When he pulled into the driveway, his heart sank. Val's car wasn't there, and he knew they'd driven her car. Thinking Gracie would know where Addy was, he got out of the truck and walked up to her door and knocked. Gracie opened it and scowled at him. "Nick Martin, what are you doing here?"

Nick felt like a scolded schoolboy as he ducked his head. "Looking for Addy."

"Well, Addy's left with Val. She's going to spend the night with her. I'd say you better leave her alone for a while. Until she has time to cool down. I can't believe y'all were still doing that silly bet."

"I know. I know." Nick nodded then waved as he turned to head back toward the truck. "Okay. Thanks, Gracie."

He hopped inside the cab and headed toward his house. *What do I do, God? Do I give her time to cool down, or do I try to get in touch with her?*

"Do not let the sun go down while you are still angry." The verse from Ephesians pricked at his heart. He couldn't control if she chose to stay angry, but he did need to attempt to reconcile with her. He needed to apologize.

Waiting until he pulled into his driveway, he took out his cell phone and selected her name in the phone's memory. It rang several times before her voice mail picked up. He waited for the greeting and then the beep. "Addy. It's Nick. I'm sorry. I was wrong. I was actually going to apologize to you, your brother, and Mike. I was on my way to do just that. I—"

His voice faltered. He cared so much for her. He loved her. He knew he did, but he didn't want the first time he said those words to be in a voice mail message. He wanted to say them in person, to be able to take her cheeks in the palms of his hands and whisper them to her then kiss her soft mouth.

Just the thought of the kiss she'd given him sent his insides into a frenzy. He didn't have a lot of experience with girls. He'd always been so determined to get his farm set up and stable, and he'd enjoyed being on his own. But her kiss—it made him realize how much he was missing out on. It made him long for what he saw in Wyatt and Gracie, even in his mom and dad.

He swallowed. "Addy, I care about you. So much. I want to talk with you in person. Please call me back."

Nick closed his phone and stuck it in his pocket. He walked into his house. Addy was supposed to clean the next day. If he didn't hear from her tonight, he should be able to talk with her in the morning.

He walked into the kitchen and grabbed a water bottle from the refrigerator. He leaned against the cabinet and stared at the kitchen table. He could see Addy sitting there, cutting her steak, dropping butter into her potato. He'd told her things had changed, and they had. More than he ever could have imagined when she came back to River Run only seven weeks before.

Seven weeks ago he was content to sit at that table by himself and eat a steak warmed on the grill and a baked potato cooked in the microwave. He'd never be content to do that alone again. He needed Addy. He wanted to see her sitting at that table every day for the rest of his life.

With a long sigh, he pushed away from the cabinet and walked into the living room. He plopped into his recliner, leaned back, and closed his eyes. *Things have definitely changed.*

Chapter 11

Nick woke up especially early the next morning. Addy never called him back, but he knew she would show up at his house in a few hours to clean. She might be angry with him, but she always proved true to her commitments. If she wasn't going to come, she would have called.

He needed to do something nice to break the ice. He needed something she would see right when she walked through the door to let her know he was sorry. He snapped his fingers. He knew just what to do.

Grabbing a pair of scissors from the catchall drawer, he headed out the back door and toward the flower garden his mom had started years before when the whole family lived in the house. He didn't tend the garden as his mom had. It wasn't that he didn't like flowers. He liked them just fine. They just weren't a priority; therefore, they were always surrounded by various weeds. To Nick's eye, some of them were just as pretty as the flowers.

He remembered purplish pink had been Addy's favorite color when they were growing up. He cut as many different variations of the colors as he could find as well as a few smaller white flowers. He should have listened to his mother a little better when she told him the different flowers. He was pretty sure he'd gathered a couple of irises, which he thought were kinda ugly. But he'd gotten some really little white flowers that he thought might make them somewhat nicer.

Shrugging his shoulders, he walked back to the house and into the kitchen. He looked underneath the sink. His mom used to keep vases there years ago, but he was pretty sure she'd taken them all with her. Pushing through several plastic bags and a box of dishwasher soap, he confirmed his concern. He didn't have any vases.

He tapped his lips with his index finger. What could he put the flowers in? He opened several cabinets until he reached the one that held his cups and glasses. In the back, he saw a tall, clear plastic glass he'd gotten from an amusement park. He pulled it out and frowned at the picture of a roller coaster on the front. *It's way too early to traipse into town to get flowers. Even the grocery store isn't open yet.*

With a sigh, he filled the cup with water. *I'm afraid it's all I've got. It'll have to do.*

He clipped the stems of the flowers the best he could. He did remember his mom used to cut them diagonally. He stuck them in the cup and fiddled with them until they were arranged pretty well. He placed them in the center of the kitchen table. He knew she came in the back door, through the mudroom. The kitchen table would be one of the first things she saw.

He grabbed his favorite cap and pushed it on his head. Hopefully she'd simmer down a bit before he came up here to talk to her. She deserved an apology. She deserved to know how he felt, and though he didn't deserve her forgiveness, he hoped he'd get it today. He was itching for another kiss like the one that kept him up last night.

Making his way outside, he headed to the barn to start on his chores. The morning passed by slower than soup beans took to soak. And nothing seemed to go right. Every tool he touched needed mending. Every step he took required him to take two back to fix a problem. It was almost ten o'clock when he looked up the hill at the house. Addy's car was in the driveway just as he knew it would be.

His heart thumped against his chest as he headed toward the house. He needed to clean up, even if just a bit, before he saw her. Reaching the house, he grabbed the water hose and washed off his hands. He walked into the mudroom and dried them on a towel he kept hanging by the back door.

"Addy?" he called. He swallowed the knot in his throat. He could hardly wait to see her, but he didn't want to scare her by coming into the house almost two hours before he normally did.

"Addy?" he called again when she didn't answer. He stepped into the kitchen and heard the vacuum cleaner running upstairs. Deciding to use the time to clean up a little better, he slipped into the downstairs bathroom and washed his face and combed his hair.

He opened the bathroom door. A woman held a glass fish-shaped paperweight over her head. She dropped it onto the ground and placed both hands over her heart. "Nick, you scared the life out of me."

"Becky? What are you doing here?"

She cupped her hand against her cheek and puffed out a breath. "I got back from my cruise last night. Addy had planned to clean today for me, just one last time. But she called this morning from Val's and said she didn't feel well.

Told me she'd clean for you if I couldn't. But I'm fine, so I came on over."

Nick's heart seemed to fall out of his chest and slam into the floor. If she'd called to tell Becky she couldn't come, then he was certain she'd seen he'd called her and left a message. He was sure she was avoiding him. Not that he blamed her.

Becky pointed to the flowers at the center of the table. "For Addy, I presume." She clicked her tongue. "I always thought you two would make the cutest couple. Once she grew up a bit."

Nick felt numb. He nodded then walked out the back door. He pulled his cell phone out of his pocket and opened it. Pushing her number, he waited while the phone rang until the voice mail picked up again. "Addy, please call me back. I need to talk to you. I'm sorry."

─☙☙─

Addy could hardly believe Southern Designs Unlimited had called and asked her for an interview. She'd spent the last three days working diligently on Sarah's hotel. She'd decided on mahogany furniture and a pale yellow and burgundy pattern for the lobby's chairs and love seats. The pattern was dark enough to hide spills and soils, but the yellow in the fabric would allow a wonderful light into the space. She'd even decided on two shades lighter and one shade darker than the yellow color in the fabric to paint the trim and walls. During that time, she'd also done some serious soul-searching, begging God to reveal Himself to her. She knew she had to talk to Nick, even though she had avoided his numerous phone calls over the last few days.

God wasn't going to let her get away with not reconciling with Nick, but she also hadn't expected to get an interview with one of the best design companies having offices in Kentucky and Tennessee. *One thing's for certain: I can't spend too many more nights sharing a room with Val. I'm a clean freak, but her compulsiveness is killing me.*

Addy took a deep breath as she walked into the office building. Her old boyfriend, Trevor, worked in the same building, and she really didn't think she wanted to deal with seeing him again. At least not right now. She pushed the elevator button, waited for it to stop on her floor, then got on and selected the fifth floor.

Alone in the elevator, she lifted a quiet prayer for discernment up to her heavenly Father. She'd felt so confident about staying in River Run; she wasn't sure that God had changed course in that area, but with finding out about the bet and then this sudden interview—*God, show me Your will.*

The doors opened, and Addy made her way to the correct office. She told the secretary who she was and then sat in a black leather chair and took in the design of the room. The decor was more contemporary than she would have imagined for Southern Designs. In fact, with the black and pewter accents and bold shapes and sizes of the furniture and paintings, Addy felt a bit discombobulated. This room didn't epitomize what she believed to be *Southern* at all. Her mother would definitely wrinkle her nose.

The door to the inside office opened, and a tall, exceptionally thin, dressed-to-the-nines man waved her inside. After shaking her hand, he walked behind a large mahogany desk, so large it looked like it would gobble him up once he sat down. He motioned for her to take a seat across from him. She did, and when he sat, just as she assumed, the man seemed to get lost behind the furnishing monstrosity.

This room's decor flowed from the waiting area, which was an excellent design feature, but Addy couldn't help but want to scrunch her nose at the design. It simply wasn't her style at all, and she was surprised at how uncomfortable she felt. However, she did notice a terrific square, beveled mirror on the far wall that would look wonderful in Sarah's hotel.

She tried to listen as he spoke about what the job entailed and what it offered, but she found herself squirming in her chair at the uneasiness that cloaked her in the office. The man wasn't threatening, the secretary had been as nice as she should be, but she just didn't feel at home.

"I'm not sure if I mentioned on the phone, but the job is based in Jackson, Tennessee, so you would have to be willing to relocate."

Addy's mind shifted into overdrive when she heard those words. She'd been to Jackson one time in her life, for a cheerleading competition back in high school. She hadn't enjoyed the city at all. When she thought of Tennessee, she thought of mountains and valleys, black bears and wildlife; however, Jackson was flat, and it was a city, a huge city.

Not that there was anything wrong with that. The people there had been as nice and friendly as they could be—and the Casey Jones train exhibit they'd ventured through had been cute and nice—but it wasn't a place she wanted to live. Especially after having spent the last two months in River Run. She needed the hills and the open air.

"So what do you think?" He clasped his hands together and rested them on the oversized desk.

Addy shook her head. "I'm sorry." The man's name escaped her. She was sure he had told her, but for the life of her, she had no idea what he'd said. "I'm sorry. I'm not able to relocate." She stood and extended her hand.

He frowned as he shook her hand. He hadn't expected her to be the one to turn him down. And his confusion made sense—who would turn down Southern Designs Unlimited?

Me. I would.

Addy continued. "Thank you so much for your time." She hefted her bag over her shoulder and turned and walked out of the office. Blowing out a sigh of relief, a soft blanket of peace washed over her at the decision. She nodded to the secretary then walked out the door.

"Addy?"

A familiar voice sounded to her right. She turned and saw Trevor motioning for her to wait. Once he reached her, he gave her a quick hug. "I'd heard you had an interview here today."

"You did?" Addy had been worried about seeing Trevor again, but with him standing in front of her, she was surprised at how nice it was to see him. He had been a good boyfriend, and as he looked at her now, she knew he'd have been much better as a friend.

"Yeah." He looked down at his watch. "I was just heading to lunch. You want to go with me?"

"Sure."

Addy followed Trevor onto the elevator. He pushed the first-floor button and turned toward her. "So, how'd it go?"

"It's not the job for me."

"Ah." He trailed the back of his index finger along her jaw, just as he had when they were dating. "Sorry 'bout that."

Addy stepped back to put a bit of space between them. "I'm not. It wasn't a right fit."

They walked to the deli they'd eaten lunch at more times than she could remember when they were dating. Trevor ordered his usual sandwich, as did Addy. With food in hand, they found an open booth and sat down to talk. Lunch with Trevor was nice. She enjoyed catching up with him.

Out of her peripheral vision, she saw a familiar figure walk through the front door. She turned and furrowed her eyebrows. "Nick?"

⁓⁂⁓

Nick thought he would scream when he saw Addy walk into the little sandwich place with that lawyer-looking guy. Who was he anyway? They obviously knew each other, the way they were laughing and carrying on.

He couldn't believe he was here to begin with. Nick hated the city. He especially hated the dead center of it, where every other road was one-way and you had to walk fifteen blocks to get to where you were going, waiting on lights to change and cars and people to move. Nick needed the open air, the open space. He felt trapped in a cardboard box every time he walked into the city.

But the woman wouldn't answer his phone calls. He'd waited three days, trying to give her a chance to cool down, but he couldn't take it any longer.

He took off his cap as he walked straight up to Addy and the fellow's booth. This was one of those times he was thankful to God for his tall height and the width of his shoulders and chest and arms, all from the real labor of a hardworking farmer. He had to work hard to keep from snorting like a bull down at the city slicker sitting across from his Addy. And proud though it was, and he knew God was working on him with his pride, Nick still wanted the man to feel a bit uncomfortable with Nick standing over him.

"Hello, Addy." He hadn't realized how tightly his teeth were clenched until he had to practically spit the words out at her.

She glared up at him, and he realized this was going to be even harder than he'd imagined. "What are you doing here?"

"You won't answer my phone calls." He placed his fists on the table and leaned closer to her face. "I need to talk to you."

"Well, what if I don't want to talk to you?" she spit back at him.

"Addy, do we need to—"

Nick turned and scowled at the suited-up man sitting across the booth from his Addy. The guy's face turned three shades of red; then he looked at his watch and cleared his throat. "Sorry, Addy. I've got to go." He scooted out of the booth and hurried out the door.

"Humph," Nick growled. "He'll take good care of you."

Addy stood to her full height, which was still several inches shorter than him. She lifted her chin and lasered him with a look of complete contempt. "That was real mature, Nick. Real mature. Just like the little bet you boys have."

She grabbed her purse and clipped on high heels out the door. She was all dolled up today in a straight black skirt and pretty green blouse that made it nearly impossible to look away from her eyes. Of course, now all he was looking at was her walking out the door away from him. "Wait, Addy. I need to talk to you."

On the curb, she turned on her heel quicker than he'd expected, and he slammed into her. She started to lose her balance, and he grabbed her around the waist and pulled her to himself. The fury in her eyes subsided for the briefest of moments, and Nick dipped his head, anxious to taste her sweet lips again.

She pushed away from him. "What do you want, Nick?"

He spread his arms. "I'm sorry, Addy. The bet's off. I forfeited. It was stupid. I was stupid."

Addy didn't respond. She stood staring at him for what felt like forever. The warmth of the day beat down on his neck, and again a wave of claustrophobia washed over him as he stood on the road in the middle of the city. The cars, the horns, the people—it was overwhelming.

Addy continued to glare at him as if she wanted to punch him in the nose and be done with it. He'd lost her trust. If he hadn't been such a fool about that bet, he could be holding her in his arms right now. But he'd lost her trust, and he needed to earn it back.

An idea formed in his mind. "Addy, I'm sorry, and I mean it, but I have a favor to ask of you, too."

Addy placed her hands on her hips, cocked her head, and squinted at him. "What?"

"Would you be willing to redecorate some of my house?"

Addy rolled her eyes. "Nick, I don't know about—"

He grabbed her hand in his, relishing the softness of her skin. "I'm serious. I want to hire you."

She looked down at their hands then up at his eyes. "Nick—"

"Please."

Addy gently pulled her hand away from his. "I shouldn't be doing this." She peered up at him, lifted her chin, and set her jaw. "Okay."

Thank You, Lord. It isn't much, God, but it's a start.

Chapter 12

Addy couldn't believe Nick showed up in the city. He hated the city. In the years she'd known him, she couldn't think of a single time he'd driven outside of River Run unless he'd been forced to get something for the farm. He'd probably willingly gone on a field trip to a city of some kind when he was in school, but did that really count? Since he was five years older than her, Addy wasn't even sure that he'd done that.

She shook her head to clear her thoughts. Nick insisted they visit some shops to give him some ideas for his living room. The whole idea made her nervous. It brought back the memory of her painting his wall and switching around his furniture and him getting so upset with her.

"So what color would be good to paint the walls?" Nick's question brought her mind back to the present.

"Probably a neutral color." She pointed to a shop just a block ahead of them. "We'll look at different wall options in there."

Addy had to lengthen her stride again to keep up with Nick. Sneaking a peek at him, she had to bite her bottom lip as she took in the dark waves peeking out beneath his worn cap. He wore a plain green T-shirt and well-worn Wrangler jeans. She held back a giggle as she thought of him being completely out of his element.

She believed he was sorry about the bet, and she thought he did care about her. But she couldn't help but acknowledge the difference in their actions. At the fairgrounds she had wrapped her arms around him, kissed him soundly on the lips, and admitted she loved him. He had barged in on her lunch with Trevor, practically forced her to redecorate his house, but hadn't mentioned anything about loving her.

Her heart stung at the truth of it. *God, help me not to think of that right now.* She swallowed back the emotion that threatened to make a visible display. *I need to talk with You about it later.*

She cleared her throat and reached for the door of one of her favorite paint and wall-covering stores. Every color and texture imaginable assaulted her senses, and she basked in the beauty of them all. She couldn't help but believe heaven captured every color in complete beauty. All she had to do was take a walk on her daddy's farm, and she knew it would be true.

"Wow." Nick sounded surprised when he stepped in behind her. "I didn't know there were so many colors."

Addy smiled up at him. "This is my favorite shop." She led him to a wall of neutral colors. "Your living room is a wonderful size, but the ceilings are a bit low, and you have a lot of furniture that's really in too good of shape to get rid of unless you're planning to donate it to someone."

Nick scratched his jaw, seeming to contemplate her words. He snapped his fingers. "You know what, Mom was telling me the other day about a family two counties over who lost a lot of their stuff in a fire. I think they were needing some furniture. Let me call Mom real quick."

Addy picked out a few colors while Nick talked to his mom on the phone. If he ended up buying new furniture, they'd really need to look at paint samples after he made the purchase.

He clicked his phone shut. "They've been given a lot of things they need, but they do still need a couch."

"Okay." Addy placed the samples back in their places. "Well, let's go look at furniture first. You'll want to have that before we decide on paint."

"I want to keep my couch."

Addy frowned. "Oh—okay. I thought you meant—"

Nick grinned. "You can still help me pick something out for them, but I like my furniture. It's just the right mixture of soft and firm when I want to sprawl out and watch a University of Kentucky Wildcats game or take an afternoon nap."

Addy punched him in the arm and grinned. "You knew I thought you were going to give away your furniture."

He laughed as he feigned being hurt from her punch. "I know. But I do want to see if we can find a couch for them."

She clicked her tongue as she pulled the paint samples off the tray on the wall again. "I'll need to take these to your house to be sure we pick the right color, but I'm leaning toward this one."

She held out a swatch of a light taupe color that held just the slightest hint of green. With his dark brown leather recliner and brown-and-taupe-colored couch and love seat, she felt sure that a deep green accent color would go nicely in his farmhouse. "What do you think?"

Nick nodded as he picked a bright purple sample from the wall. "I figured you'd like this one."

Addy laughed as she took it from his hand and put it back in its place. "Raspberry is my favorite color, but I think that's a bit much."

She picked up the color she adored, a deep cream color with just a slight lavender hue, so slight she would have to use purple accents on the walls or floral arrangements for the color to even be detected. "This is my favorite."

Nick pretended to inspect it. "I guess it's pretty."

"It's definitely pretty." She took the sample and put it back in the tray. She scooped up the ones she wanted to place against his wall and slipped them into her purse. "Let's go look for some furniture. I'll need to go pick up my stuff at Val's apartment then stop by your house to get some ideas before I can head home."

"Sounds good." He scratched his jaw. "I suppose that means we'll be getting back around five."

"I can drive myself, Nick."

"You don't have a car."

Addy opened her mouth to disagree when she remembered she'd been so upset at the fairgrounds that she'd ridden back with Val. She clamped it shut and scrunched her nose. "You're right."

He put his arm around her shoulder. "I'll get you home."

⁂

Nick dug his hand down in his front jeans pocket and touched the color sample he'd picked up at the shop. A terrific idea formed in his head when he and Addy walked into that shop. It would take a lot of work to get the cabin fixed up right, but Addy was worth it. He'd built it to be his own special hideaway, but as soon as he earned Addy's trust again, it would be transformed into their special hideaway.

He'd have to get some help from his buddies. Drew knew quite a bit about electrical wiring, and Mike had put a septic system in for the house he was building on his folks' land. He'd be able to order the parts he needed through Wyatt without anyone else knowing about it. In a month's time or less, he'd have the place fixed up for her.

He pulled into the parking lot for Val's apartment. He shut off the engine and opened the door.

Addy put her hand on his arm. "You don't have to go with me. I only have a bag." She opened the truck door and hopped out. "I'll be right back."

Nick watched as Addy scaled the steps leading to the apartment. *So this is where Addy's lived the last few years.* A smile formed on his lips as she made her way up the stairs. It was a nice enough place, but it didn't suit his Addy. She had an eye for fashion and design, but she was a country girl at heart. If he had his way, she'd truly be his country girl before too long.

He pulled the sample out of his pocket and looked at the color. He'd drive back up tomorrow morning after he took care of a few chores and pick up the paint. The lady who worked there could help him pick out a few things to put around the cabin. He'd want to get a nicer bed.

His cheeks warmed as another idea came to his mind. It was the perfect place for them to spend their wedding night. Addy might want to travel somewhere different for their actual honeymoon, and even though he didn't like to go far from home, he'd be willing to do it for her. But the cabin would be the perfect place for their wedding night. It was the place he realized he was falling in love with her—even if he hadn't put exact words to what he was feeling at the time.

Addy opened the door to the apartment and headed down the steps. Nick slipped the sample back into his pocket. He could hardly wait to get home and call the guys. He knew they would help him. They'd probably hit him up to fish in his pond a few mornings a week as well.

She opened the door and stepped into the truck. He grinned at her. "Ya ready?"

"Yeah."

She smiled at him, but Nick knew the smile didn't quite reach her eyes. She was still hurt by the way he'd treated her. He couldn't blame her. He'd have to prove how he felt about her. For now, he'd just be content knowing he would see her while she fixed up his house. He'd try to make it take as long as he could so he could show her how he felt.

She could paint his walls pink and hang flamingos from the ceiling for all he cared. After pulling onto the interstate, he sneaked a quick peek at her. Her gaze was fixed out the windshield.

He cleared his throat, trying to think of something to say. With the city quickly fading behind him and a lot of land in front of him, Nick sighed a breath of relief. "Whew. It sure is good to see a little bit of country."

He rolled down his window and sucked in a long breath. "Smells a lot better, too."

Addy giggled. "I was definitely surprised when you showed up at the deli."

"Well, you wouldn't answer my calls."

She turned and flicked the bill of his cap with her fingertips. "I'm talking about seeing you, you big overgrown country boy, in the city. You were like a fish out of water."

Nick's heart warmed at the endearing tone in her voice. He tapped the top of the steering wheel. "I suppose I don't exactly fit in the city. Makes me feel like I'm suffocating."

Addy's tone became somber. "It's so funny you'd use those words. Just today, at my interview, I thought the same thing. Like I was suffocating."

He tapped her hand, fighting the urge to wrap his hand around hers. "That's because you don't belong there any more than I do."

Addy looked out the passenger window. "You're exactly right. I just wish I knew what God wants for me. I'm twenty-three, living with my parents, and only doing odd jobs." She twisted the strap of her purse between her fingers. "But I trust God. He knows what He's doing with me."

Nick bit his tongue. Every bone in his body wanted to scream that he knew what he wanted her to be doing. He wanted her to be marrying him, living on his farm, and designing houses or whatever she so chose from River Run. But he didn't say anything. Not yet.

She had to trust him again. He wanted her to look at him with that slight glint of adoration she'd shown up until she heard about the bet. He didn't want her to idolize him or fawn over him, but he needed her to respect him—to look at him like he was the only man for her. He didn't realize how much he needed that until he saw the hurt in her eyes when he'd let her down.

Lord, I'm sorry it took me acting like a fool to see what You wanted for my life. Help me show her how valuable and precious she is.

Chapter 13

It took three days to get the necessary legal papers to be able to install a septic tank and put in a cistern for his cabin. Only three days. Nick knew God had performed a small miracle on his behalf. Now, if He would work an even bigger one.

Addy had already picked out a paint color for his farmhouse's living room and was working on different shades of what he thought she said was sage for the kitchen. He was as attentive as he could possibly be when she talked to him about it, but really all he wanted was for her to be there with him. She could do whatever she liked, and if it made her happy, he was fine with it.

Nick flipped open his phone and pushed Drew's number. When Drew's voice sounded over the line, Nick said, "I've got the permits. You ready?"

"Yep. Wyatt got the materials in yesterday. Dad and I can go pick up one load, and Wyatt will bring another, if you can go get the backhoe."

Excitement welled in Nick's heart. "Well, of course I can. I'll have Mike drive it over. He's been waiting for me to call."

He closed the phone and shoved it into his pocket. Jingling his keys in his hand, he made his way to the pickup. *God, it's happening. We're going to get that cabin so dolled up Addy won't know what to think.*

He hopped into the cab, turned the ignition, and the engine roared to life. *I'd do anything for her, Lord.*

He picked up Mike then drove to the supply store, paid for the backhoe rental, and within half an hour he was headed back to the farm. He'd spent the last three days, while he waited for the permit, mowing out a road of sorts to his cabin so they could get the equipment back there. With Wyatt's help, he'd picked out a simple sink and toilet and a fancier Jacuzzi tub.

After the first day, he'd realized he'd need more help than just the guys, so he told his parents and Addy's parents of the plan. Any concern he may have had about them not liking the idea of the match was squelched when he saw the elation on their faces.

By the time Nick got back to the cabin, Drew, his dad, Bryan, Wyatt, and

Nick's dad were already there, putting the walls in the bathroom addition to the cabin.

"It's about time." Bryan walked toward him. Mike hopped out of the backhoe, and Bryan jumped inside. "I've been getting anxious to dig a couple of holes."

Nick walked to the addition and helped his friends finish putting up the drywall. With mounds of piping laid out in a certain order on tarps all around the cabin, Nick wanted Bryan to hurry up so they could fix the septic tank and cistern.

Thankfulness swelled within his heart as he watched his family and friends tackle the project. He was fortunate to have friends and family who knew so much about construction. But then they'd built his parents' home together as well as Mike's home. It would just be a matter of time before Drew would be ready to build his own place. They'd always helped each other out, no matter what the need.

Mike wiped sweat from his brow then patted Nick's shoulder. "It's gonna look nice, Nick."

Wyatt stood and arched his back. "Yep. It sure will. I can't believe you built this place out here and didn't tell anybody about it."

Nick shrugged. "I'd have gotten around to it. I just had this notion to put a pond back here, to have a place to kinda get away. This was always my favorite spot on the farm when I was a kid."

His dad walked up beside him. He pointed to a wooded section on the other side of the pond. "Yeah. I remember. You had a little deer stand just over there. I used to have a time getting you to come down from that thing, even when it was so cold I thought my toes would freeze off."

Nick smiled at the memory. "And you didn't even mind the cold, Dad."

"No, I didn't."

"I didn't either." Nostalgia wrapped itself around him as he remembered being a preteen boy sitting in his deer stand, practically swaddled in hunting clothes with hand warmers in his gloves and foot warmers in his boots. Several oak trees dotted the bank of where his pond now stood. Does and their fawns used to venture onto the field to nibble on the treat. Of course, he wasn't interested in shooting the does and their babies, so he'd watched them glide through the natural dips of the field. He often thought it would be the perfect place for a pond. Looking out at the man-made pool, he knew he'd been right.

"Well, you're going to have to let us fish out here now, ya know." Drew's voice broke him from his reverie.

Nick laughed. "I know. I know. If y'all want to come out early tomorrow, we could fish then."

"Wouldn't I love to." Drew smacked his hands against his pants. "But I'm thinking we'll have to get a few things done on our farms before we head out here."

Wyatt nodded. "I don't have a farm to worry about, but I will need to check inventory before I head out here."

Nick scratched his jaw. His project was causing a lot of extra work for his friends. He needed them to know just how much he appreciated them. "Guys, listen, I can't thank you enough—"

Drew raised his hand to stop him. "Don't even say it. You'd do it for every one of us in a heartbeat."

Nick nodded. He would. He'd help his friends in any way he could.

"Besides, this is my sister we're talking about." Drew pointed to his chest. "And I expect the very best for her."

Nick peered into Drew's eyes. "I can promise you this. That's what I intend to give her."

⁂

Addy put the paint roller back in the pan. She'd finally finished Nick's kitchen. Taking a quick break, she walked into the living room and plopped onto the couch.

The room looked very nice. She'd rearranged the furniture so that the focal point of the room was the original brick fireplace. Since Nick was adamant about keeping a television in the room, she'd persuaded him to purchase a plasma one to place above the fireplace. It was her least favorite thing about the room, especially since she wasn't a big TV watcher, but it was much better than it had been before.

The back door opened, and Addy hopped off the couch. She looked at her watch. It was already lunchtime. She hadn't realized it was so late. "If Mom hadn't made me help her get the curtains down this morning," she muttered under her breath, "I would have been here much earlier."

She swiped strands of hair away from her eyes with the back of her hand as she walked into the kitchen. The place was a complete wreck, as she hadn't even begun to clean up the paint.

Nick's gaze scanned the room. "Looks like you've been working hard."

"Yeah." Addy fought back the embarrassment she felt. Nick had hired her to do a job, and she'd never had anyone walk in on her lounging on a couch while there was a mess in the kitchen. "I got here a little later than I'd planned. Mom decided she wanted me to help her get down the curtains so she could clean them."

She smacked her hand to her hip. "Even though Aunt Becky was right there, she just had to have my help."

A mischievous grin spread across his lips, the same grin he'd sported the time he stuck a lizard inside her dollhouse. If she had a dime for all the times Nick and her brother had tried to scare the life out of her—she blew out a breath. "I'm sorry this place is such a mess."

"No problem. You'll get it done." He swatted the air then pointed to a paper bag on the counter. "I brought some lunch from the diner. Lacy picked out your food, so I hope you like it."

Addy's stomach growled at the mention of food. She patted it and chuckled. "I guess I am a little hungry."

"Then let's eat." Nick moved the paint pan and brushes off the plastic-covered table then put the hot plates of food on the table.

The heavenly smell of fried chicken wafted through the room. Addy grabbed water out of the refrigerator and some silverware from the drawer. "I noticed you're running low on water bottles."

Nick cleared his throat. "It's been pretty hot out. I've been thirsty."

Addy pulled off paper towels from the roll and handed one to Nick. "There're like four whole containers missing." She looked at the ceiling, trying to do the math in her head. "That's close to a hundred bottles, Nick."

Nick shrugged, but Addy could tell he was keeping something from her. Not that missing water bottles meant anything to her. They were his, for him to do with as he pleased. He'd just been acting weird the last week.

They sat across from each other, and without asking, Nick grabbed her hands in his and started to pray.

A longing for this to be her norm assailed Addy's heart. She wanted this lunch, this prayer, this room, this man to be part of her daily life. He'd been kind and considerate to her like he'd never been before since she started fixing up his house. He'd been gracious when she needed to work on the hotel, and at moments, too many moments, she'd thought she detected love for her in his gaze.

But he never said it. And it made her crazy.

God, I've promised to let You guide my life. I feel at peace with You being in control, but I'm dying when it comes to Nick. I told him I love him. I told him straight to his face. He hasn't pushed me away like he did when I was a kid. In fact, sometimes I think he feels the same way. Do I just finish his house and then leave him alone? I don't want to keep torturing myself with friendly lunches and shopping trips if he doesn't love me.

She looked up from her plate and saw that Nick had been staring at her. His face reddened, and he peered down at his food, stabbing his potatoes with the fork.

Ugh, Lord. I don't know how much longer I can take this.

❧

"I don't know how much longer I can take this." Nick leaned against the outside of the cabin. The sun was especially hot, even for July, and he took off his cap and wiped the sweat from his forehead with the back of his hand. "I wanted to tell her the truth at lunch today."

"Hang in there, buddy." Wyatt patted his shoulder then took a long swig from his water bottle. "When I'd decided I wanted to ask Gracie to be my wife, I thought I would have to scream it over the mountains before I could get that ring to come in. I—"

"Ring? I haven't even thought about a ring." Nick wiped his hand down his face. "I think I'm trying to do too much."

"Don't worry. We'll get you through it. The cistern and the septic tank will be finished in less than a week; then we'll start on the wiring." Wyatt pushed away from the cabin. "Didn't you say you need to go pick up the bed frame and mattress?"

"Yeah."

"Well, why don't you head into town, pick up the furniture, then swing by the jewelry store and see what you find?"

Nick shook his head. "I'm not leaving y'all to do all the work. It's not—"

Wyatt pointed toward the septic tank. "Look, your dad and Drew's dad are laying the pipe. Drew's just standing there watching them. He's an extra hand. And I'm just standing here chomping the jaw with you. We can handle this right now."

Nick looked down at the guys. "I don't—"

"Hey, y'all," Wyatt cupped his hand around his mouth and yelled. "Tell Nick to head into town and pick up the furniture."

"That sounds great," his dad called. "When you come back, bring some more glue for the pipes."

"And some more pipe cleaner," Bryan added.

"And some more water," yelled Drew. "We're on the last package."

Wyatt smacked his hands together. "See that. They need you to head into town."

"All right. Fine." Nick pulled his keys out of his front pocket and hopped into the truck. He stuck his head out the window. "Is there anything you need, Wyatt?"

"I've got a hankering for something sweet. See if Gracie's made any cookies."

Nick laughed. "All right."

He drove down the trail until he could see his house. Addy was sitting at the table on the back porch. It looked like she was painting something. He waved to her, noting the look of confusion that etched her expression as she waved back.

He knew she wondered what he was doing at the back of his property every day. With her fixing up his farmhouse, it had been quite a chore making sure she wasn't there when the guys showed up or when they had to transport materials.

He grinned when he thought of the frustration she'd expressed at her mom making her help take down curtains. Amanda had done the best job of keeping Addy in the dark about what Nick had planned.

Knowing he didn't want to ride around town with the furniture in the back of his truck, Nick picked up the supplies he needed to get first then drove to the jewelry store.

A bell sounded above his head, and a wave of cool air smacked his face as he walked inside. A man in a suit and tie extended his hand to him. "Welcome. How may I help you?"

Nick cleared his throat. "I'm looking to buy an—" The words stuck in his mouth. It was the first time he'd actually said them out loud. "Engagement ring."

The man's face lit with pleasure, and Nick couldn't help but wonder how much money the guy was going to be getting out of him. And he'd spent a bushel of money already. Thankfully, having spent the last nine years as a bachelor and having been diligent to pay off his loan to his dad and having been blessed with good cattle sales, Nick had the money to spend. But still, he was beginning to learn that a wife would cost him a lot of money.

He thought of Addy's sweet smile, her beautiful green eyes, her excitement when she painted the mural at the church. She was worth every penny.

"What price range are you looking at?"

Nick shrugged. He had no idea how much an engagement ring would cost. It had only been in the last few months that he'd even entertained the idea of liking Addy, let alone marrying her. "Why don't you just show me a few things?"

The man's eyebrows raised, and his features shifted to that of a vulture about to devour its prey. Nick wasn't fazed by his expression. He might be ignorant about jewelry, but he wasn't about to let the man take advantage of him either.

The guy lifted an exceptionally large diamond ring from a tray beneath the glass and held it out to Nick. "This ring is a beauty. The one-carat diamond is registered perfect and is accented by two smaller diamonds on each side, as you can see."

Nick held the ring between his index finger and thumb. It was the gaudiest thing he'd ever seen. Not at all what he would want to give to Addy.

"It's a terrific price at only. . ."

Nick thought he would swallow his tongue when the man said the ring cost several thousand dollars. Who in his right mind would buy that? Not Nick. He was a simple man, with simple thinking, and to him it was a downright sin to spend that much money on a trinket of jewelry.

Nick pushed the ring into the man's hand. "I don't think so. How 'bout I just look a little bit. Which ones are engagement rings?"

Obviously flustered, the man took the ring and placed it back in the tray, pointed to the trays of engagements rings, then sat on a stool behind the counter.

Nick's gaze traveled the rows of rings. Some were too simple, only a single circle- or square-shaped diamond. Addy was a designer. She would want something unique. But she was also practical. He knew she wouldn't want something gaudy.

A ring caught his eye. He pointed at the glass. "Can I see that one? Second tray, second row, fourth from the left."

The man lifted the ring out of the tray and handed it to Nick. It had a white band with five diamonds on the top, but it had an older look to it.

"That's a very nice setting," the man said. "It's an antique style. The largest stone is one-third carat with the next two stones one-fifth each. The last two are very small, as you can see. The square design around the largest diamond was a popular design about a hundred years ago."

The man didn't need to say any more. Nick knew this was the ring he wanted. When he asked about the price, he felt good about paying that amount. Having called Addy's mom to find out her ring size before he came, he learned they'd have to alter the ring. He paid the man then folded the receipt and put it in his wallet. "How long until it's ready?"

"One week from today."

Nick grinned. They only needed one more week to finish the cabin. "Perfect."

Chapter 14

Addy had finished redecorating Nick's kitchen the day before. He'd paid her for her services. Now she had no reason to go to his house. No reason to see him except on Sundays at church. She pinched her straw between her index finger and thumb and twirled it around several pieces of ice.

"What's the matter, Addy?"

She looked across the booth at her friend Gracie. With Nick's house and the hotel complete, she'd invited Gracie to the diner for lunch as a celebration of sorts. Since Gracie's morning sickness had finally subsided for the most part, she had accepted with joy.

Addy shrugged, feeling the weight of sadness pressing down in her chest. "I guess I just feel so uncertain. I wanted to celebrate the completion of the jobs, but now—"

She peered into Gracie's eyes. "What am I supposed to do? I have no job. No job prospects. Nick's not—"

She stopped. She was tired of wishing and praying that Nick Martin would think of her as more than a friend or a little sister.

Gracie reached across the table and placed her hand on Addy's. "God knows what He's doing with you. He has a plan. You know He does."

"I know that in my head, but right now, I sure don't know that in my heart."

"You still have to work on my nursery, remember? And you agreed to lead the middle school girls' Bible study on Wednesday nights."

Addy willed herself to feel encouraged by her friend's words. "Yes. I know. And I'm excited about that. I remember how much we both learned from Miss Faye when we were that age."

"Right. And when people see what you've done with Sarah's hotel—you know she's been bragging about it to everyone."

Addy's spirits lifted as her face warmed. "Yes. I had heard that. That's what I've been told."

"I'm sure you'll be getting calls from people who'll want to enlist your services. You could work right out of River Run."

"That would be a dream come true." She took a drink of sweet tea. "To stay right here with my family and friends. I'd love that."

Gracie cocked her head and pursed her lips. "Oh, I think you'll be staying."

Addy studied her friend. Everyone had been acting so weird the last few weeks, looking at her strangely and saying things that just didn't quite make sense. Gracie shoved a bite of food into her mouth then grinned at Addy, as she used to when they were kids.

"What do you know, Gracie?"

Gracie shoved another forkful of coleslaw into her mouth. "I don't know anything."

"Yes, you do. You can't lie to me, Gracie. Does Sarah have someone lined up to call me about a job?"

Gracie shrugged and took a long drink of tea then shoved another forkful of food into her mouth.

"I'll figure it out, Gracie. You know I'll get it out of you." Her phone rang from inside her purse. She pulled it out and answered the call. Addy listened as her mom told her someone had stopped by to see her and that she needed to come home.

Addy pulled some money out of her purse and placed it on the table. "I have to get home. I've got a visitor." She squinted at her friend. "But I will find out what you're keeping from me."

───※───

Four days had passed since Nick purchased the engagement ring. He was alone at the cabin painting the color Addy said she loved on the walls. Almost everything was complete. Mike would install the wiring over the next two days. His dad would be coming out tomorrow to help him get the Jacuzzi tub installed.

Realizing it was almost four o'clock and he still hadn't had lunch, he walked into the bathroom and turned on the sink. "But I have water and plumbing."

He opened the cooler and pulled out a ham sandwich and soft drink. With the table and chairs and bed all covered in plastic while he painted, he had nowhere to sit except to shut the cooler lid and park himself on top of it.

The room looked good. He just had a few touch-ups to do on the walls, then he'd remove the plastic and move the furniture close to the places it needed to be. His mom and Amanda planned to drive out after Mike got the electric running and put some feminine touches to the room.

He shoved a huge bite of sandwich into this mouth. The room had grown rather warm in the heat of the day, but with it being surrounded by large trees, he knew he was much cooler in his cabin than he would be outside. "Once the electric's running, I'll put in the air conditioner."

The little cabin originally had only one window, but once he decided to add electric, he knew he'd want to go ahead and purchase a window unit to cool the place down in the dead of summer. He just wanted it to be a comfortable place for Addy.

Pushing the rest of the sandwich into his mouth, Nick wadded up the baggie and shoved it inside the cooler. He grabbed a paintbrush and finished touching up the paint. Once satisfied with the work, he rinsed out the brushes and pans and packed them into his truck.

Anxious to see the place in some semblance of order, he pulled the plastic off the furniture, folded it, and placed it in the corner with the tools they would still need for the electric. Everything else he packed in the back of his truck.

The windows were bare of curtains, but he had made up the bed with the sheets and comforter Amanda picked out. It was very girlie. Even though the main color was some kind of tan, it still had purple flowers and bows in various places. But he didn't mind. He knew Addy would love it, and that was what mattered.

He grinned as he leaned against the door and inspected their hard work. It had been sweat-pouring, backbreaking labor, but it looked really nice; he was proud of all they'd accomplished.

You've put Your hand of blessing on this project, Lord. There's no other way for me to think of it. We couldn't have gotten all this work done had You not allowed it. You blessed me with wonderful family and friends. Please bless me with Addy as a wife as well.

His cell phone vibrated in his pocket. He pulled it out and looked at the screen. It was Drew. Opening the phone, he pushed the button. "Hey, Drew. What's up?"

"You've got to get over here quick."

Nick's heart jumped at the sound of urgency in Drew's tone. What if something had happened to Addy or to his parents? He yanked his keys out of his pocket and jumped in the cab of the truck. "What is it? What's wrong?"

"It's Addy."

Nick's gut churned, and a wave of nausea washed over him. "What is it?

What happened? Is she hurt?"

"No, she's not hurt, but you better get over here quick."

"What's wrong?"

"There's a city slicker sitting at my kitchen table trying to sweet-talk her. That's what's wrong."

Fury replaced fear. A vision of the scrawny business suit–covered guy who hadn't had the guts to stand up for her at the sandwich place flashed through his mind. There was no way that guy was going to sweet-talk his Addy.

He yanked the truck into gear and barreled down the trail. *God, give me grace. Give me patience. And give me words. Because if You don't, I'm liable to use my fists.*

Addy could not believe Trevor was sitting at her parents' kitchen table drinking a glass of her mother's sweet tea. First of all, he hated sweet tea. He must have just felt obligated to drink it when her mother offered. Second of all, she was fairly frustrated with Trevor for slipping out of the deli as he had when Nick showed up.

He'd made it perfectly clear for the second time that he would not be there for her when she needed it. The first time being when he broke up with her shortly after she'd graduated.

It was obvious her parents didn't like him, as her dad sat at one end of the table, a scowl wrapping his face, and her mom stood leaning against the kitchen sink. If Mom liked him, she'd be sitting at the table talking his ear off. But then Addy had always known in her heart that they wouldn't like Trevor.

When she was dating him, she had moments when she felt he looked down his nose at her for her "hillbilly" upbringing. She'd always brushed the feelings off as her being supersensitive to the stereotype some people had about those who were raised in the hills of Kentucky. Seeing him look down his nose at her mother's beverage, every sip and squirm in his chair as if he'd be attacked by a mouse at any moment, confirmed the feelings she'd sometimes had.

"What was it you said you do for a living, son?"

Addy looked across the table at her dad. He was trying to be nice to Trevor. She had to give him credit for that, but the scowl on his face gave away that he sure didn't want to.

"I'm a computer programmer," Trevor said.

"Mmm." Her dad nodded his head back then looked over at his wife. "Amanda, I suppose we ought to go check on the garden." He looked at Addy. "Give them a chance to talk."

Addy didn't want her parents to leave the room. She had no desire to be left alone with Trevor. For the life of her, she had no idea why he would be here. Or why she had ever been interested in him.

She tried to beg them to stay with her gaze, but either they weren't taking the hint or they weren't going for it. She watched as her parents walked out the back door toward the garden.

She clasped her hands together and placed them on the table. "How's everything been, Trevor?"

"Not so good." He looked up at her. The sincerity in his gaze made her stomach roll, and she bit her bottom lip. "I can't stop thinking about you since we had lunch at the deli. I was such a fool to let you go."

Addy didn't know what to say. She watched as he pushed the chair back and stood. He paced the floor, placing one hand against his forehead. "I thought I was doing the right thing breaking up with you. At the time I just couldn't see us staying together, but now—"

He walked around the table and touched a strand of her hair. "I want you back."

Addy stood and stepped away from him. "I'm sorry, Trevor."

He stepped toward her again. "Don't say that. I really care about you. You could come back to the city. You could—"

Addy shook her head and waved her arms in front of her.

"No, Trevor. I'm sorry. I'm going to stay in River Run. You were right to break up with me. You and I aren't—"

"Addy, we could make it work."

"I don't want to make it work."

Addy walked toward the front door with Trevor following her. She pushed open the screen and stepped out onto the porch. "I'm sorry you drove out here, Trevor. I don't mean to upset you, but I won't lead you on either."

Trevor exhaled a long breath then walked to his car. Addy followed him and stood beside the driver's door as he opened it. He looked past her, and his eyes widened.

"Addy, wait!" a familiar voice sounded from behind her. She turned and saw a red-faced man stalking toward them. "I won't let you do this."

Addy felt her jaw drop. "Nick?"

⚜

"Listen, buddy, I'm sorry you drove all the way out here and all." He nudged the guy, who once again was all too willing to run from him into his car.

Nick shut the door and tapped the hood. "Sorry, man, but you're not going anywhere with Addy."

"Excuse me." Addy placed her hands on her hips. "This is not your concern. What do you care if I go somewhere with him?"

Nick nodded his head at the man. "See ya, mister." Then he scooped Addy up into his arms and headed back toward his truck.

"Nick Martin, what are you doing?"

Addy twisted in his arms, but he wasn't about to let her down. He'd waited like a fool for too long, and he wasn't going to let her get away. "I need to show you something."

Addy stopped squirming and jutted out her chin. "What if I don't want you to show me something?" She punched his shoulder.

He put her down beside the passenger door of his truck. He opened the door then turned back to her. Fury lit her eyes, making the green deepen. He couldn't help it. He reached up and gently touched her cheek with the back of his hand. She sucked in her breath. "Please, Addy. Can I show you something?"

She looked away from him but stepped up into the cab. "Fine."

Nick wanted to howl his excitement as he skipped around the front of the truck and hopped into the cab. He looked to his left and saw Bryan standing beside the house. Her dad gave him a thumbs-up, and Nick tipped his cap. The truck roared to life, and Nick headed back to his farm. With his Addy.

Addy didn't talk to him the whole way, but that was okay with Nick. His mind swirled with what he should say to her. Should he get on his knee? Should he kiss her first? What if she said no?

He sneaked a quick peek at her. He couldn't handle it if she said no. *Please, God, don't let her say no.*

He didn't have the ring. It wouldn't be ready for three more days. He wanted to propose to her the right way. And the cabin wasn't completely done. It didn't have the electric yet, and his mom and Amanda hadn't had a chance to give it some finishing touches. But none of that mattered. He had to do this now. He wouldn't let her go back to the city, not without him putting up a fight anyway.

Nick pulled onto the trail that led to his cabin. The truck bounced to and fro as he drove over the rough ground. At one point, Addy fell against him, but she grabbed the door handle and pulled herself away.

She's madder than a hornet right now. Please, Lord, soften her heart. I love her.

Nick pulled next to the cabin. He looked at Addy. He could tell all the equipment and leftover supplies lying on the ground surprised her. "Have you been working on the cabin?"

"Yep." He opened the door and ran across to her side before she had a chance to get out. Opening her door for her, he extended his hand. She stared at him for several moments. "Please let me help you out."

Hesitantly she placed her hand in his. It took every ounce of strength within him not to scoop her up in his arms and carry her to the cabin. But he didn't want to scare her or make her angrier with him. He guided her to the cabin door then opened it and waited for her to go inside first.

Her eyes widened in surprise as she looked around the room. "You've done a lot of work."

"Yes, I have. We made a bathroom, too." He walked past her and opened the door, exposing a hooked-up sink and toilet. "We're going to finish the Jacuzzi and put in some electric in the next few days."

Addy looked up at him. "We?"

"Yeah. Your dad, my dad, Drew, Wyatt, and Mike have been helping me." He pointed behind them to the bed. "Your mom picked out the comforter and stuff."

"My mom?" Addy furrowed her eyebrows. She wrapped her arms around her chest and shook her head. "Nick, I don't understand."

Nick swallowed. Heat washed over him. He'd never felt so nervous, so vulnerable. "Well, I hadn't planned to do this for a few more days, but when Drew called and said that city slicker was at your house—"

"What's Trevor got to do with this?"

"Absolutely nothing." Nick grabbed her hands in his own. He caressed her palms with his thumbs. The confusion in her gaze melted him, and he lifted her hand to his cheek. Brushing it softly with the back of her hand, he noticed tears pooled in Addy's eyes.

"I love you, Addy."

She bit her bottom lip as a tear slipped down her left cheek. He brushed it away with his thumb then lowered himself to one knee. "I don't have your ring. It won't be finished for three more days."

"You already have it?" Addy's voice squeaked, and she sniffed as she looked down at him.

He kissed her knuckle. "Yes, Addy, I do. I want you to be my wife."

"You love me?"

He stood to his feet and cupped both sides of her jaw in his hands. "Yes,

I love you. More than I ever dreamed possible. I love you, and I want you to be my wife."

Addy grinned, and then a little giggle slipped from her lips. Nick leaned down and pressed his lips against hers. She wrapped her hands around his neck and deepened the kiss. He forced himself to push her away and smiled down at her. "Is that a yes?"

"Of course that's a yes."

Addy punched his arm, much harder than he expected. "Ow." He rubbed the spot and grinned. "I still love you."

She placed her hands on her hips. "It sure took you long enough."

He wrapped his arms around her again and planted a firm kiss on her lips. "I'll never take that long again."

Epilogue

Nick could hardly wait for the wedding to start. It had been ten long months since he proposed to Addy at the cabin. Since then, he'd spent almost every day trying to show Addy how thankful he was that she'd chosen him as her fiancé.

Though she'd done a good deal of the planning, he'd tried to help out in any way he could. He'd folded handmade invitations and sealed them in envelopes. He'd built and painted a wedding arch Addy designed. Even his finger had come in handy to hold bows that she'd wanted tied just perfectly.

All the effort and planning had paid off. Their church looked amazing. Of course, her colors were raspberry and silver, but he had no complaints. The color had actually started to grow on him.

God seemed to be smiling down on them, as the weather was sunny and warm with almost no humidity. April had been exceptionally rainy, and he'd been a little concerned about the early May date, but he couldn't have asked for a nicer day.

As the time drew nearer, he made his way to the front of the sanctuary. He peered out at their family and friends sitting along both sides of the pews. He looked to his right at his best man and groomsmen, Drew, Mike, and Wyatt. His heart filled with thanksgiving.

Wyatt made a face out into the crowd. Nick turned and saw his young son sitting in Gracie's mother's lap. She held his little hand up toward his dad, making the infant wave. The baby smiled and cooed, and Nick found himself looking forward to the day he and Addy would have their own child.

Pastor Wes leaned toward him and whispered, "Okay, it's time."

Nick cleared his throat and stood to his full height. He looked down at his tux, swiping away any dust or wrinkles from the front. His groomsmen took his cue and straightened as well.

The music sounded, and the ushers escorted in his parents and then her mother. The music changed, and Nick's cousin from several counties over made her way down the aisle. Nick sneaked a peek at Drew, who wrinkled his nose.

Melody and Addy had become fast friends soon after the engagement. She'd only been visiting for a few weeks, but she and Drew had already gone toe-to-toe on every subject that had been brought up in the presence of both of them.

Melody took her place at the far end; then Val began her descent down the aisle. Next was Gracie and then their flower girl and ring bearer. Nick was beginning to think everyone they'd ever known was going to walk down the aisle before he'd get a chance to see Addy.

Finally, the music changed one more time—to that of the wedding march. He sucked in his breath as the ushers opened both doors at the same time. He caught sight of his beautiful Addy and felt tears in his eyes.

He swiped them away. Nick Martin didn't cry, especially not at a vision as beautiful as her. Her dress was so pretty. He didn't know the names of all the laces and trinkets and silky stuff that draped all the way down her body. He just knew they looked beautiful on her.

Some lace covered her face. He remembered from the rehearsal that once her dad brought her all the way to Nick, he'd pull the lace back, give her a kiss, then give her to Nick. He was trying to be patient, but it was taking them too long to get to him.

They finally made it in front of the minister. Bryan lifted her lace and kissed her cheek; then Nick drew in a breath as she turned toward him. Her face glowed, her eyes sparkled, and Nick felt sure he'd never seen a more beautiful creature in his life.

He took her hand in his, and they faced their minister. Nick tried to focus on Pastor Wes's words. He believed them to the core of his being. He was giving his life to Addy—and only Addy—for the rest of his days. God brought them together, and nothing would separate them.

Nick caressed Addy's hands with his fingertips as he repeated his vows and listened as Addy repeated hers. They exchanged rings, the symbol of their unending love for each other. Pastor Wes's voice lifted through the sanctuary. "By the power vested in me by the State of Kentucky, I now pronounce you husband and wife." He looked at Nick and winked. "You may kiss your bride."

Nick didn't have to be told twice. He cupped her cheeks in both his hands and gently pressed his lips against hers. "I love you, Addy Martin."

She inhaled. "I love you."

⁂

Addy waited for Nick to come around to the other side of the truck to help her out. The sweet man had thought of everything. He'd already laid several plastic tarps on the ground between where he'd parked the truck and their little cabin.

The sun would be setting in a matter of minutes. Their wedding and reception had been beautiful, lovelier than she could have planned or imagined. But now she was ready for alone time with her husband.

Nick opened the door, took her hand in his, and helped her out of the cab. She looked toward the back of the truck, which was covered with various sizes of balls and plastic chains. "I think they did quite a number on your truck."

Nick laughed. "I think you're right."

Lifting the front of her dress, she took several steps on the plastic and faced the pond. As the sun began to set, its reflection bounced off the water. The myriad blues and pinks and purples that covered the sky nearly took her breath away. "This is the perfect honeymoon evening."

Nick stepped behind her and wrapped his arms around her waist. He bent down and whispered, "Any evening would be perfect for me. As long as you are part of it."

Addy giggled and turned around to face her husband. She lifted her head and gently kissed his lips. Nick lifted his hand and trailed his fingers through the length of her hair. "I love you, Addy Martin."

Addy sucked in a deep breath and closed her eyes. "Do you have any idea how long I've waited to hear those words from your lips?"

He frowned. "I told you I loved you several times today."

Addy shook her head. "Not those words." She fiddled with the collar of his tux. "Though I definitely like to hear them." She lifted her hand up to the back of his neck and ran her fingers through his short waves. "I mean Addy *Martin*."

Nick growled as he scooped her up into his arms. "I definitely made you wait too long, Addy Martin."

His shoes scrunched against the plastic-covered ground toward the cabin's door. "But once I figured out my foolishness"—he pushed open the door with his hip and stepped inside—"I took care of that real fast."

Addy wrapped her arms tighter around his neck and kissed his cheek. "Yes, you did. I'm glad you came to your senses."

He gently placed her on her feet but didn't release her from his grip. Addy felt she would melt under the burning look in his eyes. He touched her cheek once more, and Addy felt her knees start to falter. He lowered his lips to her ear and whispered, "Me, too. Because, Addy Martin, for me. . .you were made to love."

BETTING ON LOVE

Dedication

To New Hope Baptist Church in Versailles, Kentucky. You have been Albert's and my church family since we were newlyweds (as you know, we were still babies ourselves). You have loved us through all of life's ups and downs. I am so thankful to know each and every one of you. I love you all so much. God is so good!

Chapter 1

Drew Wilson stared at his sister's bridesmaid. The girl was entirely too cute to be a diesel mechanic. He gulped down the last of his punch in an attempt to stave off the taste of the green ice cream and lemon-lime drink. *Who would have thought up such a disgusting mixture, and why does everyone think they have to have it at their wedding?* He scraped his tongue against the roof of his mouth, trying not to gag at the aftertaste.

Looking back at Melody Markwell, he took in how the silver, shiny dress hugged her body in a way that he was sure it could never hug any other diesel mechanic he'd ever known. And the pinky purple belt thing around her waist—what was it his sister had called it? He chewed the inside of his jaw. *A raspberry-colored sash.* Not only did the silky strip wrap around her skinny waist in the most froufrou bow he'd ever seen, but it also matched the color of her lips, which were a bit too plump in his opinion.

And her hair—well it rolled all the way down her back like a mud-covered hill on a wet spring afternoon after he and his buddies had four-wheeled up and down until their tanks were dry. He cocked his head. Okay, he had to admit her hair looked quite a bit prettier than a muddy hill, which was proof enough that the woman couldn't really be a diesel mechanic. At least not one of any account.

That national certification license she liked to spout off about didn't mean anything, even if he didn't know anyone in town who had one.

He tossed the clear plastic cup into the trash can. Sucking in his breath, he stepped toward the woman who grated on his nerves something fierce. Of course, the dark-haired nuisance just had to be standing close to his newly married sister, Addy, and her husband—one of Drew's best friends—Nick, as well as several of their friends.

"It sounds like it's just a spark plug." Melody's voice lifted through the air like a little bird. More proof that she couldn't be any kind of mechanic. "Tomorrow I'll come out and give it a check. Won't take me five minutes to fix."

Drew bit back the urge to gag. The woman thought she knew everything about everything.

"I'd appreciate it," Gracie, Addy's best friend, answered. "Wyatt just doesn't know much about vehicles. We usually ask Drew, but he's always so busy. . . ."

Drew cleared his throat. "Don't ever hesitate to ask me. It's no trouble for *me* to fix your car." He knew he'd emphasized the *me* a bit too much, but he didn't care. Melody didn't need to fix his friends' vehicles. He'd been helping them just fine for years.

Gracie jumped and placed her hand on her chest as she turned toward him. "Drew, you scared the life out of me. I didn't know you were there."

He looked at Melody Markwell, the woman who'd walked into his town thinking she could do everything from helping his sister organize a wedding to fixing every vehicle in the county. Not that he minded a self-reliant woman. He'd been raised by a strong mother and alongside an independent sister, but this Melody had some kind of chip on her shoulder. And she was too cute. And she invaded his thoughts at the oddest moments. And he didn't like that one bit.

Melody squinted and glared at him. He smirked when she lifted her little chin up at him. "I'm sure *I* can figure it out without a problem."

Noting the challenge in her tone, he straightened his shoulders and crossed his arms in front of his chest as he peered down at the slip of a woman. "I guess we'll have to wait and see."

Melody opened her mouth, but the sound of someone clapping stopped her from making any kind of retort. He looked over and saw his mother wave her hands in animated anticipation as everyone turned their attention her way. A broad smile lit up her face, and he knew she and Nick's mom, who had been best friends all their lives, were ecstatic about the union of their children. "It's time to cut the cake."

Drew nodded at Melody and Gracie then made his way to his buddy Mike, who stood in the far corner. The whole day was making him sick to his stomach. Sure, he was glad to see his sister so happy, and he liked that the fellow she snagged was not only a solid Christian but also one of his best friends. But getting all dressed up in a monkey suit just to stand around choking down the frothy punch—he yanked at the collar of his shirt—it just seemed to be a waste of the time he could have spent working on the farm.

He most definitely liked beating Nick at the no-women bet he, Wyatt, Mike, and Nick had made several years before. After watching another buddy succumb to a life of working long hours only to go home to a needy wife and whiny kids, the four of them had made a bet that none of them wanted to lose: The first three to get married would have to help plan and pay for the wedding of the guy who waited the longest. Something none of them intended to take part in.

With Wyatt and Nick having already given over to the female wiles, Drew was a sure win. Mike was a great guy, but he couldn't win a bet unless the rest of them handed the prize over to him. And Drew had never been one to hand a win over to anyone.

Drew grabbed Mike's hand in a firm shake. "How's it going?"

"Just standing here watching another one of us get reeled in."

Drew glanced at his sister and Nick. She had just shoved an oversized piece of cake into his face. Nick gripped both her hands in one of his and held them in the air while he rubbed his cake-covered face against her cheek. Drew wrinkled his nose. Seeing his friend and his sister so lovey-dovey made his stomach turn.

He looked back at Mike, two years his junior, and guffawed at the horrified expression on his face. He patted Mike's shoulder. "Well, we both know you're next to fall."

Mike shrugged off Drew's palm. "I don't know about that. I have just as many prospects as you." He lifted his hand and connected his index finger to his thumb to make a zero.

Drew blew out a breath. "Are you kidding? You and Lacy have been making moon eyes at each other for nearly two years."

Mike's face reddened, and he stammered as he did every time someone said something that was a bit too close to the truth. "We have not." He nodded toward Melody Markwell. "What about that gal over there? Nick's cousin? She seemed to get under your skin fast enough."

Drew snorted. "You said it. The woman gets under my skin like a tick burrowing its head into flesh so it can suck out the blood of its victim." He shook his head and almost chuckled at how true the analogy was. "No. I don't believe that gal's a threat to my bachelorhood."

"How 'bout Terri Fletcher?" Mike motioned toward the tall, thin girl who stood close to Drew's mother. Terri had always reminded Drew of Olive Oyl from the old *Popeye* cartoons. Not only was she almost as tall as Drew and as thick as a blade of grass, but she even wore her black hair tied in a knot most of the time. "She's had her sights set on you since the ninth grade," Mike said.

Drew flared his nostrils. The woman had been quite the nemesis to him throughout high school and a few years following. That is, until he'd let her know in direct terms that he was in no way interested in pursuing romantic notions with her or anyone. "I don't suppose I've got my sights set on Terri either."

Mike shrugged. "I guess we'll wait and see."

Drew turned his attention back to Nick and Addy. Melody walked up to his sister and handed her another napkin to wipe the cake off her face. The sunlight from the window seemed to dance around Melody, probably from the diamond-looking thingies she'd stuck all over the top of her head.

He exhaled a sigh of disgust. The woman looked downright adorable. Even prettier than a newborn fawn. The truth of it grated Drew's nerves and twisted something on the inside. He didn't want to think about what that something was.

<hr />

Melody folded the last raspberry-colored tablecloth and laid it in the box Addy's mother had given her. Laughter and squeals from children romping on the playground seeped through the windows and door, tempting her to slip off the rhinestone-studded heels and join them.

She peered around the room. Addy and Nick's wedding party and family had spent the last few hours cleaning up after the ceremony. The sanctuary and fellowship hall were undecorated and freshly scoured, ready for Sunday services the next morning. Warmth crept up her neck and cheeks when she remembered the look of longing in both Nick's and Addy's eyes as they headed for their first evening as husband and wife to the cabin he'd built.

Peals of laughter filled the room again, and Melody bit her bottom lip. She knew it wouldn't be proper to roughhouse with a bunch of kids in her fancy silver bridesmaid dress. Despite how much fun she'd had getting all dolled up for her cousin's and Addy's big day, she longed to let down her hair, both literally and figuratively, and just have a good time in the spring sunshine. She wondered how long it would take her to get the rhinestone twirly things out of her hair. Aunt Renee would have to help her when they got back to the house.

She looked out the window, watching as the children struggled to push the merry-go-round fast enough. She smiled at the determined expression of a little guy who couldn't have been more than five.

Kentucky was especially beautiful in the spring when the dogwood and honeysuckle, daylilies, tulips, and irises bloomed to breathtaking perfection. This May sky didn't contain even a trace of the showers that so often dripped, sprinkled, and even poured during the fifth month of the year in the Bluegrass State. Today, the sun smiled upon River Run, and the breeze blew with just the slightest kiss to the cheek.

Melody couldn't stand it any longer. She kicked off her shoes, picked them up, then raced out the back door. After dropping the heels on the picnic table, she scooped up a handful of her dress and made her way to the merry-go-round. "You want me to push you?"

"Yeah!" The little boy she'd been watching jumped onto the merry-go-round and wrapped his legs and arms around one of the metal bars. She knew he was Dana's—the church custodian's—great-grandson, but she couldn't remember the boy's name.

Melody nodded to the two redheaded girls, Beth and Becca, twin grand-daughters of Sherri, the soloist in the wedding. Melody figured they were probably about the same age as the boy. "You ready?"

The girls cheered and giggled as they locked their arms around the bar and each other.

"Okay. Here I go." In an attempt to keep her dress as clean as possible, she continued to grip the satiny material with her left hand and pushed bar after bar with her right.

The kids squealed with delight, and before Melody had a chance to think through her actions, she hopped onto the merry-go-round with them. The wind felt amazing whipping through her hair, and she bellowed out along with the children. Losing her grip on the bar, she started to slip, and the little guy grabbed hold of her arm. "I got ya," he said. His face grimaced as he held tight to her arm.

She smiled at the youngster. "Thanks, buddy." It was nice to see a boy who was so chivalrous. Her experience with the male gender had been that most of them didn't even begin to have that quality.

As the merry-go-round started to slow down, a figure in the parking lot caught her gaze. Her cheeks warmed when she was able to make out the confused expression on Addy's brother's face. Embarrassment welled in her chest at how silly she must appear. A grown woman should never jump and scream on a merry-go-round in a satin bridesmaid dress. And to do so in front of Drew Wilson only made matters worse. *That man knows how to get under my skin like no one I've ever known before.*

Lifting her chin, Melody determined she would not allow the man to make her feel uncomfortable, inferior, or whatever it was she felt every time she was around him. She hopped up and brushed the dirt and wrinkles from the shiny dress.

"Push us again!" one of the twins squealed.

Melody smiled down at them, noting how much they looked like their grandmother. "I'm afraid I need to help the grown-ups finish packing things into the cars."

"Aww...," the girls groaned.

The little guy jumped off and lifted his left hand in the air as if to stop traffic. "It's okay." He grabbed the bar with his right hand. "I'll push."

Melody lifted her hand to high-five the child. "Thanks, buddy."

If she ever had a son, she would teach him to be as kind to girls as this little one was. She sighed. She loved children, but there was no way she'd ever have a son to raise. She wasn't willing to date, let alone marry, any man.

The boy smacked her hand then focused back on the merry-go-round. Melody turned back toward Drew. She noted the humor etched on his expression and couldn't decipher if he was inwardly laughing at her or amused by her. She didn't particularly want him to be either. The man had been nothing but a half-empty glass and a condescending chauvinist since she arrived in River Run. He'd made it abundantly clear he didn't believe women could do mechanic work as well as men. Given the chance, she'd have no problem showing him different. She averted her gaze and walked past him.

"Melody."

She stopped when he said her name. There was no telling what smart-aleck comment he would have to say about her playing on the merry-go-round with the kids. She turned and looked at him, ready to verbally spar in any way necessary.

"Mom's grilling hamburgers and hot dogs for all of us. She already has everything ready." He looked away from her, and she wondered why he seemed suddenly uncomfortable. "I'm supposed to tell you to come."

"I was planning on it."

"Did he tell you we're gonna play cornhole, too?" Mike walked up beside Drew and patted his shoulder. "The only person who's ever beat Drew just left on his honeymoon."

Her heart filled with excitement, and the thought of beating Drew Wilson at the game sent it to pounding. "I love cornhole. I haven't played in ages."

Mike raised one eyebrow. "You any good?"

Teasing, Melody blew on her knuckles then brushed her shoulder. "Back home I was town champion two years in a row."

Drew grunted and rolled his eyes.

Fire blazed through Melody's veins at the man's pompous attitude. She wished she'd known they'd be playing cornhole. She'd have practiced a bit to ensure she whipped up on Drew Wilson. The man desperately needed to be knocked down a few pegs. "Maybe you and I will have a chance to play, Drew."

He gazed back at her. Challenge lit his eyes. "I'm sure we will."

⁂

Melody couldn't help but watch Drew as he glowered in the far corner of his family living room. Pride puffed up her chest and filled her gut. So much so, she couldn't even finish the hot dog she'd started eating.

Gracie sat beside Melody. Her plate was filled with a loaded grilled hamburger; potato salad made by Drew's mom, Amanda; and her aunt Renee's coleslaw. The food was delicious, and Melody wished she had room in her stomach to finish off her plate.

"Where's that big boy of yours?" Melody asked.

Gracie pointed her fork toward Wyatt, who was making his way to Drew and Mike. "His dad's letting me eat first."

"I would have held him while you ate."

"You need to eat, too." She took a bite of potato salad then wiped her mouth with a napkin. "Besides, Drew probably needs cheering up after you whipped him twice at cornhole."

Indescribable satisfaction swelled within her. "That man needed to be knocked down a few notches. He's entirely too cocky."

Gracie laughed and swatted her hand. "Aw, Drew's a great guy. He just always wins at everything. After a while, you can't blame the guy for simply expecting it."

Melody remembered the mixed expression of shock and horror on Drew's face when she sank the corn kernel–filled beanbag into the hole for her first win. "Then I'm glad I could help him get a taste of losing."

Gracie lifted her fork in the air and shook it back and forth. "Be careful, Melody. You know what the Bible says—pride comes before a fall."

Melody tried not to roll her eyes. She didn't know what the Bible said, and she really didn't care, either. It had been abundantly clear in the months she'd spent living with her aunt and uncle that they were Holy Rollers. Evidently, years before, when her mom and dad were still married, before her dad skipped out on them, her mom had been religious as well. But Melody had very few remembrances of church or the Bible or God. Her mom worked too hard and too many hours to worry about spending time with Melody, let alone fret about going to church. Her mom had given up on God and everything else when her dad left, so He must not be that great.

Melody pointed toward Drew. "You saw how the overgrown boy acted. He practically stomped off after I beat him the second time. He hasn't even so much as looked at me since. No 'good game,' 'congratulations,' or anything."

Gracie pushed a stray strand of blond hair behind her ear. Melody felt a niggling of jealousy at Gracie's beautiful light hair, eyes, and complexion. Everything about the woman was feminine and dainty. Though she was on the short side and she had a small frame, Melody felt like a dark-haired, dark-eyed workhorse beside her new friend. "He has definitely been acting strange the last few months. Probably because his little sister just married one of his best friends."

"Or maybe he's just a male chauvinist pig."

Gracie frowned. "You have Drew pegged wrong. He's a good Christian man." She took a drink of her sweet tea. "By the way, are you planning to come to church tomorrow?"

Melody wrinkled her nose. Church seemed to be all everyone in this town ever talked about. She'd agreed to go a few times with her aunt and uncle, but she didn't really care much for it. All the preacher ever talked about was having a personal relationship with the Lord. Well, she'd done just fine without that personal relationship for twenty-four years. Why would she all of a sudden have to have it now? "I don't know."

"Afterward, you could come over for lunch then take a look at our car."

Melody squinted. "I thought Christians were supposed to rest on Sunday."

Gracie leaned toward her. "Will I be able to convince you to come to church if I promise you can look at my car?"

Melody grinned at Gracie's sneaky motives. "Possibly."

Gracie smacked her leg. "Then by all means, after church you can come look at my car."

Melody shook her head. Since she'd moved to River Run, she'd been working as much as she could to build up her name as a trustworthy mechanic in the area, and Gracie knew she'd like to have the good word of the owner of the town's hardware store. "Fine. I'll be there."

Chapter 2

Drew grabbed the supplies for the house he was going to build then walked up to the counter of the hardware store. In just a few more days he'd have the ground leveled; then he and his friends could start working on the foundation. Having bought the land from his dad several years before, Drew had finally saved enough money to build a modest home.

After fixing up the cabin Nick had built on his land, Drew had no doubt he and his friends had the know-how to build a small home. Unlike Nick, Drew wasn't in a rush. They could work on it a bit at a time until it was done. He'd have his own place and no debt. He could use his money as God guided instead of forking it all over to a bank.

"This all you need?" Wyatt scanned the first item.

Drew nodded. "For now anyway."

Wyatt picked up the spark plug and furrowed his eyebrows. "What's this for?"

"The dump truck. I'm pretty sure that's all that's wrong with her."

"Is it broken or just not running well?"

"Won't start up like it should."

"Are you sure it's just a spark plug? Melody came over to the house yesterday after church, and she fixed Gracie's car in no time flat. I was sure it was—"

Drew lifted his hand as he peered at his friend. "I believe I know a bit more about vehicles than you."

Wyatt raised his hands in surrender. "Hey, don't be so defensive, man. I wasn't insulting your abilities. I was just saying Melody really seems to know what she's talking about—"

Drew clenched his hand then pounded the counter with the side of his fist. "And you don't think I do?"

"What is the matter with you, Drew? Why does she get on your nerves so bad?"

Drew thought of Melody in the long silver dress she wore as Addy's bridesmaid. She'd looked amazing with the sides of her thick, dark hair tied in a knot at the back of her head and the rest of it flowing in long curls down her back.

129

Her dark eyes held such depth and mystery. When she walked down the aisle, for a moment, Drew nearly lost his breath.

Then he'd watched her play with the kids on the merry-go-round. Her expression and body language had been of complete freedom and bliss. Her laughter rang through the breeze with the children's, and he'd found himself again drawn to her as he'd never been drawn to a woman before.

Then she'd challenged him to cornhole. The Melody he'd seen when she first arrived in River Run exposed herself. Melody couldn't simply have fun with the game. She had to win. She had to gloat. Sure, the gloating had only come from her expression, not her lips. Still, Drew had noted it all the same.

She was the same way when it came to mechanics. She had to prove to everyone that she was the best, that they should trust their transportation to her and no one else. And after years of looking after the vehicles of his family and friends, he took offense to her waltzing into River Run and stomping all over his toes.

Drew finally looked at Wyatt. "The woman thinks she knows everything."

"You mean about vehicles?"

Drew nodded his head. "That's one thing she thinks she knows it all about."

Wyatt leaned forward against the counter. "She *is* a nationally certified diesel mechanic."

Drew rolled his eyes. "Who cares?"

"And she's good."

"A lot of people are good. I'm good."

Wyatt lifted one eyebrow. "Are you jealous of a *girl*, Drew Wilson?"

Drew folded his arms across his chest and growled. "Do I need to whip some sense into you? It's been a few years since I've done it, but you know I can. Of course I'm not jealous of her. It's her cocky attitude that gets on my nerves."

"She did beat you at cornhole." Wyatt's mouth curved upward just a tad on the left side, and Drew felt a real urge to punch his friend in the face. Wyatt lifted two fingers in the air. "Twice."

Anger boiled within Drew, and he pointed his finger at Wyatt. "Now, look here. . ."

Wyatt backed away from the counter. "Actually, you two are a whole lot alike. You're both so stinkin' competitive. Have to be the best at everything. But you're a Christian, and she's not."

Drew's fury started to simmer. He knew Melody wasn't a Christian. Addy had prayed for her every night at the dinner table before she and Nick got married.

Wyatt continued. "Gracie prays for her constantly. She really likes Melody, but the woman's got some kind of wall built up all around her. She doesn't want to let anyone in. Not even Gracie, and you know how easy it is for people to open up to Gracie."

Drew blew out a long breath. "Addy feels the same way. Nick said Melody was raised by her mom, just the two of them. I guess her mom had to work a lot of hours. Nick said he thought things were kind of hard for Melody."

Anger washed across Wyatt's face as he handed the receipt to Drew. "As long as I have breath in this body, I'll do everything I can to take care of Gracie and our son. I'd never leave her to fend for herself. I don't understand a man who could do that."

Sobered and feeling thankful for his mother and father, Drew grabbed his bag off the counter. "I've got to head on over to the homesite. I'll talk to you later."

His heart felt heavy as he made his way back to his truck. He loved the Lord with all his heart, soul, mind, and strength. At least he'd always believed he did. Sure, he knew he was a bit competitive and could be a bit mule-headed at times. He wasn't perfect, but he always wanted to be sensitive to God's guiding and what God wanted from him.

After turning the ignition, he prayed silently as he started down the road. *God, Wyatt's right. I have been defensive when it comes to Melody. I don't know what it is about her that rubs me the wrong way. Forgive me, Lord. Help me be a better witness for You.*

He slammed his brakes when a small mutt ran into the middle of the road. The contents of the hardware bag fell out onto the floor of the truck. He saw the spark plugs, and an idea popped into his head.

He groaned as he lifted his cap off his head, wiped the sweat off his brow with the back of his hand, then placed the cap back on. "God, isn't there some other way?"

His heart felt as if it had been nudged again, and Drew cringed as he took the cell phone out of his pocket. "God, I wouldn't do this for anyone but You."

Hands filled with various vegetable seedlings, Melody followed her aunt Renee outside to the newly tilled garden. She felt like a fish out of water helping her aunt with plants and flowers. Melody knew everything there was to know about cleaning a house, doing laundry, and even fixing all kinds of things from televisions to microwaves to car engines, but she'd had absolutely no experience messing with Mother Nature.

"Okay, Melody." Aunt Renee set down the plants then pointed to the right side of the huge garden area. Melody followed her lead and placed her plants on the ground. "I'm going to have you put the cucumbers over there. They need plenty of room to spread out."

Melody nodded. "Okay. Which ones are the cucumbers?"

Aunt Renee picked up a tray with six plants. She handed them to Melody with a wry grin. "The ones with the picture of a cucumber on the tag."

"Make fun of me all you want, Aunt Renee." Melody smiled as she gently touched the dainty green leaves on the plants. "You're the crazy one for letting me touch these poor things."

"You'll be fine." She handed her a small shovel. Melody had never seen one so small. It was kind of cute. "Plant them about a foot apart."

Melody nodded. She headed to her spot then surveyed the area where she was to plant the cucumbers. A foot apart seemed awfully far, but she didn't know anything about gardening, so she'd have to trust her aunt.

Melody knelt down and touched the soft earth. It actually felt nice and cool and squishy between her fingers. Her aunt had fussed all morning about getting the garden out about a week and a half later than she normally did, but Nick and Addy's wedding had taken precedence over the garden.

Might as well get to it, Melody chided herself. She wasn't sure how deep to dig. She glanced over at her aunt, who appeared quite busy with what Melody believed were the tomato plants—although she had no idea why her aunt was placing circular wire contraptions over the small plants.

She shrugged. If the plants had to be a foot away from each other, they probably needed to be around a foot deep. She gazed at the small plants. But the cucumber seedlings were probably only six inches tall at the most.

Just do it. If I can fix an engine, I can plant a cucumber.

She stuck the small trowel into the earth and shoveled out several shovelfuls of dirt. Once she had a good-sized mound beside the hole, she firmly stuck the plant inside then covered most of it with the mound.

I would say the plants need plenty of water, so I'll build the dirt up around the plant; that way it will kind of be like a bowl to catch the rain.

Still unsure if she'd planted it deep enough, she looked at the small bit of cucumber plant that stuck out from the circular hole she'd created. She had no idea if it looked right or not. Peering over at her aunt, she watched her put another wire contraption over another plant. Blowing out her breath, Melody decided it was good enough and started a hole for the next plant.

Once she'd finished three more plants, she realized a shadow fell over her. She looked up to find Aunt Renee standing over her with her hands on her hips.

"Melody, what are you doing?" Her aunt's voice was calm and smooth.

Melody furrowed her eyebrows, unable to see her aunt's expression because of the sunlight. "I'm planting cucumbers."

"Are you planting them or burying them?"

Melody cupped her hand over her eyebrows trying to shield the sun. "What do you mean?"

A smile bowed Aunt Renee's lips, and she turned toward the other side of the garden. "Roy, come over here. You gotta see this."

Melody watched as her uncle walked toward them. She looked down at the cucumber plants, trying to figure out what her aunt thought was so humorous. She'd planted them a foot apart. She'd stuck them in the ground, even made kind of a bowl shape around them allowing them plenty of opportunity to hold water. A little bit of each plant stuck up from the top.

She stood and wiped her hands on her hips while her uncle made his way beside them. An obnoxious laugh snorted from Uncle Roy's mouth when he looked at her plants. "Melody, what were you thinking?"

She crossed her arms in front of her chest, trying not to feel foolish or defensive. "What?"

Aunt Renee bent down and pulled the first plant out of its crater. She filled most of the hole then gently placed the seedling into a much smaller hole and pushed dirt around it. "The plants need to be closer to the top to get the sunlight. And you want the dirt to go downward, away from the plant. The plants would drown the other way around."

"I told you I don't know what I'm doing." Melody tried to smile as she spoke through gritted teeth. She tried to swallow back her embarrassment as she thought of the many times her mother had chided her about her need to do everything right the first time—her need for perfection.

"You're doing fine. You're learning. You gave us a good laugh this morning." Uncle Roy patted her back. "Remember the last time you got a good laugh from me."

Melody's mind replayed the time Uncle Roy had tried to fix his muffler with wire and duct tape. She'd been both appalled and tickled by the mess he'd made of the poor car part. She grinned. "I sure do."

Aunt Renee shook her head, obviously remembering as well. She pointed to the buried cucumber plants. "Go ahead and fix those. You know how to do it now."

Melody nodded and bent down to her work as her aunt and uncle walked back to their spots in the garden. Her cell phone vibrated in her pocket. Flustered, she tried to wipe as much dirt as possible onto her jean shorts then dug into her pocket for the phone. She pulled it out and pressed the TALK button. "Hello."

Silence. She pulled it away from her ear to see if she'd lost the connection. She didn't recognize the number, but they were still connected. She put it back to her ear. "Hello," she tried again.

The caller cleared his throat. "Hello, Melody?"

She pulled the phone away from her ear to look at the number again. She furrowed her brows. The caller sounded an awful lot like Addy's brother, Drew. But surely he'd be the last person on the planet to call her. She placed the phone back against her ear. "Yes, this is she."

The caller cleared his throat again. "Umm. This is Drew—Addy's brother."

A sudden panic gripped her heart. The only reason he'd call her was if something happened to Addy or to Nick. Maybe he'd called her because he didn't know how to tell Uncle Roy and Aunt Renee that something happened. "What's wrong? Did something happen to Addy and Nick?"

"What?" He sounded confused. "No. No. As far as I know they're fine. Haven't heard from them, but then I wouldn't expect to." He chuckled then stopped. "I need to ask a favor of you."

Suspicion filled her gut. What would Drew Wilson want from her? A rematch at cornhole? To try to make her look silly? He'd made it abundantly obvious he thought she was just a silly little woman. Pride swelled within her, and a slow grin formed on her lips. But she'd proven herself better than him in every way he'd challenged her.

"Did you hear me? I need your help," he said.

"Okay. What do you need?"

"The dump truck I'm using. It doesn't start up well. Sometimes I can't get her going at all. I was wondering if you'd come look at it."

Melody squinted. "You can't fix it yourself?"

"I need your help."

Even over the phone, she could tell saying those four words had taken a lot out of him. And even though she felt he was probably up to something, Melody was itching to have the opportunity to work on some heavy machinery. "Okay. I'll come over after lunch. Your house, right?"

"Actually, it's at my homesite. I'm building my own house. I'll meet you at my parents' house and bring you on out here."

"Okay." Melody clicked the phone off. Bending down she tried to focus on the cucumber plants once more. Her heartbeat sped up, and a knot twisted in her gut. It was kind of weird. She'd never been so excited to see an oversized truck.

Chapter 3

Melody admired Kentucky's idyllic scenery as she followed behind Drew's pickup. He'd invited her to ride along with him, but she'd insisted she might need the tools packed in the back of her truck. Now she could drink in the rolling grass-covered hills dotted with trees of various kinds and sizes. Cattle grazed on the right side of the road, and Melody smiled as two calves chased each other in the field.

The old gravel road took them past a slightly swollen, rolling creek. She wondered about the crawdads that most definitely lived within it, reminiscing about a time when she and some friends spent an afternoon fishing for the small lobsterlike critters.

The ride was peaceful, serene. It was beautiful, awe inspiring. She thrilled at the idea of living in such a place. Though she'd been raised in a small town, her mother could only afford a small apartment in town. She'd relished the times she'd been able to romp the countryside with friends, always longing to live close to Mother Nature and away from people. People didn't treat each other right. They lied. They abandoned. They mistreated. It was one of the reasons she loved machines so much. She didn't need someone else to help her work on one. It was a solo activity, most of the time anyway. The road grew narrower and less traveled. For a moment, the trees seemed to grow thicker around them. Then they opened up into a beautiful cleared-out field.

Melody took in the machinery, spying the dump truck she assumed she was to look at. She noted the flags marking the spot of Drew's future home. Just beyond the markings, she saw a good-sized pond. He'd practically be able to cast a line from his back porch. The idea of it made her smile.

Drew stopped his truck then hopped out. Melody followed his lead. He swiped his hand across the expanse of the place. Pride radiated from him. "Here it is." He looked down at her, and Melody was surprised that his gaze held a hint of need for approval.

She swallowed the knot in her throat. It was the first time she'd noted any kind of vulnerability in Drew, and if she could allow herself to be honest with him, she'd tell him how amazing she thought the place would be. Instead, her defenses took control, and her words came out flat and elusive. "It's nice."

A trace of hurt flashed across his expression. He nodded toward the dump truck. "There it is. Let's go take a look."

Without a backward glance, he walked toward the machine. Melody inwardly chided herself. He'd wanted her to praise the land, and it was worthy of a few accolades. The place was amazing.

She could just picture a small ranch home—brick or log, she wasn't sure which she would picture. Either would be beautiful. A full front porch would extend the length of the house with a porch swing on both sides. She wondered if he'd put his bedroom in the back of the house, so he could build a deck off it so that he could sit outside and look out over the pond.

She shook her head. What was she thinking? She had no business thinking about how Drew Wilson should set up his house. She didn't even like the man. She didn't like any man. Well, except Uncle Roy. He'd proven to be different than any other man she'd ever known.

"Let me show you what she's doing." She watched as Drew hopped up into the cab of the dump truck. He shoved in the key and turned the ignition. The truck groaned and whined before she finally puttered to life. He turned it off and started it again. This time the machine jumped to a quick start.

Drew turned it off then hopped back out of the truck. "Well, that's what she's doing. One time she'll start right up. The next time she whines and carries on until she finally decides to run. Occasionally, she just won't start at all."

Melody nodded. "Oil's good? Filter's good?"

"Yes."

"What about the starter?"

"It should be fine. Replaced a little over six months ago."

Melody noted he'd had trouble answering the second question. She sneaked a peek at Drew. It was obvious that asking for her help was hard on his ego. "Okay. Let's have a look inside."

Melody looked around the engine. It needed some new spark plugs, but that wouldn't cause her to vary the way she started up as much as Drew was describing. Melody hopped into the cab and examined the ignition. The problem was as obvious as the nose on her face. He needed to change the plugs and put in a new ignition.

She looked at Drew. His hands were shoved down deep into his jeans pockets. A scowl wrapped his features. Not only was he a self-proclaimed

Mr. Handyman, but many people around town agreed with his belief and sought him out for help with their stuff. There was no way he could have missed what was wrong with this truck. The problem was too simple. He was just acting like he didn't know what was wrong. But why?

Gazing out at his property, she realized something she hadn't thought of before. They were alone. Way back in the heart of the Bluegrass State, and they were completely and utterly alone.

Her chest tightened, and her heart raced as she remembered running through the county park back at her own stomping grounds. At fourteen, she'd only wanted to practice for the high school cross-country team. She'd discovered running long distances took her mind off her worries of her mom having to work so hard to provide for them. She didn't have to think about how her mom rarely talked to her when she was home, almost ignoring her completely. It allowed her to breathe in the clean air and blow out the constant concerns and stresses and worries.

Then the man grabbed her. He seemed to have come from nowhere and everywhere all at the same time. She felt his strong, large hand wrapped around the top of her arm, so tight she thought her bone would crack. His breath smelled of cigarettes, strong and stale.

She shook the thought away. She would not allow herself to go there. She'd put that behind her, never to be thought of or relived again. She wouldn't allow it now.

After hopping down out of the cab, she stared at Drew as she straightened her shoulders and crossed her arms in front of her chest. "Why did you ask me to come out here?"

A puzzled expression wrapped his face. "I think the reason is obvious." He pointed to the truck.

She squinted at him. "Really? It's not so obvious to me why you asked me here. What *is* obvious is what's wrong with the truck. It's an easy fix." She pointed her finger at his chest. "And you and I both know you know how to fix it."

His face flamed red, but Melody knew she'd hit him right between the eyes. He did know how to fix that truck. He'd brought her out for a different reason. Knowing men as she did, she believed it couldn't be an honorable one.

Balling her fists, she broadened her stance, preparing herself for a physical battle if the need arose. She'd taken self-defense, and she now knew how to take care of herself. "So, why would you bring me all the way out here—all alone?"

Drew looked at the expanse of his place once more then peered back at her. Realization at what she was asking seemed to dawn on him, and he took a few steps back shaking his hands in front of his chest. "No way."

Melody cocked her head. "Well, then explain."

Drew's expression turned grim, and he set his jaw. "Don't flatter yourself, Melody. I only wanted help with my truck."

Taken aback by his words, she sucked in her breath. Was he insulting her? Was he saying he was too good for her? Of all the arrogant, egotistical men—

He spoke again. "I take offense at what you're thinking. You need to go on home."

Feeling as if she'd been sucker punched, Melody tried to lift her chin. She could feel the start of tears forming in her eyes. In less time than a cow can swish her tail, she'd gone from fearing he'd try to take advantage of her to feeling unwanted, unworthy, and unattractive. "I'd still like to know why you asked me here."

"Obviously, you wouldn't understand. Go home." Drew turned and walked toward his truck.

Without hesitation Melody hopped into her own pickup, started it, and headed down the gravel road toward the main road. The unwanted tears she'd been able to hold at bay now streamed freely down her face. She felt perplexed that he'd asked her help for something so simple. Even more so, she was an idiot. A foolish woman. How could she have been worried and ready to fight if Drew had intended to get her alone, and then offended that he had no desire to be alone with her?

⁂

Drew couldn't remember the last time he'd been so insulted. Melody actually believed he'd driven her out to his place to take advantage of her. He fumed as he grabbed the spark plugs he'd bought for the dump truck out of the cab of his pickup.

Sure, he'd called for her help, and yes, he did know how to fix the dump truck. He looked heavenward. "But God, that's what I thought You wanted me to do. I know the woman doesn't know You, and I know she and I don't always see eye to eye on most things."

He shrugged his shoulders then grabbed his toolbox out of the bed of the pickup. "Okay, we have yet to see eye to eye on anything. But still, I thought You were telling me to call her out here—make her feel needed or wanted or whatever it is that silly woman needs. I just wanted to be a good witness."

You can't do that by fibbing. His spirit spoke within his heart.

He let out a long sigh. "I know."

With a heavy heart, he changed the spark plugs in the truck. Though he hated to admit it, his heart ached a bit that she hadn't been more excited about his homesite. Every bit a country girl, he thought she might swoon over the pond that made up much of his backyard.

He growled at his thinking as he tightened the spark plugs. What did he care what she thought? She drove him to insanity. Always having to win everything. Always having to prove herself to everyone.

"Actually, you two are a whole lot alike. You're both so stinkin' competitive. Have to be the best at everything. But you're a Christian, and she's not." Wyatt's words flooded his mind anew.

She was a lot like him. He knew she was. Which also meant she wouldn't back down from anybody for any reason. She thought he had tried to hoodoo her out here to fix his dump truck. She'd thought he'd had an ulterior motive.

Well, the truth was he did have an ulterior motive, but it wasn't impure in any way. He just wanted to do right by his faith.

God knows the heart.

He grabbed the rag out of the back pocket of his jeans then wiped the sweat from his forehead. "You don't care much about my actions if my heart ain't right, do You, Lord?" He shoved the rag back in his pocket. "The world has plenty of do-gooders, but this is about me and You."

Drew pushed away from the dump truck. He walked to the oversized blue cooler he'd been using for water bottles. He opened the lid and grabbed one out. After shutting the lid, he plopped onto the top of the cooler. Resting his elbows and forearms on the tops of his legs, he ducked his head. "God, You know I'm awful prideful. Sometimes it works good—when it comes to farming or building things or odd jobs. I always do a good job. But sometimes that pride makes me not such a nice person."

He lifted his gaze up to the heavens. The summer sky was a beautiful clear blue with just a smattering of cotton candy–like clouds. The midday sun was hot, and he twisted off the cap to the water then took a long swig. He ducked his head again.

"Something about Melody really rubs me wrong, and I'm not myself when I'm around her. I don't like who I am, and I know You don't either. Forgive me again, God. Show me how to be a witness to that woman."

He stood and stretched his back. The long hours keeping up the farm and working on his new home had stretched, pulled, and stiffened his muscles, especially in his back. He made his way back to the dump truck and checked the oil once more and the starter. Everything looked good.

Knowing she should be ready for business, he hopped into the cab and turned the ignition. Nothing. Not even a whine or a groan.

He turned the key and pulled it out of the ignition. Shoving it back into place, he twisted again. Still no sound. *You've got to be kidding me.*

He hopped out of the cab and looked at the engine again. The spark plugs looked good, as did the engine, the starter—everything. It all looked to be in good working order.

Jumping back in the cab, he tried to start her one more time. Still no sound. *I cannot believe this.*

Drew stomped back to his pickup. He fumed as he drove toward town. His cell phone buzzed, and he pulled it out of his front pocket. Seeing Mike's name on the screen, he pushed the TALK button. "Mike, I need your help."

"Okay. I need a favor as well, but go ahead. What's going on?"

"The dump truck won't start."

"I thought Melody was going to take a look at it."

Drew clenched his teeth so tight he felt his jaw would break. He gripped the steering wheel. "She did come by, but she left."

"What did you do?" Mike's tone flattened.

"I didn't do anything. She came out here and looked at it." Drew spit out the words. He could feel his blood pressure rising. He had to get that dump truck working so he could finish leveling off the site to get the foundation going. He didn't have time to play games with some crazy, two-bit woman.

Mike spoke again. "She couldn't fix it?"

"She *wouldn't* fix it. The woman thought I brought her out here to charm her or something."

Mike's guttural laugh sounded over the line. "You? Make a move on her?"

His friend's words struck a nerve, and Drew suddenly felt the urge to grab hold of Mike and punch him a good one. It wouldn't be such an amazing feat for Drew to find the woman attractive. Melody was a very pretty girl, and when she wasn't around Drew, she seemed to be fairly nice.

He knew they had their no-woman pact and all, but it was obvious Wyatt and Nick didn't care much about it. Maybe he didn't care so much anymore either.

Drew shook his head. What was he thinking? He wasn't about to even consider that spitfire in any kind of romantic notion. The idea was preposterous. He barked at Mike, "Will you help me or not?"

"You know I'll help you, but I know—by far—less about vehicles than you do."

"I know." Drew clicked the phone off and focused on the road. He really was trying to catch the wind asking Mike for mechanical help. If Nick were back from his honeymoon, the two of them together could probably figure it out, but Nick wouldn't be back for well over another week. Drew wanted to be working on the foundation by then.

If that woman hadn't gone and gotten all hoity-toity, she could have fixed the truck, and I would have been leveling the ground right now. Admitting he needed her help tasted as bitter as battery acid, and he didn't like it. Not one bit.

Chapter 4

Drew had given up. He'd worked on the dump truck for a week with no success. Mike looked at it, even though Drew knew that wouldn't do any good. Drew's dad looked at, as did Nick's dad, Roy, and another one of the town's mechanics. Drew could have whooped his own tail when Roy figured out it was the ignition. After he and Roy fixed it, the rotten truck still wouldn't run. Obviously, Roy had been wrong.

He tossed the wrench he was holding to the ground. It was ridiculous that the truck wouldn't run. From the eye of a mechanic, it had every reason to work. He'd borrowed and rented the heavy machinery he needed, and he was on a tight schedule with some of the equipment. He bit back a growl. *I can't get started on the foundation if I can't finish leveling out the ground.*

He wiped sweat from his brow. It was still early June, but Drew knew the summer months would pass him by all too soon. Though not in a big hurry for completion, he'd still hoped to have the house built by fall, the electric and plumbing all ready before winter, and to be living in his new house by Christmas. *At this rate, I'll have to spend another year living with my parents.*

At twenty-six and with two of his best buddies already married off and his baby sister married to one of them, Drew was beginning to feel like quite a moocher still living in his parents' house. He had no plans of landing himself a wife, but he sure needed to feel like he was his own man. Not sleeping under his daddy's roof.

He growled as he walked toward what should have already been leveled land. He folded his arms across his chest and stared out at the pond. He'd spent many a night dreaming of sitting on his own back deck and watching the moon bathe the water with light.

His last option in getting the truck working again was to call Melody. The idea churned his stomach. He'd heard she'd taken a job at AJ's Auto Shop and that everyone in town was singing her praises when it came to her mechanic abilities. There were people coming from their neighboring towns with their trucks and tractors to see if the "pretty little woman," as many of the old-timers called her, could fix their vehicles as good as they'd heard. So far, she seemed to have surpassed everyone's expectations.

Drew shook his head. The notion of that little gal digging around and under those oversized vehicles just didn't seem right. She was too arrogant, too small, even a little too pretty to be doing a job like that. She should be tending the garden or cooking. . . . Drew let out a huff. The woman could fix a truck, but he would bet his best head of cattle that she couldn't cook a decent meal if she tried.

What do I care if the woman has a way with mechanics or if she can or can't cook? Again, he thought of Wyatt's scolding that Drew was too competitive. *And why would I feel so threatened by the woman?*

He picked up a small stone, walked closer to the pond, then threw it, watching as it skipped along the top of the water. All these thoughts weren't getting him anywhere. He needed to find someone to fix the dump truck, and he didn't care if he was being silly—he had no intention of asking Melody Markwell for help. Instead, he'd just have to pay extra to have someone drive down from Lexington or Louisville.

He turned and headed toward his pickup. He'd have to go home and call around to find out who he needed to get to look at it. The sound of gravel crunching beneath tires drew his attention to the road. He smiled and waved when he realized it was his dad. Then he saw who was in the passenger seat.

He groaned and squinted to the heavens. *Lord, help me to be nice. I can't stand that woman.*

His dad stopped the truck then stepped out of the cab. He patted Drew's shoulder a bit too hard. He understood his dad meant for him to be nice. If he could say it out loud, he'd assure his dad that though a war of fury was raging inside him that his dad would go behind his back like that, Drew would make every attempt to be a gentleman to the much-too-cocky and snappy gal. His dad cleared his throat. "Brought you some help for the dump truck."

"I see that." Drew tried to smile as he spit the words through clenched teeth. Everything in him wanted to tell her to go home. He couldn't believe she'd thought he'd bring her out here for sinister motives. Not only did it go against everything he believed as a Christian, but it also hurt his pride that she would think him that kind of guy.

Melody hopped out of the cab then grabbed her toolbox from the bed of the truck. She walked toward Drew. "I'm doing this for your father, and only because he agreed not to sell his 1967 Mustang until I've had the chance to save enough money to buy it."

Drew gasped. He looked at his dad. "Your Mustang? What? Dad, what is she talking about?"

His dad waved his hand in front of his face. "I was planning on selling her in a few months. Melody's taken quite a liking to her, and I knew she'd be in good hands if Melody bought her off me."

Melody headed to the dump truck. Drew stared at his dad. "Since when were you going to sell the Mustang?"

He nodded to the woman who now had the upper half of her body stuck underneath the steering wheel of the truck. "Since I saw that little lady's eyes light up the first time she saw it."

"But you love that car."

His dad looked at him. "Really? You think so? I bought that thing three years ago, and I still haven't taken the time to get her running. Melody'd have her on the road in a week's time."

"But you don't just sell your car because—"

"No buts. I want to do it." His dad crossed his arms in front of his chest and leaned against his pickup. He nodded toward Melody. "That woman's a good girl. God wants her. She's had a hard life, and she hasn't decided yet if she trusts Him. In every way I can, I want to show her that she can."

Drew watched as Melody worked on the truck. His dad's words stung, and he had a feeling his dad intended for them to. He walked to Melody and cleared his throat. "Do you need any help?"

"Nope." Her tone sounded tense, but he wasn't sure if it was from concentration on the truck or frustration with him. He figured it was probably a little of both.

"I appreciate you doing this." He tried to sound kind and sincere. At the moment, he felt more like a scolded little pup.

"No problem."

He heard a popping noise, and then she lifted herself out of the truck and swiped her hands along her hips. "All done. She should work for you now."

"Are you kidding?" Drew looked at his watch. "That fast?"

She pointed toward the ignition. "Try her out."

He hopped into the truck and turned the key. The oversized machine roared to life. He turned it off then started it again to ensure it wasn't a fluke. Sure enough, it started up again. "I can't believe it."

He studied the ignition. He couldn't tell what she'd done, and he couldn't bring himself to ask her either.

Melody picked up her toolbox and walked back toward his dad's pickup. Drew jumped out of the dump truck and grabbed her arm from behind. On what seemed to be a reflex, she jerked around with her fist clenched. He let her go but stared into her well-guarded eyes. "I just wanted to thank you."

She relaxed a bit and nodded her head. "You're welcome."

Drew watched as she got into the truck beside his dad. She'd jumped like she was terrified of him. He'd never seen a woman so ready to fight at such a simple touch. She had a reason to fear being alone with a man. He saw it for the briefest moment in her eyes. His heart pounded, and anger flamed within him as he thought of what may have happened to her. He'd never allow a woman to be mistreated.

Melody hated Sundays. She'd been living with her aunt and uncle for several months, and the first few months she'd been able to talk her way out of going to church services with them. But the last three months, between Aunt Renee and Uncle Roy, and Gracie's and Addy's constant prodding, Melody had to succumb to their requests or listen to them harp at her for the rest of the week.

She wiped her sweaty palms against the sides of her faded blue jeans as they walked into the pristine white building. They may have been able to get her to go with them, but she absolutely refused to get dressed up. It had been hard enough wearing that silver silky thing in Addy and Nick's wedding. There was no way she'd be dolling herself up for a place she didn't even want to go.

"How ya doin', Melody?" The plump and short, balding pastor grabbed her hand in a tight squeeze.

She nodded and plastered a smile to her face. "I'm fine. Thanks."

He patted the top of her hand. "It always makes my day to see your pretty face come through those doors."

Normally, Melody would deck a man for saying something like that to her, but the pastor's expression and tone was so genuine and sweet, Melody had never been able to allow herself to get mad at him. "It's good to be here."

The words slipped from her mouth, even though she knew they were a lie. It wasn't good to be there. Not to her. She hated sitting in that padded wooden pew beside her aunt and uncle and looking at the wooden cross the church people had hung above a pool of water. If she remembered right, her aunt had said it was a baptistery, whatever that meant.

She felt like such a hypocrite going to church. She didn't believe in God. Well, maybe she believed in Him, but she didn't think He was this all-present, all-knowing, all-caring being like her family did. He certainly hadn't been very present in her life.

If He was all the terrific things her aunt and uncle talked about, then why did He let her dad leave? Why did her mom work all the time and ignore her when she was home? Why did that guy try to rape her? Why did her mom up and decide to get married again?

Those were only the whys about her own life. She had a plethora of whys when it came to the really bad things that happened in the world. The people who were abused by their parents. The people who were murdered. Car accidents. Drug abuse. Drunk drivers. Hurricanes. Tornadoes. The list literally went on and on and on.

If God was in control of all the world—the whole wide world—and He loved the world so much that He gave His only Son, as her aunt liked to remind her, then Melody wanted to know why He allowed so many bad things to happen.

She shook her head. No. Either there wasn't a God, or He just liked to keep Himself out of all the happenings of the world. Whichever of the two was true of God, she wanted nothing to do with Him.

The only being who could control her life was Melody. She had been the one who tried to fight off the man who attacked her. She had been the one who helped her mom in every way possible while growing up. She was the one who got herself through diesel mechanic school and then worked hard to be one of the best at it. She was the one in control, and she didn't need to attend some feel-good church service to make her think all the things she couldn't explain would be all right in the end.

"Hi, Melody."

Melody turned at the sound of her name. She smiled at one of the older ladies in the church. Sweet, tiny Bonnie suffered from rheumatoid arthritis. Over the years, her hands had gnarled until she had almost no use of her individual fingers. Melody knew the woman had to be in pain most of, if not all, the time. Yet Bonnie always wore a smile on her face. She even painted wooden ornaments her husband cut for her. The woman was a true encouragement in never giving up, and her sweet spirit drew Melody.

"Hi, Bonnie." Melody reached toward the woman and wrapped her arms around her. Bonnie felt more like a grandmother to her than a church acquaintance, and she made sitting through church every week worth it.

"I made these for all the ladies. I got them done a little early, but"—Bonnie held up a small flag pin—"they're to wear on the Fourth of July."

Melody took the wooden pin painted in red, white, and blue. "Thank you so much."

Bonnie waved. "Church is getting ready to start. You have a good day."

Melody stared at the pin as Bonnie walked to the other side of the sanctuary. *Why would God allow that kind woman to live in constant pain?*

Why is that woman so kind?

Melody blinked at the second thought. She had no idea where it had come from. She wasn't sure what to think about it either. Her brows furrowed as she lowered herself into her seat. She felt her aunt and uncle beside her, and she nodded to Gracie and Wyatt from across the aisle, but she felt perplexed by the thought.

What did make Bonnie different?

She looked at her aunt and uncle. The music leader instructed the congregation to stand as the first song of the morning began. She never actually sang the words but mouthed along with everyone instead. She studied her aunt's and uncle's faces. She knew there was something different about them. Even when she was a girl, she could tell they had a peace, a joy that she didn't understand.

Oh, she'd seen them fuss before. She remembered one time when she was a little girl and Uncle Roy hadn't started the grill when Aunt Renee thought he had. She and her mom had all the food ready, and not only was the grill not hot, but it was out of propane as well. Aunt Renee was not happy, and she made sure her husband knew it. But even then, the way they handled their fight, they were different.

The music finally ended, and Melody sat and prepared herself to listen to their preacher for forty-five minutes or so. Today one of the women walked to the podium and picked up the microphone. Music started, and she began to sing. She had the most beautiful, soothing voice, and Melody was instantly drawn into the song. Something about being able to call down angels to destroy everything, but instead Jesus had died for all of us.

The song ended, and Aunt Renee leaned over and swiped moisture from her eye. "I love that song, and no one sings it like Tammie."

Melody nodded but continued to stare at the front of the church. This time the preacher did walk to the podium. Most of the time, she tried to envision the engine of whatever vehicle she needed to work on. Today he talked about storms of life and how we wouldn't know the answers to all our questions this side of heaven. "Some things we just won't understand," the pastor's voice boomed through the sanctuary.

Why not, God? Why won't You tell us?

She inwardly chided herself for talking to a being that she wasn't completely convinced existed. She looked around her at all the people she'd met over the last few months. Spying Drew and his parents on her right, she studied him. He'd been on her like grease on a muffler practically since the day she'd moved to River Run. He didn't like her mechanical know-how one bit. It was obvious he was threatened by her. But he was supposed to be a Christian as well.

She thought about him thanking her when she fixed his dump truck and about how offended he'd looked when she'd accused him of taking her to his homesite alone for wrong reasons. He was gruff and grumpy, but if she were honest, he'd never been cruel to her.

"Let me close with what Jesus told us in John 16:33." The pastor's voice interrupted her thoughts, and she turned her attention back to him. "God's Word says, 'I have told you these things, so that in me you may have peace. In this world you will have trouble. But take heart! I have overcome the world.'"

Melody bowed her head as the pastor led the congregation in prayer. Her mind whirled with everything she'd heard this morning. It was more than she wanted to think about. In fact, a slight headache had started to pulse above her left eye.

So God warned them they'd have trouble. Told everyone it was part of life on earth. But that didn't explain why. She needed to understand why. The pulse above her eye quickened. Actually, she needed a nap.

Once the service had been dismissed, her body tightened when Drew started to walk toward them. He extended his hand to her. Knowing she couldn't be rude in front of everyone, she shook his hand. He was so much bigger and stronger than she was. Something about that made her feel uncomfortable and protected at the same time.

Lifting her chin to force the vulnerable feelings that washed over her to pass through, she peered into his cool eyes. Sincerity and warmth shown from their depths, and Melody found herself swallowing a knot that had formed in her throat.

"I wanted to thank you again for fixing the truck."

He held her hand a bit too long, and Melody felt a thrill at the coarseness of his palm—proof that he was a man who didn't shy away from hard work. She pulled her hand away and tried not to flinch as his kind gaze became almost more than she could bear. "Again, you're welcome."

Today of all days, she did not need to endure the kind side of Drew Wilson. She wanted the man to be normal with her, to fuss and fight with her, to do something that was not so attractive.

She gasped at the thought. The last thing she would think of Drew was that he was attractive. Sick with herself for the thought, she wiped her hand on her jeans and wrinkled her nose.

Drew's expression changed. He must have thought she meant she was disgusted to have touched his hand. Fury swept across his face. A smile tickled the side of her mouth as she knew he was about to light into her. *Now that's the Drew I need to see.*

Lifting one eyebrow, she cocked her head. "Something wrong, Drew?"

"Not a thing." Drew whipped around and walked out of the sanctuary.

To his credit, he didn't fuss at her within the church's walls, but she knew he wanted to. She smirked. A good Christian wouldn't get so bent out of shape so fast.

As she walked down the aisle to the door, she tried not think about the fact that Drew hadn't given in to his anger but had walked out the door before saying an unkind word.

Chapter 5

Melody woke up with a start. She flung off the covers and sat up, wiping the sweat from her forehead. Twisting her body, she allowed her legs to fall off the side of the bed. She placed her elbows on her knees and cupped her cheeks with her hands. She took long, slow breaths, in and out, in and out.

The nightmare had returned. This was the third time in only one week she'd awakened this way. It didn't make sense why they would happen now. It had been over ten years since that day. She thought she'd gotten over it—put it in the back of her mind forever. And yet here it was—like the cobra being charmed out of its basket by the sound of the flutelike instrument—the nightmare had returned.

She could still smell his stale cigarette breath, still feel his firm, strong grasp. She'd never felt so alone, so scared, so vulnerable. Though she'd tried to fight him, in less than a moment, the man had complete control of her. He'd pushed her down in the bushes. When she remembered like this, she could still feel the small twigs break beneath her weight and the stronger ones claw at her back.

Just above her tailbone, she'd hit a root from a tree that towered just a few feet away. The deep bruise it made stayed with her in color and in pain for nearly a month. When she tried to scream, he'd cupped her mouth with one hand and blew into her face trying to shush her. His breath had parted her bangs, and droplets of his spit smacked her eyes.

Fear like she'd never known gripped her as she realized with each breath that he had more and more control of her. *How could this be happening? This isn't happening,* raced through her mind time and again.

Then as quickly as he'd attacked her, he was gone. A blond-haired woman with a little baby in a stroller in front of her reached her hand down to Melody. She held some kind of black device in her other hand. It looked like a container of mace.

"Let me help you," the woman said as she brushed leaves and twigs out of

Melody's face. Panic, embarrassment, and fear wrapped themselves around her again, and Melody pushed the woman away and raced back to her house. She'd locked the door and shoved a chair beneath the doorknob until her mother got home.

Blowing the memories out with a long breath, she padded out of the bedroom and into the bathroom. She turned on lukewarm water and washed her face. Opening her eyes, she stared at her reflection in the mirror. She looked tired. She was tired.

She didn't want this nightmare to come back. Though she had begrudged the money she spent on it, Melody was able to convince her mother to enroll her in a self-defense class after that day. Melody knew how to defend herself. She knew when and how to fight and get away. If anyone ever caught her off guard again, she was prepared. *Of course, I'll never allow myself to be caught off guard again.*

Thankful that it was morning, even if it was a bit earlier than she'd intended to wake up and the sun had not yet made its appearance, Melody brushed her teeth and her hair then slipped on a pair of shorts and a T-shirt. Not ready for breakfast, she walked outside to Aunt Renee's garden.

The small plants had grown so much. She knelt beside the cucumbers, her designated row, and pulled weeds that had started to grow around them. She and her aunt had to be consistent in plucking the weeds out of the garden. The vegetables wouldn't be able to grow if the unwanted foliage overtook them.

She wanted the nightmare out of her mind, but while plucking the weeds, she began to wonder if she would always deal with that particular mental weed—if she would continuously have to fight the fear of what could have happened.

Sometimes she didn't feel strong enough. She'd never admit that aloud. Everyone believed she was strong enough for anything, and she wanted them to believe that. But there were times, like this morning, that she wanted nothing more than to succumb to the fear she felt.

"You're out bright and early."

Melody jumped at the sound of Aunt Renee's voice behind her. She turned and stood, forcing a smile to her face. "Yep. I woke up early."

Her aunt waved her hand across the garden. "Looks like you've been busy."

Melody looked down. She had weeded a lot more than she'd realized. She must have been deep in thought. She chuckled. "I suppose I have."

"You wanna make some pancakes before the girls come to get you?"

Melody sucked in her breath and covered her mouth with her hand. "I completely forgot."

"How could you forget a shopping trip?" Her aunt winked and wrapped her arm around Melody's shoulders as she guided her toward the back door. "They're coming at eight, right?"

"Yeah." Melody looked heavenward, realizing the sun had already risen. *How could I have possibly missed a sunrise? I must be losing my mind.* "What time is it?"

"It's a little after seven." Aunt Renee opened the back door and guided her inside. "Why don't I make the pancakes while you go get cleaned up?"

Melody stopped, placed her hand on her hip, and grinned at her aunt. "Are you suggesting I don't look good enough for a shopping trip?"

"Not suggesting, honey. I'm telling you straight-out."

Melody laughed as she made her way to the hall bathroom again.

"Maybe keep your hair down today. It's so beautiful," her aunt's voice sounded from the kitchen.

Melody didn't respond. She almost never wore her hair down in public. She didn't want to look girlish or vulnerable, as she sometimes felt. After a quick shower, she put on fresh clothes and brushed and blow-dried her long, dark hair. It was pretty. Thick and wavy, heavy as it could possibly be. Taking a deep breath, she decided she'd let it fall down her back as her aunt suggested.

She opened the drawer to put her brush away and spied the mascara she'd used for Addy's wedding. A little brightening of the eyes might not hurt either. After all, she was going shopping with friends. Before she could change her mind, she swiped on a coat of the black stuff and then surveyed her reflection. She looked a lot more feminine, but she still felt like herself. A part of her actually enjoyed it.

Wonder what Drew would think. . .

Ugh. She wanted to knot her hair into the tightest bun possible and scrub the mascara from her eyes at the thought. She refused to care what Drew Wilson thought about her appearance. The man drove her crazy.

She walked out of the bathroom and back to the kitchen.

"Well, lookie here!" Uncle Roy jumped up from his seat and hugged Melody. He placed a soft kiss on the top of her head. "Prettiest girl I've seen in a long time."

Aunt Renee wiped her hands on a dish towel. She walked to Melody and pushed a long strand of hair over her shoulder. "Honey, you are absolutely beautiful. And such a natural beauty, too."

Melody's cheeks warmed at her aunt and uncle's praise. She rarely received compliments about her appearance. They usually came in the form of her mechanical abilities. She couldn't deny their words felt nice.

"Thank you." Trying to change the topic, she pointed to the pancakes on the table. "These mine?"

Her aunt nodded, and Melody slid into the chair and swallowed down two pancakes before she heard Gracie pull into the driveway. She hopped up and placed her plate in the sink. "Thanks, Aunt Renee."

"You have fun."

Her aunt's words sounded from behind as she raced out the door. Gracie's whistle pealed through the air when Melody stepped off the front porch. "Look at you!" she squealed.

Melody's face warmed as she walked to the car and slipped inside. "I don't look that different."

"Oh yes, you do, and this settles it." She flipped a strand of Melody's hair. "We're going to find you a cute outfit or two while we're out. You're entirely too pretty to wear coveralls, faded blue jeans, and old T-shirts all the time."

Melody rolled her eyes. "Just go pick up Addy and her friend. What's the girl's name?"

"Val. She and Addy were roommates in college. You'll love her."

Melody nodded and stared out the window. This morning she'd had the nightmare that had terrorized her too many times already in her life. Now she was going shopping with a group of girls who wanted to transform her into a pretty woman. It seemed the most ridiculous thing she could do, and yet she wanted to change. She wanted to feel different. Maybe a change in the way she looked would do the trick and help her put the past behind her.

When they pulled into Addy and Nick's driveway, Melody jumped out of the car and raced to the front porch to give Addy a hug. She hadn't seen her friend since her wedding. Taking in Addy's beautiful, long, blond hair and glowing green eyes, Melody smirked at her. "Someone sure looks happy."

Addy bit her bottom lip and giggled. "Being married is a lot of fun."

The tall, thin woman with bright red hair clipped in the shortest, spikiest hairstyle Melody had ever seen extended her hand. "You must be Melody. I'm Val, Addy's roommate from college."

Addy moved her eyebrows up and down. "I hear we're doing a bit of a makeover on someone today."

Melody giggled, a sound she never thought would come from her own lips. "Believe it or not, I'm going to let you."

Addy clapped her hands then brushed her fingers through Melody's hair. She looked at her friend, Val. "With her dark hair and eyes, she'd be beautiful in yellow. Don't you think, Val? I've always wanted to wear yellow, but I'm too fair."

"Oh, and soft pink. She'll look gorgeous," Val added.

Melody felt dizzy as they led her to Gracie's car. "What were we going shopping for to begin with?" she asked as the three women continued to talk about the colors Melody should wear.

"Sweetie, we were going to try to make you over all along." Gracie smacked the top of the steering wheel. "We thought it would be a battle, but you're already willing. Wonders never cease."

"Amen, sister." Addy lifted her hand for Gracie to give her a high five.

"God is always working, even with the small stuff," Val added.

Melody's body stiffened. It was always about God with these people in River Run. Even with Addy's friend it was about God. She didn't need God, and He definitely wasn't involved in the small stuff.

She closed her eyes. She wouldn't let the little comments ruin her day. She needed a change—something to get her mind off her past. She'd enjoy acting like a girl. For today anyway.

As they did at least once a month, Drew's parents invited Roy and Renee, Nick and Addy, and Melody to their house for a cookout. He'd felt anxious about seeing Melody again. She'd seemed pressed on his heart all week. The girl needed Jesus. It was as obvious as a car's need for gas. Today Drew was determined to keep the peace with the woman and be a good witness to her.

Roy and Renee pulled into the driveway. Drew could hardly believe his eyes when Melody stepped out of the car. She didn't even look like herself. Her hair cascaded like a waterfall almost all the way to her stomach on one side. Even from a distance, he could see long dark eyelashes framing chocolate-colored eyes. She wore a light pink sundress and carried a small purse in her left hand. Even at the wedding, she hadn't carried any kind of purse.

The woman was a vision. He hadn't been able to get her out of his mind since Sunday, having felt her inner struggle with God. Now he'd never be able to get how beautiful she was out of his head either.

"Do you need some help carrying anything?" Drew hollered to Renee.

"Come get the deviled eggs," she called back.

Drew nodded to Melody as he walked past her to the car. She held a dessert in one hand, probably Renee's homemade blackberry cobbler, and a bowl of coleslaw in the other. He grabbed the eggs from the car and shut the door.

Roy nudged Drew with his elbow. "She's awful pretty all dolled up like that, ain't she?"

Drew lifted his eyebrows. "She sure is."

He followed Roy into the house and placed the eggs on the table. Sitting beside his new brother-in-law, Nick, in the great room, he tried to watch the baseball game on television, but his gaze kept wandering to the women gathered around the kitchen counters.

He believed Melody even had a shade of pink lipstick or lip gloss or whatever it was called on her lips. He noticed how full they were. Though he'd inwardly criticized them at the wedding, he could tell they were just the perfect shape and size for a kiss.

He wrinkled his nose at the thought as Nick's elbow landed hard into his ribs. He frowned at his lifelong friend. "What was that for?"

Nick raised his eyebrows and nodded toward the women. "You gonna be next to fall? Mike gonna win the bet?"

Drew huffed. "I thought the bet was off."

Nick shrugged. "Technically, it is. Addy would string me by my neck if she thought it wasn't." He twisted until he could stare full into Drew's face. "I'm just wondering if you're gonna be next to fall."

Drew shifted on the couch as he lifted his left foot to his right knee. He brushed the hem of his blue jeans with his hand. "I don't know why you'd think that."

" 'Cause you got a thing for my cousin."

Drew whispered to his friend, "First of all, I don't have a thing for your cousin. Second of all, your cousin is fighting God something fierce. She's not even an option for me to have a thing for."

Nick's expression sobered. "I know. My family keeps praying for her. She's going to church with them every week, and God's Word never comes back void." He sighed. "But it's still her decision to accept Him, and so far she hasn't."

The women laughed, and Drew turned his attention back to them. He felt an urgency for Melody to accept Christ into her life. Seeing her dressed as a woman, noting how tiny she truly was, Drew felt an overwhelming need to protect her from all harm. He realized he truly cared about her.

"All right, guys"—Drew's mother waved at the men—"come get your plates."

Drew loaded his plate with the best straight-from-scratch foods in River Run: coleslaw and potato salad, baked beans and deviled eggs, pickled beets and sweet tea. Even the hamburgers came from one of his dad's best Anguses. He spied Renee's blackberry cobbler over on the kitchen counter, and his mouth already salivated at the thought of biting into the dessert.

If it weren't for the fact that he, his dad, Nick, and Roy all had to work hard on their family farms, all four of them would be as big as barns from the good cooking these women whipped up. Roy actually had put on a few pounds since he'd had to retire early, but the Wii game Renee bought him had helped him keep the weight under control.

After saying grace, Drew scooped up a forkful of coleslaw and shoveled it into his mouth. Surprised by the sour taste, he gagged and spit the food back onto his plate. He covered his mouth and looked at the peering eyes of his family and friends around the table. His face warmed, as he knew his mother would reprimand him for being so rude. But he hadn't meant to. He loved Renee's coleslaw. If he was unsure about the taste of a dish, he'd take a small bite first. But he knew hers was the best in the county, and he'd scooped the mouthful in. With the bitter taste—well, it just popped right out.

"Drew!" His mother's voice sounded tense.

"I'm sorry. I got too big of a bite." He averted his gaze from Renee. He didn't want her to think he didn't like her cooking.

"It's okay, Drew," Renee said. He looked at her as she took a small bite of the coleslaw. Her face scrunched up as if she'd just bitten into a lemon. She wiped her mouth. "It's not your fault. I must have forgotten the sugar."

"You didn't forget the sugar," Melody growled as her face flamed the brightest red Drew had ever seen. "I forgot the sugar." She smacked her napkin on the table, and tears welled in her eyes as she stared at Addy, Renee, and his mom. "I'm never going to be like you." She pushed away from the table and walked down the hall and into the bathroom.

"I'm sorry." Drew felt like a complete and total heel. Melody must have made the coleslaw and forgot a main ingredient. He glanced at Renee. "You know I love your coleslaw. I just took a big ol' bite, and when it hit my tongue, it just came right back out."

Roy lifted his hand. "It's all right, Drew. You didn't aim to hurt Melody's feelings."

Renee added, "Let's just not make a big deal about this. It's best we just go ahead and act normal. She'll feel better when she comes out if we're all acting normal."

Drew tried to eat the rest of his food. It all tasted the same—bland. He didn't overly like Melody, but he didn't want to hurt her feelings or embarrass her, either. She never came out of the bathroom. He could hear Addy trying to talk to her, and he considered trying to go back to the bathroom and apologize, but he was afraid it would make her more upset. With a sigh of frustration, he decided he should go outside with the other men.

They started a game of cornhole. Drew and his dad against Roy and Nick. It would be an easy game, as it always was. He and his dad could whip up on Roy and Nick even if they gave them a five-point lead from the beginning.

Drew turned when the back screen door smacked against the doorjamb. Addy and Melody walked toward two foldable chairs under the oversized oak tree. Melody had pulled her hair back in a ponytail, and Drew could tell she'd cleaned the makeup off her face. She still looked pretty, and Drew wished he could think of a way to apologize to her about the coleslaw.

"Drew, you entering the tractor pull?" Roy asked.

Drew scoffed as he looked back at the men. "You know I am. There ain't nobody got a tractor as sweet as mine." Drew gawked at Nick. "You gonna try to take me on this Fourth of July?"

Nick chortled and took a few steps back. "Oh no. Now that I'm hitched, I haven't had time to work on souping up a tractor."

"Excuse me, Nick Martin?" Drew turned toward his sister and Melody. Addy had her hands on her hips. "Are you begrudging being hitched?"

Nick raced to his new wife, wrapped his arms around her, lifted her off the ground, and spun her around. "Not in the slightest. I love my little ball and chain."

"Nick Martin!" Addy teasingly swatted his shoulders until Nick planted a long kiss on her lips.

Disgusted and yet feeling the oddest nudging of jealousy, Drew rolled his eyes and looked back at Roy. "Guess the only competition I've ever had won't be showing up."

"I'll be there." Melody walked toward them, her arms crossed in front of her chest.

"What?" Drew frowned.

"I'll be competing in the tractor pull."

Drew laughed.

"I'm serious."

Drew widened his stance and placed his hands on his hips. He let out a long breath. "I'm sure you are serious, but you have no business competing in the tractor pull."

"Why?" She cocked her head and squinted at him. "Because I'm a just a little, wimpy woman?"

There she went with the "little, wimpy" comments again. He had never suggested she was wimpy; however, she was little—tiny in height and frame.

Drew spread his arms out. "Why do you have to be so competitive? Why do you have to prove yourself all the time?"

"Why do you have to be the best of everything all the time? Why can't you lose?"

Drew ground his teeth. He intertwined his fingers and lifted his hands to his lips. Inwardly, he counted to ten, willing himself not to explode and say something to her that he'd later regret. He swallowed and nodded his head. "Okay, Melody. I'll see you there."

He turned and stomped toward the house. He'd had about all he could take of Melody Markwell. Girl or no girl, at that tractor pull he was going to knock that little spitfire off her high horse.

Chapter 6

Drew checked the Continental AV1790 tank engine he'd put in the tractor. He liked this particular one because it was an American engine used to pilot heavy tanks. He hopped onto the seat of the tractor and started her up. She roared to life, just as he expected.

He smiled at the power he could feel beneath him. He wouldn't have any trouble pulling the sled. It wouldn't matter that the weights pushed forward on the sled's axles, making the front of it push into the ground. His engine would rip right through the dirt and keep pulling at a good, strong pace the full one hundred meters.

Everyone he knew came out for the annual Independence Day event that took place in the town's fairgrounds. The fact that the town allowed vending stands to start setting up last year made the tractor pull quite an event. They'd sell funnel cakes and popcorn, hot dogs and hamburgers. He'd heard someone was setting up a blooming onion stand. His mouth watered at the thought of the fried vegetable dipped in that delicious pinkish-colored sauce. After winning, he'd be sure to get one of those.

Once the truck and tractor pull finished and it started to get dark, the sheriff's department would set off fireworks. For a small town, Drew had been impressed by the good show they'd been able to put on, but then the sheriff's son-in-law had a brother in Tennessee who sold them fireworks at a discounted rate.

In the back of his mind, he still wondered about Melody's tractor and engine. He'd learned the hard way he couldn't take that gal for granted. She was a talented mechanic; he couldn't deny it. But if she had to work with what Nick and Roy had to offer with their tractor, then Drew shouldn't have any trouble showing her who was the boss of the tractor pull.

He turned off the tractor and jumped down. He'd planned to work on finishing up the foundation of his house today, but he had to make sure the tractor was ready first. The tractor pull was in a little over a week, and he'd never be able to show his face in town again if Melody beat him.

He spotted Mike's truck driving along the dirt road leading to the barn. He waved at his friend, and Mike parked and stuck his arm out the window. "Whatcha doin?"

Drew patted the tractor. "Getting ready for the pull. Did you hear Melody's planning to race?"

"I heard." Mike patted the side of the truck. "The woman's just itching to prove herself."

"She sure is."

"Sounds like someone else I know."

Drew squinted at Mike. "Now, what's that supposed to mean?"

"Not supposed to mean anything." He motioned for Drew to get in the truck. "Come on. It's lunchtime, and I'm heading to the diner."

Drew's stomach growled when Mike mentioned food. He hadn't realized it had gotten so late. Noting the sun high in the sky, he realized he'd been out working on the tractor longer than he thought. If he didn't watch it, he was going to get behind on his farmwork. "Sounds good. Take me by the house to clean up a bit."

He got in the truck, and Mike drove to the house. Drew hurried into the bathroom and washed his face and hands and changed his shirt. Most everyone went to the diner just as they were after a hard morning's work on the farm, but Drew's mom would have his hide if he didn't at least clean up enough that he wasn't covered in dirt and the smell of cows and sweat. After running a brush through his hair, he went back outside and got in the truck with Mike.

As they headed to the diner, Drew's thoughts jumbled with all he needed to do for the house and the farm, and yet now he was worried about not having his tractor fixed up enough. When he thought rationally, he knew his competitiveness with Melody was ridiculous. Normally, he'd never even consider competing against a girl in a tractor pull.

It was her attitude. He just couldn't get past how the woman thought she needed to beat a man, him in particular, at everything. He bet if he had his mom show him how to stitch a quilt, that fool-brained woman would try to make one that looked better.

He should challenge her to a cooking duel. She'd proven she wasn't any good in the kitchen. Drew sighed at his mean thought. She'd been so embarrassed over the coleslaw, and he'd felt lower than the gum stuck to the bottom of a shoe that he'd been the one to inadvertently call her out on it. Mike and

Wyatt both warned him that he and Melody were a lot alike when it came to their competitive nature. When Drew was honest, he knew it was true.

Mike pulled into a parking space, and the two got out of the truck and headed inside. Drew watched as Lacy's eyes widened when Mike walked toward her. She smiled and blushed when she led them to their usual booth.

Drew shook his head at Mike as the man tried to act as if Lacy's obvious attraction didn't affect him. "I think I may try something different today," Mike said, staring at the menu.

Drew chuckled. "You're not going to try anything different. You're just avoiding eye contact with me, as you do every time we come here and you get a first look at Lacy."

Mike narrowed his eyes. "I am not."

Drew folded his arms on top of the table. "Oh really. What are you going to have different, Mike? You're not going to have meat loaf and mashed potatoes? You and I both know how much you love the meat loaf and mashed potatoes."

"No. I'm not. I'm going to have the Salisbury steak today, or maybe I'll have the country ham." Mike folded the menu and smacked it against the table.

"I don't know why you don't just ask the woman out on a date. You two have been making goo-goo eyes at each other for two years. It's ridiculous. The bet is off. Addy made us call it off."

"Oh really." Mike grabbed the utensils rolled in a paper napkin between his fingers and pointed them at Drew. "So, why don't you go on a date?"

Drew huffed. "There's no one I like."

Mike leaned back against the padded booth. "Really. If you weren't so mule-headed, you'd see there is a woman you like. And you like her a lot."

Drew's ire rose, as he knew exactly who his friend was about to say. Wyatt mentioned her, as did Nick, but all three of them seemed to have lost their senses. Melody Markwell was his number one nemesis, not someone he'd be interested in. "And who would that be?"

Lacy walked up to their booth before Mike could respond, which was lucky for Mike, because Drew planned to kick him hard if he'd said that woman's name. His ire was quickly replaced with humor as he watched his friend swallow hard then look up at Lacy. She averted her gaze from Mike, and Drew grinned as her neck and cheeks blazed bright pink. "What can I get you boys?"

Drew stretched his hands out in front of him. He enjoyed watching the two of them squirm in each other's presence. "Well, Lacy," Drew started, "I think I'm going to try something different today. Give me the country ham and mashed potatoes."

He handed her his menu and grinned when Mike looked up at him and wrinkled his nose and narrowed his eyes.

"What about you, Mike?" Her voice squeaked. "You gonna try something different?"

The woman's tone seemed to plead with him to try something different, as if ordering a Salisbury steak instead of meat loaf would suddenly give him the courage to ask her on a date. He watched as she held her breath. For a moment, Drew felt kind of bad for Lacy. He knew she'd never in a million years ask Mike on a date first. It went against everything they'd all been raised to believe. Of course, when he thought about it, he didn't know why it was so wrong for a gal to ask a guy for dinner. It wasn't as if it would hurt anything, but still he had to admit he'd rather be the one asking the girl out on the date.

Drew's attention shifted back to his friend and Lacy as Mike handed the menu to her without looking up. "No. I'll get the usual. Meat loaf and mashed potatoes."

Lacy let out the breath and nodded. "Coming right up." She tucked the menus under her arm and headed back to the kitchen.

Drew burst into laughter as he smacked the table with his hand. "The usual. Really? Mike, I would have never guessed it."

"Laugh at me all you want, Drew. I'm not the only one avoiding women."

Drew laughed again, but this time Mike's words didn't seem so comical. Over the last few weeks, he'd spent more time stewing over what Melody was thinking, doing, or feeling than he had over his farm or the home he was building. It was sobering to think Mike's point was all too true.

Melody lifted Gracie's baby boy out of his high chair. At five months, little Wyatt had grown so much. She wiped the dribbling of rice cereal from his lips with the MOMMY'S LITTLE HELPER bib he wore around his neck. She kissed his fat cheek then cooed at the boy. "Tell your mommy I said thanks so much for inviting me to lunch."

Wyatt Jr. widened his mouth into a full, toothless smile. A cackle escaped as he twisted his body and grabbed at the strands of hair that had fallen out of her ponytail. He was always excited after he'd gotten some food in his belly, and he absolutely adored pulling her long hair.

"We love having you over for lunch," Gracie said as she laid plates of ham sandwiches and baked chips on the table. "Do you want me to take him so you can eat?"

"No. I like holding him."

"But you only have another thirty minutes."

Melody looked at the clock above the table. Her lunch hour always flew by too quickly when she was able to spend it with Gracie and Wyatt Jr.

"That's okay. I can hold him and eat." Melody shoved a bite of sandwich into her mouth. Little Wyatt tried to reach for her mouth as she chewed. She leaned toward him and Eskimo kissed his nose. "It's my turn to eat now, big guy."

Gracie sat across from her and started to talk about her morning. Melody genuinely enjoyed hearing about Wyatt's projectile vomiting and soiled-through diapers. Even though she'd never been a huge fan of men and marriage, she'd always been drawn to children. She hated that she'd probably never have any of her own.

An image of Drew Wilson popped into her head, and she wondered for a moment what his children would look like. She envisioned three rowdy, blond-haired, stair-step boys chasing after a cow. A tiny dark-haired girl fought through the tall grass, running after the boys. She shook her head. Why would she think of that egotistical man? Sometimes the notions her mind conjured up made absolutely no sense.

Gracie continued, "This morning I woke up later than usual, and I didn't have a chance to get my shower before Wyatt woke up. I knew I was going to be miserable for the whole day."

After taking another big bite of sandwich, Melody tickled the baby's chin, and he cackled again. "Was Mommy going to be miserable for you today?"

Gracie tapped the tip of Wyatt's nose, causing him to laugh again, as she went on. "I prayed for God's intervention. I didn't want to be grumpy just because I woke up late. But then he took a morning nap." Gracie clasped her hands. "I couldn't believe it." She reached over and tickled Wyatt's toes. "This little guy is a wonderful nap taker in the afternoon, but he almost never goes back down in the morning. It was like God's precious gift to me this morning."

Trying to respond in a supportive manner to her friend, Melody raised her eyebrows and nodded. She got so tired of the God-did-this, God-did-that stuff she was inundated with by her family and friends. It was as if these people couldn't take a step without praising or praying to God about it.

She loved her aunt and uncle, and the friends she'd found here were some of the very best she'd ever had. She wouldn't do anything to change them, but she really got tired of it. If Gracie lost her favorite pen, she'd pray about it and say God helped her find it. If she was nervous about taking Wyatt Jr. to the doctor for his shots, she'd pray about it and say God gave her peace. If the sun shone high and the breeze blew perfectly, she'd say praises about how good God was to them. To be honest, Melody was just plain sick of it. The whole wide world didn't revolve around God.

"It doesn't?"

She wanted to growl at the still, small voice that seemed to creep up within her at the weirdest moments. Every time it did, she was forced to think about if she had a few things wrong.

Over the last few weeks, she decided she did believe there was a God—or at least some kind of higher being. The sermons and the comments from her family and friends had made enough sense, and it was true that creation was entirely too intricate and too perfectly put together not to have been formed by something.

So if something did form all of creation—the oceans and mountains, the rivers and valleys, the animals and plants, and the intricate weavings of all those things—would it make sense that the world revolved around it?

Holding the baby with one hand, she rubbed her temple with the other. She'd had more headaches in the last few months than she'd had in her life, and she was still having nightmares. Only now they were about her dad leaving when she was five.

She barely remembered the man, and she definitely had no recollection of him leaving them. He'd gone in the middle of the night when she was asleep. And yet, for several nights in a row, she'd envisioned him walking out the door and not looking behind him in her dreams.

She'd begun to dread nighttime. She'd grown weary of asking herself why God allowed so many bad things to happen. Now she'd have new questions to invade her thoughts: *Does the world revolve around God? And if the world does revolve around Him, then is Gracie's approach of talking to Him and about Him every day the right way to have a relationship with Him? But again, if the world revolves around God, why does He allow bad things to happen?*

Melody scrunched her nose. It was like a constant circle of unanswered questions. Her brain had never worked this hard before moving to River Run, even when she was learning all she needed to know about mechanics. The pulsing in her temple deepened. "Gracie, do you have any ibuprofen?"

"Sure." Gracie got up and walked to the cabinet. "You have another headache?"

"Yeah."

"Maybe you should see a doctor." Gracie grabbed a water bottle from the refrigerator and handed it to Melody. "You've been looking tired a lot lately."

"I haven't been sleeping well."

Melody placed both pills in her mouth and with one swig of water swallowed them down. Hopefully, they would kick in soon after she got back to AJ's garage. She still had a long day ahead of her with a transmission to fix, and she wanted to look over Uncle Roy's tractor engine one more time. In only a few days, she'd be whipping up on Drew at the fairgrounds.

"I know you may not. . ."

Melody looked up at her friend when she started to talk and then stopped. Gracie bit her bottom lip as if unsure if she should continue. Melody furrowed her eyebrows. "We're friends. You can tell me anything. What's wrong?"

"I was just wondering if you'd let me pray for you."

Melody shrugged. "I don't care. Pray all you want. I'm getting ready to go."

Gracie shook her head. "No. I mean right now. Before you leave. Out loud."

Melody's body stiffened, and she let out a long breath. It was one thing to sit through a church service and bow her head when the pastor told her to or to sit at the dinner table while someone prayed over the food, but to actually have Gracie pray for her—Melody wasn't sure how she felt about that. She gazed over at Gracie, whose expression seemed to plead for Melody to allow her to do it. With a long sigh, Melody nodded. "Okay."

A smile brightened Gracie's face, and before Melody could protest, she grabbed her hand and squeezed. "Oh dear Jesus, I praise You for my wonderful friend Melody. I love her so much, Lord. I'm so glad she moved to River Run. Thank You that she comes and eats lunch with Wyatt and me."

Melody had to clear her throat. Tears started to pool in her eyes. Gracie was thankful she came over for lunch? It was the highlight of Melody's day to be able to see them.

Gracie continued, "She's been having headaches, Lord. A lot of them. And she looks tired, God. I don't know what is causing all this, but I pray You will heal Melody. Draw her close to Yourself. Thank You, Jesus. Amen."

Melody had to swallow and blink several times to keep from crying outright in front of Gracie. She handed the baby to his mother and grabbed her coveralls off the chair. After slipping back into the grease-covered garment, she nodded to her friend. "Thanks, Gracie."

Before Gracie could wrap her in a hug, which Melody knew would be coming if she didn't get out of that house fast enough, Melody left. A knife seemed to be stuck in her heart, and it twisted with every step she took. The pulsing in her head grew stronger, and either God wasn't listening or He was saying no to Gracie's request. Either way, Melody was sure of one thing: Gracie had something that she was beginning to realize she wanted. A relationship with God.

Chapter 7

Melody rolled onto her back and stretched her arms as far as she could above her head. The sun peeked through the cracks of the closed blinds. Groggy, she gazed at the alarm clock on the nightstand. Nine o'clock!

She sat up in a hurry and flung her legs over the bed. I'm late for work. The sleep fuzzies in her brain began to clear, and she remembered she didn't have to work today. She smiled just before a yawn took over her mouth.

Hopping off the bed, she padded across the room and peered out her upstairs bedroom window. Her aunt's car was gone. She'd probably already headed to the store for her weekly grocery trip.

She drank in the beautiful countryside just across the road. Full, lush trees blanketed the hillside and seemed to roll like waves atop the ground and along the sky. She could see Nick and Addy's house and barn just before the tree line. Endless rows of wooden fences spread out before her eyes with more cows than she could count grazing in the fields.

Running her fingers through her matted hair, an overwhelming sense of refreshment welled within her. She'd slept the whole night without a nightmare. No would-be rapist threatening her. No father walking out. For the first time in weeks, she felt rested. *I wonder if Gracie's prayer had anything to do with it.* She blinked as she pushed the thought aside.

Normally she'd head straight to the shower and get ready for her day before heading to the kitchen for coffee and breakfast. But she loved to sit on the back deck and look out at her aunt's full vegetable and herb garden. The flower garden was equally amazing, bursting in reds, yellows, whites, and purples. She'd grown to need the time she spent basking in the early morning's slight breeze while she sipped her java. If she waited until after a shower, the sun would be too hot to enjoy the coffee on the deck. She grabbed the bright pink fuzzy robe her aunt had given her as a hand-me-down and slipped into it.

Knowing her uncle was most likely watching one of the morning news shows or playing on his Wii, Melody traipsed down the stairs then hollered down the hall, "Uncle Roy, I can't believe I slept this late."

She walked into the living room. He was sitting in his recliner watching a news show, just as she expected. But he was resting at an odd angle, slightly hunched to one side with his elbow resting on the arm of the chair and his hand cupping the side of his face.

Her heartbeat quickened, and her stomach churned at the pensive expression on his face. "Uncle Roy, are you all right?"

He tried to look up at her, but his eyes squinted, and he didn't seem to have the strength to lift his chin. "My head. . ." His words slurred, and his mouth seemed to drag on one side.

Panic welled within her, but she forced herself to remain calm. She raced into the kitchen, grabbed the phone, and dialed 911. The dispatcher answered.

"I believe my uncle is having a stroke." Melody could hear the anxiety in her voice even as she tried to remain steady. As she relayed their address to the woman, Melody grabbed a plastic bag from under the sink. The woman told her he could start vomiting at any moment. She needed to watch to be sure he didn't choke.

The thought of it spurred a sob within her chest. She sucked in her breath, willing herself to stay in control of her emotions. Racing back into the living area, her heart pounded at the sight of Uncle Roy slumped farther in the chair. She pushed back the recliner to shift him in what appeared to be a more comfortable position.

The dispatcher continued to ask her what her uncle was doing, when his eyes opened wider as if in panic. She placed the bag under his mouth just before he started to vomit. Tears pooled in her eyes, and she tried to swallow them back as she asked the dispatcher, "How much longer until they'll be here?"

"Just a few more minutes, honey," the woman tried to reassure her. She kept talking, but Melody only heard a jumbling of words from the woman.

Seconds seemed like hours. Melody felt so helpless, so out of control. There was nothing she could do to help her uncle. He kept trying to talk to her, and Melody tried to understand what he said, but his words slurred together; plus the dispatcher continued to ask questions and make comments.

Melody sat close to him, watching to be sure he didn't vomit again and choke, or fall and hurt himself worse, or stop breathing. She could tell his body continued to tighten, and she knew at any moment he could pass out or die.

The thought of him dying sent a wave of fear and nausea through her body. She loved this man. He'd been the only consistent male in her life. He'd always been good and caring and fun. She didn't want him to die.

She heard the distant sound of sirens, and relief washed over her. The piercing noise grew closer, and she looked out the front bay window. She saw the ambulance approaching and looked back at her uncle. "Help is coming, Uncle Roy. Hang on. They're coming."

The ambulance pulled into the driveway, and two men jumped out of the front. They dashed around the back of the vehicle and pulled out a gurney. Melody swung open the front door, waving them inside. The older, gray-haired one came through the door. "Where is he, ma'am?"

As he spoke, his gaze scanned the room for her uncle. She pointed to the recliner, but he was already rushing to him. The younger man pushed inside the door, and the two of them began to assess her uncle.

Her body began to shake with relief that they were there but also with fear they couldn't help him. Realizing she needed to call her aunt, she ran back to her bedroom and grabbed her cell phone off the nightstand.

She pushed her aunt's number as she made her way back to the living room. They had already loaded Uncle Roy onto the gurney and were wheeling him out the front door.

"I'm going with you!" she hollered. The younger man nodded for her to come on.

"What's going on?" Her aunt's voice sounded over the phone. Melody hadn't realized the line connected. Before she could respond, her aunt continued, "Are those sirens in the background? Melody, are you there?"

"Yes, Aunt Renee." Melody tried to sound calm as she stepped up into the back of the ambulance. Just realizing she wasn't dressed but in her pajamas and pink robe, she scrunched her face. She wasn't immodest, and she hadn't had time to dress. Her uncle's health was most important.

"What's going on?"

"It's Uncle Roy." Melody sat on the benchlike seat in the back of the ambulance while the older emergency technician connected him to a machine. "I think he's having a stroke."

"What?" Aunt Renee's voice heightened, and Melody knew her aunt was going to panic.

"We're on our way to the hospital. Meet us there."

"I'm coming," her aunt said. Crackles and rustling sounded over the line, as Aunt Renee must have forgotten to push the END button on the phone. Melody could hear the beeping of the car when she opened the door. Her aunt's audible prayer sounded over the line. "Oh dear Jesus, please heavenly Lord, don't take Roy. Not yet. . ."

Melody pushed the END button on her phone and shoved it deep into the robe's pocket. She looked down at her uncle. In the midst of all that was happening in his body, his face still glowed of a peace she didn't understand. But his body seemed to still be tightening. He looked to be completely paralyzed on one side.

And there was nothing she could do to help him.

She'd tried to make him comfortable. She'd kept him from vomiting all over himself. She'd called the ambulance. But she couldn't heal him. She couldn't make him better. She had absolutely no control, and she hated it.

⁓

"Come on, son. We've got to go!"

Noting the urgency in his dad's voice, Drew tossed the shovel against the barn wall and jogged to his dad. He pulled off his gloves and hopped into the cab of the truck as his dad started the engine. "What's going on?"

"Gotta get to the hospital."

A myriad of reasons to rush to the hospital whizzed through his mind. His mother was most likely at the grocery store with Renee. Could they have had a wreck? Did something happen on the farm to one of his friends? Did Melody get hurt trying to fix a vehicle? "What happened?"

"Roy's had a stroke."

"How? When?"

"Apparently Melody woke up and found him hunched over in his recliner. She called the ambulance and got them there in a hurry." The truck bounced through a large pothole in the road, but his dad didn't slow down. "But your mom doesn't know if he's all right yet or not. They're at the hospital. Half the church is already there praying."

Drew stared out the windshield. Within moments, trees and fields gave way to buildings and streetlights. They passed a subdivision, then a gas station, a couple of fast-food restaurants, and then a grocery store. Finally, they made it to the hospital. Drew recognized several of the cars and trucks in the emergency parking lot. He saw Doris shuffling to the door after having just had hip replacement surgery only two months before. Her sisters, Joanne, Maggie, and Betty hustled behind her, fussing that she needed to slow down.

He was thankful for the outpouring of love his church family was sure to drape over Renee and the family. Many prayers would storm heaven's gates for Roy's recovery. But Drew still worried about what was happening at that moment.

Without a word, he and his dad rushed into the emergency room. His mom saw them, ran to them, and grabbed her father in a hug. She released him then gripped Drew's hand. "He's going to be okay."

Tears streamed down her face, and a smile brightened her lips. She squeezed Drew's hand then grabbed his father's hand with her other one. "He had what's called an ischemic stroke, and they were able to give him some medicine." His mother released their hands and called over to one of their church friends, "Anita, what did the doctor say that medicine was called?"

"Tissue plasminogen activator."

His mom turned back toward Drew and his dad. She laughed and patted his dad's chest. "What she said. But the important thing is he's going to be okay. They have to watch him for bleeding, but his prognosis is good."

"God is so good." His dad's praise was barely above a whisper as he swiped his hand down the entirety of his face.

"Your buddy's going to be okay." His mom nudged his dad's shoulder. "Come sit down."

Not ready to have a seat, Drew watched as his parents sat beside their pastor and his wife, Joan. They'd spent far too much time in a hospital with Joan having battled cancer in two separate parts of her body over the last few years. God had mercifully healed her both times.

Drew scanned the room. He felt humbled by the care and concern his church displayed. Behind him he could hear some of the ladies making a calendar of who would prepare which meals for the family and on what days. He knew his dad and several of the other men would probably argue over who would have the privilege of mowing Roy's one-acre yard.

On the far side of the room, Drew spotted Melody wearing a bright pink robe. Her hair stuck out at odd angles all over her head. She had her elbows propped against her knees, and her face was buried in her hands. Sweet, quiet Wanda sat beside her with one hand on Melody's back.

Feeling prodded by the Holy Spirit, he made his way to them. Wanda stood up slowly. "Here, honey. I'll let you sit here. I've missed my morning medicine, and I need to go take it."

Hesitantly, Drew sat beside Melody. She didn't move, aside from the rising and falling of her back. He clasped his hands in front of him. Should he touch her back as Wanda had? Would she be offended? She most definitely didn't seem to be the kind of girl who would appreciate an uninvited touch of reassurance.

His mind kept imagining what she must have felt walking into the living room to Roy having a stroke. She must have been so afraid, and it must have seemed like forever until the ambulance arrived. He didn't even want to think about how it would feel to fear someone he loved might die before help could arrive.

If it were him, he would be on his knees in prayer, clinging to God for help, wisdom, and comfort. But Melody didn't have that.

He looked at her robe and hair again. It was obvious she had just awakened when it happened. She probably hadn't eaten or brushed her teeth. He knew she must feel every bit as uncomfortable as she was afraid.

No matter what she thought of him, he had to show her that he cared. He had to at least try to comfort her. Slowly, he wrapped his arm around her and squeezed her shoulder. "I'm sorry, Melody."

She turned toward him, buried her face in his chest, and wrapped both arms around him. Her back heaved with the sobs she seemed no longer able to hold back. He pulled her closer and patted her back. Every protective urge he'd ever felt prickled his skin. He'd do anything to make her feel better, to assure her he'd do everything in his power to keep her from pain.

Without thinking, he lowered his lips to the top of her head. Though tangled, her hair was still soft and smelled of shampoo. He raked his fingers through a portion of the long hair against her back. "It's okay, Melody."

She continued to cry, and he didn't let her go. He'd hold her for the rest of his life if she'd let him. Anything to take the tears away from this beautiful, strong, competitive, almost always difficult creature.

A shadow fell over him, and he looked up and saw Renee. She bent over and rubbed the back of Melody's head. "You did good, honey. Why don't you let Drew take you home to change?"

To his surprise, Melody lifted her head and nodded. She stood, and Drew got up and placed his hand in the small of her back. He still felt the need to protect her.

Renee's eyes were red rimmed and her nose was puffy from tears that had shifted from fear to rejoicing. She touched Drew's shoulder. "Please stay with her a little while."

Drew nodded. He wouldn't have a problem with that. He had no intention of leaving Melody alone. After getting the keys from his dad, he guided her to the truck, opened the door for her, then raced around to the driver's side and got in. They didn't speak as he drove to Roy and Renee's house. He pulled into the driveway and parked. Looking over at her, he noted her furrowed brows as she bit her bottom lip. He knew she was remembering having left there only a few hours before in an ambulance.

Once he got her out of the truck and into the house, he tried to lighten the tension she felt. "You go get cleaned up, and I'll find something for us to eat." He looked at the clock. "It's almost one o'clock. I bet you're starving. I know I am."

She didn't say anything as she puttered down the hall and up the stairs. A few moments later, he heard water running in the shower. He rummaged through the refrigerator to see what Renee had that he could fix for lunch. The pickings were slim, as she had been going to the grocery store when Roy had the stroke.

He found a little bit of sliced turkey and bread. He made a couple of sandwiches then cut apple slices and put them on two plates. Spying some packaged chocolate chip cookies, he put a few on each plate as well. Not sure what she'd drink, he decided he'd let her get that herself when she was ready.

She finally made it to the kitchen wearing cutoff sweatpants and a T-shirt. Her hair was tied in a knot at the back of her head, and her face was scrubbed clean. To his surprise, her bare feet exposed toenails painted a bright pinkish orange color with a small white flower on her big toenails. He wondered if his sister had something to do with that.

He smiled when she looked up at him. "Hey. I made us some lunch. I wasn't sure what you'd want to drink."

She opened the refrigerator and grabbed a soft drink. Popping the top, she nodded as she sat down in the chair across from his. "Thanks, Drew."

They didn't talk as they ate their sandwiches, apples, and cookies, but Drew noted that she did eat. In fact, she ate everything on her plate. She must have been starving. She stared off into space, and Drew prayed for the right words to say to her.

"It was good you got Roy to the hospital so quickly."

She nodded.

"They believe he's going to make a full recovery."

She gazed at Drew. Her eyes pooled with tears. "I was so scared. I thought he was going to die right there in the living room. I didn't know what to do."

"You did exactly what you were supposed to do."

She shook her head. "But I couldn't help him. Not really. I could make him comfortable and keep him from vomiting all over himself, but I couldn't fix him. I couldn't make him better. I couldn't control—" Her voice broke, and she sucked in a deep breath. She picked up a paper towel and patted her eyes.

Drew reached across the table and patted her hand. "Melody, you did everything right. Just like Renee said, you did good."

Melody shook her head. "I had no control."

Drew furrowed his eyebrows, beginning to see the basis of Melody's need to be the best for the first time. "None of us do. Not really."

Chapter 8

The next morning Drew woke up long before the sun. Several of his friends were supposed to come over to start framing his house. After spending the afternoon with Melody and most of the evening at the hospital, he'd forgotten to tell them they'd wait until next week.

He started down the stairs to get the coffee brewing before his dad woke up. The strong aroma filled his nostrils before he made it into the kitchen. He saw his dad already dressed in work clothes and boots, sitting at the table with a steaming mug pressed against his lips. He set the mug down and looked at Drew. " 'Bout time you got up, son. I thought we had a house to frame today."

Drew furrowed his eyebrows. "Dad, I just assumed we'd wait. What with Roy's stroke yesterday, and—I'm sure no one is going to show up."

"I guess I'm no one," Nick's deep voice sounded from inside the pantry. He held a dainty, rose-framed container of sugar in his left hand and his fish-decorated coffee cup in his right.

Drew grinned at how ridiculous his oversized friend looked pouring sugar from that container into the oversized mug. "Nick, what are you doing here? You should be with your dad."

Nick guffawed. "Are you kidding? Dad's mad as a hornet that he couldn't be here. You know how the man is. He was carrying on, even while slurring his words, that he was slacking on his part."

Drew pursed his lips. He knew Nick was probably telling the truth about that. Roy never shirked on a task he'd told someone he'd do. Nick's and Drew's dads had raised both of them to be that way. If a person told someone they were going to do something, they had better do it. A man's only as good as his word. He'd heard Roy and his dad say those words so many times they used to make him sick.

Drew scratched at the stubble on his jaw. "Well, I think the three of us will have our work cut out for us. Won't be easy framing the house with just us."

"Now why would you think that?" His dad scooted his chair back and leaned his arm against the table. "Mike and his dad and brother, as well as about five guys from church, are all coming to help get that house framed. It's just a little ranch house. We'll have it done by the end of the day."

Drew's jaw dropped. "They're all coming?" He scratched his head. "I just assumed—I mean, Roy had a stroke, and we all lost a good part of a day's work on the farm." He nodded toward Nick. "Not that we minded. You know Roy's health comes first."

Nick lifted his hand to stop Drew's words. "Enough of that, sleeping beauty."

Drew looked down, noting that he still wore the basketball shorts and white T-shirt he'd worn to bed.

Nick shooed him with his hand. "Just get your tail on up those steps and get ready. We've got a house to frame."

Drew turned and climbed the first two steps. He looked back at Nick. "Roy's really doing good?"

Nick swallowed hard, and Drew knew yesterday had nearly scared the life out of him. Drew couldn't imagine how he'd feel if it had been his dad lying in that hospital bed. It was bad enough that it was Roy. He was like an uncle to Drew.

Nick nodded. "He really is. I've already talked to Mom this morning." He cleared his throat, probably warding off a show of emotion. "We're very thankful."

"How 'bout Melody? She was still pretty shook up when I left yesterday."

"Melody is so hard to figure out." Nick leaned against the pantry door. "Usually she has something to say or argues about everything. But she was real quiet yesterday. I can't tell what's going on in her head."

Drew nodded then headed back up the steps. Melody was a hard one to read. No doubt about that. But yesterday he felt he'd seen a little insight into her "problem."

The woman needed to be in control. It was no wonder she hadn't accepted Jesus as her Savior. Becoming a Christian was all about faith and being willing to give up control of her life to follow Jesus. As long as Melody clung to being in control of her life, she could never accept Christ.

Drew's heart felt heavy. She had to know she didn't really have control of anything. She had to see it in her life and in nature. There was no controlling a tornado or a flash flood. She couldn't decide who was willing to seek her mechanical abilities or even how other people drove their cars. Yesterday she momentarily lost control at the hospital and allowed him to comfort her with a hug and kind words—something he knew she would normally never do.

God, help her to see that the most control she will ever have over her life or circumstances is when she gives it up to You. . .when she has faith that You will give her peace and hope in whatever life brings her.

Drew sighed as he realized anew what a terrible witness he had been. His competitive spirit was really just that—a competitive spirit. He loved to battle and win. And he had to admit he was really not very good at losing at all. It was actually something he really needed to work on—losing gracefully.

But his competitive nature wasn't about him controlling the world around him. He wanted to win, but Melody needed to. Realizing the difference between them weighted his heart with conviction about the way he'd allowed his pride to get wrapped up in their ridiculous battles.

God, forgive me. Draw Melody to You. Whatever it takes, may she give her life to You.

<hr />

The doorbell rang, and Melody hopped off the couch and opened the front door. A woman from the church stood on the porch with several deli sandwiches in her hands. "Hi. I brought some lunch."

Melody forced herself to smile to be polite. They'd already had so many visitors, and they had more food than they'd be able to eat in a week. More than anything, Melody just wanted to have a little time alone. She waved to the woman. "Come on in."

"Thanks, Melody." The woman walked through the living room and into the kitchen and placed the sandwiches on the table. She extended her hand. "I'm Sheila. Can't remember if we formally met."

"And I guess you already know I'm Melody."

"Is that Sheila?" Aunt Renee called from the back of the house. She walked into the kitchen and gave Sheila a quick hug. "Roy's resting. Thanks so much for bringing us lunch."

"I didn't have time to cook, as I have to be at work in thirty minutes, but I was sure to pick up food I know Roy can eat."

Aunt Renee turned toward Melody. "Sheila's a nurse."

Melody took in the pastel-flowered nurse uniform top and blue pants. "I can tell."

Sheila looked at her watch. "I better be going. Tell Roy we're praying for him." Sheila walked back to the front door. "Oh. . .I almost forgot. Sarah gave this to me at youth group last night and asked me to give it to you." She pulled a homemade card out of her purse.

Aunt Renee chuckled. "The girl got her nose out of a book long enough to make him a card?"

"Yep."

"That was so sweet of her."

"She's a good kid." Sheila raised her hand. "I gotta go. I'll see you later."

Aunt Renee shut the door behind her. She opened the card and read the contents to Melody. The teenager's sentiments were kind and heartfelt, and her aunt had to brush a tear out of her eye. "Will you put this on the table with the others? It will make Roy's day to see all these things once he wakes up."

Aunt Renee gave the card to Melody then gripped her free hand. "I'm so thankful our Roy is going to be okay."

Afraid her emotions would get the best of her again, she looked away and mumbled, "Me, too."

Melody walked into the dining room, taking in the magnitude of cards her aunt had stood up on the table. Several vases of flowers sat around the room, most of them either various shades of blue or adorned with blue ribbon. It was obvious his church family understood Uncle Roy's fanatical feelings about the University of Kentucky Wildcat basketball team. The kindness shown by his church family would overwhelm him once he was able to see all they'd done.

And the food! In addition to the cold cuts and baked dishes, fresh vegetables and fruits, several people had also brought over dishes just for her and Aunt Renee: desserts rich in chocolate that they were supposed to indulge in whenever Uncle Roy took a nap.

Her cell phone buzzed in her front pocket. She pulled it out and looked at the number on the screen. It was her mom. Melody had called her the night before to tell her about Uncle Roy, but she'd gotten the voice mail and had only been able to leave a message. It had been so long since Melody talked to her. Her heart raced with a need to hear her mom's live voice, to know she was all right. She pushed the TALK button. "Hello, Mom."

"Hi, Melody. I got your message. How is Roy?"

"He's doing good. They were able to get him medicine at the right time. He should make a full recovery."

"That's great."

Melody could hear her mother's husband talking in the background. She couldn't make out what he was saying, but he sounded frustrated. Melody sucked in her breath. She really didn't like that man. "How have you been, Mom?"

Her voice sounded muffled, and Melody assumed her mother had put her hand over the phone so Melody couldn't hear her talking to her husband. It was apparent she was more concerned with getting back to her new husband than she was about her brother-in-law's health. Or talking with her only daughter. Their relationship, as strained as it had been all the years after her dad walked out, seemed to get worse instead of better. Melody wondered if it was easier for her mother to simply put all of the painful past behind her and start fresh with the new guy.

Her mother's voice sounded again. "I'm sorry, Melody. Frank and I were just getting ready to head to town. I'll talk to you later."

Before Melody could respond, her mother hung up. She sucked in a deep breath and bit her bottom lip as she pulled the phone away from her ear and clicked it off. She would not focus on her lack of a relationship with her mother. She bit her lip harder. She refused to feel sorry for herself.

Aunt Renee walked into the dining room. She held a piece of paper in her hand. "Melody, could you do me a big favor?"

Grateful for the opportunity to think of something else, she turned toward her aunt. "Absolutely. Anything."

"You know I didn't get to finish my grocery trip, and even though I don't think we'll need much food for a while. . ."

Melody chuckled. "I think you're right about that."

"We still need toilet paper and toothpaste and several other things. Would you be willing to go for me?" She held out the paper. "Addy offered to go, but I thought you might like to get out of the house for a while."

Melody nodded. "Of course, I'll go." She was glad for the excuse to go somewhere. When AJ insisted she not come in to work today, she'd been grateful for his kindness, but she also knew that sitting around the house would make her feel antsy. She'd want to be working on something, but her tractor was ready for the tractor pull on Friday, and they'd weeded the garden two days ago. Aside from cleaning the house, which she did not like the idea of doing, and it didn't need it anyway, she really had too much time on her hands today. She added, "I may stop by Gracie's on the way home."

"Yes, you do that. It will do you good to get your hands on that sweet little guy."

Melody chewed the inside of her lip. Her love for Wyatt Jr. was apparent to everyone. The little guy had her wrapped around his chubby finger.

She took the list, grabbed the keys off the counter, and headed out the door.

It didn't take long to get everything on her aunt's list, especially since most of it had been marked through because of all the food they'd been given.

She pulled into Gracie's driveway and saw Gracie pushing Wyatt in the swing in the backyard. Melody honked, and Gracie scooped Wyatt into her arms, making him wave his chubby hand at her. Melody got out and made her way through the gate and into the backyard. "Hey. Thought I'd stop by for a minute."

"I'm so glad you did."

Wyatt leaned over, reaching his arms out to Melody. She cooed at the baby and took him from his mom. "Come here, you rotten stink."

Wyatt cackled and grabbed for the strands of her hair that had fallen out of her ponytail. Pushing them behind her ear, she Eskimo kissed him. "This boy only loves me for my hair."

"I don't know about that." Gracie patted his diaper-padded bottom. "The boy knows when he's got someone hooked."

Melody tickled his neck. "That's because you're a smart boy, aren't you?"

Gracie motioned toward the back door. "Come inside. Let's get a glass of sweet tea."

Melody followed her then sat on the couch in the great room. She plopped Wyatt on her lap so that he was facing her. He reached for the buttons on her shirt, and Melody picked up his oversized key ring off the end table and handed it to him.

"How's Roy doing?" Gracie walked into the room, handed her a glass, then sat on the love seat.

"He's doing remarkably well. He should make a full recovery." She grinned. "He's even planning to go to the tractor pull."

"Praise God!" Gracie practically shouted through the room. Little Wyatt looked at his mother as if she'd lost her mind. She grabbed his arm and lifted it in the air. "Say, 'Praise God,' my little man."

Today Gracie's outburst didn't upset Melody. She was too overwhelmed to be aggravated. Wyatt cackled, and Melody spied something in his mouth. "Uh-oh, buddy, what's in your mouth?"

Gracie squealed. "Did you see it?" She pulled down on Wyatt's lower lip. "A tooth!"

"What!" Wyatt shook his head to get his mother's finger away from his lip. Melody put her finger on his mouth to try to get another look. He bit down, and she felt the small, hard tooth. "Wyatt Jr." She lifted the baby in the air. "You're not allowed to get teeth." She gently twisted him back and forth. "You're supposed to stay a baby." He cooed, and slobber oozed out of his mouth and hit Melody on the forehead.

She brought him back down to her lap, and Gracie howled. She handed Melody a cloth diaper. "Well, that's what he thinks about that."

Melody wiped her forehead. "I guess so." She handed the toy keys back to Wyatt, and he shoved them into his mouth. Melody frowned. "Seriously though, he's growing up so fast."

Gracie sighed. "Believe me, I know it." She swatted Melody's arm. "Don't worry. I'm sure you'll have plenty of babies of your own."

Melody snorted. "I doubt that."

"Why? Don't you think you'll get married?"

Melody scrunched her nose. She'd always thought she'd never in a million years want to get married, but having watched her aunt take care of her uncle since his stroke and watching him respond to her—something had changed inside her. Uncle Roy and Aunt Renee, Drew's parents, Wyatt and Gracie— since moving to River Run, Melody had witnessed some good marriages. From everything she'd seen between Addy and Nick, they would be very happy as well. If she could have a marriage like that, then maybe she wouldn't mind so much.

The feel of Drew's strong arms around her flooded her mind and rushed through her. She'd felt protected and cared for. When he'd kissed her head, though she knew it was in innocence, for a moment, she'd wondered what it would be like to feel his lips against hers. The idea of it scared her, and she pushed the thought away.

She looked at her friend, who still waited for her to answer. She shook her head. "No. I've never thought I would get married."

Chapter 9

D rew inhaled the sweet aroma of diesel engine smoke and grease and even a dabbling of sweat. Nearly the whole town had come out for the tractor pull and fireworks. In addition to the concession stands, the women's auxiliary had set up several portable, inflatable games. There were two with slides, one made like a cage for the kids to jump in, and another that was an obstacle course. The high school cheerleaders had set up a face-painting tent. They even had several people who'd set up tents to sell all kinds of crafts—fancy pillows and quilts, knickknacks, and belt buckles. There was even a Christmas decorations tent—on the Fourth of July! The tractor pull was becoming a town festival of its own.

With his tractor already pulled up to the starting line, he looked around for Melody and her tractor. As luck would have it, she was one of the final two tractors, and he'd have to race her.

Different places raced different ways. Mostly people simply timed each tractor, and the winner took all, but Drew liked the way River Run did it.

Tractors raced against time the first round. They'd take turns driving the one hundred meters to see which two tractors could pull their sled the fastest. At the end, the top two tractors would race each other for the ultimate prize: a big ol' trophy, a $250 gift certificate to Wyatt's Hardware Store, and bragging rights for a year.

Granted, he'd seen many a fellow make it to the finals with a good time in the first round but then have to drop out because his engine blew or something else broke on his tractor. But if a guy built his tractor tough enough, as Drew always did, it would be able to withstand the challenge. Melody's had come through looking pretty good as well.

And tonight she would come out the overall victor.

It was still hard on his pride to think about it, and in his mind, he knew that his losing wasn't going to make Melody see the need to give her feigned control of her life over to God. But maybe if she saw him lose and handle it the way he should, the way Mike always handled loss, then maybe she'd see that Drew didn't have to win at everything. She needed to see there were more important things in his life than taking home the prize.

Mike walked up to him and grabbed his hand in a firm handshake. "I still can't believe it's going to be you against Melody for the championship."

"I know. It's crazy, isn't it?"

Mike raised his eyebrows. "I'll tell you what it is. That woman's your match." He extended his arms. "Never in my wildest dreams would I have ever imagined a person, let alone a girl, would be able to get the best of Drew Wilson." He pointed to a stream of smoke. "And yet, here she comes."

Drew saw Melody driving around the tractor of a guy from another county. She'd fixed up Roy's old John Deere just as Drew expected. Even from a distance he could tell she'd done a lot of work to the old girl.

A slow smile bowed his lips. Melody had done a good job. She truly was quite the mechanic. In a way he couldn't quite explain, Drew was kind of proud of her.

"Just so you know, and it's no offense"—Mike patted Drew's shoulder—"but I'm betting on Melody."

Drew noted the gleam in Mike's eye, and he knew his friend was only trying to mess around with him. But for the slightest moment, Drew's competitive pride reared up within him, and he felt the urge to jump on his tractor seat and blow Roy's old tractor out of the fairgrounds. Shaking off the feeling, he returned the pat on Mike's shoulder, only a little firmer than Mike must have expected, because he flinched under the pat. "She's exactly who'd I'd put my money on."

Mike frowned, but Drew nodded to his friend then turned his attention to Melody. She pulled up to the starting line and stepped down from the seat. He nodded to his friend. "Excuse me, Mike. I'm going to go wish my rival good luck. In a matter of speaking, anyway."

Drew walked toward Melody. He didn't believe in luck, and he never uttered the words to his opponents, but he wanted to be able to say something to Melody before their race.

She had the helmet stuck under her arm as she looked over the outside of her tractor. He grinned as he couldn't help but admit she looked kind of cute in Nick's much-too-big-for-her racing garb. He extended his hand to her. "Hey. I just wanted to wish you luck."

She pursed her lips and glared up at him. "I didn't think you'd believe in luck."

Caught off guard, he stepped back and dropped his hand. "You're right. I don't. But I wanted to—"

Fire lit her eyes, and she moved toward him like a rabid dog about to attack. "Look, Drew. Don't try to be nice to me so you can knock me off my game and win this championship." She poked him in the chest with her finger. "You're just going to have to take being beaten by a girl."

With a huff, she walked away from him and stuck her helmet on her head.

Aggravation streamed through him. The woman never gave him a break. Never. She always thought the worst of him. No matter what he did. He'd tried over and over to be kind to that headstrong, two-bit polecat, but she simply would not have it.

He strode toward his own tractor. Grabbing his helmet, he stared at his nemesis. He shoved it on his head and tapped the top to be sure it was in place. *Little lady, you're going to eat my dust.*

⁂

Melody stepped up and into the seat of the John Deere. She had no idea why she had been mean to Drew. Just edgy. The last few days had her in a whirlwind of frustration. She was confused about everything in life. But she shouldn't have snapped at him like that.

He had been so kind to her the day he brought her home from the hospital. She knew then that he had a good heart. Truthfully, deep in her gut, she'd known it long before then. His need to always come out on top had just struck a chord somewhere down deep inside, and she'd done everything she could to show him up.

She looked toward the bleachers. Uncle Roy had insisted on coming to the tractor pull. He still didn't have all his strength in his hand, and his face still fell ever so slightly on the left side. His speech slurred, but she could understand everything he said. Since his right hand hadn't been affected, he still played his Wii, which made Melody chuckle. He didn't play it quite as much, as he needed rest, and Aunt Renee made him rest. But Melody knew as soon as he could he'd drive them crazy with the video game once again.

Fearing he'd not be able to sit without back support the whole time, Aunt Renee brought two folding chairs for them to sit in. She'd set them up close to the bleachers, as Uncle Roy loved to chat with everyone who passed his way.

Tonight he didn't have any trouble finding people to talk to him. Melody watched as one person after another stopped to shake his hand or give him a hug. First, it was Cindy and Tricia. Melody thought of them as the Bobbsey twins. Everywhere they went, they went together.

Then it was Lana. Then another lady. Melody tried to remember her name. The woman's husband wore a long beard, white as snow, and he drove an old historical train for tourists. He was the most welcoming man she'd ever met in her life, practically squealing, "Well hello, Melody!" each time he saw her. She snapped her fingers. Sue. That was the woman's name.

Melody's attention was diverted as Drew hopped onto his tractor seat. She wanted him to look over at her. She needed to apologize, but he kept his gaze straight ahead. He looked tense and furious. She couldn't be sure, but she imagined that if he took off that helmet the veins in his neck and forehead would be bulging with fury.

The track was ready. She knew they were about to start, and she needed to get her mind off Uncle Roy and off Drew Wilson and onto the race. She looked at the finish line. Surprisingly, she didn't care much about this race. She just wanted to be done with it.

AJ signaled for her to let him know if she was ready. After giving a thumbs-up, she glanced once more back at Uncle Roy. Another woman from the church, Rhonda, was bent over, giving him a hug.

Rhonda had confused Melody since the first time she met her. Ten years before, Rhonda lost her sixteen-year-old daughter to a heart defect. It was sudden and unexpected, and when Rhonda talked of the girl, it was obvious she had been a pride and joy to her and her husband.

What Melody didn't understand was that despite the loss, Rhonda was filled with joy. She headed up the kitchen ministry at Uncle Roy and Aunt Renee's church, organizing the meals that were taken to families in the church who were in crisis, organizing Thanksgiving and Christmas dinners for families in the community in need, even cooking dinner every Wednesday evening before church services.

Melody simply didn't understand the woman. Gracie's little boy, Wyatt, wasn't even Melody's son, but if God took him, she would be devastated. Rhonda had the right to be devastated.

"I have told you these things, so that in me you may have peace. In this world you will have trouble. But take heart! I have overcome the world."

The scripture the preacher had spoken about filtered through her mind. She'd gone home and searched in her aunt's Bible for that scripture, memorizing it because it bothered her so much.

Old English lessons washed through her thoughts. She'd taken many an extra lesson as she'd struggled so badly with reading in school. Sentences ending in a period were a statement or a declaration. "In this world you will have trouble," and "I have overcome the world." They were declarations made by Jesus. "But take heart!" It was written with an exclamation point. Jesus was exclaiming or shouting to the people, "Take heart! Don't give up. Don't give in."

I'm not supposed to give up. Not supposed to give in.

But why do so many bad things happen? Horrible things? Why doesn't God stop them? Why don't You stop them, God?

She peered at Rhonda. Tears welled in her eyes as the woman reached down to hug her aunt. Rhonda had lost her daughter. Her child. It didn't seem fair. Didn't seem right. Why? Because bad things happen. But Rhonda didn't give up. She didn't give in.

Humbled to her core, Melody's view of God began to shift. Bonnie wasn't being punished with gnarled hands. She was able to show love and kindness despite continuous pain. Gracie wasn't being ridiculous with her constant conversations with and about God. She trusted Him with every aspect of her life.

The gunshot sounded, signaling the start of the race. Drew's tractor shot forward, but Melody didn't care. She closed her eyes and allowed the tears to stream down her cheeks. *Forgive me, God. I am a sinner. Please accept me anyway. I long for what Gracie and Uncle Roy and Aunt Renee and Bonnie and Rhonda have—for what they have with You.*

She opened her eyes. The heavens didn't part, and she didn't see Jesus in the sky, but she knew she was different. Something inside her had changed.

Looking ahead, she saw that Drew had already reached the finish line. He jumped off the tractor, threw off his helmet, and let the loudest whoop she'd ever heard peal through the air.

He raced the full one hundred meters back, pointing both index fingers at her. "Take that, little lady. Now, get off your pedestal, and—"

"Drew, I don't even care about the race." She jumped down from the tractor, stood on tiptoes, and wrapped her arms around him in a quick hug. "I've accepted Jesus into my heart."

Drew's eyes seemed to bulge out of their sockets as he took a step back. "What?"

"I'm a Christian." She clapped her hands. For the first time in her life, all dressed in protective gear with grease smearing her face and her hair knotted up to fit a helmet, she felt like a giddy schoolgirl. "Aren't you excited?"

Before Drew could respond, AJ walked toward them holding a microphone in one hand and the trophy in the other. "Same ending as last year, folks. This year's tractor pull winner is—"

Melody pushed Drew toward AJ. "Run over there and get your trophy." She waved toward her aunt and uncle. Confused expressions marked their faces, and she could hardly wait to tell them what had happened.

"Melody." Drew tried to step toward her. Sadness wrapped his face for no reason she could understand. This was the happiest day of her life.

She shooed him away. "Go on. Get your trophy. I've got to talk to Uncle Roy and Aunt Renee."

Throwing her helmet on the ground, she rushed to her aunt and uncle.

"Melody, what happened?" Uncle Roy asked as she wrapped her arms around his neck.

"Is the tractor not working right?" asked Aunt Renee.

New tears swept down her cheeks as she shook her head. "No. Everything is fine. Everything is wonderful. I've accepted Jesus."

"You what?" Aunt Renee's eyebrows lifted.

"You did?" Uncle Roy smiled.

"Did I just hear correctly?" Gracie hollered as she stepped toward Melody. "You accepted Jesus?"

Melody nodded, and Gracie smashed her with the tightest hug she'd ever experienced.

"Melody's a Christian!" Addy's voice sounded from the bleachers three seats behind them.

"I heard," Nick said. Melody giggled as he tried to make his way down the bleachers to her.

"Praise the Lord," said someone.

"God is so good," said another.

"He doesn't want any to perish," responded yet another.

"I knew you were going to come over to the light side," Nick said as he towered over her. "Now come give Cousin Nick a proper hug."

Before Melody could protest, Nick threw her over his shoulder as he had done when he was a teen and she was a girl. He twirled around several times then plopped her back on her feet. When she was little, he'd let her go just to see her wobble around then fall to the ground. This time he held her in a bear hug. "I'm so happy for you."

Allowing a peace that goes beyond understanding to envelop her whole being, she sucked in a long breath. "Me, too."

Chapter 10

Drew was a dog. He was lower than a dog. He was the scum on the bottom of the dog's paw. He wasn't even worthy to be on the bottom of the dog's paw. He covered his face with his hands. He couldn't believe he had acted that way.

Standing on his own farm, mending his own fence several days after the tractor pull, his face still warmed with embarrassment at the memory of it. *God, You even told me to let it go, to show her care and encouragement, to not be so consumed with winning, but like always, my pride got the best of me.*

He'd wanted to dig a hole and hide inside it when AJ announced Drew the ultimate winner of the tractor pull and handed him the trophy. Almost no one in the stands seemed to give a care about his win. Everyone he knew surrounded Melody, congratulating her, while everyone else looked down at her, confused by what had happened.

I should have just thrown that trophy on the ground and rushed over to give her a hug like the others. But he hadn't. Shame had wrapped itself around him, and Drew grabbed the trophy, loaded up his tractor, and headed straight home. Conviction at his behavior had eaten him alive ever since.

He finished hammering the broken fence post back in place then looked at the cows that grazed beside him. Thinking he'd brought a treat, several made their way toward him when he jumped inside the fence. He watched as one of them lifted her head. Her mouth was full of grass, and she chomped at it with no apparent concern in the world.

"Life's pretty easy for a cow." He reached out and petted her nose. Her calf moved close to her and grabbed hold of one of her teats. The cow didn't so much as take an extra blink. She didn't have to worry about pride or embarrassment or admitting she was wrong. She just had to eat and feed her calf.

"You need to talk to her."

Drew didn't move at the sound of his dad's voice behind him. He'd heard someone walking up. He figured it was either his mom or dad coming to give him a bit of advice. He continued to stare at the cow and her calf. "I know."

"Waiting around isn't going to make it any easier."

He twisted around and looked at his dad. "Boy, don't I know it. I haven't slept in three days. I'm humiliated even out here all by myself, just me and my cows." He gripped the fence post. "Her salvation is the best thing in the world. I'm happy for her and thankful to God, and I can't even tell her."

"Sure you can. You've had to eat dirt before."

Drew laughed at the grin that spread across his dad's face. He was definitely right about that. On more than one occasion in his life, Drew had been overzealous about a competition and ended up landing face-first on the losing side of embarrassment. But it had been awhile since he'd drunk from that bitter cup, and it didn't taste so great going down. "I know. I'm just not sure how to do it."

"Give her a call. It's as simple as that."

Drew let out a long breath. His dad was right. She deserved an apology and his congratulations. And God simply wouldn't let him rest until he'd made things right. "You're right."

His dad patted his back. "I gotta get to work. See you later, son."

Drew put the hammer and extra nails in his toolbox and loaded it onto the truck. He didn't have service on his cell phone on this part of the farm. Driving closer to the house, he prayed God would give him the right words to say to Melody.

He looked down at his phone again. He had service. She'd be at work, and he probably should wait until she got home to call her, but if he didn't do it now he was afraid he'd lose his nerve.

Exhaling a long breath, he dialed AJ's number and asked to speak to Melody. She sounded confused when she answered the phone, and he assumed she probably didn't have too many people calling the shop asking to speak specifically to her.

He cleared his throat. "Hi, Melody. It's Drew."

"Hey." She sounded happy to hear from him. Something he would have never expected.

His hands started to shake, and Drew cocked his head to hold the phone against his shoulder. He stretched his arms out in front of him then wiped them against his jeans. "I need to talk to you."

His voice sounded too high, too anxious, even to his own ears. He cleared his throat again.

"Sure. Can it wait until after work?" Melody sounded chipper but anxious to get off the phone.

Drew closed his eyes. He shouldn't have called her right now. What was he thinking? Of course he could talk to her when she got off, but where? Should he just call her again? Now that he was talking to her, it just seemed wrong to say all he had to say over the phone.

An idea popped into his mind, but he wasn't sure she'd be willing to spend time alone with him at his place. He shrugged. It wouldn't hurt to ask. "Would you be willing to do a little nighttime fishing with me?"

"Absolutely. I love to fish. Where should I meet you?"

Her quick response encouraged him that she would accept his apology. At least she wasn't afraid to be alone with him. "Do you remember where my homesite is?"

"Yep. I'll meet you out there after dinner."

"Okay." He pushed the END button on his phone and stared at it. Melody probably knew as well as he did that they wouldn't catch many fish in his pond after dinnertime. They'd have to wait until closer to dark or until the early morning. But she knew they needed to talk. *I just hope she's willing to forgive me.*

Nearing seven o'clock in the evening, the weather was still hot and humid. Melody knew she and Drew wouldn't be catching any fish for at least another hour or two. But she and Drew had some reconciling to do, and she'd been anxious to share with him all God had shown her just in the last few days.

As they sat on the bank of his pond, she could feel in her spirit she needed to wait for Drew to do the serious talking first. She baited her hook and cast it out into the water. "So, what kind of fish you got in here?"

"Bluegill and some bass."

Melody nodded. She thought Drew might say a little more than that, but he'd been visibly nervous since she pulled up. His hand actually shook a bit when he cast his line, and the breaths he took were so big and deep, she could see his chest moving up and down as if he'd been running a race.

Trying not to make him feel any more anxious, she focused on the land before her. The pond was beautiful. Several trees towered over it on the left side of the water. But on the right bank a single strong old tree stood. It had the most enormous branch, probably twelve feet high, that was perfect for a swing. Drew had already done a lot of work to the bank just behind the house.

He even had a small dock of sorts with a paddleboat tied to it.

She looked back at his house. He had the bones all up. Foundation laid. Frame in place. Outside walls up, even if they were still rough. She knew he still had to do the drywall and electric, some plumbing and other stuff, but he'd gotten a lot accomplished in the last several weeks. "The house is really coming along, Drew."

"Yep."

She blew out her breath and stared at the pond. Maybe she should be the one to start the serious talking, but her spirit still seemed to nudge her to wait. She thought about the call she'd made to her mom to tell her the good news about becoming a Christian. Her answering machine picked up. Melody left a message, but that had been two days ago, and her mom still hadn't called back. *God, I will just pray every day that she accepts You, just as Uncle Roy and Aunt Renee and everyone here prayed for me.*

"Melody, I need to talk to you." Interrupting her thoughts, Drew's words came out fast but quiet.

"Sure."

He started to open his mouth, but her bobber dipped under the water, and a tug pulled at her line. She whooped. "I think I got one!"

She released the tension then started to reel in her fish. When it was almost out of the water, she grabbed her line and lifted up the small bluegill. She laughed at the little thing that couldn't have weighed more than a pound. "Definitely not a keeper."

"But it's a fish."

"You're right about that, and who'd have thought I'd catch one at this time of day and in this heat?"

She bit her bottom lip to shut her mouth when Drew gawked at her. A knowing expression marked his face. "So you did know we probably wouldn't catch many."

She shrugged. "I'm a country girl, Drew. I've been fishing all my life."

Drew's laugh filled the air around them. His muscles seemed to loosen, and he relaxed. "I need to apologize to you, Melody."

His tone was somber and serious, and Melody knew he meant every word he said. She sat still, peering down at the cooler. She just couldn't seem to look him in the eye.

He continued. "My pride got the best of me. I don't have to tell you that I'm very competitive by nature."

A quick giggle slipped through her lips, and she pursed them shut. Sneaking a peek up at him, she saw that he was grinning at her. She gazed back down, but he put his thumb under her chin and lifted her face until her gaze met his. "You accepting Christ is the best thing I've heard in a long time. I want you to know that even though I was acting like a jerk, I had been praying for you almost nonstop."

Melody's heart pounded in her chest. She wasn't surprised. All along she knew which buttons to push on Drew Wilson to incite his competitive fury. He'd been the best competitor she'd ever challenged, and she'd fully enjoyed most of their battles.

"Drew, I wasn't innocent. I knew how to make you mad, and I enjoyed seeing you get angry. I'm sorry, too." She placed more bait on the hook. "As far as me being a Christian," she said as she cast out her line once more, "it is the best thing that's ever happened to me."

She shifted in her chair so that she was sitting on her left foot. "I can't stop reading my Bible. It's the funniest thing, because I hate reading. I've started with John because that's where Aunt Renee told me to start."

"Where are you in John?"

"Oh, I've finished it. I'm in Acts now." She pointed to her rod. "But isn't it interesting that Jesus was all about fishing, and here we sit—fishing."

Drew chuckled. "You're right."

"I don't know why it took me so long to give my heart to Jesus." She cocked her head. "Actually, yes I do. I have a really hard time giving up control of anything, and that would include my life."

Her bobber dipped under the water again. She pulled back against the tug on her line. "I've got another one." Reeling in again, this time she pulled in a much larger bass. Grabbing its bottom lip with her left hand, she yanked out the hook with her right. "Look at that!"

Drew lifted his eyebrows. "Now, that's a keeper."

"It sure is." She waited while Drew opened the cooler so that she could place the fish inside.

"We'll have to have a cookout with the fish we catch."

She studied Drew for a moment. Once they'd said their piece, she was really having a good time with him. "That would be great." She bit her bottom lip. The urge to tease him welled inside her until she simply couldn't hold back. She elbowed his arm and winked. "You have realized I've got two fish to your none."

Drew leaned back and howled. "Yes, you have. And Melody Markwell"—he reached over and pinched her cheek as if she were a little child—"tonight I might just let you catch them all."

"Oh, you might, huh? You want to make a bet?"

Chapter 11

Drew was absolutely, one hundred percent, over-the-top smitten. Melody Markwell was everything he never realized he wanted in a woman. She was naturally beautiful. He remembered how gorgeous her amazingly long and silky brown hair looked blowing in the wind while they were fishing. Even pulled back in a ponytail, it was gorgeous.

And her eyes. Deep, dark brown. They were filled with such intensity and depth. So much truth. And when she teased him about her catching more fish, they had sparkled with delight. He could stare into those depths all day if she'd let him.

And her lips. Well, her lips were just downright difficult for him to be around. Thick and almost pouty, he had to stop himself from kissing her on more than one occasion the other night.

But more than her perfectly sun-kissed skin and her tiny frame, he was falling for who she was. Her inner strength drew him, as did her competitive nature. They'd always have fun battling over one thing or another.

But now with her zeal to know more about Christ and her honesty about what she understood and felt and thought, she inspired him to be a better Christian. She encouraged him to learn and study God's Word more.

I'm falling for her, God.

There was no use denying it or trying to dissuade it. He didn't want to push it away. He'd spent too much time worrying about pride and winning. He didn't want to waste another moment on any of that.

Needing to talk with his friend, he'd driven to Mike's house. He knocked on the front door. Joe, Mike's little brother, answered it. The teen wasn't so little anymore. He was nearly as tall as Drew and as broad as his big brother, which didn't say a whole lot, as Mike was quite a bit smaller than him or Nick or even Wyatt. Still, the kid had grown up a lot.

"Hey, Drew." Joe grabbed Drew's hand in a firm handshake.

Drew was surprised at how strong Joe had become. If he remembered right, the boy was going into high school this year. He was probably a great help on the farm now. But then Drew wondered why the kid was standing in the door barefoot in shorts and a T-shirt. He obviously wasn't helping Mike and his dad at that moment. "I'm looking for your brother. You know where he is?"

He pointed around the back of the house. "In the back with Dixie."

"She have her pups?"

Joe nodded, but he turned his head toward the baseball game that was on the television.

Now that Drew came to think of it, the reason he'd been surprised at how much Joe had grown was because he hadn't seen Joe at church in a while. He frowned as he wondered what could be going on. He knew Joe played for a traveling baseball team that took him away from church some Sundays, but it had been quite a few weeks since Drew remembered seeing him. Drew waved. "Okay. Thanks."

Joe didn't respond. He simply shut the door, and Drew walked around the house and toward the shed. He spied Mike leaned up against the door, one leg crossed in front of the other. He was such a softy when it came to the animals having their babies. Mike was a good balance to him and Nick and Wyatt. Not the strongest in any physical way, Mike was the one with a good head and a tender heart.

"Hey, Mike."

Mike turned and put his finger up to his mouth. "Not too loud, man. You'll make Dixie nervous. She just settled in to nurse her brood."

Drew peeked in the shed door and saw the dark lab with several babies fighting for their spot to feed. Dixie saw him and let out a low growl.

Drew lifted his hands. "I'll move, Dixie girl. Don't get mad."

Mike pulled the shed door closed then looked at Drew. "She's just a little protective of her pups."

"How many did she have?"

"Six. Four boys and two girls." Mike studied him. "So what's up?"

"I need to talk to you about Lacy."

Mike rolled his eyes and blew out a breath. He walked away from Drew toward the barn. "I'm not talking to you about Lacy." He lifted his hand. "Just because you're dying to win that bet since Melody's been showing you up doesn't mean you need to hound me to ask that girl out on a date."

Mike's words stung, and part of Drew wanted to lay into him with both barrels. But he knew he couldn't fuss at Mike. His friend was right. Drew had been especially hard on Mike when it came to Lacy, and it probably had a lot to do with the fact that Melody kept kicking his tail every time they competed against one another. He'd been spending a lot of time learning to be on the losing side of the stick over the last few months.

"That's not exactly why I'm here." Drew shifted his feet. "Actually, it is sort of why I'm here."

Mike lifted his eyebrows and crossed his arms in front of his chest.

Drew spread open his arms. "Look, man, I've fallen for Melody. I'm crazy about the girl. I came over here to tell you to ask out Lacy anytime you want. I'm throwing in the towel and going after Melody. You win. I lose."

Mike furrowed his eyebrows and stared at Drew for a moment. Then he smiled and punched Drew in the shoulder. "It's about time you came to your senses. That girl is perfect for you."

Drew sucked in his breath at the thought of asking Melody to go on a date, on a real date with him. It made him as nervous as the worm being baited on the hook, but Mike was right. She was perfect for him.

"I know." Drew extended his hand to Mike. "I can't stay. I just wanted to let you know I'm out. You win."

As he walked back to his truck, he imagined talking to her, fighting with her, kissing her soft lips. And now, he could worship with her. *God, a year ago I would have laughed if someone had said I'd want this, but Melody has changed my mind and my heart.*

The wheels in Drew's mind churned as he tried to think of the best way to tell her how he felt. As much fun as they'd had the other night fishing, he was sure she'd give him a chance. Still, he'd never asked a girl out before, and Melody was special. He had to do it right.

Since the day they'd planted it, Melody realized she loved working in her aunt's garden. She pulled another weed from the cucumber row she had planted almost two months before. Just as her aunt said, the plants had grown big and sprawled out along the ground. She had to pick up and dig around stems and leaves to find all the weeds.

She thought about how she had dug huge craters and nearly buried the poor things. So much had changed since that day. Drew and Addy returned home from their honeymoon. Uncle Roy had a stroke and amazingly was almost fully recovered. Baby Wyatt had gotten two teeth. She'd accepted Jesus.

Her heart swelled. It was the best, most exciting change she'd ever experienced. She still didn't understand a lot of things, and Aunt Renee warned her that God's Word promised she'd still have a bunch of problems to deal with and the world would still have a lot of bad things happen in it, but she felt such peace. She prayed God would give her faith no matter what happened in the future.

Finished pulling the weeds, she stood up, wiped her hands on her blue jean shorts, then grabbed her Bible off the back deck table. She walked along the small stone path her aunt had built. It led to a good-sized flower garden that surrounded a large shade tree. She sat down on the bench and watched as a small cardinal flew up above her and perched on a branch.

God's creation amazed her. With a slight sigh, she picked up her Bible and opened to where she had a bookmark. She'd been reading about these two guys, Paul and Barnabas, who were traveling all over the place telling people about Jesus. She didn't understand all of it, but apparently some of the believers who were Jews didn't like the idea of "other" people being able to accept Christ.

The thought baffled her a little bit. Aunt Renee tried to explain that in the culture of the time, different groups of people didn't associate with each other. She just didn't quite understand why some of them wouldn't want everyone on the planet to be able to accept Jesus.

She wanted to tell the whole world about Him. She'd probably driven Gracie crazy talking about all she was learning about Jesus. She smiled at the thought. *It would serve her right for all those days she drove me nuts talking about God.*

More than anything, she wanted her mom to know Jesus. She still hadn't called Melody back. It stung, and a part of her wanted to wash her hands of her mother. But when she thought of how much she'd changed since accepting the Lord, she couldn't help but want the same thing for her mom.

She shifted to get more comfortable on the bench. She'd really liked the part in Acts where the guy—if she remembered right, it was Paul—talked about how after he'd stopped persecuting Jesus and accepted Him, this other guy came along and touched him, and then something that looked like scales fell off Paul's eyes. Then he could see, and he went to tell everyone about Jesus.

Melody had instantly felt a connection with that man, Paul. Not only did scales fall off her eyes so that she could see that she needed Jesus, but now she could also read His Word. It wasn't as if she couldn't read at all. She'd learned the basics, and she'd been forced to sit through plenty of "special" classes in school to help her along. But she just couldn't read very well.

Since she fell in love with Jesus, she couldn't seem to put her Bible down. She read it all the time. She didn't understand everything, and she had to ask a lot of questions of Aunt Renee and Gracie, but she was starting to get it. A lot of things were beginning to make sense.

She peered down at her Bible and began to read again. The two guys she'd been reading about, Paul and Barnabas, had a disagreement and decided to go their own ways. It made her a little sad, and she wondered why Paul didn't want to give Mark a second chance. Evidently, he'd skipped out on them when the pressure got hot in another town.

"Hey, you mind if I interrupt you for a second?"

Melody gazed up at Drew. He was already enormous compared to her, but with her sitting on a bench and him standing, he really towered over her.

She patted the empty side of the bench. "Only if you have a seat. I'll strain my neck trying to look up at you."

Drew chuckled, and she noticed that his neck and cheeks turned red when he sat beside her. She also realized he smelled pretty good, like a light, woodsy cologne. And he'd gotten a haircut. She could see a white line along his neck where his hair had guarded it from the sun.

He cleared his throat and leaned forward, placing his elbows on his knees. He clasped and unclasped his hands. Why was he so nervous? His acting that way was making her feel squeamish.

He finally spoke. "So have you enjoyed vacation Bible school?"

She sat up. "It has been a complete blast. Those senior ladies in the kitchen are a hoot. I was a little nervous when Audrey asked me to help out in the kitchen." She elbowed his arm. "We both know I'm not the best cook."

He chuckled.

"But those women have been so kind to me, and they've all promised to teach me how to 'find my way around the kitchen,' as they put it."

Drew swiped one hand through his hair. He gazed out over her uncle's fields then looked back at her then back at his hands. "They're all wonderful. That's for sure."

She continued, "And Addy is amazing with music. Every chance I got I'd sneak a peek in the auditorium. She had those kids jumping and dancing and singing and shouting. Part of me wanted to just run right in there and join them."

"You should have."

Melody ducked her head. "I did." She giggled and held up two fingers. "Twice."

He smiled at her, but he didn't respond. Instead, he cleared his throat again, and Melody couldn't help but wonder if he'd come down with a cold or if he had a sore throat or something. "Have you got a cold? Do you want me to get you a drink?"

Bright red patches covered his neck and cheeks again, and Drew shook his head. "I was just wondering." He leaned back against the bench and wiped his hands on the front of his jeans. "Well, the Bible school picnic is Sunday evening. And I wondered if you'd want to go with me."

Melody shrugged. She didn't see any harm in that. She and Drew were friends now. Of course she'd be willing to go with him to the picnic. They were having cornhole and horseshoes and volleyball. She chuckled inwardly. She'd be his best competition. She may have given her heart to Jesus, but she was still going to whip up on Drew every chance she could. "Sure. Everyone will be there. It sounds like fun." She teasingly punched his arm. "I'll need a friend to whip at cornhole."

His expression fell as he stood up. A hesitant smile bowed his lips. "Great." He smacked the side of his leg. "I'll pick you up at five."

Melody frowned as she watched Drew walk away. That was weird. She'd never seen Drew act that way.

<hr/>

She didn't get it, Lord. She didn't understand that I was asking her on a date.

Drew leaned back against the seat in his truck. He smacked the top of the steering wheel then turned the ignition. The truck grumbled to life a little slower than she normally did. Ignoring it, he shifted her into REVERSE and pulled out of the driveway.

I wanted it to be perfect. When I saw her sitting under that tree reading her Bible, well, I thought there wasn't a better place in the world to ask her on our first date. But she thought I was just asking her to ride to the church with me—as a friend.

He stared out over the countryside as he made his way back to the homesite. He'd left his dad alone working on the electric because he wanted to ask her in person. And he had asked her. And she had said yes. But a lot of good that did. They were going as friends.

He pulled into what would soon be his driveway and turned off the truck. His dad walked out of the house and wiped sweat from his forehead. It was an awfully hot day in July, and wiring a house sure didn't cool a fellow off. "How'd it go, son?"

"She said yes." Drew walked past his dad and back into the house.

"That's great." His dad followed behind him. "So why are you upset?"

"She thinks we're going as friends. It was obvious she didn't understand I was asking her on a date."

His dad laughed as he grabbed a water bottle out of the cooler. He wiped the outside of it against his forehead before he unscrewed the top and gulped a long drink. "Maybe that's for the best."

"What?"

His dad lifted his hands in surrender. "At least for right now. The girl's only just accepted Christ, and the two of you were at each other's throats just before that. Dating you might be a bit more than she can think about right now."

Drew chewed on his dad's words. He might be right. But at the same time, Drew didn't wait for anything. He wasn't one to sit on something and stew about it. If he wanted it, he went out and got it. He tried to follow the Lord's leading, and there were times he had to take things a little slower, but for the most part, he just set his mind to something and went after it.

"I don't know, Dad. I just think I botched up asking her out. You know I'd never done it before."

"Let me ask you something, son. Is going to a church picnic really going on a date?"

Drew lifted his eyebrows and shrugged. "I don't know. It's somewhere I wanted to go with her."

"When you take a woman on a date, you want it to be somewhere that you can get to know each other. Somewhere where everyone you know in the world isn't going to be there. Do you get what I'm saying?"

"So asking her to the picnic wasn't really like asking her on a date?" Drew pursed his lips. "You could have told me that to begin with."

A low chuckle escaped his dad's mouth as he shrugged. "Maybe so, but I thought you might want to figure it out on your own. That's how you usually like to do things."

Drew wrinkled his nose at him. His dad didn't have to point out that Drew was mule-headed. He knew it all too well.

Merriment still lit his dad's eyes as he swatted Drew's arm. "Come on, son. Right now I need you to help me get this wire through the wall."

Drew helped his dad as his mind replayed his invitation to Melody. She talked with such ease with him now. The transformation had been so dramatic and sudden. He knew she still had her spunky, competitive spirit, and he loved that, too.

He'd just wait until they were at the picnic, and then he'd ask her again. This time he'd make sure she understood he wanted to take her on a date. Especially now that he understood taking her to a Bible school picnic wasn't a real one anyway.

Chapter 12

Melody waited in line to load up her plate with several homemade foods at the Bible school picnic. Standing behind her, Drew pointed to tiny pieces of bread with some kind of dressing and cucumbers on top. "See those? Nelli Jo makes them. They're delicious."

Melody grabbed one and placed it on her plate. She'd never been to a potluck picnic of this sort until she'd come to visit her aunt and uncle. Most everything she and her mother ate came from a box or can.

He pointed to another dish. "There's Mom's potato salad."

Her mouth watered as she put a spoonful of Drew's mom's potato salad on her plate.

As they made their way down the line, she looked back at Drew's plate. It was already piled up with food, and they hadn't yet made it to the coleslaw. She wasn't going to tell Drew until after he'd tasted it, but she'd made it again. Only this time, Aunt Renee helped her with each step, and she hadn't forgotten the sugar.

"Oh, yum." He pushed some of his food toward the middle of the plate with his fork. "I have to make room for Renee's coleslaw."

He scooped up a big spoonful and dropped it on his plate then peered at Melody. A blush spread across his cheeks, and he started to open his mouth. She looked away from him, knowing he was probably remembering the last time he thought he was eating Aunt Renee's dish. *Well, this time he won't be disappointed.*

With her plate as full as she could get it, she walked over to the folding chair Drew brought for her and sat down. Though it was hot for late afternoon in July, the enormous shade tree they sat under kept it from being unbearable—as long as the insects left them alone. She swatted at a fly.

Drew joined her and set his plate in his chair. "I'm going to go get a drink. What would you like?"

"Sweet tea, of course."

He winked. "Of course."

He made his way to the table set up with several two-liter bottles of sodas as well as pitchers of lemonade and sweet tea. She noticed how strong he looked in the maroon T-shirt that hugged his true-farming-boy's muscles. As always, he wore jeans and boots. She wasn't sure she'd ever seen him without them. The white line along the edges of his haircut was now a bright red, sunburned from the hours he spent outside.

Drew was a good man. A hard worker. He was God-fearing. And he wasn't hard to look at either. He'd make such a good husband. Her face warmed at the thought.

He turned back around with two cups in his hands and made his way toward her. She averted her gaze even though she knew he didn't know what she was thinking. She didn't have those kinds of silly notions floating around in her mind. She knew all kinds of girls who dreamed of the boy they'd one day meet and marry. She didn't have those dreams. Hers were always about getting away.

Taking a bite of her food, she tried to shoo the thought away. She wanted to feel normal in front of Drew, to enjoy their friendship.

"Mmm. Renee, the coleslaw is wonderful."

She looked up, and Drew had lifted his empty fork in the air at her aunt, who sat on the other side of him.

"Melody made it." Her aunt nonchalantly nodded toward her then continued to talk to the woman sitting beside her.

Drew turned to her. His eyebrows raised in surprise. He nodded. His eyes gleamed with just a hint of mischief. "Good job."

She placed her hand against her chest and batted her eyes, feigning arrogance. "Did you doubt I could do it?"

He blinked and cocked his head to one side. "Yes."

Melody swatted his arm for his teasing, and Drew laughed outright. "You gonna play me at cornhole?"

"Absolutely." He leaned close to her. "Now that you're a Christian, you gonna let me win?"

She wrinkled her nose. "Absolutely not."

He made a fist and gently tapped her jaw then pulled her ponytail. "That's my girl."

Melody's jaw dropped. "What are we? In seventh grade?"

Drew pinched her nose. "I happened to like seventh grade."

"Well then, I'll do you like I did every other thirteen-year-old boy when I was in middle school."

In one quick motion, she dropped her plate to the ground, jumped up, moved behind Drew, and wrapped her arm around his neck in a headlock. She rubbed his head with the knuckles of her free hand and yelled, "You want a piece of me, big guy? You think you can mess with me?"

Laughing, Drew hopped up to his full height, but Melody didn't let go even though her feet were dangling in the air. Reaching around his back with one arm, he grabbed her around the waist and twisted her until she was in front of him.

For a moment, panic set in as she realized Drew was so much bigger and stronger than she was. They were only playing, but fear flooded her for a brief moment. He must have seen it in her eyes, because he let her go.

Knowing she shouldn't be afraid, she tried to laugh as she lifted her hands up. "You got me."

She looked around, noting how many of their church friends were covering their mouths and giggling at their antics. Uncle Roy even appeared downright amused. She pointed at Drew and tried to chuckle. "He got me there. Beat me that time."

Drew had already sat back down. He gazed at her with too much intensity. He was trying to read what had happened. God was working on her heart, teaching her to trust. She just wished she could completely get over her past.

Drew's hands wouldn't stop sweating as he drove Melody back to Roy and Renee's place. He'd been puzzled about her reaction to their horseplay before the kids performed their Bible school program. He thought he saw fear in her gaze, but that didn't make sense. He'd never given her any reason to be afraid of him. The only thing he could figure was that she got embarrassed teasing around like that in front of the whole church.

He liked that she'd gotten so spunky with him. She didn't back down for anything, even though she probably didn't weigh a hundred pounds soaking wet. He snuck a quick peek at her in the passenger's seat.

She was tired. It had been an eventful couple of weeks for her. If he knew her well at all, he figured she'd spent plenty an evening staying awake far too long trying to soak in more of what the Bible said. Then she'd have to get up early to head over to AJ's for work. He loved that she was so excited, but a girl needed her rest.

Several times she'd started to lay her head back, but he'd hit a pothole, and she'd wake back up. He tried to be careful, but there wasn't much a man could do with these old country roads and his pickup.

He huffed. Here he had been so mad that she didn't understand he was trying to ask her on a date to the church picnic. His dad had been right. That wasn't no kind of date. A date would be just the two of them going to dinner or seeing a movie or whatever it was people liked to do. His idea of a perfect date would be going fishing and then frying up the catch, but he probably wouldn't mind eating dinner somewhere nice either.

His heartbeat sped up as he got closer to the house. He was determined to ask her. In fact, he'd made up his mind that he would not pull out of Roy's driveway until he had.

Trying to get up his nerve, he slowed the truck just a bit. No sense in getting there any faster than he already was. His stomach started to churn. *Please, God. Help me through this. I've helped cows birth their calves, killed more copperheads than I can count, but the thought of asking this woman on a date absolutely terrifies me.*

Unable to go any slower, he finally had no choice but to pull into the driveway. Melody smiled at him as she reached for the door. "Thanks for the ride, Drew. It was fun."

She turned the handle, and Drew thought he might be sick at any moment. She couldn't leave. He had to ask her on a date. He reached across her and pulled the door shut. She gawked at him in surprise. A mixture of anger and panic flashed across her face. He sat back in his seat. "Wait a minute, Melody. I want to ask you something."

She stared at him, and for a moment Drew wondered if reaching over her like that had been a bad idea. He couldn't think that through right now, though. He had to get up the nerve to just spit it out.

"Okay?" Melody's tone was sarcastic, and he knew he needed to say it and quick. Grabbing the steering wheel, he gripped it with all his might. "I was wondering if you'd like to have dinner with me sometime."

He blew out a long breath. There, he'd said it. He'd finally gotten the nerve to ask her out. Now he only needed to hear her say yes. He looked at her, but he couldn't read the expression on her face.

"I'm sorry, Drew. I can't."

Before he could respond, she opened the door, stepped out, and raced into the house.

<hr />

Melody lowered into Gracie's oversized leather recliner and nestled Wyatt close to her chest to feed him his milk. Already a little grumpy and ready for his afternoon nap, Wyatt whimpered and reached for the bottle. She stuck it in his mouth, and he closed his eyes and gulped it down. "I still can't believe Drew asked me out."

She rocked the chair, and Wyatt reached up and grabbed a strand of her hair and twisted it around his hand. In a matter of moments he would be fast asleep.

"I'm not surprised." Gracie popped a chocolate-covered peanut into her mouth. "It was obvious he was falling for you."

"How so? All we ever did was fight."

"That was how we knew." She popped another peanut. She pointed to the almost-empty plastic container. "You know this is why I'm still not losing my baby weight."

Melody grinned. "How would us fighting make you know he liked me?"

Gracie gave her an exasperated look. "Do you know how many girls have hit on Drew Wilson over the years?"

A niggling of jealousy crept up Melody's spine. Just how many women had liked Drew, and why did it bother her that they had? She looked down at Wyatt. His bottle was already almost gone, and he'd fallen asleep. She gently lifted him up to her shoulder and patted his back. "No. I guess I don't."

Gracie flipped her hand. "Let me tell you, there have been plenty, but he's never given any of them the time of day. Until you."

Wyatt burped, waking himself. She continued to pat his back, and he snuggled into her shoulder until he had fallen asleep again. "I never chased after him."

"I know."

"So, why?"

"Melody, you've always been a terrific person, and you're beautiful, even if you do try to hide it behind a ponytail." Gracie popped another chocolate-covered peanut in her mouth then waved her arms in the air. "And now that you're a Christian, you are simply a–maz–ing."

Melody bit her bottom lip and grinned at Gracie's dramatics. She sobered and closed her eyes. "I can't go on a date with him."

"Why?"

Melody took a long breath. She wasn't sure she wanted to tell Gracie.

Chapter 13

Drew spent the last several days trying to get over Melody's rejection. He'd wanted nothing to do with women before her, so he should be able to just move on with life as normal. Yet he couldn't get her out of his mind.

He'd tried putting all his effort and energy into the house, and he'd gotten a lot accomplished, but he'd also had to redo things because he couldn't concentrate properly. Most of the plumbing and electrical work was finished except for the more cosmetic things.

About to install the kitchen sink, he moved a few scrap boards and stray nails in search of the supplies he needed. He hollered into the other room, "Nick, have you seen a marker?"

Nick walked into the kitchen holding a black one in his hand. "Looking for this?"

"Yep." He pointed to the template he'd already taped in place on the counter. "Just need to mark this, and I can cut my hole."

Drew outlined the template then picked up the drill, ready to drill holes in each corner. He was getting kind of hungry, as he and Nick had been working for quite a while, but he figured he could at least get the hole cut into the countertop.

"Hang on, man." Nick lifted his hand to stop him. "Look, it's a bit off center."

"No way." Drew inspected his markings. They did seem a bit off, but he'd measured twice before he'd taped down the template. Exasperated, he pulled out a tape measure and measured both sides. Sure enough, Nick was right. He'd almost drilled holes a full three-eighths of an inch off center. He placed his hands on the counter and ducked his head. "I don't know what's wrong with me."

"I've got a hunch."

Drew turned around and leaned his backside against the counter. He crossed his arms in front of his chest. He'd worked so hard on this house. Didn't owe a penny for it, and lately, he'd been wasting a lot of pennies with little mess-ups like the one Nick just prevented. "Your hunch is probably right."

Nick grabbed the cleaning spray and a paper towel off the floor. He sprayed the counter then wiped off the marker. "Don't give up on her. She just needs some time."

Drew scoffed as he pointed at his own chest. "Me? Give up? When have you ever known me to give up on anything?"

Nick threw the towel at Drew's chest. "Never. And that was what I wanted to hear."

Drew didn't want to give up on her, but his pride stung a bit, too. Part of him couldn't stop thinking about her, day and night. That part told him to just keep praying and that when the time was right she'd want to go on a date with him. The other part of him wanted to throw in the towel, to somehow get her out of his mind for good.

He glanced at his watch. "It's getting pretty close to lunchtime. I think I'm going to take a break."

"Yeah. I've got to go. I promised Addy I'd come home for lunch."

Just as Drew figured, his sister, Addy, had his best friend on a tight schedule. Nick used to do what he wanted when he wanted. Now he always had to do things with Addy. He never thought the day would come, but Drew wanted that with Melody.

They left the house and got into their trucks. Drew stuck his arm out the window. "Thanks for the help. See you later."

Nick nodded then drove off. Drew made his way into town. He planned to grab a bite of some real food at the diner before he headed back to work on the kitchen sink again. Maybe a little protein would help his overworked mind to focus better.

He passed AJ's shop, and it felt as if a knife twisted in his gut. She was there. He was sure of it. AJ had been as tickled as a boy who got his first bike on Christmas ever since Melody started working for him. From what Drew heard, they could hardly handle all the work she'd brought in. AJ had even hired another worker to do nothing but oil changes.

He pulled into the diner's parking lot. It would be so easy to just walk over there and talk to her. They were friends, and there wouldn't be anything wrong with him saying hello to a friend. He envisioned her rejection and how she didn't even look back to say good-bye as she rushed into Roy and Renee's house.

He was probably the last person she wanted to see. But he cared about her, and he wasn't a quitter. He couldn't just give up on his feelings without at least finding out why she'd dismissed him so quickly.

Fighting the urge to walk over to the shop, he made his way into the diner. Mike had a lot to do on the farm today and wouldn't be meeting Drew for lunch. Wyatt and Nick rarely ate with them anymore, now that they were married. But Drew didn't mind being alone today. He was tired of thinking, but he really didn't want to do any talking or explaining either.

The place was unusually busy, so Lacy simply took his order, brought out his food, and left him alone. He was glad for that. The meat loaf was good. It was always good. But it didn't do much for the ache that just wouldn't leave his gut.

God, I can't stand this. I have to try again. At least get her to tell me why she doesn't want to go on a date with me.

Before he could change his mind, Drew paid the bill and walked straight to AJ's. He saw the most adorable, coverall-covered, female legs stuck out from beneath a truck. Not wanting to startle her, he waited until she'd slid herself out from under it. Her eyebrows lifted in surprise when she saw him.

"Hello, Melody."

She sat up and pulled a cloth from her front pocket. She started to wipe her hands, and Drew thought by the sparkle that seemed to light her eyes that she was happy to see him. "Hi, Drew."

"I need to ask you a favor."

She averted her gaze but still nodded. "Okay."

His mind raced trying to think of something he needed her help with. He couldn't come up with anything, but he had to have some reason, some favor to ask of her. He needed the chance to talk to her. "I need you to come look at my tractor."

She looked back at him with an unconvinced expression across her face. She opened her mouth to say something then shut it. Smiling at him, she nodded her head again. "Okay. I'll come by after work."

Drew's spirits lifted. She was going to stop by his house. He was going to have the opportunity to talk to her again.

He waved and almost tripped over his own feet as he walked out of the garage. The only problem was there was nothing wrong with his tractor. A twinge of guilt tickled his conscience, and he knew he was going to have to head out there and pull a belt off that tractor.

Melody was going to tell Drew the truth. She prayed for guidance as she drove out to his house. It seemed like forever since she'd been there. She remembered how much fun they'd had fishing together. He'd been so cute when he apologized for the way he acted at the tractor pull, and she knew he had been sincere.

It had been several weeks since she drove through the thick patch of trees. She gasped when she reached the clearing. The house! It looked like a house. And he'd made it a log cabin. It had a porch that extended the full length of the front. Surely he'd have a deck on the back. It only made sense.

Wondering what it looked like inside, she knew she wouldn't be able to ask Drew about it. For a moment, she imagined a dark brown leather couch and love seat around a stone fireplace. She'd seen the coolest lamps with stick bundles as pedestals that would look perfect in a log home. She loved deep red accents, and she knew the color would look perfect as part of the rug and possibly in a few pictures in the home Drew had built. *What am I thinking? Why am I decorating his house in my mind?*

She shook the thoughts away. She didn't know what he would think of her once she told him everything. She should just get over her past. She'd put her trust in God, and Drew would probably think she should no longer have this fear of losing control. But a girl didn't change something overnight that had gripped her for so long. God was working on her heart, but she wasn't ready to date.

Drew already stood beside the tractor he needed her to look at. She grinned. She knew he didn't need her to look at it. The man knew how to fix a broken belt. If it was even broken.

After parking the truck, she hopped out and walked over to him. Before she could say hello, he handed a belt to her. "I can't lie to you. I took it off to get you to come out here."

Despite her nervousness, Melody laughed outright. She grabbed the belt from his hands. "Thanks for the honesty. Now you get to help me put it back on."

"Not a problem." They worked together, and in no time the belt was back on the tractor, and it was running as it should.

He handed her a rag to wipe off her hands. "Melody, I have to just be honest with you. I'm really attracted to you. I think you're something special. I'd really like you to give me a chance."

Melody closed her eyes. Unlike most girls, she hadn't dreamed of this moment. She didn't seek out attention from boys. She tried to avoid them, tried to beat them at every game they played.

But she did like Drew. She was drawn to him as she'd never been drawn to a man before. There were moments when she could lose herself in visions of dating him. Then she'd think about her reaction to their playing at the church Bible school picnic. She didn't want to have that kind of response to her boyfriend, one of fear because he was bigger and stronger than she was. Drew didn't deserve that.

No. She wasn't ready to date. Not Drew. Not anyone. She peered up into his beautiful eyes and shook her head. "I can't."

He placed his hand against the tractor. "Why not? I know I wasn't the best witness to you. I've come to realize it's because I was so intrigued by you that I acted as I did. I know you've been interested in me. I've seen it in your eyes."

Melody sighed. Her heart pounded beneath her chest. She didn't want to tell him what happened. She'd never really shared it out loud, except with her mom on the day it happened. She couldn't even make herself share it with Gracie the other day. Besides, her fear went deeper than her attacker. It was also a lack of trust in men because of her dad.

"It's really not you."

He huffed and looked away from her.

She continued. "I know that's just a saying, but it's the truth." She paused, blew out a breath, then said, "When I was fourteen, I was trying out for the cross-country team. I loved that I could run and take my mind off my stresses at home. So I went for a jog in the park. It was early, and no one was really out. . . ."

She stopped and swallowed the knot in her throat. Her hands started to tremble, and she shoved them into her coverall pockets.

Drew peered down at her. Concern etched his face. "What happened?"

She felt tears pooling in her eyes. The words were hard to say out loud. They were embarrassing, humbling. If she hadn't been out so early, she never would have been confronted. She swiped her eyes with the back of her hand and lifted her chin. She was determined to tell him the truth.

"I was jogging, and a man grabbed me. I didn't know where he came from. He was just there." She touched her arm where his hand had gripped her. "And he was stronger than me. He threw me on the ground."

"Did he rape you?" Drew's voice was low, and his expression was serious. He looked like a bear about to protect his cub. She knew he wanted to find the man who'd hurt her, and in truth his reaction warmed her heart.

She shook her head. "Praise God, no. A woman pushing her baby in a stroller happened by and scared him away. But now, I still get afraid. I still—"

"That was the look you gave me when we were playing at the picnic. I couldn't figure out why you had fear in your eyes."

"You see, I shouldn't have. You haven't done anything to scare me, and yet I had a moment of panic because you are so much bigger and stronger than I am."

Slowly he reached up and touched her cheek with the back of his hand. She willed herself not to flinch then relished the feel of his warm skin on hers. He wouldn't hurt her. He would protect her. "Melody, I would never hurt you."

"I know." She pulled his hand away from her cheek. "But I'm not ready. I don't know if I'll ever be ready."

※

Drew wanted to find the man who'd hurt Melody and rip him apart, limb by limb. Only a no-good coward would do such a thing to a woman. If he'd happened upon the scene that morning in the park, he'd have whipped that man's tail.

He sucked in a long breath and exhaled extra slow. He had to settle down. He couldn't change what had happened to her. All he could do was show her how different he was than that disgusting man. He could be her friend. He could pray for her.

God, I know exactly what I can do for her.

Drew looked at Melody. The sun was starting to set. The pink and orange glow of the sky behind her made her look like a perfect character drawn in a picture. He'd seen that beautiful, long hair flowing down her shoulder only a few times, and now he longed to pull out that rubber band and watch it drop down to her waist. Every girl he knew caked makeup on her face. But not Melody, and she was still indescribably beautiful.

It will be hard for me not to want more from her.

His Spirit seemed to encourage Drew. *"I will give you strength."*

He started to reach out his hand to touch a stray strand of hair that brushed her cheek. Coming to his senses, he shoved his hand in his front pocket. "Tell you what. I still want to be friends."

Melody lifted her chin and gazed up at him. The vulnerability in her eyes was almost more than Drew could handle. "I'd really like that. I really want you to be my friend. I really do."

Drew bit back a grin at her emphatic reply. In his gut, he knew she did care for him. She probably wanted him to be more than a friend, and she needed him to be patient. *You know patience isn't my strong point, Lord.*

"You can do all things through Me."

He cleared his throat and went on with his idea. "How 'bout we meet out here a couple times a week for Bible study and maybe a little fishing." He pointed to the big old oak tree on the right side of the pond. "I'll set us up a bench or a table or something over there for our studying."

Melody's eyes lit up, and she clapped her hands. "Would you put up a swing? That branch is perfect for a. . ." Her face turned crimson, and she ducked her head and lifted her shoulders as if she'd just gotten caught doing something mischievous. "Sorry. I just think it'd be such a fun place to swing. It's perfect, and—"

Drew lifted his hand. "Consider it done." He pinched her nose. "And you'll be the first to swing on it."

She put up both her fists like she was going to box him. "You don't want me to put you in a headlock again."

Drew laughed and shook his head. "So, when do you want to start?"

Melody shrugged. "Tomorrow night?"

"Tomorrow night." Drew led her back to her truck and opened the door for her. She seemed hesitant and embarrassed as she hopped inside. "I can hardly wait."

She leaned her arm out the window. "Thanks for being patient with me, Drew."

Drew wasn't sure what to say.

She started the truck and shifted it into gear but kept her foot on the brake. She peered out across the expanse of his property, seeming to drink in every intricate detail. "It's absolutely beautiful out here." She smiled at him then drove off.

He waved as he whispered, "One day you will share it with me."

Chapter 14

Melody was elated that she and Drew would be studying God's Word together. If there was a man in all the world whom she wanted to help her overcome her fear and need for control at the feet of her Father, it would be Drew Wilson. Though it made little sense to her, she wanted to do something, to look prettier than she normally did when she went to Drew's later that evening.

She only had an hour for lunch, and Gracie wasn't expecting her today, but she raced to her house anyway. Melody didn't know exactly what she wanted Gracie to do, but surely the woman would have some ideas.

She knocked on the front door, and within moments Gracie opened it. A full grin spread her lips. "Melody, it's so good to see you. Come on—"

Melody interrupted her friend and sped into the house. "I need your help."

Gracie furrowed her eyebrows as she shut the door. "Okay. Is something wrong?"

Wyatt squealed from inside his playpen and reached up to Melody. Unable to withstand any fussing from that precious boy, Melody scooped him up into her arms. He immediately reached for her hair. "Nothing's wrong. I've agreed to do Bible study with Drew, but just as friends."

"Okay?" Gracie still looked confused.

"And I want to do something about my hair."

"What's wrong with your hair? It's gorgeous."

Warmth trailed up her neck. "I mean, I don't want to wear it up in a ponytail, and I don't know what to do with it."

Gracie squinted and cocked her head. "I thought you were going to be just friends."

Melody huffed and shifted Wyatt to her other hip. "We are." She nestled her nose into the baby's neck, avoiding eye contact with her friend. "I just want to look a little prettier."

Gracie lifted her eyebrows and slowly nodded her head. "I see."

Melody rolled her eyes. "I'm not ready for Drew to be my boyfriend, but when I am ready—"

"You want Drew to be your boyfriend."

Embarrassed by the conversation as she simply hadn't considered falling for someone, Melody dug her face into Wyatt's chest. The boy squealed and grabbed her hair with both hands. She mumbled into his shirt. "Will you help me?"

Gracie laughed as she pried her boy off Melody's head. "Of course." Wyatt screamed and reached for Melody. "If my son will let me."

Melody walked to one of the straight-back dining room chairs and sat down. She reached for Wyatt again. "Here, I'll hold him in my lap. You fix my hair. But tell me what you're doing so I'll know how to do it."

"Sounds great."

Gracie left the room and within moments returned with a brush and a fat curling iron. Melody listened as Gracie talked about rolling the bottom of the back of her hair under and rolling the sides along her face. It felt nice to have someone fix her hair.

"Make sure whatever you're doing isn't hard to do, or I'll never do it."

Gracie snorted. "Melody, your hair is naturally amazing. I'm doing hardly anything at all."

To Melody's surprise, only ten or fifteen minutes had passed when Gracie said she was done. She handed Wyatt to his mom and walked into the bathroom to see what she'd done. It was too hot, and her hair was too long to let all of it fall, so Gracie had pulled up the sides in one big clip at the top.

She'd left just a few curled strands touching each cheek. Slight curls flowed from the clip and all the way down her back. Some of them were shaped from the curler, but most were there naturally. Melody looked pretty but not too different. She still felt like herself.

She bit her bottom lip and smiled when Gracie and Wyatt came into the bathroom and looked at her reflection as well. "It looks good, Gracie."

"You're such a natural beauty. What I wouldn't give for that hair." She lifted a curl in her hand then winked into the mirror. "Have fun with your friend."

"God's getting me there. I just know it."

⁓⁂⁓

Drew had gotten up extra early to get his work done on the farm. It had been a challenge keeping up the farm and building his house, but God blessed him with extra strength the last few months. The fact he'd been unable to sleep several nights fretting over despising Melody or falling in love with her had also helped him.

This morning he'd wanted to get a swing up on the tree as a surprise. He knew she wouldn't expect him to have it up so fast, but in order to do it, he'd had to make an unplanned trip to town to get what he needed. He'd also stopped by the diner to pick up a pitcher of their homemade sweet tea, as he knew she really liked it.

He set up two benches on the other side of the tree. He kept moving them so that they angled correctly away so that the sun didn't smack either one of them in the eye. Then he realized it would be near time for the sun to set once they met, so he arranged them again to be able to enjoy the sunset.

I feel like a girl fussing over my company coming over. He wrinkled his nose as he thought of the times his mom and sister had raced around the house, picking up blankets and moving pillows so that it looked nice before their guests arrived. He spread out his hands after he moved the bench one more time. *It's fine, Wilson,* he cajoled himself. *We're going to be focusing on God's Word, as friends.*

He heard a truck coming up the gravel road. He knew it was her. He took the Bible off the top of the cooler that held the sweet tea and placed it on one of the benches. Wringing his hands together, he knew it was ridiculous to be this nervous. His biggest concern was that he wouldn't be able to simply meet with her as a friend. *But I have no choice for now, God. Help me wait for Your timing.*

Melody parked beside his almost-finished house as Drew made his way around the pond toward her. She stepped out of the truck, and Drew gasped. That long, amazing, dark hair flowed freely all the way down her back except for a clip at the top of her head to hold up the sides.

She wasn't dressed up, but the blue jeans she wore looked like a mix between shorts and full-length jeans. They kinda hit just below her knees, but they looked really cute on her. Kinda feminine. And her top was a light pink. Pink! It was plain—no lace or frills like what Addy would wear—but it still looked very pretty on Melody. He swallowed hard, thankful he still had a little ways to walk to collect himself before he got to her.

Drew noted that she seemed to not know exactly what to do as he made his way to her. The breeze blew at her hair, and she just kinda kept swiping it away from her face with her fingers.

"Hey," he said when he reached her. "You look really pretty."

"Thanks." She stared out over the pond, and he noted the blush that spread along her neck. She glanced at him then looked away. "You got the swing up."

"Sure did, and you're going to try it out after our Bible study." He reached out and touched her arm. "Come on."

He let go of her right away so that she wouldn't feel uncomfortable then led the way back to the tree. She sat down on one of the benches and placed her Bible in her lap, and Drew sat across from her. He noticed she'd also put on some pink paint on her lips. Not real dark. It looked pretty, but all these little things she'd done were going to make it doubly hard for him to concentrate on just being friends.

"I thought we'd start with one of the fishing stories in the book of Matthew, if that's all right with you," Melody offered. She didn't look up from her Bible but focused on finding the right page. "Since we both love fishing and all."

"Sounds great to me. What chapter?"

"Fourteen." She twisted the cloth bookmark in her Bible around her index finger. "If you don't mind, I'll read it. I'm not a good reader, but I understand better when I'm the one reading."

"That's fine. You want me to pray first?"

"Okay."

Melody bowed her head. Drew wanted to reach over and take her hands in his, but he knew she might not be ready. He wasn't ready. If he touched her, he wouldn't be able to focus on the scriptures. He said a quick prayer to bless their time, the whole time praying in his heart that God would help him be a good friend.

When he'd finished, Melody looked up at him and smiled. She seemed more at ease as she started reading God's Word. Drew was surprised at how much she stumbled through the passage, but he had to give her credit that she never stopped. She'd fight to pronounce a word, conquer it, then go on to the next.

He thought of Melody's competitiveness and her need to be in control. Between a father who'd left her and her mother, a man who'd tried to rape her, and the struggles she'd obviously faced in school, Drew understood why Melody sought to be in charge of every area of her life. She'd been knocked down a lot, but she was a fighter and always determined to come out on top. *Now that You're the head of her life, God, she is already victorious.*

She finished reading, and they talked about Jesus feeding the multitude with only a few fish and loaves of bread. She marveled at the miracles Jesus performed. She put her index finger against her lips. "But did you notice what it says Jesus did?"

Drew shook his head.

She lifted her hands in the air and looked up at the sky. "He lifted the food up to God to bless it. Did He really have to do that? Wasn't Jesus able to do the miracle on His own? It seems to me that He could have, but He got God's blessing first." She lowered her voice and her hands. "He kind of gave it over to God."

Drew knew she was talking about control and trust and faith and handing all of it over to Jesus. He felt humbled by the innocence of her words. He wanted so much for Melody to date him. He prayed the friendship stage wouldn't last too long, but he'd been looking at it from the wrong perspective.

Anew, he inwardly took his feelings for Melody to the foot of the cross and laid them down. God knew when and if the time was right, and Drew would trust Him with it.

Once they finished their Bible study, Drew said a short prayer of thanksgiving for their time together. When he opened his eyes, Melody leaned forward on the bench and patted his hand. "Thanks, Drew." She raised one eyebrow as she glanced over at the swing then back at him. "Can I swing now?"

Drew laughed. "If I can push."

"*If* you can push. Buddy, I was gonna *make* you push." She hopped up from the bench and jumped onto the swing. She bounced up and down a few times as she looked up at the branch. "You sure this can hold me?"

"Are you doubting my ability to tie knots, or are you suggesting I'd enjoy watching you fall on your tail?"

Melody pursed her lips and twisted her mouth. "Hmm. Both."

Drew moved behind her and grabbed both ropes above her head. "You're not going to fall, little lady."

He gave her a good push, and she swung forward with a squeal. He continued to push her from behind as she lifted her legs forward and backward, going as high as she could.

Her youthful spirit was like a balm to his tired soul. He'd been so wrapped up in competition and pride for so long that this woman, who could beat him at almost any sport she set out to challenge him at, made him sit back and smile. She was a lot of fun, and Drew had needed to learn not just to win, but to have fun. He was going to enjoy having her as a friend.

Chapter 15

A month had passed since Melody started having Bible studies with Drew. Her faith in God had grown so much as she learned about Paul's adventures in telling others about Christ. He'd endured so much pain and so many trials, but he never gave up on his faith.

But when Drew suggested they read about some of the women from the Old Testament, Melody had been more than intrigued by the strength and faith of Deborah, the judge who led the Israelite people to battle. She'd marveled in Ruth's faith to walk away from her people and all she knew, and in Esther's courage to go before the king.

So many people—men and women—had endured all kinds of troubles and problems, and they'd stayed true to God. But what she loved more than anything was that God had stayed true to them. Not everything was easy. She'd read that with her own lips, but God had remained faithful. She could trust Him.

"Melody, will you go get a couple more cucumbers out of the garden?" Her aunt's voice sounded from the kitchen.

"Sure, Aunt Renee." Melody made her way out the back door. As they did at least two times a month, Drew's parents, Drew, and Addy and Nick were all coming over for dinner. Now that Roy had recovered, he enjoyed whipping up on everyone at the Wii tennis game. She was thankful he'd had a good report the last time he went to the doctor.

Addy and Nick pulled into the driveway as Melody walked back into the house with several cucumbers loading down her arms. Careful not to mess up her sundress, she dumped them in the sink to be washed then received a hug from her cousin and then from Addy.

Addy held her at arm's length. "I knew that dress would look pretty on you."

Melody smiled. "I'm glad you talked me into it."

Addy turned her around. "Bright colors look so good with your dark hair and eyes, and as dark as you've gotten this summer. . ." She swatted her hand through the air. "You needed some bright colors."

Melody glanced down at the plain bright yellow dress that had just a touch of embroidery at the bottom. "I really do like it."

Addy leaned close to her and whispered in her ear. "Drew will like it, too."

Melody felt as if a patch of butterflies fluttered through her heart. She and Drew had gotten to know each other so well over the last month. They'd fished together and played games together; she'd even helped him pick out some stuff for his house. Though she loved Addy and Gracie was her best girlfriend, Drew had truly become her best friend.

They'd prayed earnestly for her mother together, whom she'd only talked to one time in the last month and for only a few short minutes. They'd shared hopes and dreams. He'd even let it slip that he wanted as many children as God allowed. She hadn't admitted to him that she felt the same. She finally felt ready to be more than friends with him.

Drew and his parents walked into the house. He smiled and winked at her as he pointed from his shoulders to his knees. He mouthed the words *I like your new dress.*

Addy leaned toward her and whispered, "Told ya."

Melody giggled as she walked toward Drew's mom and took a dish from her hands.

"Thanks, honey." She peered around the room. "Where's Renee?" She glanced back down at Melody and smiled. "By the way, I like your dress."

"I'm here." Renee walked out of the back room wiping her hands on a towel. "The hamburgers should be almost done. Is everyone hungry?"

Roy nudged Drew's dad's arm. "She's joking, right?"

He shrugged. "I suppose, because we're always hungry."

"Oh hush, you two." Aunt Renee swatted at them. "Give us a second to get spoons for all the dishes."

Melody hadn't realized Drew walked behind her until he touched her arm. With his other hand he crooked his finger, gesturing for her to follow him. They walked through the mudroom and out the back door.

He gently touched the side of her face with the back of his hand. Closing her eyes for just a moment, she thrilled at the touch, having not felt any fear with him in a long time. When she opened her eyes, he pressed a soft kiss on her forehead. "You are absolutely beautiful, Melody."

She bit her bottom lip, unsure how to respond.

"I brought you something." He pulled a small yellow daisy from behind his back. He stuck it behind her ear. "Matches your dress perfectly."

Melody giggled. "I can't wear this to dinner." She took it out from behind her ear and twirled the stem between her fingers. "But it was sweet of you."

"Come on, everybody. Let's eat." Her uncle Roy's anxious voice sounded from inside the dining room.

Melody wrinkled her nose. "We'd better get inside, or we're gonna get in trouble."

Drew motioned for her to go first. She walked back into the house. Yes, she was definitely ready to add more than friendship to her relationship with Drew.

Drew was going to ask Melody on another date. He wouldn't do it today. They'd enjoy dinner with their families, probably play some cornhole, and Roy would whip all of them at tennis on the Wii. But their next Bible study session, he was going to ask her.

He'd already planned where they were going. There was a nice restaurant right on the Kentucky River. It was a little ways from River Run, but he'd heard it was worth the drive. As soon as she accepted, he'd make reservations for them to have a sunset dinner on their patio. Seeing Melody in that beautiful yellow dress, he could hardly wait to take her on a date, just the two of them.

"Could you pass me some more of that potato salad?" Roy asked.

Drew handed him the bowl, but not before scooping a bit more out for himself.

"Hey, now. No one said you could get some, too." Roy smiled at Drew. "I hear the house is almost done."

He swallowed his bite of food. "It is."

"When you going to have all of us for a cookout?"

He wiped his mouth. "Well, I'm still finishing the back deck."

"It looks really good, Uncle Roy," Melody added. Drew looked at her, and she grinned. He knew how much she loved the idea that he'd put a door on his bedroom that connected to the deck. One day, when she agreed to be his wife, she would be able to enjoy sitting on that deck, watching the sunrise in the mornings.

Drew agreed. "It does." He pointed to Melody. "And Melody's helped a lot."

"I haven't done much."

"Sure you have."

His dad smacked his hand down on the table. "When are you two lovebirds gonna quit going round and just decide you like each other?"

Drew watched as Melody's face washed bright crimson. His mom swatted his dad's arm. "Bryan, that is up to them. You don't go blabbering out things like that."

Drew opened his mouth to say something. He didn't know what he would say, but anything to ease Melody's embarrassment. The phone rang before he could speak. Renee picked up the cordless phone from the hutch that sat behind her. A deep frown wrapped her face. "Oh no."

She stood and walked away from the table. Drew and everyone watched as she covered her mouth. "Oh no. How?"

The room grew quiet as an eerie feeling blanketed them. Something had happened. Drew tried not to let his mind wander with possibilities.

"Where is the family?" Renee's eyes filled with tears as she raked the fingers of her free hand through her hair. "I'm so sorry. So very sorry. Yes, we're all together. I'll tell them."

She clicked the phone off and looked at the family. She cupped her hand over her mouth. Drew held his breath as he waited for her to talk. "There's been an accident."

Roy had already started to shake his head. "What happened, honey?"

"Mike's little brother, Joe. He was boating at the lake with some friends yesterday. The kids stayed out too late, swimming when it was too dark. They couldn't find him until this morning. He drowned."

⁂

Melody felt like she was in a daze as she moved forward with Aunt Renee and Uncle Roy in line at the funeral home. She didn't know Mike's family very well, and of the three of Nick's good friends, Mike was the one she knew the least. Still, to have his little brother, only fourteen years old, die so suddenly. It was awful, and her heart broke for the family.

She waved to Drew, Nick, Addy, Wyatt, and Gracie, who all stood at the far corner of the room. Baby Wyatt wasn't with them. She assumed Gracie's mom was taking care of him.

They moved a few more steps forward. A large man still blocked her view of Mike, but she could see his mom and dad. Their faces were red and puffy from probably having cried for days. The man moved forward, and Melody saw the exhaustion and sadness that etched Mike's face. He had his arm around his mother's shoulders, and she knew he tried to be strong.

They moved forward again. Her aunt wrapped her arms around Mike's mother. "I'm so sorry." She patted the woman's back. "So, so sorry."

Uncomfortable and unsure what to say, Melody simply mumbled her condolences and shook Mike's parents' hands. She reached Mike and shook his hand as well. She wished she knew what she could say to ease some of the hurt he felt, but what could she say? If she were in his place, there wouldn't be words to make her feel better. She whispered, "I'm sorry, Mike."

Mike's expression remained blank as he looked past her. "Me, too." He paused for a moment and took a deep breath as he scanned the long line of people still waiting to give their condolences. He patted her back. "Thanks for coming."

Melody made her way to Drew and their friends. Gracie grabbed hold of her hand and squeezed it. "It's awful, isn't it?"

Melody didn't know what to say. She simply nodded.

"Mike said he wasn't supposed to be out there." Wyatt's voice was low. "Their dad told him they didn't need to be out swimming that late."

Nick shook his head. "I guess Joe had been giving them a hard time lately. It can be awfully difficult being a young teenager."

"Yeah. We did some stupid stuff that could have landed us hurt—or worse," Drew added.

"But God protected us," said Nick.

Melody furrowed her brows. Then why wouldn't He protect Joe? She needed to go home and search the scriptures, to spend some time in prayer. Aunt Renee told her things would still happen that she wouldn't understand, but now that something had happened, she wanted to understand why. She looked up and saw that Drew was staring at her. He knew what she was thinking.

Chapter 16

Drew hadn't been able to have Bible study with Melody for a week. He'd spent a lot of time working, praying, crying, or simply being there for Mike and his family. They supported one another and spent a lot of time trying to bask in God's comfort, but they still struggled with Joe's death. He also spent a lot of time listening.

Today she was coming over. He'd missed seeing her, and he worried that Joe's sudden, unexpected death would cause her to stumble in her new faith. She already struggled with wondering why God allowed bad things to happen. Truthfully, he wondered why some bad things happened. Joe wasn't where he was supposed to be, but Drew couldn't count the times on all his fingers and toes that he and his buddies had gone swimming after dark, not to mention the times they'd disobeyed their parents.

"For the wages of sin is death. . . ."

He closed his eyes, remembering when he'd learned that wages didn't mean "penalty." It meant "payment." Growing up, he'd always thought the verse in Romans was saying that the punishment for sinning was to die, but that wasn't what the scripture said. It said the payment he received for sinning was death.

"But the gift of God is eternal life."

But instead of letting him suffer for all eternity, Jesus had saved him. In terms of eternity, he was saved. God could have taken him the night he fell out of the fort he and his buddies set up when they were eight, after his mom had told him not to climb up in it. Nick could have died when he was a teenager and was driving his dad's pickup too fast in the rain. He hit a slick spot and slammed into a tree. They could have and should have died, but God had chosen to spare them.

He'd chosen to take Joe.

Drew let out a long breath and sat on the bench. He picked up his Bible and held it between his hands. Peering out over the amazing creation God had formed, he whispered, "I don't know why, but I have to trust You."

He placed the Bible back on the bench and stood and walked to the edge of the pond. He bent down and picked up a few smooth stones and skipped one across the top of the water.

He was nervous about Melody's reaction to Joe's death. For all Drew knew, she may not even show up for their Bible study. He feared she'd decide the whole faith thing wasn't worth it, because bad things still happened, and she couldn't control them.

Listen to me, God, I sound just like Melody. Here I am stewing about her. You're big enough to handle my worries and her worries, and the whole wide world's problems if we'd only give them to You.

He skipped another rock. It had been a hard week. It hurt to let Joe go. It hurt to watch Mike and his parents in so much pain.

But the week also confirmed for him that he loved Melody. He didn't just care for her. She wasn't solely his friend. She was the woman he wanted to marry. He wanted to sit on these benches and read and study God's Word with her every night. He wanted to hold her close and to have her work hard alongside him. If she'd have him, he'd pack her up in his truck and take her wherever he could to marry her tonight.

He looked at his watch. Melody was nearly a half hour late for their usual Bible study time. Then again, she may not show up.

———✧———

Melody couldn't believe she was running so late. She'd missed seeing Drew something fierce all week. His friend and family needed him, and she'd never do anything to keep Drew from helping someone in need.

He probably thinks I'm not coming. She looked down at her greasy coveralls. She knew her hair was an absolute wreck. She'd always cleaned up before going to Drew's for their Bible study time. She'd even starting dabbing on perfume the last few times they met. Today she simply rushed out of the shop and headed straight for his house.

AJ told her she didn't have to stay to help. It was after five, and he'd planned to just tell the woman to bring her car back in the morning. But when Melody saw the lady and her three small children waiting in the lobby and how tired the woman looked in her factory uniform, Melody simply couldn't make her come back the next day. She'd probably have to call in sick and lose money she most likely needed. All the car needed was a couple of new gaskets. It really didn't take her that long.

She looked at the clock on the dash of the truck. She was almost an hour later than usual. For all she knew, Drew may have given up on her and left. Her stomach growled. *If he's not there, I'm running through a fast-food restaurant.*

But she wanted him to be there. She needed to see him. A week without him proved to her how much he meant to her. He was more than her best friend. She loved him.

Through a lot of prayer and Bible study, she'd learned that a part of her may always have moments of fear when it came to men being bigger and stronger than she was. It was kind of like a scar from the experience she'd had. It was there, and sometimes she noticed it, but it wouldn't hurt or bother her unless she allowed herself to focus on it.

She couldn't change that her dad left her mom. She couldn't change that the man attacked her in the park. But with God's help, she could control how she reacted to the memories of those things.

She drove through the thick wooded trees and into the open field. She saw Drew's log house. He was living in it now, but he hadn't been able to take her on the official tour since he'd finished just before Joe's death.

Looking at the tree, their tree, she spied Drew standing beside the pond. He skipped a rock across it. She could tell he'd cleaned up for her, as he always did. He must have heard the truck, because he turned, and if she saw right, he seemed to offer her a hesitant smile.

She snuck a peek in the rearview mirror. Just as she feared, she had grease smeared across her left cheek, and stray hairs clung to her temples and forehead from working all day.

God, help me not to be consumed by what I look like. I just want to enjoy seeing Drew and spending time in Your Word.

The night before she'd looked over the chapter they were going to study. It was 1 Corinthians 13. Her aunt had winked at her, saying it was the "love" chapter. And it was. It talked of love being about patience and kindness. It wasn't proud or rude or angry.

The verse that stuck with her was verse 7. "It always protects, always trusts, always hopes, always perseveres." She'd gone to bed repeating the verse over and over in her mind. Drew had shown her that kind of love, and it made her realize just how much she loved him as well.

She parked the truck and jumped out. He was walking toward her, and she looked down at her coveralls once more. She noticed that even her hands were dirty. *I can't believe I didn't even wash my hands.*

"I thought you weren't coming." Drew's smile had deepened.

She swept her hand down the front of her coveralls. "I wasn't sure I would make it. A woman came in late needing some gaskets fixed, and I just couldn't turn her away. I know I look a mess." She lifted her hands. "I should have at least washed my hands, but I knew I was running so late, and I didn't want you to worry, and. . ."

She took a breath, realizing she was babbling. Her nerves were getting the best of her. She wanted to look pretty the first time she saw Drew again. *My thoughts have changed a bit, huh, God?*

She bit her bottom lip to hold back a smile. "I'm really glad I made it."

"Me, too." He lifted his hand and touched her cheek with the back of his hand. Her heart beat faster. "I missed you this week."

"I missed you, too."

At any moment, she thought her heart might beat out of her chest. She wanted to scream out just how much she missed him, how much she loved him. She wanted to wrap her arms around his neck, and for the first time feel his lips pressed against hers.

He smirked, and for a second she wondered if he could read her thoughts. He picked at a patch of sweat-dried hair against her temple and wrinkled his nose. She noted the gleam in his eye when he said, "Would you like to clean up a bit?"

She lifted her hands palms first in front of him and acted as if she were going to wipe them on his shirt. He flinched, and she laughed. "Do I have to?"

He pointed to the house. "Yes."

She feigned a pout as she stomped onto his front porch and through the front door. The house looked beautiful. Just as she'd suggested, he'd bought dark brown leather furniture and accented with bits of red in the living room. She made her way down the hall.

"I'll give you a tour when you get out."

She turned to see Drew standing inside the front door. She nodded and walked into the bathroom. Turning on the water, she gasped when she caught sight of her full reflection. She really was a mess.

She scrubbed her face clean and pulled the ponytail out of her hair. She didn't have a brush, but she spied a comb on the counter. She couldn't get all the tangles out of the mass with just a simple comb, but she could at least make herself look presentable.

Unzipping her coveralls, she wished she'd worn something nicer beneath them. Of course that wouldn't make much sense when she had to spend eight hours a day working on vehicles. She sighed. *Oh well, the cutoff sweats and T-shirt will have to do.*

She sniffed under her arms and wrinkled her nose. She could seriously use some deodorant, and she wished she had her toothbrush. Spying men's spray deodorant on the shelf above the toilet, she giggled. *Should I use it or should I not?*

Not wanting to stink, she decided to take her chances on smelling like a man and sprayed a little on. *Maybe he'll think it's just from working with the guys all day.*

As presentable as she could get herself, she folded the coveralls over her arm and walked back into the living area. He smiled at her and winked. "Much better."

He sniffed the air. "Do I smell my deodorant?"

Warmth raced up her neck, and she shrugged. "At least I don't stink."

Drew smacked his leg, bent back his head, and laughed. "Melody Markwell, I really did miss you this week."

She laid the coveralls on the back of one of the wooden chairs around the dining room table. She loved how the house was so open. He'd made it so the living room and dining room and kitchen all shared one big area. The house was small, but the design made it seem so much bigger. "Do I still get a tour of the house?"

"Absolutely." He stood, and she followed him down the hall. He pointed to the first door on the right. "You've already seen the bathroom." He opened the second door on the right. "This is the guest bedroom." She nodded at the room painted a plain white with nothing more than a bed and dresser inside. It definitely looked like a guy had decorated it, but then she liked simple. But maybe not that simple.

He turned and opened the door on the left. "Here's the master."

Not sure she felt comfortable going into his bedroom, she just peeked inside. Again, he didn't have pictures or any decorations, only a huge bed, dresser, and armoire that held a TV. But just as she'd envisioned and suggested, he'd put in french doors along the back wall. The simple brown curtains were open, and she could see they opened up to an enormous deck that was probably only twenty yards from the pond. "It's beautiful, Drew."

"Thanks. It means a lot to me that you feel that way."

A sudden wave of emotion washed over her. She stepped away from the door and walked back down the hall and into the living area. She looked back at the puzzled expression on his face, but unable to talk without crying, she walked outside the door.

She stared up at the sky. The sun still shone bright, and it was still hot and humid. Her stomach growled again, and she patted it to be quiet. *I love him, Lord. I love him. I want to tell him, but. . .seeing his house—I could imagine it being our house, his and mine.*

"Melody, what's wrong?" Drew stepped out onto the front porch.

Still unable to say anything, she sat on one of the porch swings and started to rock. She tried to look up at him and grew flustered again. She stood up and grabbed one of the poles and gazed at the wooded area in the front of his house.

"Melody?"

She smacked her hip. "Who would have ever thought I'd be so nervous?"

"Why would you be nervous?"

She spread open her arms and smacked them down on her thighs. "Because I love you. I love that you're God-fearing. I love that you're hardworking. I love that you're competitive, and that you're protective, and that you're my very best friend. I love the way you get sunburned along the base of your hair every time you get a haircut. I love—"

Drew wrapped his arms around her, and before she could say another word, he pressed his lips against hers. She inhaled and closed her eyes at his sweet touch. Feeling weak, she wrapped her arms around his neck. He pulled away, looked at her lips, then kissed her again, then again. She giggled when he pressed his lips to hers a fourth time.

"You have no idea how badly I've wanted to do that."

Melody unwrapped her arms then placed her hands on her hips. "I think you just wanted to kiss me before I kissed you."

He cupped her cheeks with his hands and kissed her again. "You're right about that."

He pulled her close to his chest and wrapped his arms around her back. She felt another soft kiss on the top of her head before he released her enough to lift her chin so that he could look into her eyes. "I love you, Melody."

She lifted her eyebrows and smirked. "I said it first."

"But I kissed you first."

"Oh yeah, well—well. . ." She searched her brain for a comeback. "Well, I'm going to ask you to marry me first."

"Oh no, you're not."

Melody gasped when Drew pulled a small box out of his front shirt pocket. He bent down on one knee and took her hand in his. "Melody, I've been carrying this ring around with me for a month. I knew one day God would show me when I could give it to you."

Her heart beat so fast she thought it would take flight and soar out of her chest. He opened the box, and she gazed at the gorgeous marquis diamond. It was simple, just like her. It was perfect. "I love you, Melody. Will you marry me?"

Her hand trembled as he touched the ring to her fingertip. Unable to speak, she nodded, and he pushed it all the way up her finger.

A sudden wave of excitement surged through her, and she flung herself into him for a big hug. He lost his balance and fell backward. She toppled toward him, and they bopped heads.

He sat up and rubbed the place that was already turning red. "So this is how it's going to be?"

She laughed as she felt to see if she, too, had a bump forming. With her other hand she punched his arm. "Every day."

He reached over and pinched her nose. "I'll take it."

Epilogue

May

Drew could hardly wait for the wedding to just start already. He'd been waiting all morning to get the thing going, and he was just about to lose his patience. He didn't care about all this fancy dressing up and the pink and yellow flowers and the white lace and whatever else they decorated the church with. Now the food afterward, he was okay with that part of this whole wedding gig. But all the froufrou stuff—he just wanted to make Melody his wife.

He already knew her long dark hair fell like perfect waves all the way down her back when she didn't knot it up in a ponytail. He already knew her eyes were the deepest, darkest brown he'd ever seen and that he could get lost in them. He knew she had the prettiest lips of any woman he'd ever known, and that she had a tiny yet remarkably strong frame.

He didn't need to have a big old fancy wedding.

The music started. Finally. He cleared his throat and lifted his shoulders. At least she wasn't going to make him wait too awfully long to see her since she'd decided to just have Addy and Gracie as bridesmaids. It broke his heart that her mom said she couldn't make it to the wedding. He still hadn't met her in person, but he and Melody continued to pray for her every night.

Addy walked toward them first, and Drew blew out his breath. His sister had told them last night at the rehearsal that she and Nick were expecting their first child in six months. He snuck a peek at Nick. He'd always heard that women glowed when they were pregnant, but it was Nick doing the glowing. He shrugged. He supposed it would be nice to have a little niece or nephew.

Gracie walked down next. She was huge with her second child. She looked like she was going to pop at any moment, but God answered Melody's prayers with a yes. She'd prayed every day for months that her friend would wait until after the wedding to go into labor. And she had. Although if Drew were a

232

betting man, and Melody told him she'd wring his neck if he did any more of that, he'd wager that Gracie would have that baby before they got back from their honeymoon. That had actually become Melody's new prayer, as she wanted her to wait until they got back.

Drew shook his head. Melody would be appearing next. He already knew she was beautiful. He'd tried to be supportive about the whole wedding bit, but if he'd had his way, they'd have been married the day after he proposed. And she could have worn her coveralls for all he cared.

The wedding march sounded, and everyone in the church stood. Melody and Roy moved from behind the left wall and into the center aisle.

Drew sucked in his breath. He couldn't remember how to let it out. She was an angel. She was amazing. Gorgeous. Stunning. Her long white dress didn't have any sleeves at all. It was simple, but it hugged her body to perfection, and Drew felt light-headed that she was the woman God had given him to marry. A see-through material hung from the top of her head all the way down her back.

That beautiful hair of hers was all tied up in knots at the top of her head, but she had curls that framed her face and fell along her shoulders. But it was her eyes and her smile that absolutely blew him away. She looked at him as if he'd made her the happiest woman in the world.

He felt humbled that Melody would love a man like him. *God, You're too good to me.*

She and Roy finally reached him at the altar, and Drew took her hands in his. The ceremony went by so fast that Drew could hardly remember anything he said. The beauty of his bride and the fact that she'd allow him to be her husband mesmerized him. The only words he'd heard were "I do." They were the two best words he'd ever heard in his life.

"You may kiss your wife," the pastor said, and Drew's chest puffed up so full he thought it would burst.

He'd promised himself that he wouldn't embarrass her with a long, drawn-out kiss in front of all their family and friends. Her gaze was glued to his as he bent down and lightly touched her lips with his. He smiled and stood to his full height.

"Oh, I don't think that's good enough, buddy," Melody whispered. Gripping his shirt with her right hand, she pulled him down to her and kissed him with everything in her. Drew felt woozy when she let him go, and again he inwardly praised God for having this woman to deal with.

The pastor coughed back a chuckle. "I present to you Mr. and Mrs. Drew and Melody Wilson." She squealed when Drew lifted her into his arms and carried her down the aisle. He could hardly wait to take her home.

He placed her on her feet at the front door of the church so they could shake hands with everyone as they left. Leaning over, he whispered, "I love you, Mrs. Wilson."

She lifted her chin and kissed his lips quickly. "I love you, Mr. Wilson." She kissed him again.

He growled. "You know I expect a lot of those tonight."

She cocked her head and smirked. "Betcha I can give you more kisses than you give me."

Excited anticipation filled him. "Now that's a bet I'd like to make."

GAME OF LOVE

Dedication

To my dear friend and critique partner Rose McCauley. I met this wonderful woman at the first national ACRW (now ACFW) writing conference. Since then she has been one of my greatest encouragers. From laughing off my scatterbrained ways when I forget clothes for conference, to inviting everyone who enters the store where I'm signing to buy one of my books, to editing two to four chapters a day for a week (which she did for this story), Rose has been a constant smile in my life. Thank you, Rose. I love you.

Chapter 1

Johanna Smith took a step away from the wedding cake table and wiped her brow with the back of her hand. She admired the three-tiered, buttercream fondant-covered creation her mother had designed. Light yellow and light pink roses overlapped each other and covered the top of the cake. White fondant that her mother had made to look like ribbons circled the bottom of each tier with a small bouquet of yellow and pink roses resting on the left side of the middle tier and on the right side of the bottom tier. "Mama, this is the prettiest one yet."

A full smile framed her mother's lips. "Thanks, Johanna." She wiped her hands on the front of her dark blue denim skirt then pointed at the cake. "I had such a time with the flowers on the middle tier. I was afraid they'd never look right."

Johanna stepped closer to the cake, inspecting the part her mother mentioned. Her mother had to add an extra few roses to that bouquet to get it to sit properly, but her mother had a natural touch when it came to decorating pastry, and the cake looked exquisite. "If it tastes as good as it looks, they're in for a real treat."

"Made-from-scratch French vanilla on the top and bottom tiers and dark chocolate on the middle one—it better be good."

Johanna chuckled softly. "Mama, your cakes are always delicious." She peered around the barn-turned-reception-area. Normally, one of her younger sisters would have helped their mother deliver the wedding cake, as Johanna veered away from crowds. But she'd been so intrigued by the idea of holding a reception in a barn that she'd wanted to see how it looked.

Her gaze drank in the perfectly arranged bales of hay along three walls of the barn. Bouquets of pink and yellow roses, baby's breath, and daisies had been tucked into the hay bales in various places. Yellow and pink iridescent balloons hung from the rafters above the bales. The barn doors stood open, and the white satin sashes wrapped along the top and sides of the opening created a wedding arch. Large light yellow bows and pink roses were tied every few feet all the way around.

Several circular tables, twenty or more if Johanna guessed correctly, rested along the center of the barn floor. Some of them were already decorated with the smallest hay bales she'd ever seen, probably only one foot long, that held smaller versions of the same bouquets gracing the bales lining the walls.

She looked at her mother, who also drank in the elaborate decorations. "This has got to be the most beautiful barn I've ever seen."

"It smells wonderful, too."

Johanna sucked in a deep breath. The scent of roses mingled with hay hovered in the air, but the soft scent of the horses that lived in the barn still lingered. The mixture brought a smile to her lips. "It's perfect, isn't it?"

"It is, but we'd best stop dawdling."

Johanna turned back toward her mother, who began to work feverishly gathering the supplies. After scooping up her mother's touch-up instruments and a few small plastic bags, she sneaked one last peek at the open room. Not usually one to fret over froufrou things, Johanna couldn't stop the niggling of desire to be planning her own wedding.

She was young in the world's eyes. She knew that. But she and her family had never lived by the world's standards. Her father, a conservative minister of a small country church in Hickory Hill, had raised her to love the Lord above all else. She'd been taught how to be a lady and how to take care of a home while learning all of her precollege schooling at her mother's hip. And she'd witnessed a love between her parents that she'd longed for since her early adolescence.

Besides, she felt much older than her peers. Though she'd stayed in her parents' home, she'd graduated from a nearby college with a degree in English. She enjoyed her job at the public library in the nearby town of River Run. But her heart longed for a husband and children to care for. *Maybe the children could wait a few years. I am only twenty-one. But still, I'd love for God to reveal His husband for me.*

Knowing her mother would be unhappy with her meandering, Johanna turned on her heels and stepped forward. She slammed into something solid. The man looked as surprised as Johanna when her mother's touch-up materials fell to the ground, as did a cardboard box of small plastic bottles of bubbles. On impact, several of the bottles popped out of the box and spilled all over the floor. Johanna gasped at the unexpected collision and placed her hand on her chest as she stepped backward. Her heel didn't quite reach the floor as she smashed a bottle of bubbles, sending the soapy substance squirting out of the side. She lost her footing and started to fall backward when the man in front of her reached forward and grabbed hold of her then smashed her into his chest.

Heat rushed up her neck and wrapped around her cheeks as she gathered her balance then pushed away from him. She found it hard to speak past her embarrassment as she peered up then away from the very handsome, all-dressed-up-in-a-tuxedo fellow. "I am so sorry." She bent down and started to pick up the bottles and toss them in the cardboard box that had landed to her right.

A frustrated sigh seeped from the man's lips, making her feel even worse. "It's okay," he mumbled.

She leaned forward to reach a stray bottle, grabbed it, then flipped her head back to look up at him to apologize once more. The top of her head connected with him. Hard. A slight squeal slipped from her lips, and a moan fell from his. She touched the top of her head and looked up at the guy. Blood trickled down his bottom lip.

"Oh my. I'm so sorry." She reached in the front pockets of her capris, praying she had a tissue of some kind in one of them. She—didn't. She looked around the room. The only tissues or napkins she spied were already part of the table decorations. She looked back at the man. He hadn't moved, just stood sucking blood from his bottom lip and staring at her as if she'd lost her mind.

Tears welled in her eyes, and she tried to bite them back. She loathed her typical, horrible nervous response to any situation that had her flustered. Painfully shy—and having lived most of her life sheltered in what she deemed the best of ways—she'd never fully learned how to handle an embarrassing situation such as this.

The expression of complete reproof and disdain tracing the man's face shook her already melting countenance. Growing more mortified by the second, she noted a dot of crimson blood on the front of his white shirt. Before the tears could stream down her face, she scooped up her mother's materials and raced out the door, leaving the man with the bulk of the mess to clean up.

I should go back. I shouldn't just leave the mess to that man. I'm just so embarrassed. I'm never that clumsy.

She reached the van. She simply couldn't go back now. Thankful her mother still arranged things in the back, Johanna slipped into the passenger's seat. She pulled down the visor and peered at her reflection. Her cheeks were flushed and her eyes red and puffy. She blinked several times and gently patted her cheeks. After loosening her ponytail, she pulled down a few long blond strands around her temples to help disguise her eyes. She did not want to have to explain her emotions to her mother.

Her mother's voice sounded from the back of the van. "It looked as if they're going to have a beautiful reception."

"Yes." Johanna tried to sound emotionless as she sucked in a few more breaths. The expression of contempt in the man's perfect blend of green and blue eyes still seemed to float around in her mind, and she inwardly chastised herself that she continued to feel waves of embarrassment.

"I don't really know the family, but they seem like wonderful Christians. You'd think we'd know more people from River Run. After all, we only live ten miles from here." A loud snap sounded from the rear of the van, and Johanna knew her mother had put the backseat in place.

"Mmm-hmm." Johanna lifted the visor and patted her cheeks one last time. She was a grown woman. Rationally, she knew she shouldn't get so upset. She sat up straight and braced herself for her mother to get in the driver's seat. Praying her face looked normal, she sucked in her breath when her mom slipped inside.

She could feel her mother's gaze upon her for what seemed like an eternity. Finally, turning to face her mother, she said, "Mama, I—"

Her mother patted her leg. "Johanna, I know you long for a husband and a home of your own. The time is coming. I'm not sure why Gavin drags his feet, but—"

Johanna looked out the window beside her seat. Her mother misunderstood her emotions. At that moment, she was not longing for her future life. And she hoped Gavin dragged his feet until, well, until forever. His mother and her mother had always presumed the two would make a match one day, but she didn't have the slightest interest in Gavin Mitchell. And she felt certain he would agree with her sentiments. At least she hoped he would.

She found nothing wrong with the guy. Gavin had been born one month before her, and they had spent their entire lives together, from playpen to school lessons to Sunday outings. He was a good Christian man and a true friend. But that was all.

She continued to stare out the window as her mother began to talk about all they needed to do when they got home. Johanna couldn't listen. All she could think about was a pair of blue-green eyes filled with contempt. Though she tried to squelch the feeling, she wondered what they'd look like if the man smiled.

⁓

The day just couldn't get any worse for Mike McCauley. It should have been a day of celebration. The last of his friends tying the knot with the woman of his dreams. Which meant that not only should he be happy for his lifelong buddy, but he should also be celebrating the fact that for once in their friendship, he'd beaten his three best friends in a bet. A feat he had never accomplished before.

The whole thing had started innocent enough. Seven years ago, Mike and his friends, Wyatt, Nick, and Drew, watched as another friend tied the knot. Still young and foolish, the four of them made a bet that whoever was the last of them to get hitched won, and the losers had to help plan and pay for the winner's wedding.

Wyatt had been the first to fall, marrying his high school friend Gracie. Then Nick married Drew's sister, Addy. And now, Drew, the man who won nearly every bet the four made, decided to lose the bet and marry Nick's cousin Melody.

Mike was the winner, and yet he was the biggest loser of all.

He looked at his reflection in the bathroom mirror. After that woman practically body slammed him in the barn, he'd had to run over to the main house to try to get the blood out of his shirt. He didn't have to go too far, only 150 yards or so to the main house. In fact, they were using the house to keep the food warm as well as a restroom facility, as needed, but he still didn't have time to be running to unnecessary places. He had to be at the church in thirty minutes.

Growling at his reflection, he'd succeeded in making a quarter-size red stain out of what had been a tiny drop of blood on the white shirt. Not to mention that his bottom lip was slightly swollen around the teeth marks where he'd bitten down hard when his mouth collided with the woman's head.

He'd never seen the blond-haired woman before. He hoped never to see her again. At least not today. He had enough to deal with today.

Even though it had been nine months since his brother drowned, it would still be the first time he'd seen a lot of these friends and family in a group setting. He'd been praying for strength for weeks, especially since he would be bombarded with condolences, comments, and promises of continued prayers. His parents would be attending the ceremony but not the reception. His mother still carried a lot of bitterness and anger in her heart regarding God's sovereignty. She hadn't been to church or rejoined any of her usual activities since Joe's death. She simply stayed home, only visiting briefly with those who hadn't given up on visiting with her on her good days.

Trying one last time, he pumped a dab of liquid soap onto a paper towel then tried to blot it against the red spot. It simply would not come all the way out, and it was located in a place he could not hide. With a deep sigh, he threw the paper towels in the trash then walked out of the bathroom.

He gulped when he saw Lacy McRoberts standing in the kitchen doorway. She caught his eye and smiled. He lifted his hand in a hesitant wave, and she made her way toward him. Mike willed himself to remain calm as his heart beat fast and hard against his chest. A cold sweat washed over him, and he shifted his weight to be sure his extremities still worked.

He'd had a crush on Lacy for years. Three, to be exact. At first he'd just been too bashful to admit his feelings for her. Then he'd decided not to pursue her because he thought he might be able to win the bet. Then he found himself longing for what he saw happening between Nick and Addy, and he almost asked her out two years ago, but Drew picked at him a bit, and Mike grew determined to wait a bit longer. After all, he had to beat Drew at something.

Then Drew fell for Melody, and Mike determined to ask Lacy on a date. But his brother died in the accident and all he could think about was his grief and holding on to God and caring for his parents. *But, Lord, today is the day. I promised You that today I'd ask her. It's time to move forward.*

"Here she comes. You gonna ask her out?"

Mike jumped at the sound of Nick's voice behind him. He turned and saw his friend wink as he carried a small circular table out the back door. With friends as exhausting as his, it was no wonder Mike hadn't asked the woman out. At the end of the day, he was just flat-out too tired.

"Hi, Mike."

Mike turned again, and Lacy already stood in front of him. He wondered if she'd heard what Nick said. He couldn't imagine that she missed it. It wasn't as if Nick's deep voice didn't already boom through a room even when he whispered. Mike cleared his throat. "Hi, Lacy." He nodded toward her purple dress. "You look pretty."

"Thanks. So do you." Mike sucked in his breath when her gaze took in the length of him. She frowned as she pointed to the bloodstain. "What happened?"

He touched his finger to his mouth. "Bit my lip."

"Oh no."

Mike stiffened when she reached up and touched his lip. He'd never known her to be forward in any way, but then he'd never really known her outside of the diner, either. Not since they were kids, anyway.

She rummaged through the small silver bag that hung from her shoulder. "I always keep a stain remover pen with me."

She pulled out the orange device and pulled off the top. Mike felt his cheeks warm when she flattened his shirt against his chest with her left hand then dabbed the pen against the spot with her right.

She stepped back and put the lid back on the pen then smiled up at him. "All gone."

He prayed his neck and cheeks weren't as red as he feared as he looked down at the spot. Sure enough, she'd gotten the stain out. He looked back at her and smiled. "That is terrific. Thanks so much." He laughed. "I was afraid I was going to be in big trouble."

Lacy giggled then twisted her lips into a pout as she touched his bottom lip again. "I wish I could do something to help you with that."

He'd never known the woman to be so bold, and yet he'd never felt so attracted to her. He liked the perkiness in her personality, something he'd never seen at the diner. Before he'd only been attracted to her looks, but maybe she was a woman who would keep him on his toes as well.

The shyness he'd always known tried to creep its way up his spine. He could feel himself starting to back away. *God, help me move forward. Open my mouth.*

He cleared his throat. "Lacy, would you like to go to dinner with me this week?"

Squinting at him, Lacy bit her bottom lip. She crossed her arms in front of her chest and studied him for what seemed like hours. Finally, her mouth broke into a smile and she nodded. "Mike McCauley, I seriously thought you'd never ask."

Chapter 2

Johanna grabbed her Bible and journal off the nightstand and shoved them into her tote bag with the embroidered bookworm on the front. She pulled a sweater off the hanger and put it on. Though often warm in Kentucky in May, the early hours were still quite cool. As she did every morning, she planned to greet her Savior early in the day with the rising sun.

She walked quietly down the hall. The family's golden retriever hopped up off his bed in her parents' room and joined her. She and Max were the only two members of the family who enjoyed early rising. With the wafting aroma of the coffee she'd preset to brew, she pulled her mug out of the dishwasher, added a spoonful of sugar, a bit of milk, and then the warm, delicious-smelling java. She looked down at Max. "Ya ready?"

Max wagged his tail and walked in a circle, whimpering. Johanna opened the back door. The cool, damp air kissed her face, and she zipped up her sweater then slid her feet into her old loafers. She hefted her bag up on her shoulder and pressed the fingers of her right hand against the mug for additional warmth as she shut the door behind her and Max.

In a matter of moments, the sun would rise. She quickened her pace as she walked toward the pond at the top of a slight hill behind their house. Reaching the top, she placed her bag on the bench her father had made several years ago for her to use in this favorite spot. She pulled a hand towel from the bag and spread it out on the bench to avoid getting wet from the morning dew. She sat and watched the horizon.

As if God had been waiting just for her, an orange haze peeked up from the hills to the east. A bright yellow mound rose from beneath it, giving way to the top of the yellow-white mass of the sun. The plush green springtime grass and lush trees seemed to stand taller, more confidently, as light and warmth bathed them.

"Dear Jesus, Your creation is amazing."

Welcoming her day with the sunrise and a prayer to her Lord had been a ritual since she turned thirteen years old, and she never grew tired of the wonder and majesty of His glory. She opened her journal and wrote her first of the morning's praises, as well as concerns. One concern that weighed heavy on her heart was her sister Amber's desire to attend public school this fall for her senior year.

Johanna had loved being taught by her mother and father, but she was also content with the simpler things, including solitude and inner reflection. Her youngest sister, twelve-year-old Bethany, was a lot like Johanna. Amber, on the other hand, was boisterous and social. She exhibited a special giftedness in music and, at almost seventeen, longed to share her talent in a public setting with the hope of gaining a scholarship of some kind.

Johanna finished her scripture reading and writing and looked up at the still pond waters before her. Her mind drifted to the blue-green eyes of the man she'd bumped into. She touched the spot on her head where they'd collided. It still ached, and she wondered if his bottom lip had swollen and to what degree. Had he been able to get the blood spot out of the white shirt? Wearing a tuxedo, he must have been a member of the wedding party. For all she knew, he was the groom.

She cringed at the thought of having busted the groom's mouth on his wedding day. *Lord, I pray he wasn't the groom.*

She'd seen the man for only a brief few moments, but she felt sure she would spot him in an instant. Her mind continually replayed his strong, freshly shaven jaw and chin, straight nose, and full, dark eyebrows, just a shade darker than his sandy-brown hair. But it was his piercing blue-green eyes that haunted her.

She brushed the thought away as she gathered her journal and Bible and shoved them back in her bag. She made her way down the hill and back to the house. Almost an hour had passed. Her family was sure to be up by now. Amber was probably already practicing on the piano while Bethany got her shower. Daddy was most assuredly sitting at the kitchen table talking with Mama while she finished the biscuits and gravy.

It was Tuesday, her day off, and she knew her mother would want her to help fix the birthday cake orders that had to be finished by Wednesday night. Johanna wasn't as good at the decorating, but she could do the baking just fine.

She opened the back door and startled at the sight of Gavin sitting at the kitchen table eating breakfast with her daddy. Her mother looked at her and smiled. If Johanna didn't know the woman better, she'd have thought the look was of pure mischief. Mama placed her hand on Gavin's back. "Hurry up and get ready. Gavin's come to get you. Remember you promised Sandy you'd help her with spring cleaning today?"

She plopped her tote bag onto the table. "I'd forgotten." She nudged Gavin's shoulder, as he was still her friend despite their parents' matchmaking attempts. "You get here early enough?"

Gavin wiped his mouth with a napkin and swallowed down a large bite. "I don't deny it. I knew if I got here early enough, your mama would feed me."

Mama clucked her tongue. "With your mother's last boy as young as he is, I bet she's hardly able to keep up with the laundry. You tell her Johanna will help out any time she needs her."

"Of course I will." Johanna squinted at her mother. She had no qualms with helping Sandy, but she wanted her mother to stop trying to set her up with her friend. She looked back at Gavin. "Just give me a minute to change."

"Don't I get a 'good morning'?" Her daddy stood to his feet and opened his arms. He towered over most men in height and girth, and Johanna always felt loved and protected when he was near.

"Absolutely." She wrapped her arms around the overgrown teddy bear of a man then lifted her face and planted a slight kiss to his jaw. "Have a good day, Daddy."

He patted her back and released her; then she raced up the stairs to change clothes and freshen up. She'd completely forgotten about her promise to help Sandy. There'd be little rest to be had at the Mitchell home. With Gavin being the oldest of seven brothers and the youngest still breastfeeding, Johanna could only imagine all Sandy would need her to do.

She pulled her hair up in a quick ponytail and stared at her reflection in the mirror. "Give me strength today, Lord Jesus."

With Bethany finally out of the bathroom, Johanna wiggled her way in and quickly brushed her teeth and washed her face before Amber could complain about needing a shower. Feeling refreshed, she made her way downstairs and grabbed a granola bar from the pantry.

She walked into the kitchen and spied Gavin helping her mother put the dishes in the dishwasher. He would make a good husband one day, but she just didn't feel romantic about Gavin. And though she'd been raised knowing marriage was every bit as much about commitment and friendship as it was love, she still wanted the love. The eros love described in the Bible. A love like Solomon and the Shulamite woman.

Her cheeks warmed, and she pushed the thought away. She cleared her throat. "I'm ready, Gavin."

He turned and grinned at her. "Pretty as always."

Mama's knowing yet mischievous smile returned, and Johanna wanted to scold her own mother.

"We'll be leaving now, Mama." Without waiting for her reply, Johanna walked out the back door and toward Gavin's work truck. She hopped inside the passenger's seat and buckled the belt.

Gavin slid in beside her and started it up. "Matchmaking again, huh?"

"As always."

Gavin's deep, guttural laugh sounded through the cab. "They'll never give up."

"I know it. Your mom's going to do the same thing while I'm at your house."

"Yep."

She drank in the rolling hills around her. Gavin lived deeper in the country than she did, and it was nothing surprising to see all kinds of wildlife—raccoons, squirrels, rabbits, and deer. The coyotes she wanted to stay away from, but she knew they mainly showed their faces at night.

Gavin's voice filled the cab again. "I don't know what they're thinking. You and me are just friends."

Johanna shrugged without looking at him. "Always have been."

"Yep. Just friends."

Something in the tone of his voice or in the way he said it didn't sound quite right. She looked at her friend, the guy she'd shared a playpen with. He was her friend. Just her friend. So, why did he all of a sudden look so serious?

⋙◆⋘

Mike had never felt so nervous. He still had a few days to stew over his date with Lacy. Now he wished he'd just asked her out the day after the wedding. He hadn't planned anything fancy, just a sit-down dinner. He thought he'd drive her into Lexington, where she'd have a bigger selection of restaurants to choose from. But he couldn't focus on his work for fretting over a silly dinner.

Knowing he needed a few things from the hardware store anyway, Mike decided to head into town. Hopefully, he'd be able to talk with Wyatt a bit. Maybe his friend could give him some advice to quell his nerves.

He hadn't told his parents about the date. Since his brother's death, his mother had become overly worried about him and his father. She'd even been to the hospital a few times with severe panic attacks. Though he saw his folks every day at the farm he and his father shared, he tried not to overwhelm them with any of his own concerns, including his first date.

Finally arriving at the hardware store, he walked inside to the sound of a bell over his head. He nodded to his friend who stood behind the counter. "How you doing?"

"Awful." A whiny, female voice sounded in Wyatt's place.

Mike looked against the wall behind the counter and saw Gracie sitting in a chair with a laptop propped on her bulging stomach. Though he'd never tell her, he couldn't imagine how the small woman's belly could get so big. She looked as if she carried a couple of basketballs under that shirt, and both of them fully inflated. Her face seemed all splotchy, and even her nose seemed a little wider and flatter, which really weirded him out.

"Honey, you're doing great." Wyatt bent down and kissed the top of his wife's head. "It'll be any day now."

Gracie stuck out her lower lip farther than Mike believed possible. "No, it won't. Melody put a curse on me. She and Drew won't be home for another week, and I won't be having this baby until then." She pushed on the top of her belly while lifting her shoulders and trying to take a breath. "And, I can hardly breathe."

Mike didn't know what to say. She did look rather uncomfortable. Even more so than she had a few days before at the wedding. He knew Melody had told Gracie she'd prayed the Lord wouldn't let her deliver until they returned from the honeymoon. But he was pretty sure that didn't equate to Melody putting a curse on her. He tried to think of something positive. "Where's little Wyatt?"

Big tears pooled in Gracie's eyes then streamed down her cheeks. "I'm so fat I can't even take care of my own son."

"Now, Gracie." Wyatt kneeled beside her and rubbed her arm. "You know that's not true. Mom is keeping him while you work on the shop's books. And I told you I'd do them this week."

She sat up, wiped her eyes, and scowled at Wyatt. "Are you saying I can't do my job? I always take care of the books."

"No, honey. I'm saying you need a break. Why don't you take a break?"

The tears returned. "I know I'm an emotional wreck." She looked at Mike. "I'm sorry. Let Wyatt help you with whatever you need."

Wyatt looked at Mike. Obvious by his strained expression, he needed to be needed, and not by Gracie. "What can I help you with?"

"Well, I—"

Wyatt walked around the corner and grabbed Mike by the arm, guiding him toward the plumbing supplies, which just happened to be in the back of the store. "Tell me I love my wife."

"Wyatt, you love your wife."

"Of course, I love my wife, but the last few weeks of pregnancy are absolutely exhausting. Nothing tastes good, and yet she craves everything. Her stomach hurts, her back hurts, her feet hurt. You know what else? My head hurts."

Mike had to bite back a laugh at Wyatt's serious yet frustrated expression.

Wyatt continued. "I begged her not to come to the shop today." He pointed at his chest. "I admit I need a break, every bit as much as she needs to rest. But I begged her to let me do the books." He smacked the back of his right hand into the palm of his left. "But she wouldn't hear of it."

"Maybe you could take a quick break, and you and I could go pick up some lunch for her."

Wyatt snapped his fingers. "That sounds like a great plan." He headed back toward the counter. Mike followed him into the office area behind the counter space. Gracie was as curled up as a nine months pregnant woman could be on the love seat. Wyatt gently closed the office door. "I'm glad she's sleeping. She doesn't rest well. I won't be able to leave now."

"You want me to pick something up for you?"

"No. I'm going to try to get the books caught up before she wakes up."

Mike chuckled. "That sounds like a good idea." He walked to the front door.

"Hey." Wyatt's voice stopped him. "Did you need anything?"

For a few moments, Mike had forgotten his anxiety about the date with Lacy. And Wyatt had enough going on. He didn't need to add anything else. "No." He waved as he opened the door. The bell sounded again, and Mike hoped it didn't wake Gracie. "I'll see you later."

He headed down the sidewalk toward the Main Street Café. He preferred the diner's food, but he simply couldn't patron there again until after his and Lacy's date. As he walked down the sidewalk, he noticed a woman several yards in front of him with her head down as she rummaged through her bag.

He recognized the woman, but he couldn't quite figure out from where. Not only was her face lowered, but the wind blew wisps of her long blond hair in front of her as well.

As the distance between them shortened, Mike wasn't sure if he should veer to the left or right. The sidewalks were too narrow. The woman hadn't looked up, and she continued to walk down the center.

Mike stepped into the street to let her pass, but the woman shifted herself to the left and still bumped into him with her elbow. Hard.

"I'm so sorry." She looked up.

Mike's mouth fell open. "It's you."

Recognition wrapped her features, and she turned bright crimson. Her light-green eyes with flecks of brown seemed to flash with the deepening color of her skin.

She pulled her hand out of her bag, and several items fell out. He bent down to help her retrieve them. He chuckled. "Don't bend down with me this time. My lip has only just healed."

He stood up and handed her the lip gloss and pen that had fallen in the street. Tears welled in her eyes, and she stepped back. "I'm so sorry."

Before he could respond, she hurried down the sidewalk. *There must be something about me making women cry this week.*

He walked into the café. As long as it wasn't Lacy doing the crying. As anxious as he felt about their date, he looked forward to the fact that they were finally having one. He didn't want to do anything to mess it up.

Chapter 3

Johanna twisted her long hair into a ball then fastened it with a clip. The morning had been quite hectic as she made sure she had everything needed for the afternoon's "Spring into a Good Book." Conveniently, the county's preschool and kindergarten were located right next to the public library. Throughout the year, the school and library joined forces to encourage literacy among the students.

Today the library hosted a fairly involved event with three stations for the children to visit. The head librarian had recruited a local farmer—Johanna believed she said the man's name was Nick—to bring a live calf for the students to see and pet. He planned to talk with them about the many duties of a farmer in the spring. Johanna would read a book to the children about the spring, and then Nick's wife, Addy, would help the children plant a seed in a small plastic cup to take home.

She tried to focus on the children who would be coming down the school's steps and over to the library's outdoor area at any moment. Instead, her mind replayed the walk down Main Street, as she'd rummaged through her purse for lunch money. She'd run into the man again. Literally.

She'd spent enough time worrying over that man. Then to run into him again? What were the chances? She knew his face would be imprinted in her mind for weeks to come. This time he hadn't looked angry. Actually, he'd seemed amused that she'd run into him a second time.

Well, she wasn't amused. She was fully humiliated. He must think her a complete klutz. The truth was she was actually quite careful and meticulous about things. She liked things to go as planned.

The school door opened, and the children started toward the library. The teachers faced a challenge keeping the children from racing to the calf and the other activities. But safety came first.

Mrs. Love, the head librarian, arranged the students into groups of three and sent them to each station. One tall, dark-haired boy stuck out his bottom lip and crossed his arms in front of his chest when she pointed him toward

Johanna. "I don't want to listen to her read. I want to see the baby cow."

Johanna settled the rest of the children on the quilts she'd laid out for them to sit on, while the boy became more agitated with Mrs. Love. The older woman tried to scoot him toward the quilts, but he dug his heels into the ground. "I don't want to listen to no stupid book."

"Young man." Mrs. Love placed her hand against her chest.

Knowing the older librarian had little experience with children, Johanna rushed to Mrs. Love and the boy. She knelt down to his level and rested her hand on his arm. "You know what? I really need someone to help me turn the pages of the book. Do you know anyone who could do that?"

He grunted and shook his head.

"Hmm. Well, it has to be someone who wants to learn about the springtime. Someone who one day might grow up to be one of River Run's best farmers, because he will have learned the things a farmer needs to do in the spring."

The boy's expression softened, and he uncrossed his arms and raised his hand. "I want to be the best farmer in River Run."

Johanna smiled. "You do? Well, could you turn the pages for me?"

The boy nodded and grabbed hold of Johanna's hand. If the overgrown tyke pulled her heartstrings any tighter, she'd burst into tears for sure. "But I still get to see the baby cow, right?"

"You definitely still get to see her."

"Okay."

The afternoon grew hotter, but the students became more inquisitive and excited about all they were learning. By the time the last group had gone through, Johanna thought she would have to take a nap on the quilts spread on the ground before she'd be able to do anything else.

Knowing that wasn't an option, she folded the quilts then walked over to Addy to help clean up the plastic cups, seeds, and soil. "Thanks for doing this today. I think the kids really enjoyed it."

Addy looked at her. "I think I had as much fun as they did." She waved her hand in front of her face. "I am a bit warm from the heat." She opened her water bottle and took a long drink. "I'm just barely past the first trimester of my pregnancy. I'm still not quite over the sickness part."

Johanna clasped her hands. "Congratulations. Then we appreciate your willingness to help out today even more."

Having already loaded the calf, Nick joined them. He placed his palm on Addy's cheek. "You look a little flushed. I think it's time for you to get home and get some rest."

Addy laughed and shook her head. She looked at Johanna. "You'd think I was fighting some kind of illness the way this man worries over me." She gazed up at her husband. "Pregnant women are supposed to get flushed, Nick."

"Well, when my pregnant woman gets flushed, I want her to rest."

Johanna felt a niggling of jealousy at the obvious love between them. That was what she longed for. Her mom and Gavin's mom kept slipping hints for the two of them, but she didn't feel that way toward her childhood friend. She wanted a man to look at her as if God had created her just for him. She wanted commitment and friendship, but she wanted more. She wanted a man who protected her and loved her with all his heart.

"I think your husband is right. You need to go on home." She swept her hand across the outdoor area. "There's very little left to do. Go home and rest." She extended her hand. "It was my pleasure to meet you, Addy." After shaking Addy's hand, she shook Nick's. "And you, too, Nick."

"It was our pleasure to meet you." Nick patted her shoulder with a strength he must not have realized he had. "I hope we'll get the chance to see you again."

She nodded, though she knew it wasn't very likely. She worked at the library in River Run, but she and her family lived about ten miles down the road in Hickory Hill. Unless the couple started visiting the library, and today was the first day she'd seen them there, she'd probably never see them again.

⚬⚭⚬

Mike sat on the edge of his brown leather couch. He placed his elbows on top of his legs then rested his chin on his fists. The laptop, sitting on the coffee table in front of him, was actually sticking its tongue out at him. Originally, he'd put the screensaver on there because he thought it was funny. Right now, it wasn't so funny.

His article deadline loomed the next day—the same day as his date with Lacy. He'd never been late on a deadline. Not even when his brother passed away. He knew he'd been preoccupied with Drew's wedding, and he and his dad were overwhelmingly busy on the farm with spring planting, but this proved ridiculous. He had one day to write the entire article, and he still didn't even know what to write about.

He stood up and grabbed his writing fishing pole out of the corner. His buddies made fun of him for keeping the first fishing pole his dad ever bought him in the corner of his living room. But they didn't know he sometimes used it as inspiration when he struggled with an article. They didn't even know he wrote articles.

And he didn't want them to know. Nick and Drew had always been so competitive, trying to beat each other at everything from cornhole to cattle farming. They'd even made a bet about who could keep their mom's flowers alive the longest when they were kids. Being a few years younger than Drew and Nick, Mike and Wyatt never had a chance when it came to beating them.

Wyatt never did mind. He hadn't been raised on a farm, so he just enjoyed it when one of them included him. And Wyatt had spent most of every summer at Mike's house. The truth was, Mike didn't mind the losing, either. He'd found a love for words when he was no bigger than a coonhound.

Of course, he never told his friends about his adoration for reading and writing. They'd laugh him all over the farm. It still didn't stop him from taking a few community college writing classes after high school. He never graduated from college, but he landed a job writing fishing articles for one of Kentucky's largest outdoorsman magazines. Between that and farming, he lived all he'd ever dreamed.

Except having a wife and kids.

Pushing aside the thought that caused his writer's block, he pretended to cast his old fishing pole. He'd been overpowered by so many emotions the first summer his dad had taken him fishing. In a lifetime, he didn't believe he would be able to pen all he thought and felt on that day. But every once in a while, when an article just fought him to be written, he'd pretend to cast the line and a thought or memory of some kind would surface again.

He closed his eyes and tried to envision the first fish he'd reeled up with this rod. He could still see the little bluegill. It had to be the smallest one that ever lived. But he'd been so proud. Felt so accomplished.

Keeping his eyes closed, he took several slow breaths. *Help me, Lord. I desperately need an idea.*

His cell phone rang, breaking his concentration. With a growl, he looked at the screen. The screen read his honeymooning friend's name. "Drew? Why would Drew be calling me on his honeymoon?"

Dread filled his gut. No man in his right mind would ever call a friend on his honeymoon. Unless something bad had happened. Mike didn't know if he could take any bad news. Everything in him wanted to ignore the call and try to focus on his article. But he knew there would be no focusing now. Not until he knew Drew and Melody were safe.

He pushed the TALK button. "Hello."

"Hey. What's up, man?"

Mike swallowed the knot in his throat. Drew didn't sound distressed, but why else would he call? Mike placed the fishing pole on the couch and sat in the recliner, preparing for the worst. "Nothing's up with me. How are you?"

"I'm fine. The beach is beautiful, although not as pretty as my wife."

Mike heard Melody's soft giggle, and his body relaxed. If something were wrong they wouldn't sound so happy. Mike furrowed his brows and scratched his forehead. "Drew, why are you calling me?"

"Your date with Lacy's tomorrow, isn't it?"

"Yeah."

"I just called to tell you not to stress. Be yourself. We've been friends since before you were born. Remember how your mom says I was punching on you when you were still in her belly?"

Mike grinned. "Yeah."

"Well, I know you're probably feeling a little nervous. Overanalyzing everything like you always do."

Mike leaned back in the recliner and allowed it to rock back and forth. "So you think you know me so well?"

Drew laughed. "Am I right?"

Mike chewed the inside of his mouth and wrinkled his nose. "Maybe."

Drew's guffaw sounded over the line. "I knew I was. Look man, I'm calling you on my honeymoon. On my honeymoon!"

Mike blew out a breath. "I definitely wouldn't have asked you to do that."

"But I called you just the same to tell you that as goofy as it sounds coming from one of your best buddies, I want you to know you're a great guy. Put your shyness to the side and just be yourself with Lacy."

Mike smiled. "I really appreciate that."

Drew chuckled. "Think of it like this: you're the fisherman casting the line. If she's the fish God's prepared for you, she'll take the bait and you'll be able to reel her on up."

"Thanks, man. See you next week."

"I don't know. Melody and I may stay here forever." Her giggles sounded over the line before it went dead.

Mike mulled over Drew's words. *I've got an idea.* He looked at his old fishing pole, the first one he'd ever had. The one that conjured all sorts of childhood memories and emotions.

"There's a reason you didn't work for inspiration today." He placed the fishing pole back in its spot in the corner. "You conjure up all kinds of childlike feelings. This article's going to be about the marriage between the fisherman and his fish."

Johanna drove home with the annuals she and her sisters and mother would plant the following day. As a tradition, the Smith women planted flowers the day before Mother's Day. Then Sunday they treated their mother to homemade dishes, made solely by the girls and their father, for dinner after church. This year her mother had requested all impatiens in various shades of pink and white.

She pulled into the driveway and honked the horn. Her youngest sister ran out the front door to greet her. With Bethany having a natural green thumb, they'd learned to heed her advice about the placement of the flowers. Bethany opened the back door of the car and pulled out a flat. "These look really nice, Johanna. Where did you get them this year?"

"Well, Locklear's Greenhouse costs a bit more, but I thought they looked worth it. Besides, it's Mama's Mother's Day gift."

Bethany nodded. "You made the right choice."

Johanna looked toward the house. "Where are Mama and Amber?"

Bethany let out a sigh. "Fighting over math again."

"Ugh. You get the flowers. I'll go help." Johanna grabbed her purse and coffee mug out of the front seat and headed into the house. She petted Max then walked into the guest room they'd turned into their schoolroom.

Amber slouched forward in a chair, her eyes red from having been crying and her gaze focused on the wall in front of her. Her mother rested in the rocking chair that sat against the wall. She called it her calming chair whenever Johanna or one of her sisters pushed her patience. Mama had her head back and her eyes closed. Johanna knew she prayed for God's will with Amber.

Her sister wanted desperately to go to public high school. Outgoing and boisterous, she was the direct opposite of Johanna and Bethany. She learned best by talking and experimenting. She thrived in groups, like when they did group lessons in Sunday school.

"I'm just dumb." Amber's words were flat, and she continued to stare at the wall in front of her.

"Amber, you are not dumb. Don't say such things." Johanna sat in the chair beside Amber's desk. "You just struggle with math. We all struggle with something."

Amber peered at Johanna. "What do you struggle with?"

Johanna swallowed. "You know what, I didn't struggle with academics. But I struggle a lot with talking to people. You know how shy I am with people I don't know." She nudged her sister. "But you, you're naturally friendly and outgoing."

"A lot of good it does me cooped up in a house with my parents and sisters all day."

Johanna pushed a strand of hair behind her ear. She hadn't meant for the conversation to shift to Amber's desire to go to high school. She tried a different angle. "You're also the most musically talented person I know. Amber, yours is undeniably a true gift from God."

"And one I can only share with the people in my family and in my church because I am not allowed to experience anything of the world."

Johanna gazed back at her mother. Mama had opened her eyes. She wasn't angry with Amber's words. Instead, her expression etched one of true concern, of true openness to whatever God wanted for her middle daughter.

Johanna looked back at her sister. "Amber, I do not believe it is Mama's and Daddy's intention to shelter us from the world. Yes, they mean to protect and teach us what the Bible says, but look at me. Your most bashful sister works at a public library. Granted, people do not surround me every day, but you know I feel much more at home simply basking in God's nature, without speaking with anyone for hours at a time."

Amber faced her sister. Johanna's heart wanted to break in two at the anguish in her sister's expression.

"But I do need to be around people. I want to share my gift of music with everyone I meet. I want to go away to college to learn to be even better at my talent." She looked back at the wall. "All of that won't even matter if I can't understand math. I won't be able to go to college anyway."

Johanna felt her mother get out of the seat from behind them. She placed a hand on Amber's shoulder. "Go on upstairs and wash up."

Amber nodded then stood and left the room.

Johanna turned toward her mother. "Mama—"

Her mother shook her head to silence her. "Supper is almost done in the slow cooker. Why don't you head on out to your favorite spot at the pond and pray that your daddy and I make the best choice for Amber. I'll be up in my room doing the same."

Johanna nodded. She walked into the kitchen and grabbed a water bottle out of the refrigerator. She opened the back door, and Max followed her outside and up the hill that led to the pond.

She sat on the bench and lifted her face toward the heavens. She prayed fervently for her sister and that God would give her parents wisdom. Amber was so different than Johanna or Bethany. But Johanna wondered if she was really a lot like their father. Before he'd married their mother, he'd been a traveling preacher, sharing God's good news all over the southern parts of Kentucky and into Tennessee and West Virginia. She petitioned God once more to make His will for Amber transparent to her parents.

Looking back down at the calm waters, she noticed a small frog hop from beneath a leaf and closer to the water. She chuckled at the remembrances of the many times she'd caught frogs and taken them home as pets. Much to her mother's chagrin. "I think I'll let you stay at your own home," she whispered to the creature.

Her stomach growled, and she pressed her hand against it. "I think it's time I get home to mine as well."

Chapter 4

His big date with Lacy had finally arrived. Mike exhaled a long breath as she waited for him to open the passenger's door for her. At first he'd planned to see if his dad would let him borrow their car, as Mike only had a truck. But he still hadn't told his parents about the date. He wanted to see how the night went first. When she struggled to hold down her skirt and still lift herself into the cab, he berated himself for not asking.

Nervous, he shut the door too fast and almost caught her fingers. He closed his eyes before walking around the truck to the driver's side. *Calm my nerves, Lord.*

The most bashful of his friends, Mike was known for doing clumsy things when he was nervous. A vision of the woman who'd bumped into him at the wedding and on the sidewalk popped into his head. He shook the thought away. Why would he think of her at this moment?

He hopped in and started the truck. Accidentally putting the gear in neutral instead of reverse, Mike quickly fixed his error and backed out of her driveway.

Lacy crossed her legs and shifted to face him. "So, where are we going?"

"I thought we'd go to"—his voice squeaked, and Mike cleared his throat—"to Lexington. You could pick out a restaurant from there."

She mentioned a Mexican restaurant. He'd heard it was a good restaurant, but he hated Mexican food. In fact, it was his least favorite. He also noticed Lacy didn't bother to ask him if he liked it. It seemed a bit insensitive to him, but he'd never really dated before, so maybe he was wrong. He turned toward her. "Did you have to work today?"

"Yes, and I worked with Sarah. She drives me absolutely crazy. First, you have to fight her to keep her hairnet on. I mean, *hello*, people don't want your scraggly red hair in their food. Then, she always takes too long on her breaks. She leaves me to cover for her for like half an hour; then she gets all upset if I take the tips for the tables she's left stranded all that time."

Mike grew more uncomfortable as Lacy continued to talk about the people she worked with. All the things she said may be true, but he didn't think it was appropriate for her to be sharing them with him.

He pulled into the restaurant's parking lot, and they walked inside. The dark room and blaring Latino music led him to believe they wouldn't be able to have any kind of conversation. But it was the smell that almost sent him running back outside.

After taking a deep breath, he left his name with the hostess and took a pager. The restaurant entryway was packed, so they weren't able to sit together. Lacy sat on the bench close to the hostess, while Mike stood back by the door.

He looked through the menu the hostess had given them for the least spicy dish he could find. It appeared his best bet would be the tacos. Maybe this time they wouldn't give him indigestion as they had every other time he'd ever eaten them.

As the minutes continued to pass, Mike looked around the room at the burnt orange and green painted walls. Mexican blankets and paintings and sombreros hung from the walls, with a multicolored light of some kind above each table and booth. The colors were very festive, but the music was simply too loud. He could already feel a headache tapping at the front of his forehead with the beat of the drum.

He looked at his watch. They'd been waiting for thirty minutes, and it didn't seem anyone had been seated. He peered at Lacy. She seemed deep in conversation with the older woman sitting beside her.

He studied the woman he'd been so taken with for so many years. Her long brown hair was beautiful. It was sleek and straight and shone beneath the lights. Her facial features were dainty. All of them—eyes, nose, mouth, even her chin. She wore glasses, which really added to her features. She was a very pretty woman. It was the reason he'd been so attracted to her, but their conversation in the truck had taken him by surprise. Her features had twisted into an unattractiveness he'd not expected each time she spoke poorly of someone else.

He watched as Lacy leaned closer to the older woman and whispered something in her ear. The woman looked around Lacy and up at the hostess. She pursed her lips and nodded as she focused her attention back on Lacy. His date wrinkled her nose then opened her mouth and placed her finger inside in a gagging motion.

Mike looked up at the hostess. What could Lacy have been belittling her for? By the look on the woman's face, he believed she'd heard whatever Lacy said. Lacy was not the woman Mike thought she was.

Unable to take any more of the music, the smell, and most importantly the rudeness of his date, Mike took the pager back to the hostess. "Please mark McCauley off the list."

The woman frowned. "I'm sorry the wait is taking so long."

Lacy stood and peered at the woman. "If this restaurant were better staffed, it would—"

Mike lifted his hand to keep Lacy from saying anything further. He pulled some money from his wallet and handed it to the woman. "You're working very hard, and I appreciate your efforts. I hope no one has said or done anything that would make you feel otherwise."

The woman blushed, and Mike felt heat rise up his own neck and cheeks. He'd pushed aside his shyness so much in the last few weeks that he feared it was starting to get the best of him. Either that or the smell of the food finally made him sick.

He knew Lacy stood fuming beside him, but he didn't care. The woman had been nothing that Mike thought. Possibly Mike had dreamed her into something she wasn't. At the diner, when she waited his table, she'd always seemed so kind. Now he wondered if her irritations with Drew were proof of her true character. *I have to admit Drew can definitely irritate the most rational of people.*

With all the gentleness he could muster, he grabbed Lacy's elbow and walked out of the restaurant with her. She didn't say a word as he opened the passenger's door. Shutting the door behind her, he walked around to the driver's side. *God, give me grace to speak with humility and truth.*

After hopping in the cab, he started the truck. "I'm ready to head on home, but I'd love to buy you something from a drive-through. I know you must be hungry."

Lacy crossed her arms in front of her chest. She stared at him with all the contempt he expected. "What is going on, Mike?"

Her words sounded hateful and furious, and Mike knew he needed to be careful with everything he said. He cleared his throat. "Did that hostess do anything to upset you?"

She glared at him. "What are you talking about?"

"I saw you talking about her with the older woman. I wondered what the hostess did."

"You were on the other side of the room. You have no idea what we were saying."

Stealing his gaze away from the road for just a moment, he peered at her. "It was obvious by your gagging motion that you were unhappy with her.

That woman didn't deserve that."

Lacy leaned back against the seat. He couldn't see the steam rolling out of her ears and off the top of her head, but he felt confident that if it were possible, it would have been there. After several moments of silence, Lacy growled, "I cannot believe you would talk to me like that."

"Lacy, I can't believe you talked about your colleagues the way you did. It was embarrassing, and it made me feel uncomfortable. I don't need to hear such negative things about those people."

Lacy shifted in her seat. "Well, don't you just think you're Mr. Perfect. I didn't mean to burn your ears by the things I said."

"From everything I knew about you at the diner, I thought you were a Christian woman, a—"

"Are you judging my faith?"

Mike looked at her. "I guess I am questioning it."

Lacy sucked in her breath and looked out the passenger's window. Mike chewed his bottom lip. *Was that too much, Lord? That didn't feel like humility, even if it was truth.*

She'd never suggested a fast-food restaurant, and Mike had been too upset to offer again. With only a few miles to Lacy's house, Mike continued to pray that God would guide his parting words. He didn't want to be mean to Lacy, but he didn't want to be a part of her gossip, either.

He pulled into her driveway and turned off the ignition. Before he could get out, she opened the door. Mike reached for her arm, but she shrugged him away. "I don't mean to hurt your feelings, Lacy. I only want to be honest about. . ."

She hopped out of the truck and glared at him. "Thanks for nothing, Mike." Then she slammed the door.

⸎

Johanna snuggled into her bed. It had been a long day of planting flowers and baking homemade bread for all the mothers in their church family for Mother's Day. It had been a week since she'd been able to catch up on her favorite magazines.

As a lover of God's creation and an avid outdoorswoman, she devoured several magazines each month. Probably one of her favorites was the Kentucky-based fishing magazine that had gained a nationwide following. One of her favorite writers, or maybe he just intrigued her the most, was John James.

Whenever she read his articles, she always felt he wrote about River Run, and sometimes even Hickory Hill. It stood to reason a lot of places mentioned within its pages might seem like her hometown. But the descriptions in his articles sounded as if the author was someone from their area, someone who enjoyed the same places where she loved to bask in God's glory.

In her mind, she envisioned an older man, probably around five feet, six inches. He'd have a bushy white beard, and wear an aged brown fishing hat. His eyebrows would be as bushy as his beard and his deep blue eyes would mimic the color of a clear stream. He had a ready word of encouragement and a quick smile, and could easily be the grandfather of every child who'd ever wanted to learn to fish.

She found his newest article in the magazine. An caricatured smallmouth bass seemed to swim right off the page and toward a hook. She'd love to meet John James one day and find out if she was right about him.

She read the article he'd written about smallmouth bass. Every time she finished his writings, she always felt like a young girl on her first trip to the fishing pond with her mom. Something about the way he said and placed his words always brought back nostalgic feelings of childhood. She wondered if that was the reason she liked his writing so much. He wrote with pure innocence.

With her eyes growing heavy, she shut the magazine and placed it on the floor beside her bed. The distant sound of thunder lifted her lids. She looked at her bedroom door. Sure enough, Max stood in the doorway with his head lowered. The silly dog was terrified of storms. She patted the bed. "All right. Come on."

Max jumped onto the foot of the bed, and Johanna shook her head as the dog whimpered until she pressed her leg against his back. "You're such a chicken, Max."

Johanna looked at the bedroom door again. Max wouldn't be the last visitor for the night. Just as she expected, Amber stood in the doorway. She shrugged and ducked her head. "It's getting ready to storm."

"I know." She patted the empty side of her bed, thankful her parents had given her their old queen-size one.

She glanced back toward the door. Sometimes, if Bethany were already asleep, a storm wouldn't wake her. Her figure appeared in the doorway. To-night wasn't one of those nights. Johanna laughed. "Come on, Bethany. We'll make room."

Bethany settled in between her big sisters. After several shiftings, Johanna situated her legs to satisfy Max's need to have his back pressed against someone.

The room grew quiet except the occasional roll of thunder. Then Johanna heard the faint, muffled giggles from the room across the hall. She knew her parents found it hilarious that everyone got in bed with her when it stormed. Unable to resist, Johanna yelled, "Mom, Dad, I think I'm scared. I'm going to come in there and get in bed with you. Mine's too crowded."

"Oh, no you're not." Her mother laughed.

"You and Amber and Bethany and Max can all stay together in your room," her father added.

Her sisters broke out into giggles once more, and it took several minutes for the whole family to settle back down. Once they did, Johanna watched her bedroom window. Only a thin curtain covered the window of the second-story bedroom, and she could see the occasional flash of lightning.

Unlike her sisters, she enjoyed the storms. She always envisioned them as God's way of communicating with the earth and sky. He commanded His creation what He wanted, and when and how He wanted it done. She knew it was silly, just as believing thunder was God knocking down pins while bowling was silly. But she enjoyed storms anyway. They showed God's awesome majesty.

A flash of lightning and a clap of thunder sounded right outside the house, causing her to jump. Without a doubt, she served an awesome God.

Chapter 5

M ike woke up Monday morning with a heavy heart. He'd spent most of the day before with his mom and dad. It had been a hard day, being the first Mother's Day since Joe's death. He and his father had attended church, as they did every Sunday, without his mother. Then afterward, they took her to lunch.

In years past, they would drive to Lexington and take her to the mall to pick out a new summer dress. He and Joe, and if truth be told, their father, viewed it as the most sacrificial, painful task they could do for their mother. This year she refused to go, saying she didn't have anywhere to wear a new dress. He missed the shopping trip. It broke his heart to see his mother carry so much bitterness.

But it wasn't just his mother that had him feeling blue. He continued to dwell on his date with Lacy on Saturday. How could he have been so wrong about her? He'd spent years fawning after her at the diner. He should have been paying attention to who she was as a person and not just that she was a pretty waitress. *God, I've been looking at her superficially, and I know better than that.*

Trying to push the gloom to the back of his mind, he put on his work clothes. Looking outside the window, he noted the looming dark clouds and a good wind blowing the treetops. Looked like a rainy day was about to set in. That was all he needed.

He forced himself to perk up. They did need a good rain. A good, day-long, steady one. Just because he felt a little down didn't mean he needed to be taking it out on the weather. He picked up his ball cap and put it on his head. "Enough of this whining. It's time to head to the farm. Mom will have breakfast ready."

Two years ago he'd bought the old farmhouse and property that backed up to his family's farm. He'd had to do a lot of work to it. Put in a new toilet and shower. Had to tear up the existing floor and lay tile and hardwood. It still wasn't fit for a family, as it needed more insulation and new windows so it would be cooler in the summer and warmer in the winter, but it allowed him to be on his own and still farm with his father.

A drizzle started when he got in his pickup. By the time he'd reached his parents' house, a steady rain fell from the sky. He ran up to the porch and wiped his boots on the front mat, lifted his ball cap off his head, and brushed the raindrops off his shirt. Sucking in a deep breath to prepare for his mother's doldrums, he opened the front door. "Steady rain outside."

"We need it," his father called from the kitchen.

He joined his father in the kitchen and saw his mother standing at the sink, staring out the window. "Not so many years ago, you boys would have been out there getting all wet and muddy, and I'd be hollering at you to come inside."

His mother's voice was low, little more than a whisper. The pain she felt seeped through every syllable. He wished he could help her. She was already taking medicine. Though his father didn't say it outright, Mike knew his dad monitored how much she took.

Mike wanted to shake his mother, to poke into her head that she would never come out of this depression until she allowed God to heal her heart. But she was still mad at God for taking her son.

He and his father had grieved as well. Grieved miserably. Still grieved at times. But they sought God's healing. It was his own father who reminded him once that God understood the pain they felt. That His Son had paid the ultimate price for our sins. Tears had streamed down his dad's cheeks at the realization that God truly understood his pain. Mike would never forget that conversation. He'd never before known such admiration and respect for his father's strength through Christ.

"Mom, the bacon smells wonderful." Trying to change the subject, Mike sat down beside his father at the table. He picked up several pieces and put them on the plate his mother had already set out for him. He scooped up a spoonful of scrambled eggs then grabbed a couple of biscuits out of a bowl. "Would you mind to bring me some coffee?"

His mother turned away from the window and smiled at him. "Sure."

His mother was naturally hospitable, and he'd learned as a little boy that nothing pleased her more than to take care of her sons. She grabbed the pot off the coffeemaker and poured the hot liquid into a mug. The smile that didn't quite reach her eyes remained on her face until she placed the coffee in front of him then sat down beside his father.

He noticed she stared at the mug she'd given him. He looked at it and realized it was the one with a picture Joe had drawn in elementary school. This one had a stick figure of Joe with the mutt dog they'd had when he was in first grade. The little rascal had gotten out one day, ventured onto their country road, and was struck and killed by one of their neighbors. Joe had cried for two weeks straight.

Mike looked up at his mother. She placed her elbow on the table then cupped her hand over her forehead. After a moment, she rubbed her hand across her face. "I think I'm going to go lie down for a bit."

She stood, and Mike watched as she left the room. "Not a good day today, huh?"

Mike studied his father as he shook his head. His dad had aged since Joe's passing. His dark hair was now streaked with more gray than brown. Deep bags darkened his eyes. He'd lost weight as well.

His dad sucked in a deep breath. "Nope. It's not going to be a good day for your mother." He filled his coffee cup with the pot Mike's mother had left on the table. He sat all the way back in his chair. "So, tell me what's been going on."

Mike shrugged. "Nothing much. Working the farm and writing articles. Same as always."

His dad shook his head and made a loud hissing noise as he sucked air between his two front teeth. "No. Something else is going on."

Mike wrapped his hands around the coffee mug, enjoying the warmth of the brew. He had no intention of burdening his father with his inner struggle over Lacy or the fact that he was the biggest loser of all his friends. He sounded whiny in his own ears. He surely didn't want to add any more silliness to all his father had to deal with. He looked at his father but couldn't quite make contact with his eyes as he said, "Everything's fine."

His dad sat forward. "Boy, I thought I taught you better than to lie to me." He grabbed a piece of bacon and crunched a bite out of it. "Now, tell me the truth."

Mike grinned at his father. He may have been spending every day of the last several months with the stress he'd feel with a two-year drought, but he still paid attention to what was going on with Mike. It was one of the things he loved about his father. One of the things he hoped he would be able to show to his own children one day. "There's no getting anything past you, is there?"

"Nope. As long as there's breath in this old man's body"—he pointed to his chest—"I'm going to be involved in your life."

Mike couldn't hold back the chuckle at his father's words. They sounded familiar, as they were the same ones he'd said throughout his teenage years when Mike rebelled in some form or fashion. "All right. I might as well start at the beginning." He pointed to the window. Rain streamed down as if being poured straight down from buckets in the sky. "Looks like we have a minute."

His dad nodded. "God knows when a good rain's needed."

Mike chewed on the wisdom of his father's words. He scratched his jaw, noting a spot he'd missed shaving. "A long time ago, Wyatt, Nick, Drew, and I made a bet."

"The no-women bet."

Mike gaped at his dad. "How did you know about it?"

"Son, everyone in town knew about it. I thought it was quite funny. Knew it wouldn't last long, but I still thought it was humorous."

Mike peered at his father. He wondered how many things the old man knew about. He thought of the times he and his buddies went mudding without permission, and the one time in particular when they'd busted the radiator. Luckily, Drew had been able to figure out how to fix it.

His father crossed his legs. "Now don't be worrying about all the things I know or don't know. Go on."

Mike rubbed his temple. "I'd always thought it was a kind of stupid bet. I'm not really as competitive as the other guys, but it was supposed to be just for fun, and I always lose anyway. Well. . ." He paused for a moment. "I guess this time I wanted to lose."

"But you're the winner."

Mike smacked his thigh. "I know. Doesn't that beat all? The first thing I actually do win I never wanted to."

"So how does Lacy come into all this?"

"Dad." Mike placed his elbows on the table and leaned closer to his father. "How could you possibly know about Lacy?"

"I told you I'm keeping tabs. So, how did the date go?"

Mike decided it wasn't worth it to ask how his father knew about their date Saturday night. He might as well just tell him how it went. "It was awful. She's not the woman I thought she was." Mike's cheeks warmed. "Even as I say that I feel wrong to say anything bad about her to you, and yet foolish that I've liked the woman for so long."

"Hmm. Son, it's good you went out with Lacy. Now you know she's not the woman God has for you."

"I know." Mike sat back in his seat again. He looked at the empty bowl that had been full of biscuits earlier.

"Then what's the matter?"

"I shouldn't have been spending all that time pining over her. I should have just asked her out three years ago and figured it out then."

His dad placed his elbows on the table and clasped his hands. "Son, you've changed so much in the last three years, especially since your brother passed away. Maybe you weren't ready to go out with her then. Maybe you wouldn't have been as in tune to what God wants for you—until now."

His dad pushed away from the table and stood. "The rain's settling down. You wanna clean up the kitchen for Mom or go check on the animals?"

Knowing how much his father detested doing dishes, Mike said, "I'll clean up and meet you out there in a few minutes."

He thought about his father's words as he rinsed off the dishes and placed them in the dishwasher. His faith had grown since his brother passed. And though he was still naturally shy, he knew he was more confident than he'd ever been and more willing to stand up for what was right. *God, You know what You want for my life, and Dad is right—You've grown me up a lot in the last few years. I still want a wife. I want all that I see my friends have. I ask You to help me find one. The right one.*

⁕

Johanna hefted her purse higher on her shoulder then raced into the grocery store. Today was Amber's seventeenth birthday and she'd promised her sister she'd make her a chocolate crème pie from scratch.

But the day had not started well. First, her boss phoned asking her to come in for the morning because one of the workers called in sick. Knowing Mrs. Love would be shorthanded with the monthly women's book club meeting at ten, she simply couldn't decline. Thankfully, she'd had the presence of mind to place the ingredients for Amber's pie on the counter. Which was how she discovered they were out of cocoa. She couldn't believe it; they were never out of cocoa.

Johanna looked at her watch. It was 1:30. Her mother had invited several families from church over at 5:30. Johanna was really going to have to rush to get the pie finished before then. Not to mention she had to run into River Run's grocery store, one she was not familiar with.

Peering down at the list of items her mother asked her to pick up, "since you have to go anyway," she grabbed a cart and headed toward the aisle with the baking ingredients sign above it.

Thankfully, the store was almost empty, so she found potato chips and plastic cups with relative ease. Her cell phone rang. She pulled it out of her purse and pushed the TALK button.

Her mother's voice sounded through the line. "Are you still at the store?"

"Yes."

"Go ahead and pick up a couple of two-liters of something diet. I thought I had some, but I can't find them."

Johanna glanced at her watch again. It wasn't her mother's fault she'd been called in to work that morning. But with each minute that passed, Johanna feared she wouldn't be able to finish the pie her sister had requested practically every day for the last month. "Okay. I'll be home soon."

She pushed the END button and looked at the signs above the aisles for soft drinks. Spying them, she rushed toward the aisle. *I think I might have a coupon.*

She continued to walk as she rummaged through her purse. Her cart jolted. She looked and saw she'd bumped into someone. Someone wearing tennis shoes. Which probably meant the back of his ankles would really hurt. "I'm so sorry."

The man lifted his right foot a bit as he turned to face her. "No prob— You?"

It couldn't be. It simply was not possible. There stood the same man she'd run into at the barn and on the sidewalk. She was normally a very careful person, but it seemed as if some weird force propelled her to wound this man in some way.

Her cheeks warmed and her hands shook slightly until she gripped the cart handle. "I—I don't know what to say."

A smile bowed the man's lips, and Johanna couldn't help but admit how cute he was. He extended his hand. "I think I'd better introduce myself to you before you need to notify my family."

Johanna frowned. "Notify your family?"

"Yeah. The next time you run into me, you may put me in the hospital."

A new wave of warmth washed over Johanna's face and neck, but she reached and accepted the man's handshake. Her heart raced when their hands touched. She shook hands with plenty of men at church, but never with the reaction this one evoked.

He tipped his head. "Mike McCauley."

"Hi. I'm Johanna Smith."

He motioned toward her cart. "You getting ready for a picnic?"

Johanna swallowed back the knot in her throat. She seemed to have lost all the saliva in her mouth as well. "It's my sister's seventeenth birthday. We're having a cookout with our church family."

He raised one eyebrow, and Johanna noted again how beautiful his blue-green eyes were. They reminded her of the sky and grass all wrapped up into one gorgeous color. Unsure what to do, she continued, "My sister wanted me to make her a chocolate crème pie, and we didn't have any cocoa." She pointed to the container in the cart. "Then Mama asked me to pick up a few things. And now I barely have time to get home and get the pie made."

Yet another wave of heat washed over her. Only this time, a cold sweat added itself to her nervousness. She gripped the cart handle until her knuckles turned white. Needing to get out of there, she nodded. "I'll see you later." She furrowed her eyebrows. "I'm sure you don't want to see me later. I mean— well—bye."

Johanna rushed to the checkout line. God blessed her with an empty lane, and she was able to pay for the groceries quickly. Pushing the cart outside, she inhaled the warm fresh air and allowed the breeze to calm her.

God, that was so embarrassing. That man must think I'm a complete idiot.

He wasn't just "that man." She knew his name now. "Mike McCauley," she whispered.

Getting his face out of her thoughts would be impossible now. Plus she had the sound of his voice to add to her thinking. This time she noticed he wasn't wearing a wedding ring. Not the groom at the wedding.

Johanna Smith, what are you thinking? she inwardly chastised herself. Opening the trunk of her car and placing the bags inside, she shut it then walked the cart to the cart rack. With just over three hours to get home, make the pie, and help her mother with the cookout, she needed to focus on Amber's birthday.

Sliding into the front seat of the car, she looked in her rearview mirror and saw a mother cradling an infant with one arm and holding the hand of a toddler with her other hand. The little guy tripped and fell forward without bracing his fall. She hopped out of the car to volunteer her help. She couldn't stand to see a child hurt.

Chapter 6

Mike walked out of the grocery store and saw Johanna jump out of a car and rush to a woman holding a baby. Once he pushed his cart closer to his truck, he could see the woman also had a small boy with her. He must have fallen, because Johanna bent down and helped the little guy up.

The boy's screams pealed through the parking lot, and Mike saw a scrape on his chin. The boy held his palms up to Johanna and his mother, and Mike knew he probably hurt his hands, too.

He heard Johanna say, "I have a first-aid kit in my car."

He knew he was being nosy, but he watched as Johanna scooped the boy into her arms and walked to the car. The boy was too focused on his wounds to fight off the stranger who'd picked him up. The woman, who now looked on the verge of tears herself, followed Johanna to the car.

"It's so hard to try to bring both of them to the store, but my husband works double shifts a lot," the woman said as her voice cracked.

"I'm sure it's very difficult." Johanna's voice was calm. "We'll have him all fixed up in a second."

Mike watched as Johanna, still holding the screaming child, dug into the glove compartment and pulled out a large baggie of various first aid supplies.

"It's okay. We're going to make it all better. What's your name, big guy?"

"His name is Henry." The mother bounced the baby while Johanna opened a few packages of cleansing wipes.

"There now, Henry," Johanna cooed at the child as she wiped his wounds. He screamed and fought, but Johanna remained calm and continued to murmur to him in a soothing tone.

The baby in the woman's arms began to cry, and the woman grabbed a pacifier from her pocket and put it in the baby's mouth. "It's okay, sweetie." She began to bounce the baby more fervently and rocked from side to side.

"Now, this will make it feel better." Johanna opened some cream and applied it to his chin, hands, and knees. His cries shifted to whimpers when she pulled out some kind of cartoon bandages.

A few times the boy actually cackled over his whimpers when she put the brightly colored plastic strips on his hands. Johanna glanced at the mother. "Do you need some help getting your things from the store?"

"No." The woman shook her head, but Mike could tell she was shaken and overwhelmed. "I'll be fine."

"Why don't you let me help you? I don't have anything in my trunk that will ruin."

The woman sighed and smiled. "I'd really appreciate it."

Mike watched as Johanna grabbed her purse out of her car. She looked his way, and she averted her gaze. He knew she'd seen him, though.

Sneaking another peek, he watched as she carried the boy and followed the woman into the store. He knew she was in a hurry. Making a chocolate crème pie for her sister's birthday. But she'd taken time she didn't have to help out the harried mother.

He hopped into the truck cab and turned the ignition. *God, are You trying to tell me something? Is that why she keeps bumping into me?*

⁕

Johanna didn't get home until almost four. Thankfully, her father had come home from work early and helped with the food preparation. Her sisters had cleaned the house spotless, and she would have just enough time to fix her sister's pie. A warm pie tasted better than a cold one anyway.

She tried to focus on the ingredients for the dessert, but her mind kept drifting back to running into Mike at the grocery. He seemed much kinder than her first impression, and she could no longer deny the attraction she felt.

When she saw him in the parking lot, watching her— She whipped the meringue for the top of the pie with more fervor. She'd never felt so queasy inside.

Her mother walked up behind her and said, "Gavin and his family will be here in just a bit. I believe chocolate meringue is his favorite also."

Johanna nodded but didn't say anything in response. Her mother had been dropping more hints than usual, and it made Johanna anxious. She wanted to be herself around Gavin. The way they'd been for as long as she could remember.

They'd dug out earthworms for bait together, fished together, gone gigging together. She even shot her first buck on a trip with Gavin and their fathers.

I can't even think of Gavin as a husband.

She tried to envision what it would be like to kiss her playpen pal, as they used to call each other. She wrinkled her nose at the thought; then a vision of kissing Mike McCauley popped into her mind. Heat warmed her cheeks at how much she liked the idea. *God, I know nothing about this man. Or about kissing. Forgive me for these ridiculous thoughts.*

"What do you think?"

Amber's voice interrupted her thoughts. She looked at her sister who had her hands on her hips. Amber made a sweeping motion from her shoulders to her knees. The bright-pink-and-white capris outfit suited her sister to perfection. Johanna clapped. "You look absolutely gorgeous."

"And I can finally wear makeup." Amber walked closer to her and batted her eyelashes.

Several of the younger girls at their small church were already allowed to wear makeup. Her daddy detested it and wouldn't allow his daughters to wear makeup until they turned seventeen, and only as long as they wore it sparingly. "It looks really good. You did it very tastefully. Your eyes look more green than I've ever seen them."

Amber giggled. "Mama helped, of course."

Johanna hugged her younger sister. As excited as she was now, Johanna couldn't imagine what Amber would do when she found out Mama and Daddy had decided to enroll her in public high school after all.

Amber sneaked her finger into the chocolate part of the pie, and Johanna gently swatted it. "Amber, it's not finished yet."

Amber shrugged as she stuck her finger in her mouth. "Mmm. Tastes so good. And it is my birthday."

A car sounded in the driveway, and Amber jumped. People were starting to arrive. She patted Johanna's arm. "I'm so excited."

She raced out of the kitchen, and Johanna quickly folded the meringue onto the top of the pie. She put it on a cookie sheet and placed it in the oven. It would be ready in fifteen minutes. She wiped her hands on a kitchen towel and walked out the back door to welcome whomever had arrived.

It was the Mitchell family. One boy after another unloaded from the van. Mrs. Mitchell had a son every three to four years from the time twenty-one-year-old Gavin was born all the way down to their newest six-month-old addition. All boys.

Johanna couldn't help but feel a bit sorry for the frazzled woman. The boys were all healthy and strong and helped their father on the farm, but that left little to no help for her. And lots more work.

Amber already stood beside the van, ready to take the youngest Mitchell boy from his car seat. She loved children as much as she loved music, and Johanna knew one day her sister would make a wonderful mother.

Gavin slipped out of the van, unbuckled the baby, and handed him to Amber. She smiled up at him, and for a moment, Johanna wondered if Gavin and Amber would be a good match when she got older. When the idea didn't bother her, Johanna knew Gavin was not, could not, be the man for her. Though she never wanted to be a jealous person, she still would need to have some inkling of concern if she thought of the man she loved with another woman.

No. Gavin was her friend. She did love him, but not in the way her mom wished. When the time was right, she would have to talk with her mother.

Johanna looked down and realized she hadn't changed since she'd gotten home. Still wearing the long black slacks and blue blouse she'd worn to the library that morning, she needed something different to wear. After eating, they'd be playing cornhole and croquet.

After getting the pie out of the oven, she ran upstairs and pulled a pair of denim capris and a T-shirt out of her dresser drawer and put them on. She heard her name from outside the window, and she peered outside to see her mother talking to Gavin. She listened carefully as her mother said, "Johanna made a chocolate meringue pie. It's your favorite, isn't it?"

"Yes, ma'am," he responded.

"Well, I'll be sure. . ."

Johanna could take it no longer. She stuck her head out the window and yelled as sweetly as she could muster. "Mama, could I see you a minute?"

Her mom gasped as she looked up at Johanna. "What are you doing upstairs, dear? We have company."

"I just need you for a moment, Mama."

Johanna watched as her mother headed toward the back door. She waved at Gavin. He smiled up at her and winked. Again, she couldn't figure out if he was just being her friend, as he'd always been, or if he was looking for something more. Those thoughts would have never even entered her mind if her mother hadn't placed them there. She hated feeling so weird around Gavin.

She paced back and forth in front of her bed as she waited for her mother to come up the stairs. *God, show me how to say this to Mama in the right way. She's got to stop. It's not fair to me or to him. Lord, it's just not fair. And I need her to listen to me. Not to brush me off. God. . .*

"Yes, Johanna, what is it? Why are you hidden up here in your room instead of with our guests?"

Johanna studied her mother. The woman looked so much younger than her forty years. Many people often thought they were sisters when they first met them. It used to drive Johanna crazy until someone mentioned that possibly God would bless her with the look-young-forever gene as well.

Her mother lived the life Johanna yearned for. She was a wife and mother. She tended an herbal and a vegetable garden, cared for strawberries and fruit trees. She loved to fish and hunt, all the things Johanna wanted out of life. And Johanna could have them with Gavin if he offered, but she'd be missing the one thing she wanted the most. She didn't look at Gavin the way Mama looked at Daddy. She didn't love him. Somehow, she had to get her mother to see that.

"Mama, I came up here to change clothes." She lifted her chin. "I heard you talking to Gavin."

Her mother frowned. "I said nothing wrong to Gavin." She swatted at the air. "I merely told him that you'd made the pie and that—"

"Mama, stop it."

Her mother looked at her.

"Please." Johanna sat on the edge of the bed. "Mama, I don't feel toward Gavin the way you'd like me to feel."

"Gavin is a good match for you."

"He's perfect." Johanna looked up at her mother, who started to smile. "But I don't love him."

Her mother shook her head. "I have told you that marriage is about friendship and commitment—"

"But it's also about love. I want what you and Daddy have."

With a heavy sigh, her mother lowered into the sitting chair beside the door. "We didn't always have love, Johanna."

Johanna sat forward, studying her mother's face. What was she saying? Johanna had just assumed her parents had fallen in love as teens and had been in love ever since. "What are you saying, Mama?"

Her mother let out a deep breath. "When I was a young woman, I was in love. But it was with another man."

Johanna swallowed the knot in her throat and gaped at her mother. "What?"

Her mother nodded. "I was. The man's name was Jimmy." She looked into Johanna's eyes, and Johanna knew it hurt her mother to talk about it. But she had to know, had to hear what her mother was about to say.

"Jimmy really liked me, but I wasn't the only girl he liked. And after dating me for six months, Jimmy decided to marry the other girl. The girl I didn't even know had existed all that time."

Her mother stood and started to pace. "I was devastated. I couldn't eat. I couldn't sleep. I couldn't do anything. Your grandparents were worried sick about me."

She wrung her hands together. "Of course, you know your father met me in Tennessee. It's where all of my family is from. Well, when Jimmy finally did marry the girl, I went into an even deeper depression."

She sat on the edge of the bed beside Johanna. "Then a traveling preacher came through our town. He was kind to me and prayed for me and with me. I knew he cared for me more than I cared for him."

Her mother averted her gaze, and Johanna tried to make sense of what her mother tried to tell her.

"When he asked me to marry him"—her mother closed her eyes—"in my heart, I knew I didn't love him. I just needed to get away from Jimmy."

"You married Daddy to get away from someone else?"

Her mother stood again. "I'm so ashamed of the way I behaved back then. What I felt for Jimmy wasn't true love, it was selfishness and my desire to have what I wanted. Your daddy knew I struggled with my feelings, but he loved me and was patient with me, and when you came along—"

"You still didn't love Daddy even after I was born?"

Her mother walked over to her and wrapped her arm around Johanna's shoulders. "It took awhile, honey. That's why I know exactly what I'm talking about when I tell you marriage is about commitment and friendship. I love your daddy with a love that can only be explained by God. But I do love him."

Her mother kissed the top of her head. "Think about what I've said for a minute, but not too long. Amber will want you to be with her for her party."

Johanna stared at the window as her mother left the room. She could hardly believe what Mama had told her. She hadn't loved her daddy when they married. It was a love like theirs that she longed for.

She walked to the window and peered outside at Gavin playing cornhole with his dad, her father, and one of his younger brothers. He'd always been such a good friend. Maybe she was wrong not to believe she could love him.

Again, Mike McCauley's face flashed through her mind. She didn't even know the man. She had no reason to think about him as much as she did. *God,*

I'm just going to go outside and enjoy my sister's birthday. I'm leaving all the love stuff to You. She chuckled. *For right now. You know I'm probably going to bother You about it again later.*

Johanna joined her family outside. No matter where he went, she couldn't help but watch Gavin. She still didn't feel any kind of love for him, but she wondered if she could.

"It's time for presents," her father announced, and Amber squealed.

Their friends and family gathered around the folding table her father had set up in the backyard under the large oak tree.

Loving every moment of the spotlight, Amber oohed and aahed over each gift. Johanna found herself wishing Amber could open presents for her on her birthday, as Johanna always wanted to find somewhere to hide when people watched her.

Once Amber had opened the last present, her mother produced a small package from behind her back. "You have one last gift, Amber."

Amber's eyes lit with delight as their little sister, Bethany, urged her to open it quickly. Relishing her last present, Amber gingerly tore back the paper. She opened the box and pulled out the single sheet of folded-up paper. She scrunched her nose. "What is this?"

Her dad smiled. "Well, open it."

Johanna feared she would burst, she was so excited for Amber to figure out what it was. She rubbed her hands together while Amber unfolded the paper and read the top. Her sister's eyes widened and her mouth fell open. Amber jumped up from her chair and waved the paper in the air. "Is this what I think it is?"

Johanna burst into laughter.

"Is it?" Amber looked at her parents again.

Her dad stood and wrapped his arms around Amber. "It's your enrollment paper for high school. You're going to be a high school senior this year."

Amber squealed and wrapped her arms around her dad. Her mother joined the hug, and Johanna could wait no longer. She grabbed Bethany, and the two of them wrapped their arms around their parents and Amber.

Her father broke away. "Remember you're to be a light in the world. If we feel this is too much, we will take you back out of school."

"I know, Daddy."

He patted Amber's back as he addressed their friends from church. "Why don't we all go inside so Amber can play the piece she's been working on?

My girl here is planning to play in college."

Johanna grabbed hold of Amber's arm. "I'm so happy for you."

"Did you know?"

Johanna nodded. "I thought I would pop if your birthday didn't hurry up and get here."

They walked inside, and Amber sat at the piano. The room was crowded, but most of the younger children stayed outside playing games.

Amber beamed when she began to play. Her fingers moved over the keys with a grace and ease Johanna had never seen from anyone else. Happiness filled her for the pure joy that shone from her sister's face.

Johanna looked around the room. She spied Gavin watching Amber. There was something about the way he looked at her. It reminded her of the way her daddy looked at her mama.

Again, she wondered if she should feel some sort of jealousy. She didn't, and no matter what her mother had experienced, Johanna could never be the one to take that look of affection away from her sister.

Chapter 7

A few days after Drew and Melody returned from their honeymoon, Mike walked up the sidewalk to Nick and Addy's house. They'd planned a get-together with Wyatt and Gracie, Drew and Melody, Nick and Addy, and Mike. He felt like a complete fifth wheel; actually, it was more like a seventh wheel.

Before he reached the porch steps, the front door swung open and Addy ran out. She beamed at Mike. "Gracie's water broke."

Mike lifted his eyebrows and glanced back at the driveway. He hadn't noticed Wyatt's car.

"They hadn't made it here yet." Addy turned back toward the house. "Come on, Melody. Just leave the water boiling. The men can finish the corn on the cob."

"I'm coming." Melody's voice sounded from inside the door.

Addy turned back toward Mike. "It's just going to be you, Nick, and Drew. We're heading to the hospital. There's plenty of food. You all can just hang out here. . . ."

"I'm ready." Melody raced through the front door. Drew followed close behind her. She started down the steps when Drew pulled her back and kissed her lips.

Mike's cheeks warmed at the display of affection. Not because he was embarrassed, but because he realized how much he wanted that.

Melody pushed Drew away. "Honey, I've got to go. Gracie waited for us to get home. I can't ask her to wait for me to get to the hospital, too."

Drew laughed. "Melody, I don't think you had all that much say in when that woman went into labor."

Melody swatted the air with her hand. She glanced at Mike and waved. "Nice to see you again, Mike."

He nodded and then moved out of her and Addy's way as they barreled down the steps. Within seconds, the two had jumped into Addy's car and were headed down the road.

Drew opened the door wide and motioned to Mike. "Looks like it's just going to be the three of us."

Mike grinned. He was glad. It had been a long time since he'd spent time with just his buddies. Except for Wyatt's bachelor party and then Nick's bachelor party and then Drew's. But even then poor Drew had been so torn up and excited about the upcoming wedding that they weren't able to enjoy the truck pull they'd gone to.

He wondered if he'd ever have a bachelor party they could go to.

He walked inside as Nick was coming in the back door holding a plate of freshly grilled burgers. Nick bellowed, "Looks like we can eat as much as we want."

Mike surveyed the counter filled with hamburgers and fixings, homemade potato salad and coleslaw, corn on the cob cooking in a pot on the stove, and some kind of cobbler, probably blackberry, sitting on the kitchen table. The variety and volume of food had certainly improved with the additions of his friends' wives. It looked delicious, and his stomach rumbled in response.

Drew patted his back. "I think the man wants to eat."

Mike turned and grabbed Drew's hand in a firm handshake. "It's good to see you, buddy. Sounded like you were having a good time on your honeymoon."

Drew's eyes lit up, and he beamed brighter than the sun beats down on a man in the middle of a field on the hottest day of August. "It was awesome. So did you take my advice before your date with Lacy?"

Nick stopped loading his plate with food and turned toward Drew and Mike. "Wait a minute. Are you saying you talked to Mike before he went on his date? Weren't you on your honeymoon?"

Mike laughed. "Yes, he was. I couldn't believe it when I saw his number on my phone."

Drew shrugged and grabbed an empty plate. "Mike's my friend, and I wanted him to relax and enjoy his date."

Nick snickered. "He's my friend, too, but he's the last thing I'd be thinking about on my honeymoon."

Drew put down the plate and lifted his hands in surrender. "Okay. Okay. I get it." He placed a hamburger bun on the plate. "So, how did the date go?"

Mike growled. "It was awful."

"What happened?" asked Nick as he turned off the stove then jabbed a corncob with his fork.

Mike plopped an oversize spoonful of potato salad on his plate. "We weren't very compatible. I don't believe we have the same beliefs when it comes to our faith. She just— I really don't want to say anything negative. Let's just leave it with we didn't agree on a few things."

"Yeah. I was afraid of that." Drew took a bite of his hamburger then headed toward the kitchen table and sat down.

With their plates overflowing, Nick and Mike joined Drew at the table.

"That's too bad, man." Nick took a drink of his soft drink.

"I spent too long worrying over that girl." Mike swallowed a bite of coleslaw. "Now I've already got another gal floating around in my mind all the time. Course, I should be afraid of her. Every time I see her she hits me in some way."

"What?" Drew leaned closer to the table and shook a pickle at him. "Mike McCauley, the man who warded off women all through middle and high school, who had a crush on the same woman for three years, goes out with her, and finds out he doesn't like her, so he finds another girl he's interested in—in a week's time?"

Mike wrinkled his nose and gawked at Drew. "Man, I have no idea what you just said."

Nick swallowed a big bite of hamburger then laughed. "So there's a new girl. Tell us about her."

Mike told them about Johanna knocking the bottles of bubbles out of his hands and then busting his lip at the barn before the wedding. Then he shared how she'd run him off the sidewalk and then slammed into his ankles in the grocery store. He held up his leg and lifted the back of his jeans to show them the mark. "I'm telling you the woman practically ran me over with that cart."

"Hmm, a cute woman who beats up on you every time you see her." Drew shrugged. "I guess she sounds interesting, if you like to be covered in bumps and bruises."

Nick guffawed and punched Drew in the arm. "Maybe you should go for her."

Drew winced and rubbed the spot Nick punched. "Ow. That hurt. I'm still a little burned there from the honeymoon. It's above my farmer's tan line."

Mike almost spit out his food at Drew's whining. He turned to Nick. "Actually, I've been kind of thinking that myself, but I don't know how to get in touch with her. I know what she looks like and I know her name, but that's all I know."

"So who is she?" Drew asked.

"She's a cutie, long blond hair. All I know is her name is Johanna Smith.

We introduced ourselves at the store in case the next time she ran into me I'd need to go to the hospital."

Nick pulled the hamburger out of his mouth without taking a bite. "Did you say Johanna Smith?"

"Yeah."

Nick placed his hamburger back on the plate and touched his arm about midway down. "Long blond hair. Thin girl. Maybe a little shorter than Addy."

Mike nodded.

Nick smacked the table. "Doesn't that just beat all. Addy and I just worked with that gal last week at the library."

"What?"

"Yeah. Remember I told you the librarian lady had asked me to do this fair thing for the preschool and kindergarten kids and bring one of my calves for the kiddos to look at?"

Mike nodded. He had a vague remembrance of Nick telling him something about that.

Nick pointed his fork at Mike. "That girl. Johanna Smith. She was one of the librarian's helpers there. She read a book about spring to the kids." He shoved a bite of coleslaw in his mouth. "Seemed like a nice girl," he muttered. "Addy really liked her."

"The library, huh?" Mike sat back in his chair. It made sense. The library was just a ways down the road from where she'd run into him on the sidewalk. He'd have to conjure up a reason to patronize the place. After several moments, he looked up at his friends who were both staring at him and grinning. Warmth flooded his face, and he swatted at them. "Let's talk about something else. Drew, tell us about Florida."

Drew shared that Melody had talked him into going scuba diving. He raved about the various fish, stingrays, and jellyfish he'd had the opportunity to see.

Mike tried to focus on his friend, but his mind kept drifting to when he'd have an opportunity to head to the library. He could say he needed to do some research on their computers, but that would be a lie, as he had Internet availability at his home. Though he enjoyed magazines, he wasn't much of a book reader. Informational books maybe, but he did most of his reading on his computer.

I could just go in there and tell her I'd like to go on a date, rather than wait three years like I did with Lacy.

The very idea made his heart race and his hands grow clammy. If she said no, he'd be mortified. *I'm still going to be embarrassed even if she says yes.*

Drew's voice interrupted his thoughts. "And then we jumped into a pool of sharks, and one of them bit off Melody's leg."

Mike wrinkled his nose and furrowed his eyebrows. "What?"

Drew laughed. "Are you still with us, buddy? I think you went off into space for a while."

Mike squinted at his friend. "Aren't you just hilarious?"

Nick elbowed Drew's side. "I think our friend here is pining over another girl."

Mike didn't admit it aloud, but he believed he was.

<hr/>

"It's opening day for frog gigging!" Johanna exclaimed when she walked in the house after work. "I've got the gigs all ready."

Johanna and her mother had a tradition to frog gig up at their family's pond on opening night. She looked forward to the May event every year. The day before, Johanna would search the shed for their gigs, which were simply metal three-pronged forks attached to old broomsticks—homemade fishing spears. Near midnight, wearing the oldest pants and shoes they could find, she and her mother would walk and steal around the banks of the pond with a bright flashlight in one hand and the gig in the other.

Listening carefully for the distinct *varuump* of a bullfrog, they would shine the light in its eyes, freezing the amphibian for a moment, then jab the gig into the frog's body, and stick it in an onion sack. After collecting several, they'd head home, clean their catch, and the next day the family would enjoy a dinner of fried frog legs. As long as their dad didn't get anxious and make their mom fry them up with breakfast.

"Johanna." Her mother's voice sounded weak as she called from her upstairs bedroom.

"Mama doesn't feel well." Bethany walked into the kitchen. "She asked me to start dinner. Amber's in the basement doing laundry."

Johanna made her way up the stairs and into her parents' bedroom. Her mother's face was as pale as the white sheets, and droplets of sweat beaded on her forehead. She tried to smile. "I don't think I can make it gigging tonight. I believe I've caught a bug."

Johanna picked up a washrag from the end table and wiped off her mother's brow. "I believe you have." She looked at her mother's nearly empty glass. "You want me to get you some water?"

Her mother nodded. "Haven't held much down today, but I wouldn't mind to try a few saltine crackers again. The Mitchell boys started getting sick from a stomach bug right after they left the other night. I'd say I caught it from one of them."

Johanna nodded. "I'll go get you some water and crackers."

She made her way down the stairs to the main floor as Amber clunked up from the basement with a load of folded clothes. She placed the basket on the table with a huff. "Whew. Those are heavy." She turned toward Johanna. "I told Mama I'd go gigging with you tonight."

Johanna lifted her eyebrows and pointed to her sister. "You're going to go gigging with me tonight." To her knowledge, her sister had never touched a live frog let alone a dead one, though she never minded to eat her fill of Johanna and their mother's catch.

Amber giggled as she smacked and rubbed her hands together. "I know. There's a first time for everything."

Bethany wrinkled her nose and flipped a mass of long blond hair over her shoulder. "I wouldn't mind to pick up the frogs, but I don't want to kill them."

"Don't play with your hair while you're cooking," Johanna reprimanded her youngest sister.

Bethany stuck out her tongue. "Good thing you're not my boss." She stuck out her bottom lip. "You could have asked me nicely."

Johanna wrapped one arm around Bethany, who had always been the most sensitive of the three girls. "You're right. I just hate that Mama's sick. She loves gigging. Do you want to go with Amber and me tonight?"

Bethany turned back to the hamburger frying in the skillet. "No way."

Johanna looked back at Amber. "I think you're going to have a lot more fun than you expect."

She took a can of chicken noodle soup from the pantry and opened it. She poured its contents in a pan and added a cup of water. Her mother had only asked for crackers and water, but she looked so pale that maybe she could try a bit of soup, too.

Once it finished warming, she gathered the soup, saltines, and water for her mother and went back upstairs. Her mom had already propped several pillows up behind her. Johanna smiled at her mom. "I hear Amber's going with me tonight."

Her mom braved a weak chuckle. "You'll have to let me know how it goes. Hopefully, I'll feel better by tomorrow so I can enjoy your catch." Her mother frowned. "Although the thought of it right now makes my stomach turn all over again."

Johanna placed the bowl of soup on the end table. "Then don't think about that right now. Think about holding down some soup and then resting some more. The girls and I can handle the house tonight."

"I know you can. The three of you have been such a blessing."

Her mother took a few sips of water and ate a couple of spoonfuls of the soup. Johanna could tell Mama already felt fatigued again. She walked out of the room and downstairs to help her sisters.

With dinner finished and the dishes done, her father retired to his bedroom to read where he could watch over their mother, and her sisters settled into the family room to watch some evening television.

Johanna nestled down on the couch in the living area to enjoy the latest release of her favorite fishing magazine. John James wrote about his first experience frog gigging with his little brother. As the article went on, the emotion he felt toward his younger sibling became more apparent. At the close, he talked about how his brother had passed away unexpectedly.

A lone tear slipped down Johanna's cheek. She couldn't imagine, didn't even want to think about, what it would be like to lose one of her sisters. John James had such a sensitive, caring spirit, and he was able to express it with his words. Again, she yearned to meet the man one day. She didn't get all excited about autographs and pictures, but she'd still like to be able to put a face with the stories she read.

She glanced at the grandfather clock that had been in her father's family for five generations. It was ten o'clock according to the old antique. She looked at her watch to confirm it told the correct time, as it only did half the time. It did.

Anticipation swelled in her belly as she stood and made her way into the family room. Bethany had just stood up and turned off the television. Johanna noted Amber sitting on the couch, a mixed look of fatigue and dread etched her face. Bethany patted Amber's knee. "Have fun with Johanna, sis."

Johanna giggled. She hooked her arm around Amber's and helped her sister to her feet. "It's really not that bad. You liked to play in the mud when we were kids. It's just like that all over again."

Amber wrinkled her nose. "I haven't purposely played in the mud in *many* years, and I *never* recall stabbing innocent creatures when I did."

Johanna laughed out loud. "I need someone else to help me slay the bullfrogs, or I wouldn't ask you to go." She elbowed her sister's side. "I promise it will be fun."

Amber slumped away from the couch and meandered up the stairs. By the time Johanna was finally able to get her sister on her way to change into old clothes and shoes and had changed into her own grubbies, it was almost eleven o'clock. They made their way downstairs and grabbed an onion sack, two flashlights, and the frog gigs.

"I can't believe I'm doing this," Amber moaned.

Johanna hooked her arm around Amber's. "Just think of all those yummy fried frog legs we'll eat tomorrow evening."

Amber whined. "I don't think that helps."

Feeling mischievous, she winked at her sister. "We'll have to be sure to cut the tendons in their legs correctly so they don't hop out of the skillet while they're frying. Remember that one time—"

Amber wrapped one hand around her stomach. "I think I'm going to be sick."

Johanna giggled. "You know I'm just teasing you. I know how to cut the tendons."

Amber moaned, and Johanna burst into laughter.

They walked up to the pond, and Johanna sucked in her breath at the beauty of the moon shining down on the pond. "God's amazing, isn't He?"

Amber looked around. "It is pretty up here. I can see why you like to come up here so much."

Words couldn't adequately express how Johanna felt each time she walked up to the family's pond. For so many years she had been basking in her Savior from this spot. It was like nostalgia mixed with repentance intertwined with worship. She couldn't count the times she'd sat on the bench and felt as if God wrapped His mammoth arms around her in strength, forgiveness, and comfort.

"I do love this spot." She looked back at her sister. "But let's get to work. You need to listen for the bullfrog then shine the light in his eyes. If you're too nervous to gig him, motion for me, and I'll do it."

Amber nodded.

Within moments, they'd found and speared two bullfrogs. As they walked the bank of the pond, slipping every once in a while into its waters, Johanna found it increasingly difficult to keep from laughing outright. Her sister became more enthusiastic than Johanna would have imagined though she wouldn't actually kill the frog. The goofy faces Amber made sent Johanna into giggles, and she missed some that she could have gotten.

By the time they had expended their energy, the girls had collected ten frogs. More than enough for their meal the next day. Giddy and giggling, they made their way to the back door, pulled off their sopping shoes, and stripped off their pants and jackets until they stood in the shorts and T-shirts they'd worn underneath. They cleaned their catch in the sink in the mudroom to avoid making a mess in the kitchen.

Amber brushed a stray strand of hair out from her eyes with the back of her hand. "That was a lot of fun. Now I know why you and Mama look forward to it so much."

"I told ya you'd like it."

"At the party, Gavin was talking about how much fun it is. I told him he was crazy, but he insisted I should go." Her sister's face flushed. "Even if he had to take me himself."

Johanna bit her bottom lip as she studied her sister. She looked back at the frogs and continued to clean them. "He seemed to enjoy your piano playing."

Amber's voice raised a pitch. "I know."

Johanna flipped the water off her hands, wiped them on a towel, and turned to her sister. "Amber, do you *like* Gavin?"

Amber huffed. "Of course not." She shifted her weight from one foot to the other. "I mean, he's too old for me."

"Only four years, and just barely that."

"Yeah, but I'm only seventeen."

Johanna leaned against the wall and studied her sister's expression. "Next year, four years won't be too much."

"But—"

Johanna crossed her arms in front of her chest. "Just so you know, I don't like him that way."

Amber looked at Johanna. "You don't?"

Johanna shook her head.

"But Mama always acts like—"

"I told Mama I don't like him that way." She moved closer to her sister. "But you know what, I think he likes you, too."

"You do?"

Johanna nodded. "But you would need to wait a year."

Amber giggled. "I know. Besides, I want to go to college. I'm not worried about a guy right now." She looked at Johanna, ducked her chin, and smiled. "Not really anyway."

Johanna grabbed her sister in a big hug. "Let's finish these frogs up. We all have plenty to do tomorrow."

Chapter 8

Exhaustion oozed from every one of Johanna's 206 bones. It had been two weeks since she and Amber went frog gigging the first time. Since then Amber had her out at the pond and at the stream, which was a good twenty-minute trek from the house, nearly every other night. Last night she hadn't slipped into bed until well past two o'clock.

Rubbing her eyes with the back of her hand, she peered up at the top shelf of books. She'd been shelf reading—making sure all the books had been put back in correct alphabetical order—for the past two hours. The names and titles were beginning to blur, and Johanna knew she needed to take a break. But her lunch wasn't for an hour, and she really didn't have a good excuse, except that she'd been staying up too late frog gigging.

Noting that several books sat beneath the return slot, she decided to switch tasks and check them in while her eyes rested a moment. She made her way to the front desk, smiling at a young girl sprawled out on her belly in the children's section, trying to sound out the words of a picture book.

Memories of doing the same thing while perched on her mother's lap filled her with joy. The only thing that could bring her more joy would be to have a child of her own to help sound out words, to teach, to lose herself in the words of a story.

She walked behind the counter and sat on the stool. After picking up the books, she logged into the computer and started checking them in.

She felt someone standing in front of the desk before the person actually said anything. "Can I help you?" She smiled as she looked up then sucked in her breath when she saw Mike standing there. Taken aback, she lost her balance on the swivel chair and fell off the side. Mike reached across the desk to help her, but she held tight to the lip of the wooden desk, praying her feet wouldn't give way.

He drew back his hand, and the amused smile she'd noted he often wore around her surfaced again. She swallowed. "Hello, Mike."

She continued to grip the side of the desk until she feared she'd rip the wood in two. In an attempt to be inconspicuous and to try to gain control of her composure, she drew in a slow breath. Finally letting go of the desk, she swiped a strand of hair behind her ear. "Is there anything I can help you with?"

The expression on his face changed, and Johanna noted a deep-red wave trailing up his neck. For once, he looked nervous. Wanting to put him at ease, Johanna's anxiety dimmed and she smiled fully at him. She leaned forward. "I'll try not to hurt you this time."

She must have said the right thing, because Mike laughed and the tension in his expression subsided. "I'm not worried that you'll hurt me."

He cleared his throat, and Johanna waited for him to continue. He started to open his mouth, but he averted his gaze to the fishing magazine she'd brought back to the library that morning. He pointed to it. "You read that?"

Johanna bit her bottom lip and nodded. "I'm an avid outdoorswoman." She pressed her fingers under her eyes. "I've been out late frog gigging way too much lately. You can tell by the bags under my eyes."

Johanna's stomach turned. She'd said more to him in the last few minutes than she normally said to Mrs. Love in a full day's work.

He raised his eyebrows as if surprised by her admission. He pointed at the magazine again. "It's a good magazine. From Kentucky, I believe."

Johanna nodded. "Yes, but it's gained a nationwide following."

"Has it?"

"Yes." She picked it up and opened to the article written by John James. "This author specifically writes as if he's from around here. His last article was about frog gigging with his brother." She let out a deep sigh. "But his brother passed away unexpectedly. I could tell by the way he wrote, it devastated him."

"Really?"

Johanna noticed Mike looked away from her for a moment, but she continued. "I'd like to meet him. I've got him pictured in my mind as a bushy-bearded, gray-haired grandpa type with—" She looked up at Mike and noted the amused smile had returned. Embarrassed, she put the magazine back on the desk and clasped her hands. *I cannot believe I am talking this man's ear off. God, what is going on with me?*

Mike nodded. "You can continue."

Johanna shook her head and feared her embarrassment was going to turn her stomach to the point that it made its way up her throat. He really wouldn't know what to think if she upchucked all over him.

She swallowed again. "Is there anything I can help you with?"

"Actually, there is." Mike cleared his throat once more and shifted his weight. "I was wondering."

She glanced at his hands and noted his fingers crumpling the ball cap he must have been wearing before he'd come into the library.

He continued. "I was wondering if you'd let me take you for a soft drink when you get off work."

He blew out a quick breath, and for an instant Johanna wondered at how hard it had been for him to say those words. But what he said didn't seem to register in her mind. She stared at him for a moment, trying to put together his request. No one had asked her on a date before. No one.

Which made sense, because her family didn't believe in dating in the world's sense. They believed more in friendship that moved to a dating of sorts with the intent to marry.

She must have stared at him too long, because he took a step back. "It's okay if you're busy."

She peered into the blue-green eyes of the man she'd thought so much about though knew so little about. She was attracted to him as she had never been attracted to a man before, and everything in her wanted to say yes.

Then say yes, her spirit prodded.

Warmth flooded her cheeks, but she nodded. "Okay."

Mike stepped forward again; his eyebrows rose in surprise. "Really? I thought you were going to say no. What time do you get off work?"

"Five."

"Okay." He backed away from the desk and lifted his hand in a wave. "Well, I'll see you then."

"Okay." Still in a daze, Johanna watched him leave the building. She jolted back to the present when one of the books she'd been checking in fell to the ground.

Spotting one of the aides, she raced over to her and told her she needed a quick break. She couldn't believe she'd agreed. She had to call Mama.

Excitement filled him as he walked out of the library. *So she fixes homemade chocolate crème pie, helps people in need, likes the outdoors, and loves John James's articles. God, where has this woman been all my life?*

He made his way to the diner. He hadn't eaten there since his and Lacy's date several weeks ago, but the guys had talked Wyatt into having lunch with them. The poor man looked like the walking dead after working all day and helping Gracie take care of his toddling boy, Wyatt Jr., and their new daughter, Greta.

Excitement switched to dread as he walked through the front door of the diner. Maybe he didn't have anything to worry about. She could be off today, and they wouldn't have to see each other. He scanned the room, spotted his friends, and walked toward them. He didn't see Lacy anywhere.

With a sigh of relief, he sat down next to Wyatt and patted his friend on the back. "How's it going, man?"

The man looked like he hadn't slept in weeks. Fine lines strayed from red-rimmed eyes. His color looked as splotchy as Gracie's had when he saw her just before she had the baby. Wyatt muttered, "I'm living. Barely."

Nick guffawed from across the table. "You said you wanted a bus full of kids."

Wyatt looked up at him and scowled. "I don't believe I said that."

Drew chimed in. "Oh, yes, you did."

Wyatt rubbed his hand across his stubble-covered jaw. "Somebody should have shot me when I said that."

They all laughed, including Wyatt. "Nah." He turned his coffee cup right side up as a sign to the waitress to fill it up. Mike imagined Wyatt had been drinking a lot of java lately. "These days are just a bit harder on the body. She'll get into a sleeping routine soon enough."

Mike looked at Nick. "So, how's Addy doing?"

Nick nodded. "Doing well. Still having some sickness, but we go back to the doctor in two weeks."

Mike turned toward Drew. "What about you? You and Melody having kids yet?" He pointed to the other two guys. "You don't want them to outdo you now, do you?"

Drew lifted both hands in the air. "I'll surrender on that one. Be the loser for sure. I'm not ready to give up alone time with Melody yet." He winked; then he nudged Mike with his elbow. "But what about you? Did you ask the librarian out on a date yet?"

Before Mike could answer, a familiar female voice sounded above them. "I'll take your order, boys." She smirked at Mike, and he knew she'd heard what Drew said. "Mike, I assume you'll try something different today."

Mike looked down at the menu. *I guess she's working today after all.* He glanced across the table. His friends were studying their menus as well. He handed Lacy the menu. "Nope. I want the same. Meat loaf and mashed potatoes."

She took his friends' orders then stomped away from the table.

Nick leaned across the table. "What did you do to make her so mad?"

Mike shook his head and shrugged. "It wasn't a good date. I told you we disagreed on some things."

Drew punched his arm. "Geez, man. I hope she doesn't take it out on our food."

Mike didn't respond to the comment. Instead, he looked at Drew and said, "To answer your earlier question, yes. I'm taking the librarian for a soft drink tonight."

Wyatt howled. "Good job, man. Two dates in one month. You're finally coming out of your shell."

Lacy walked out from the kitchen with their soft drinks on a tray.

Mike stared pointedly at his friends and whispered, "We probably shouldn't talk about it right now."

She placed their drinks in front of each of them. "Your orders will be out in a minute."

Mike looked up at her. "Thanks, Lacy."

She glared at him and walked away. He didn't want her to be angry with him, but he felt certain that the true Lacy showed up for their date. And he didn't want to date a woman who behaved that way. Mike smiled at his friends. "Let's talk about something else."

Wyatt pulled out his phone and passed it around for them to see the latest snapshots of Wyatt and Greta. This prompted Nick to show off Addy's ultrasound picture that they'd all seen at least five times. When Drew pulled out his phone to show off the beach photos from his honeymoon, Mike feared he was going to be sick. Thankfully, Lacy arrived with their food, and they started to eat.

They had a good visit, and Mike was glad they'd been able to hang out for a while. So much had changed in the last few years. He remembered the bet they'd made to ward off women. In truth, he'd enjoyed those years. They hunted and fished whenever they wanted. Had tractor and truck pulls. Just pretty much did whatever they wanted whenever they wanted.

All that had changed for Wyatt, Nick, and Drew. Now they made late evening trips to the grocery store for items they'd never even known existed until they'd gotten hitched. They couldn't hang out on a whim or rush to a tractor pull without some kind of prior planning.

But Mike had never seen them so happy.

He paid his bill and left the tip for Lacy. He wanted an opportunity to talk to her again, but he didn't know what he would say. He couldn't take back that he thought she'd been wrong for the way she acted on their date, but he didn't want to be cruel to her either.

She seemed to avoid coming out from the kitchen, so Mike walked on out of the diner. He said good-bye to his friends, and they each went their separate ways. Mike headed back to his truck. He had four hours until he needed to be back for Johanna. He had plenty to do on the farm. Hopefully, he'd keep his hands busy enough to keep his mind off five o'clock.

Chapter 9

Johanna wasn't surprised when her father pulled up in front of the library during her lunch break. She knew her mother would hunt him down, wherever he happened to be doing handyman work for the day. He walked through the door, holding up his lunch bag. "Mind if I eat with you today?"

Johanna smiled. She knew most of the girls she worked with would be upset if their fathers wanted to know every time a guy asked them for a soft drink. But Johanna was different. She felt protected and loved that her daddy would leave his work, find her, and give her advice about the man she was meeting.

She pointed out the window to a bench beside a flower bed and fountain. "I'll meet you there. I take my break in five minutes."

"Sounds good."

She watched as her father tipped his head at an older gentleman who sat at a table perusing a magazine. He settled onto the bench but didn't take out any of his food. She knew he would wait to say grace with her. Turning back to her work, she placed another DVD in its spot.

Mrs. Love approached her. "Go ahead and take your lunch five minutes early." She smiled. "No need in making your father wait to eat."

"Thanks, Mrs. Love." Johanna went into the break area, took her lunch from the refrigerator, then joined her father on the bench.

"I'm supposing Mama called you."

He nodded and took her hand. "Let's say grace first."

Johanna bowed her head and listened to her father's genuine petition for blessing over their food and their time together. She may have felt snippets of rebellion against her parents during her early teen years, but at twenty-one, her father had proven to her time and again that he sought God's will and her best interest. Though she was attracted to Mike, she'd accept his wisdom and love and heed whatever he said.

He bit into his ham and cheese sandwich and swallowed it down with a chug of water. Johanna took a small bite of hers, as well, knowing he'd share his thoughts any moment.

"Your mama tells me a young man asked to take you to get a soft drink after work today."

Johanna nodded. "He did."

"And you accepted."

She nodded again.

"Do you know anything about this man?"

Hesitation and a sense of foolishness nibbled at her gut. She averted his gaze. "I really only know his name is Mike McCauley." Dread began to sink into her gut. "I guess I don't."

He cupped her chin with his finger, forcing her to look at his eyes. "Then why would you say yes?"

Her cheeks blazed, and she felt the foolishness of her acceptance. How could she explain to her father that she'd simply had a feeling that he was a nice man? Didn't she know that scripture told her the heart was "deceitful above all things" and that Christians were to be "shrewd as snakes and as innocent as doves"? *God, I should have talked with my parents first.*

"Johanna, I can tell you feel foolish for having accepted his offer. You should never accept a date, so to speak, from a man you do not know."

She nodded. Her father was right. "I'll tell him when he comes at five."

She looked at her father and noticed a grin forming on his lips. "Now, I didn't say that." He stuck a chip in his mouth, chewed, and swallowed. "You know your mother thinks Gavin Mitchell would be a good match for you."

Johanna sighed. "Yes, I know."

"But I have a feeling Gavin has his sights on another girl. Another Smith girl, possibly?"

Johanna couldn't hold back sharing her smile. "I believe you're right again."

She felt it nearly impossible that her father would pick up on Gavin's and Amber's interest in one another. Her mother, who was always in tune with everything happening with her daughters, hadn't even realized it.

"Which brings us back to Mike McCauley."

"Daddy, I said I'd tell him when he gets here. You're right—"

Her father held up his hand. "I happen to know who the young man is. And I know his father."

Johanna perked up. "You do? Is he a good man? I have a feeling"—she pointed to her stomach—"down deep in my gut that he's a Christian, and that he—"

Her cheeks warmed again as her father grinned at her excitement. He grabbed her hand with his left hand and patted the top of it with his right. "As a matter of fact, I believe he is a good man. A good Christian man. And you have my blessing to have a soft drink with him tonight."

Johanna leaned closer to her father. "Tell me what you know about him. Where does he work? Where does he go to church?"

Her father placed the remaining contents of his lunch back in the bag and stood. "All of those things you need to find out on your own when you talk with him tonight. Your mother and I will be praying for you. You know we feel dating in the traditional sense leads to unnecessary heartache."

He patted the top of her head as he used to do when she was a girl. "But you have to get to know a man to know if he's the one God has planned for you." He kissed her head. "See you later, sweetie."

She watched as he walked back to his truck and drove away. Glancing down at her lunch, she realized she'd hardly eaten anything at all. Though her stomach churned too much to eat all she'd brought, she forced a little down so she wouldn't be hungry the rest of the day.

Her father's words played and replayed in her mind. A good Christian man. She longed for a good Christian man. Closing her eyes, she lifted her face to the sky. *I'm so attracted to Mike, and to learn he is a Christian. . .* She sucked in her breath. *You know my greatest desire is to love and serve You, and You also know I want a husband and a family. It's what I've longed for since I was a little girl.*

She tried to rein in her feelings. Her prayer sounded too dramatic to her own mind. She didn't know this man, and she was practically planning their marriage. Not even the wedding, but their life together. *Jesus, I've never felt this way about anyone. I don't want to simply follow my heart. I want to follow Your will. Show me tonight if Mike McCauley is the man You have for me.*

⌘

Mike sat across from Johanna at the Main Street Café. He knew her to be attractive from the brief encounters they'd had, but now he saw how truly beautiful she was. He could tell she was nervous, and she seemed even shyer than Mike, but he still snuck peeks of her. When she smiled, she had the slightest dimple in her left cheek. And her teeth were perfectly straight and white. Her skin didn't have a blemish, not even a freckle that he could find. She was so naturally gorgeous he had a hard time not staring at her.

Trying to start some kind of conversation, he asked, "How was work today?"

She glanced at him for a moment and smiled. "It was good. Thank you."

She twisted the tissue in her hands until he thought the poor thing would crumble to shreds on the table. She cleared her throat. "So, what do you do for a living, Mike?"

"Mostly, I farm with my dad."

She nodded and averted her gaze back to the tissue.

The waitress arrived. She pushed the blue cap she wore off her forehead. "My name's Zelda." She pointed to the name tag on her button-down uniform shirt and winked at Mike. "I'll be helping you this evening." She pulled a notepad and pen from the apron around her waist, and Mike noticed she wore several rings on each finger. She looked at Johanna. "What can I get you, honey?"

"Well. . ." Johanna's voice came out barely above a whisper.

"Honey, you're going to have to talk louder than that." Zelda pointed the pen to her ear.

Johanna sat up and spoke a little louder. "A chocolate shake with whipped—"

"Sweetie." Zelda shook her head at Johanna. "I've been doing this a long time." She pointed to the graying hair sticking from behind her cap. "I don't have much hearing left in me. You're going to have to—"

Mike spoke up. "We'd like two chocolate shakes with whipped cream on top."

Johanna smiled at him, melting his heart.

Zelda nodded. "Would you like cherries, too?"

Johanna nodded, and Mike said they would.

Zelda grabbed their menus and tapped the side of them on the top of the table. "I'll get them right out."

The café was busy with the dinner crowd coming in. Mike wished he'd asked her if she'd like to eat dinner. He hadn't thought of it when he went to the library, because he thought she might get off earlier. He assumed she was probably hungry by now, but she was so quiet and bashful that he didn't want to ask.

Unsure what to say, he took in the fifties memorabilia around the café. The checkerboard patterned walls had vinyl records hanging on them. In the back stood an old-fashioned jukebox that played real records. Johanna had picked the perfect drink, as their chocolate shakes, made from scratch, were the best he'd ever tasted.

He glanced back at Johanna. This wasn't going as he planned. He figured she'd be shy. He couldn't be upset with her for it. He tended to be bashful as well. But they had to be able to talk about something.

A family walked in the door. The little girl must have recognized Johanna, because her face lit up and she raced to their table. "Hi, Miss Johanna, do you remember me?"

Johanna beamed and she wrapped the child in a hug. "Of course I remember you, Marly. How is first grade?"

The little girl shared about a boy who enjoyed picking on her, about the slide that had a nail popped up on the ladder that cut her foot, about the toilets that terrified her because they flushed by themselves. When her parents finally motioned for her to rejoin them, she hugged Johanna once more. Johanna whispered, "I'm glad you're enjoying it."

The little girl giggled and skipped to her parents. Johanna laughed. She looked at Mike. "Marly is so full of life." She leaned over and placed her hand beside her mouth to whisper. "She's just a little dramatic." She sat back and shrugged. "But you can't help but love her."

The child had broken the tension, and just as Mike expected, he realized Johanna was a breath of fresh air. Her genuineness shined through. Mike asked about her family, and she shared how much she cared for and respected her parents and two younger sisters.

By the time they started talking about his family, their shakes had arrived, and they laughed as they tried to get the thick shake up through the straw. Giving up, they both ate their shakes with a spoon.

He wiped his mouth with a napkin. "So tell me about this avid outdoors-woman stuff."

She spread her arms open. "I love God's creation. I love hunting and fishing and frog gigging and camping and hiking. I have a special place at my house where I fellowship with God every day."

"So, you're a Christian?" He nodded. "I had a feeling you were."

She leaned forward. "I had a feeling you were also."

"I am."

"I know. My dad found out." She covered her mouth with her hand.

"Checking up on me, were you?"

"I had to make sure you weren't trying to seek your own revenge for the many times I've attacked you."

Mike twirled the spoon in his glass then ate his last bite of shake. "You've definitely been trying to get my attention."

Johanna waved her hands. She reached across the table and grabbed his arm. "I promise I wasn't."

Realizing what she'd done, she pulled her hand away, and Mike missed the feel of her hand on his skin. He gazed down at his arm and noticed the time. He looked up at her just as Zelda passed their table with another armload of fresh burger baskets. "Johanna, it's after 6:30. Let me buy you a hamburger. You've got to be as hungry as I am. Those burgers smell delicious."

Johanna glanced toward Zelda then up at the *Happy Days* clock on the wall behind her. "They sure do. I think I'll take you up on that offer." She bit her bottom lip. "I'm going to run outside and call my parents so they won't be worried."

Mike nodded and motioned for Zelda while Johanna stepped outside. He could see her through the window talking to either her mother or father. She seemed every bit as pleased with their date as he was. *God, thanks for having her bump into me. Sorry it took three times.*

Chapter 10

Johanna couldn't sleep that night. She'd had a wonderful time with Mike at the café. Even better than she'd prayed for. She forced herself to wait until as close to daybreak as she could stand before she slipped into some clothes and grabbed her tote bag. She patted her leg for Max then headed out the back door and up to the pond.

It would be thirty minutes or more before the sunrise. She sat on the bench and basked in the cool breeze kissing her cheeks and the moonlight bouncing off the still waters. Lifting her face to the heavens, she prayed to her Master and King. *Lord, he's just what I've dreamed of. He loves You, Jesus. And he's easy to talk to. He's a farmer, God. I could continue to bask in Your land. And he's handsome.*

She stood, opened her arms, and twirled around. Closing her eyes, she reveled in the contentment of glorifying the Father and praised Him that it appeared He would give her the desires of her heart.

"Did your family tell you I stopped by your house last night?"

With a gasp, Johanna stopped spinning and turned toward the male voice. Recognizing her lifelong friend, she let out a sigh. "Gavin Mitchell, you scared the life right out of me."

"Did they tell you?"

Johanna studied his solemn expression. She'd never seen her friend so serious. He looked as if he'd slept as little as she had. "No." She shook her head and sat on the bench. She patted the seat beside her. "What's wrong?"

Gavin looked out over the water. "I don't want to sit down." He gazed back at her with condemnation filling his expression. "I know you were with a man."

Johanna's heart fell inside her chest. Why would he be angry with her? Why would he talk to her as if she'd done something wrong? The dinner with Mike had been innocent and friendly. She'd learned so much about him, and he about her. She'd found a man she hoped liked her as much as she liked him. "Gavin, the dinner with Mike was perfectly innocent, and Daddy knew—"

"I don't like it."

Johanna stood and shoved her fists beside her thighs. "Gavin Mitchell, why are you acting like this? We are just friends."

"I don't want to be just friends."

As Johanna stewed on the words he'd just uttered, her heavenly Father's sunrise lifted from behind her friend. She couldn't enjoy His glory for trembling over Gavin's words.

Johanna shook her head. "That isn't true. You know it isn't true."

"I care about you, Johanna. You know I always have. I want you to marry me."

Johanna gasped and took a step away from him. Tears welled in her eyes. She hated the emotion that always flowed first from her eyes. "You don't mean that. I can tell you love my sister."

Gavin seemed taken aback by her words. His hardened shell seemed to break, and he plopped onto the bench. "I've never uttered those words, Johanna."

Placing her hand over her chest, she stepped closer to him. "But it's obvious. To everyone. Even to Amber. Even to Daddy."

Gavin closed his eyes. He looked as if the weight of every rock in Kentucky had fallen hard upon his shoulders. He wiped his face with the palm of his hand. "I'm sorry I have given that impression. It was not intentional."

"Intentional or not, we know you care about her."

She moved closer to him and reached out to touch his shoulder. He pushed her hand away and stood. Raking his fingers through his hair, he paced in front of her. "I cannot care for her."

He stopped and faced Johanna. "Look, you *are* my friend. I do have feelings for Amber, but they don't matter." He raked his fingers through his hair again. "The truth is, I need to marry you."

Johanna squinted at him. "Why would you need to marry me?"

He flopped onto the bench again. "Last spring my father found out he has multiple sclerosis. He didn't want to tell anyone. His symptoms are getting worse."

He looked up at Johanna. His expression pleaded with her to understand. "We need help. The boys and I take care of the farm, but Mama needs help. She can't care for Dad and the baby and all that needs to be done."

Johanna frowned. "Gavin, you can get help. You don't have to marry."

Gavin looked away from her, his expression angry. "You know our farm doesn't make enough money to hire someone. We make it by God's grace alone."

Johanna tried to make sense of what he asked. Maybe the lack of sleep had twisted her ability to reason. Or maybe it had twisted his. "But there are so many ways to get help, and our church family can help, and— You don't love me, Gavin. You love Amber."

Gavin stood and smacked his thigh. "Is Amber going to give up going to high school? And college? Is she going to give up her dream to share God's Word through piano and song? I won't do that to her."

Johanna was stunned by the emotion in Gavin's voice. She could see that he loved Amber more than he'd even realized.

He reached for Johanna's hands, but she pulled away. "I'm sorry, Johanna. You and I *are* friends. I offer you the life you want, the life of a farmer's wife. You know I care for you. I would always be good to you."

Johanna stood still as a hunter who'd locked her gun sight onto a deer. What could she say to Gavin? How could he ask this?

Weariness fell over his face, and he shoved his hands into his front pockets. "Just think about what I've asked. I *would* always be good to you."

Johanna watched as her friend walked down the hill and toward the driveway. She'd been wrapped up in such happiness, she hadn't even heard him pull up. Now sadness draped itself upon her.

Mr. Mitchell had multiple sclerosis. She didn't know what all the disease entailed, but Gavin had said he was worsening. Poor Mrs. Mitchell. She already had her hands more than full.

Johanna knew Gavin's words were true that his mother needed help, and she knew they couldn't afford to hire help. She would help all she could, but Gavin was right, they would need more help than she could offer after work or after her own chores.

But how could she marry Gavin when she knew he had feelings for Amber and Johanna had such strong feelings for Mike? She thought of her mother telling her how she had loved another man but married her father. The idea of going through the heartbreak and then learning to love again tore at her insides.

But it was more than her heart involved. It was Gavin's as well. And even more than that, it was Amber's. *God, I can't be the one who breaks my sister's heart.*

<hr />

Mike's dad's voice sounded from the other side of the barn. "Well, hello there, Pastor Smith."

Stunned, Mike stopped walking and put the bag of feed he carried on the ground. *Pastor Smith? That would have to be Johanna's dad.*

"How are you?" a deeper voice responded. "I've come to see Mike if he's around."

"Didn't know you knew Mike." His dad laughed.

The other man chortled. "Well, I've been hearing a lot about him lately."

"Hope it was all good stuff."

Mike cringed. His dad loved to tease people, but the last person he wanted thinking poorly of him was Johanna's father. He sighed. *I might as well go on over to him.* He clapped his hands together, trying to get most of the dust off, and walked around the barn.

Taken aback at the size of Johanna's father, Mike raised his eyebrows. The man had to be every bit of six feet five inches and probably weighed well over two hundred pounds. He extended his hand to the huge man. "I'm Mike McCauley."

Her father smiled, and Mike noted the same dimple in his left cheek. "It's good to meet you, son. I won't keep you. I know you two have a lot of work to do, but I wanted to invite you to dinner tonight. Six o'clock."

Mike nodded. His heart sped up like a tractor going downhill out of gear. He feared it would be several days before he'd be able to see Johanna again. He'd thought about her all night. "That sounds terrific. Thank you."

Her father gave him their address and waved good-bye. His dad stared at him. "What was that about, Mike?"

"I think I've met my future wife."

His dad howled. "Your wife?"

"I'm serious, Dad." He folded the paper and put it in his front jeans pocket. "I'm going to have dinner with them tonight."

His dad squinted. "I think I'd like to meet this young lady myself."

Mike nodded. "You'll love her."

His father patted his back. "I'm sure I will."

Mike tried to focus on farmwork the rest of the day. He and his father had plenty to do, but Mike couldn't keep his mind on his work. He drove his father so crazy he finally sent him to the house to fix the loose shingles on the roof. He dropped his hammer off the roof and had to climb down and then back up—twice.

At four o'clock, his dad took mercy on him. He shooed him to his truck. "Go on home. Take a shower. Get ready to go to that gal's house. I'm afraid you're going to tear my house down if you don't get out of here."

Mike decided not to argue. He waved good-bye, hopped in the truck, and headed for home. After a long, hot shower, he tried to shave but nicked himself three times. With pieces of tissue plastered over his bloody spots, he searched his closet for something to wear. He pulled out two different shirts and wrinkled his nose at both. *I feel like a woman. Isn't this what women do? Worry over clothes. This is what Mom does.*

Exasperated with himself, he hung up one of the shirts and stuck the other one on. He finished getting dressed, brushed his hair, then pulled the tissues off his face.

Ready to go, he started the truck and headed toward her house. Praying the entire way, he allowed the Holy Spirit to calm his heart and mind.

He'd had such a good time with Johanna the night before. He knew he had nothing to worry about. Her father seemed nice. Her mother and sisters would surely be equally as welcoming.

As he pulled into the driveway, a huge golden retriever greeted him. He hoped they didn't use him as a guard dog, because before Mike could get out of the truck the animal had already tried to lick him to death.

"Max, get down."

He looked up when he heard Johanna's voice. She looked beautiful in a light green sundress. Her long blond hair fell in waves over her shoulders. Even from a distance, he could see the sparkle in her eyes.

He waved. "Hi, Johanna."

She waved back. "Hi, Mike."

He'd asked his mother if she would cut a small bouquet of flowers from her garden. The night before, at the café, he'd shared how much the flowers meant to his mother since his brother's death. He hoped she understood how special the gift was. He handed her the bouquet. "My mom cut this for you."

Johanna's lips formed a perfect O, and she lifted them to her nose. "They're wonderful. Please tell her thank you, and that I'm honored she'd share them with me."

Mike wanted to pick the woman up and twirl her around. She did understand. She was perfect for him. He wanted to reach up and touch a strand of her hair, to feel how soft it was. He wanted to lean down and kiss her perfect lips. But those things could wait.

First, he would meet her family. He followed her up the sidewalk and into the house. Her home was warm and inviting, but it was the aroma of soup beans and corn bread coming from the kitchen that demanded his attention.

Johanna pointed to the older of her two sisters. "Mike, this is Amber." Amber smiled; then Johanna pointed to the younger one. "This is Bethany."

Mike nodded and shook the older then the younger girl's hand. "It's a pleasure to meet you."

She turned toward the woman who could have easily been Johanna's twin a couple of decades before. "And this is my mother, Melissa Smith."

Mike nodded and extended his hand. She smiled and shook it, but he could tell the smile didn't quite reach her eyes. "It's a pleasure to meet you, Mrs. Smith."

"We're glad to have you, Mike." She turned toward her other children and clasped her hands. "Let's eat."

Mike followed Johanna into the dining room. The table was covered with some of the best Kentucky cooking a man could imagine. They'd fixed soup beans and homemade sauerkraut, fried potatoes, and fried green tomatoes. And the corn bread looked so fluffy that it could float off the plate. If the food tasted as good as it looked, he would ask Johanna to marry him tonight.

"It's good to see you again, Mike." Pastor Smith's voice boomed from the other side of the room.

Mike nodded. "Thank you for having me." He looked at Mrs. Smith, hoping her demeanor would soften. "The food looks delicious."

Again, she smiled, but it seemed stiff. "Thank you, Mike." She looked at her husband. "I invited another guest. I'm sure he'll be here in just a moment."

"Hello!" A man's voice sounded from the front door. "Sorry I'm late."

Mike watched as Johanna's face blanched, while Amber sat up straighter and smiled. He looked toward the door and saw a tall, dark-haired man.

"Have a seat, Gavin." Mrs. Smith pointed to the empty chair beside Amber. The woman's demeanor changed significantly in this man's presence. Mike noticed that Pastor Smith gave his wife a weary glance.

"Hello, everyone. Have I missed grace?"

"No, son. You're right on time." Pastor Smith grabbed hands with the daughter on each side of him. Mike held Johanna's hand and Bethany's. He tried not to think about how soft Johanna's hand was or how perfectly it fit in his. Her father's "amen" brought him back to reality, and he released her hand, but he noticed the flush that had crept up her neck. It made him happy to know that he affected her in the same way.

They started passing the food, and Mike filled his plate and bowl. He took a big bite of fried potatoes. They were scrumptious.

"So you must be the man Johanna had dinner with last night?"

Mike looked up at the man they'd called Gavin. "Yes. I'm Mike. It's nice to meet you."

"I think we've seen each other before."

Mike made a fist and pressed it against his mouth. "You know, I thought you looked familiar. We have a farm over in River Run. Where do you work?"

"I farm here in Hickory Hill. You're McCauley, right?"

Mike nodded. "That's right. What was your last name again?"

"Mitchell."

Mike racked his mind for where he'd heard that name before. He remembered his dad had mentioned a friend who'd gotten sick in the last year. At the time, the prognosis wasn't good. Mike's dad would have never known about it if he hadn't run into the guy when taking Mike's mother to the doctor. The man had an unusual first name. What was it? He snapped his fingers. "Is your dad's name Gorman?"

Gavin smiled. "The one and only."

Mike frowned. "How's he doing? My dad saw him last year at the doctor's office. He was worried for him."

Mike felt Johanna stiffen beside him. Gavin's face fell, and he sat back in his chair and rested his hands in his lap. "Right now, he's not doing very well."

Mrs. Smith peered at Gavin. "What's wrong with your dad?"

Pastor Smith also looked concerned. "Son, is something the matter with Gorman?"

Gavin stood and pushed his chair under the table. "I'm sorry. I'd best be going. I know I'm needed at home."

Gavin stared at Johanna, and Mike glanced at her to see if she understood the meaning behind Gavin's look. She averted her gaze to her plate, but the pain in her expression was apparent.

Gavin headed toward the door, and Pastor Smith followed him. After a few moments, Johanna's father returned and told them Gavin shared that his father had multiple sclerosis.

Mike felt horrible. No one had known. He hadn't meant to tell a family secret. He hadn't meant to upset Gavin and Johanna's family. They ate in silence, but everyone seemed finished long before their plates were empty.

Pastor Smith was the first to speak. "Amber and Bethany, you do the dishes." He nodded to Johanna. "Why don't you and Mike go for a walk? It's a beautiful evening."

Mike followed Johanna out the back door. "I'm sorry about that."

Johanna shook her head. "Don't be upset. You didn't know."

Mike studied her. "But you did?"

She nodded. "Gavin just told me today." She surprised him when she grabbed his hand. "May I show you something?"

Mike intertwined his fingers through hers. He didn't want her to let go. Her soft hand belonged in his. "Absolutely."

She guided him up a small hill. At the top sat a bench that overlooked a huge pond. "Johanna, this is beautiful."

She released his hand and sat on the bench. He watched how the fading sunlight shone through each strand of her hair. She was more beautiful than he knew how to describe.

Crossing her legs, she peered up at him. "This is where I spend time with God."

He sat down beside her and took her hand in his. She didn't pull away. "It's a perfect place."

She sneaked a peek at him. "I prayed about you in this spot this morning."

"I prayed about you a few times today as well."

She laughed and brushed a strand of hair behind her ear with her free hand. "I like you, Mike McCauley."

"I like you, too, Johanna Smith. Very much."

She stared out at the water, and he studied her profile for just a few moments longer. Lifting his eyes to the sky, he smiled into the heavens. *God, thank You for bringing her into my life. I'm going to make her my wife.*

Chapter 11

Johanna shelved another book in its proper spot. She hadn't seen Gavin for three weeks. Their family hadn't even attended church. She knew her father had visited the Mitchells' house several times. Her mother and Amber had also gone to help. Johanna had offered to clean or do laundry with Mrs. Mitchell, but her father always had something else for her to do. And he'd invited Mike for dinner at least three evenings a week.

Not that she minded.

When Johanna thought of Mike McCauley, her heart beat faster and her knees grew weak. As she picked up another book to shelve, she took in the man and woman on the cover. They looked at each other longingly. Obviously a romance. All the emotions she'd always believed to be ridiculous fancies in those kinds of books and movies now filled her with joy and wonder. She knew, whether ridiculous or not, the feelings were true and powerful.

A young boy poked her arm. She recognized him as the student who hadn't wanted to visit her station at the "Spring into a Good Book" event just a few months ago. She smiled down at the dark-haired child. He'd grown even taller since she'd last seen him. "Hi. How is your summer going?"

"Fine." He pushed his jaw forward and pointed at an empty place between two teeth. "Lost my first tooth yesterday."

Johanna clapped. "Congratulations. You're growing up."

"Got a dollar from the tooth fairy." He pointed to a woman holding a toddler and perusing the newly released novels. "That's my mom over there."

Johanna nodded.

"I'm going to first grade this year."

"Are you excited?"

He shrugged. "I don't know. School is school." He looked at the children's section. "You wanna read me another book? Another one about farming maybe?"

Pride welled within her. He'd been quite a handful during the event the past spring, and she wondered if he struggled with literacy when she'd read the book, and he'd had a hard time responding when it called for the students to help her finish some of the sentences. But he had still enjoyed himself, and she wanted to encourage him to read. She reached out her hand, and he grabbed hold of it. "Let's go pick one out."

"Mom," he yelled and pointed to Johanna. His mother looked up. "She's the library lady. She's going to read a book to me."

Her cheeks warmed when everyone in the library peered at them. His mother simply nodded and gazed back at the books.

Johanna whispered, "Remember to use a quiet voice in the library."

"Okay," he boomed in a voice almost as quiet as a lion threatened by an enemy.

Shaking her head, she guided him to the children's section. She couldn't remember the child's name, so she pointed to her chest. "Do you remember my name is Johanna?"

He nodded. "Yeah, and I'm Hunter in case you forgot."

"I had forgotten, Hunter. Thank you for reminding me."

They picked out a farming book and then settled onto the plush, shag rug. She read several sentences then encouraged him to read the easy words like "sat" and "cat" and "dog."

Just as she suspected, he struggled to sound out the words. Only going into first grade, she knew he wouldn't be a proficient reader, but he should have been able to identify letters and their sounds.

When they finished the book, Hunter grabbed another book off the shelf. This one, about cars. She read that book; then he grabbed another. After almost half an hour and several more books, Johanna looked around the library to spy his mother. The woman sat in an overstuffed chair in the fiction section reading a book, the toddler draped over her shoulder, obviously asleep.

Hunter had grown weary of reading books, but Johanna figured his mother most likely wanted her little one to rest a bit longer. She looked at her watch, but she needed to get back to work. An idea popped into her head. She pointed to a stack of books on the front desk. "Hunter, would you like to help me put those away?"

He wrinkled his nose and shrugged. "I guess."

Noting the less than enthusiastic tone in his voice, she added, "It'll take someone pretty strong to help me out. You'll have to hold several books at a time."

Jutting out his chin, he lifted his arm and bent his elbow, making a muscle.

"I'm super strong. Feel it."

Johanna wrapped her hand around the small bump and nodded. "You're right. I think you can handle it."

Hunter jumped up to a standing position. He spotted his mother and yelled, "Hey, Mom. Johanna needs someone strong. So I'm gonna help her."

His mother nodded as she laid the book in her lap and with her free hand placed her pointer finger over her lips to remind him to be quiet. She gazed at Johanna and mouthed, "Thank you."

Johanna walked Hunter to the front desk. She loaded six big books in his arms and motioned for him to follow her to the nonfiction section. It seemed to take much longer to put back all the books with Hunter's help, but he had such a good time she couldn't bear to finish without him.

His sister finally awakened, and his mother found them and told Hunter they needed to leave. Johanna knelt down in front of the child and shook his hand. "Thank you for all your hard work. You were a big help." She snapped her fingers. "I think I've got a sucker in the back. Would you like one?"

Hunter nodded, and Johanna realized she hadn't consulted with his mother. She looked at her. "I'm sorry, I should have asked you first."

Her mother swatted the air. "No, that's fine. This is the best library trip we've had in a long time."

Johanna nodded and raced to the break area. Pulling out two suckers from the leftover candy for the last children's event, she walked back out. Her heartbeat sped up when she saw Mike standing at the front desk. Hunter and his mother and sister stood next to him. She handed a sucker to Hunter and then asked his mother if the toddler could have one as well.

She nodded, and the little girl squealed with delight when Johanna handed the child-safe sucker to her. Hunter whined, "That's not fair. She didn't do any work."

Johanna gazed at Hunter. "But she took a good long nap so that you could help out."

Hunter pinched his lips. Johanna could almost see the little wheels churning in his head as he contemplated if he would accept that as a viable reason to give her a sucker. Finally, he nodded. "Okay."

His mother grabbed his hand, and Johanna watched as they walked out the door. She couldn't hold back a smile when she looked into Mike's eyes.

"You're really good with kids."

"I love kids."

"It's obvious."

Before she could respond, Mrs. Love raced up beside her and said, "I can't believe the library is still intact." She pulled a tissue from her front pocket and patted her nose. "Every week this summer, usually on Tuesdays when you aren't here, that woman brings that boy into the library. He runs around like a maniac, and she just sits in a corner reading a book."

A need to defend Hunter welled up inside her. Obviously loud and some-times difficult to deal with, mainly he was just inquisitive and bored easily and needed someone to give him one-on-one attention. He also loved to help. "He helped out a lot today."

Mrs. Love placed a hand on her chest. "I know it. I don't know how you did it, Johanna. The boy frazzles my nerves. Hopefully, she'll start coming on days when you're here."

"I hope so."

Mrs. Love walked away, and Johanna turned back toward Mike. It bothered her that her boss grew so perturbed with children who didn't sit silently with their hands folded in their laps. "He's really not so bad. He just likes attention and likes to keep moving."

Adoration gleamed from Mike's eyes, and heat swelled in Johanna's cheeks. "You are amazing, Johanna Smith."

She averted her gaze. "Not really."

"I would disagree, but I came to ask you if you'll have dinner with my family tonight. My parents are anxious to meet you."

Nervousness twisted her stomach. "Well, sure. I'll need to call Mama—"

"I've already talked with your dad. He said it's fine."

Johanna nodded. Her chest tightened and her stomach muscles twisted some more. "Okay."

Mike placed his hand on hers. "Don't be nervous. My parents will love you. You may even be the breath of fresh air my mother needs." He winked. "You've been good for me."

Johanna ducked her chin at his praise. Her feelings for Mike had deepened over the last weeks. Her father especially liked Mike and encouraged their relationship to blossom. *But Daddy doesn't know what Gavin asked me. He doesn't know they need permanent help.* She pushed the thought away.

Gavin hadn't returned any of her calls. Her heart yearned for Mike, not Gavin. And her mind couldn't quite wrap around the notion of marrying Gavin because he needed help. Even though her sister was too young and wanted to finish high school and college, and it would be possibly years before Amber was ready to settle down—there were simply no circumstances under which Johanna could accept the idea of marrying a man who loved Amber and whom Amber adored.

With dinner finished and after he and his father had cleaned up the kitchen, Mike lowered into one of the wicker chairs on the front porch. His dad swung in the wooden swing beside him. He watched as Johanna knelt with his mother beside one of her favorite flower gardens. His mother took great pride in the various patches of flowers she'd planted around the front and back yards. Together they inspected her most recent creation.

Johanna laughed at something his mother said, and his mom smiled the first genuine smile he'd seen in a long time. Johanna pointed at something, and his mother's face grew animated as she responded.

"She's a really nice girl, Mike."

"Yes. I think so."

"So, how serious are you?"

Mike took a long drink of his sweetened iced tea. He stole his gaze away from Johanna and peered at his father. "I want to marry her. Just like I said before."

His father's eyes twinkled. "I thought you might still feel that way."

"You disapprove?"

"Absolutely not. I've known her father for years. He's an honest Christian man. From everything I've seen from her, she shares all of her father's good qualities." He glanced at Mike. "Have you spoken with her dad?"

Mike leaned forward and rested his elbows on his knees. "Not yet. I've only been seeing her a little over a month."

His father pushed the swing back then turned and spit off the side of the porch. "Let me tell you a little bit about her dad. Roger Smith is extremely conservative in his beliefs. Some would even call him old-fashioned. He would appreciate knowing your intentions, and he wouldn't tell Johanna."

Mike pondered his father's advice until he noticed Johanna motioning for them to join her and his mother. He got up and stepped off the porch. "I'll think about that, Dad."

His mother started motioning for them to join them.

"What is it?" his father called.

"Johanna is begging me to take a walk." His mother acted exasperated, but her face shone brighter than it had in almost a year. "I told her I'd go only if you two went with us."

Johanna stuck out her bottom lip and batted her eyes at him and his father.

Mike laughed. "If you're going to make us."

Johanna clapped her hands like a schoolgirl. His dad reached his mother, took her hand in his, and led her onto the gravel road. Mike wanted to hold Johanna's hand. They had for a brief moment the first time she'd showed him her favorite worship spot by the pond. He still wasn't convinced she realized she'd held his hand then, or if she'd just been wrapped up in the moment. A war raged within him as he battled if he should try to hold her hand.

McCauley, the worst thing she can do is pull her hand away. He inwardly chastised himself. Grabbing her hand, he intertwined his fingers with hers. She didn't pull away. He sneaked a peek at her and noticed her neck and cheeks bloomed red. He held their joined hands up. "Is this okay?"

She peered up at him and nodded then averted her gaze.

"You know you're awfully cute when your face turns red."

Johanna gasped and punched his arm with her free hand. "Mike McCauley."

"What?" He feigned hurt and innocence. "You're cute when you aren't embarrassed, too."

She stomped her foot. "Mike."

He laughed out loud. His parents turned around to look at them then turned back around and continued their conversation.

He pointed ahead. "Look, you worried my parents."

"Mike McCauley," she hissed. "Stop teasing me or I'm pulling my hand away."

He sobered. "Don't do that. Your hand is so soft and fits perfectly with mine."

She ducked her head. "Okay."

They walked together in silence. Mike peered at his and his father's farm. If Johanna would have him as a husband, it would be her farm as well. They would work alongside each other. Their children and grandchildren would play in these fields. He'd always been a simple man, longing for a simple life. Not an easy one. He'd spend the rest of his days doing hard work. But he wanted someone to share his life with. Someone with long blond hair and a sparkle to her green-with-flecks-of-brown eyes. And that dimple in her left cheek. He wanted Johanna.

Chapter 12

Johanna tossed the cell phone in the passenger's seat beside her. She'd had it with Gavin Mitchell. It had been over a month since he'd interrupted her quiet time and announced she had to marry him because he needed help. Though head over heels in love with Mike, she seemed to dwell in some weird love triangle that Mike didn't even know existed because of what Gavin had asked.

Furious, she turned onto the blacktop road that led to Gavin's house. Normally, she enjoyed the beauty of the drive to the Mitchell home. Overwhelmed with frustration at this moment, she needed closure. Today.

She wanted to tell Gavin to forget it, that he'd stepped way out of line asking for her hand in marriage the way he had. They didn't live in the eighteenth or even the nineteenth century. There were ways for his family to get the assistance they needed. His pride alone made him feel he *had* to marry. If his mother knew what he'd asked of her, knowing he cared for her sister, she'd find his old time-out chair and sit him in a corner.

And what kind of life would his wife of duty or convenience—or whatever he chose to call it—have? Versions of the old play and movie, *Seven Brides for Seven Brothers*, danced through her mind. Adam had essentially tricked poor Millie into marrying him. He'd only wanted a wife to care for him and his brood of brothers. *Hmm. Actually, it sounds very similar.*

She'd had plenty of time to stew on Gavin's request. Everything in her wanted to punch him in the nose. How dare he think that he could ask for her hand after admitting he loved her sister? "Ugh!" She smacked the top of the steering wheel.

Her frustration with Gavin had grown the last few days as Johanna realized how deep her feelings for Mike were becoming. Amber, who was ready to start her senior year of high school in only a few weeks, still spoke privately with Johanna about her feelings for Gavin.

She turned the last right that led to his driveway. As she drove up, she spied two of the middle boys pushing each other in a tire swing hung from the old maple tree in the front yard. One of the younger ones played in a sandbox. The baby slept in a playpen under a shade tree. Mrs. Mitchell hung clothes on the line a few yards away.

When they heard her car wheels crunching on the gravel, the boys hopped off the swing and out of the sandbox and raced toward her. Mrs. Mitchell waved.

The love Johanna felt for this, her second family, filled her heart. She hugged the boys and then walked over to Gavin's mother. The older woman wrapped her arms around Johanna, and Johanna knew she would be the kindest mother-in-law ever. "What a pleasure to see you, honey. What brings you out here?"

"I'm actually here to find Gavin."

His mother pointed to the barn. "He should be about done working for the day."

Johanna nodded to the clothes. "After I talk with him, I'd love to help you with these."

Mrs. Mitchell swatted at her. "Nonsense. I'm almost finished. You go find Gavin."

Johanna peered into the eyes of the woman who'd always been like a second mother to her. "How's Mr. Mitchell?"

She smiled and her eyes lit up. "He's on some medicine that is really helping him. He's actually in the barn with the boys."

Johanna hugged the woman again. "I'm so happy to hear that."

The older woman wiped a tear from beneath her eye and sniffed. "Me, too, sweetie." She nudged Johanna's arm. "Go find Gavin."

Thanksgiving swelled in Johanna's heart that Gavin's father was doing well. She lifted up a prayer of gratitude as she made her way to the barn and heard several of the Mitchell men talking. It did sound as if they were about to finish up for the day. "Hello!" Johanna called before she reached the front of the barn.

Eighteen year-old Gabe stuck his head out from inside the barn. "Hey, Johanna. What brings you out here?"

"Looking for Gavin."

"Oh," Gabe grunted then scrunched up his face. "Don't know"—he lifted his leg and rubbed the back of it as if someone had just kicked him—"where he is."

Johanna crossed her arms in front of her chest. "I heard you talking, Gavin. Get out here."

His father's "Hee-haw" sounded from inside the barn. "I told you she wouldn't fall for no fibs."

Johanna couldn't hold back a grin. Mr. Mitchell remained as mischievous as the day was long. He shouldn't have allowed his son to try to fib to her, but the older man knew how to bring a lot of laughter to his home.

Gavin walked out of the barn, his head hung low. He peeked up at her like a pup that begged for mercy for messing on the floor.

She motioned for him to follow her. "We need to talk."

They walked several yards to the gazebo his father had built for his mother. He'd even dug her a decorative pond and put koi fish in it. Mrs. Mitchell told them it was her place to escape the chaos of all her men.

Johanna sat on the bench inside and looked up at her friend. His dark hair fell in his eyes. In desperate need of a haircut, he appeared to have missed a shave or two in the last few days as well. "Why haven't you returned my calls?"

Gavin stepped inside the gazebo and leaned against the rail. He folded his arms in front of his chest. There was no denying Gavin was a handsome man. A man whose broad shoulders and tall stature exhibited strength. Much like her father, he was big as a bear. "I guess you thought about what I asked you."

Johanna spread out her arms. "Of course I've thought about what you asked me. I haven't been able to get it out of my mind." She stood and poked him in the chest. "But you wouldn't return my calls."

He stood up straight and puffed out his chest. "What's your answer?"

Her mouth fell open. How could he possibly still want to marry her? She rubbed her eyes with her hands. She knew her mother had fallen in love with her father after they were married. She knew Gavin was a faithful and true friend who loved the Lord. But she also knew her sister cared deeply for this man, and that Johanna loved Mike. She couldn't do it. Smacking her hands against her thighs, she released a growl. She simply couldn't do it. "The answer is no."

She pointed her finger at him. "I can't believe you would ask—" Gavin released a long sigh and wrapped his arms around her. She pushed him away. "What are you doing? I said no."

"I know." He laughed and sat on the bench. "I've avoided you because I felt miserable for what I asked. It was wrong of me."

Frustration of a new kind swelled within her. "So, you just avoided me? Let me stew about what you asked? And not even tell me you were wrong?"

Gavin shrugged. "Really, I'm surprised you're here. I knew you were spending a lot of time with Mike. I knew your dad approved of him. I figured you hadn't given any more thought to what I said that morning. At least, I hoped you hadn't. I decided if I stayed away you'd know I should have never asked in the first place."

Johanna bit the inside of her lip as she contemplated whether she should pummel the man. "Gavin, we've been friends since birth. You shouldn't have avoided me."

"You're right. I'm sorry."

Johanna huffed and stomped her foot. "You're sorry, and that's supposed to make everything all right?"

He looked at her and stuck out his bottom lip. "Pwease."

She snarled at him. "Are you kidding me? You're a grown man." She punched his shoulder. "Don't act like that."

He winced and grabbed his shoulder, even though she knew he'd probably only barely felt her punch. "Does that mean you forgive me?"

Johanna blew out a breath. "Of course I forgive you."

He hopped off the seat and gave her a hug. "I knew you'd forgive me." He stepped off the gazebo and started heading toward her car. "You're right about me liking your sister."

"She definitely likes you, too."

"So maybe we'll be related one day anyway."

Johanna snorted. "I really ought to kick your behind for making me worry about this all month."

Gavin placed his hand against his chest. "I'd have never dreamed you were so uptight about things."

She swatted his arm again. "You know I'm uptight about things."

He opened the car door for her. "Well, I am sorry. Truly."

Realizing they'd walked through the yard and hadn't seen a single member of his family, she looked toward the house. "Where is everyone?"

He peered at his watch. "It's five o'clock. *Happy Days* reruns are on. Would you believe every Mitchell in the family loves to watch *Happy Days*?"

Johanna rolled her eyes and slipped into the car. "You all are crazy."

He shut the door and tapped the hood. "Yep. I better go, 'cause I'm missing it."

He waited while she started the car and drove off. In the rearview mirror, she saw him skip into the house. He was crazy, and she should be livid with him. But all she could think about was she was free to love Mike.

Mike pushed OFF on his cell phone. He'd waited until mid-August to ask Johanna's father to his house. After talking with his own father the first night Johanna had eaten dinner with them, Mike decided he wanted to fix up his house before asking her father for her hand in marriage. He had more insulation put in and new windows installed. Both of which made a huge mess, so Addy helped him with coloring up the place. With her being six months pregnant, Nick wouldn't let her do any of the work. But she picked out all the colors, and he and his friends did all the painting.

Once he finally got the house all ready, it was the beginning of August, and Amber started school. Their whole family had been as anxious as a heifer whose calf was turning a week or two before birthing time. He'd decided to wait another week. Addy's aunt Becky came out and cleaned the house up real good for him.

His mother had even come over and worked a bit on his landscape. Though she'd only attended one time, his mom had even visited a Sunday evening service with him and his dad at Johanna's church.

He paced the living room floor, trying to remember all he wanted to say. Everything in and around the house smelled good and looked good. Now he just had to wait for Pastor Smith to show up.

Crunching gravel sounded from outside the house. Mike peered out the window and saw that Pastor Smith had arrived. He exhaled a nervous breath. *God, give me the right words to say. I believe Pastor Smith respects me, but I want him to know that with me his daughter will be loved, protected, and cared for.*

Mike opened the front door before Johanna's father made it up the porch. He nodded and extended his hand. "Evening. Thanks for taking the time to come out and see me."

Pastor Smith shook his hand. "Anytime, son."

Mike stepped outside and shut the screen door. "If you don't mind, I'd like to show you around my property first."

A smile tugged at Pastor Smith's mouth, but he nodded. "Go right ahead, son."

He tried to keep his hands clasped, as they simply would not stop shaking. It was too far to walk to the barn near his parents' house, but he pointed out the farm's boundary lines and explained where the cattle grazed.

Taking Pastor Smith inside the house, he showed him the improvements he'd made—the new windows and insulation, the plumbing and floors. Mike pointed to the kitchen cabinets. "I know these are a bit old, but I wanted to wait until. . ." His face warmed. He almost said he wanted to let Johanna pick out cabinets she'd like.

Pastor Smith cupped his chin. "Until what, son?"

Mike blew out a deep breath. "Could I get you a soft drink?"

Pastor Smith nodded. "Sure." He pointed to the kitchen table. "Would you like me to have a seat?"

Mike pulled two drinks out of the refrigerator and handed one to Johanna's father. "That would be great."

Mike sat opposite Pastor Smith. He wrapped his fingers around the can, allowing the coldness to calm his nerves. Mike studied the older man across from him. It was obvious Pastor Smith knew Mike's intentions. Still, Mike wanted to assure him that he would care for Johanna.

Mike opened the soft drink and took a quick swig. "I know you know why I've asked you here."

Pastor Smith rested his hand on top of the table. "Why have you asked me here?"

"I'd like to request your daughter's hand in marriage."

"Which one?"

Mike furrowed his brows and gawked at the older gentleman. Had he lost his mind? *Which one?*

Pastor Smith let out a loud belly laugh. He smacked the tabletop. "I'm assuming you mean Johanna."

Mike laughed as well. "Yes, I mean Johanna."

"It's about time you finally asked me."

"I had planned to ask earlier, but I wanted to get some things fixed around the house, and then Amber started school. I had to wait for the right time."

Pastor Smith extended his hand, and Mike accepted the handshake. "I will be proud to have you as a son-in-law. So when will you be asking Johanna?"

"I plan to take her on a picnic at your house this weekend."

A confused expression wrapped Pastor Smith's features.

Mike continued, "I'd like to propose at your pond."

The older man opened his mouth and nodded. "Oh, good idea." He snapped then pointed his finger at Mike. "Smart man. She'll love that."

"I hope so." Mike didn't tell him about the other half of his surprise. He wanted it to be solely between Johanna and him.

Pastor Smith stood up and pulled his truck keys from his front pocket. "Your house and farm are very nice, Mike. I know you'll take good care of my daughter." He shook the keys. "But I best be going before they start wondering why their old man is so late for dinner."

Mike followed his guest to the door then walked back to his bedroom and opened the top dresser drawer. He pulled out the small box and popped it open. The ring he'd bought a few weeks ago was perfect. When he saw it, he immediately thought of Johanna. A gold band and a small circular diamond. Just like her, it was simple but beautiful. Shutting the lid, he tucked it inside the drawer again. The weekend couldn't arrive fast enough.

Chapter 13

Johanna slipped into her sweatpants and old shoes. She looked at her sister and her mother, who'd also donned their old clothes. "Mama, you get the flashlights?"

Her mom lifted them up. "Got them right here."

Johanna took one from her mother, as did Amber. Since the first time she went frog gigging, Amber never allowed Johanna and her mother to go without her.

Amber pointed outside. "I laid the gigs against the house."

With gear in hand, the three made the quick trek to the pond. Amber had yet to spear a bullfrog, though there were definitely more to be had the closer it got to fall; but she excelled at hearing their sometimes muffled *varuump* and then flashing the light in their eyes to stun them.

"Amber, how was school today?" Her mother's voice sounded from a few feet behind Johanna.

Amber huffed. "Mom, are we going to get some bullfrogs or are we gonna talk?"

"I'd like to do both."

Johanna backed up her sister. "Let's finish gigging; then we'll talk."

Her mother nodded, and the three turned their attention to the sounds of the night, most specifically their prey. Time passed quickly, and soon they were sitting side by side on Johanna's favorite bench with an onion sack filled with fifteen bullfrogs on the ground beside them.

Johanna stared at the full moon that draped its beauty on the still pond waters. Trees of various sizes and shapes stood majestically in the distance. The occasional call of a bullfrog and the constant chirps of crickets calmed her spirit.

She looked at their mud-caked shoes and legs. Their arms and hands were filthy, but happiness filled her that she could share this moment with her mother and sister.

Her mom, who sat in the middle of them, nudged Amber's shoulder. "So how was school today?"

"It was good. Mrs. Watkins is really helping me with my math. I'm still behind, but I've met a friend. Her name is Hannah, and she's helping me, too."

"That's wonderful, Amber." The relief in her mother's tone was evident, and Johanna knew her parents still prayed that they'd made the right choice for her sister.

Johanna cleared her throat. "Mike is coming over tomorrow."

"I know it," her mother said.

Johanna frowned. "How do you know it? He only just asked me today."

"I think your daddy told me."

"But I haven't told Daddy."

Her mother shrugged. "Then I have no idea."

Amber interrupted their conversation. "Gavin's coming, too."

"I knew that as well." She turned toward Johanna.

"See, your father must have asked the boys to come first."

Johanna bit the inside of her lips. Maybe that was possible. She'd thought he'd asked her in such a way that he wanted her to be sure it was okay with her family, but maybe she was imagining things.

Her mother and Amber started talking about Gavin, and Johanna found her mind wandering. She was thankful her mother had figured out on her own about Amber's and Gavin's feelings for each other. There would be no more trying to talk Johanna into having romantic fancies for her childhood friend.

But she hadn't seen Gavin since the day she stopped at his house. She'd forgiven him, but a niggling of frustration with him still bit at her gut. To her knowledge, Mike hadn't seen Gavin since that day they'd had dinner together—the day Mike accidentally told the family about his father's illness. She wondered how Mike would feel about spending time with Gavin.

"I can't help but wonder when Mike will finally propose to Johanna." Amber's voice broke her concentration.

She gaped at her sister. "What?"

Her sister lifted her hands. "What's it been? Two and a half or three months?"

"Amber." Johanna stood and placed her hands on her hips. "I can't believe you would say that."

Her mother giggled, and Johanna gaped at her as well. "Mama."

Her mother shrugged. "Johanna, it's pretty obvious to the rest of us that you are head over heels for Mike." She leaned forward. "And I believe he feels the same about you."

Johanna placed her hands over her chest. She didn't want to talk about this with them. Her heart yearned for him to ask her to be his wife. She knew they'd known each other only a short time, but their faith, their desires, their personalities fit so perfectly. Still, she did not want to share that with her mother and her sister. At least not at the same time. Maybe in the confines of the house, where a perfect stranger couldn't meander up to them and hear their conversation. Or a dear friend, the way Gavin had surprised her one day.

Her mother stood up and stretched her back. With one last giggle, she motioned toward the house. "Amber, let's stop teasing Johanna and head back to the house. We still have to clean our frogs."

Amber groaned. "This is the part I hate."

Johanna followed a small distance behind her mother and sister. Now she wouldn't be able to sleep the whole night because she'd be dreaming of Mike asking her to marry him.

Mike patted his front jeans pocket for what must have been the hundredth time. Nervousness and anticipation warred within him. He'd planned to take her for a picnic lunch at her pond, but she, her sisters, and her mother changed the plans since they'd gone frog gigging, yet again, the night before.

He chuckled inwardly. Those women frog gigged more than any man he knew. The delicious aroma of frying frog legs wafted through the living room where he sat, only somewhat watching the Reds game, with Pastor Smith. Normally, he'd jump at the opportunity to eat the Smith women's frog legs and fixings. Today he just wanted the four of them to hurry up.

The older man leaned forward in his chair. He rested his hand on the side of his mouth and whispered. "I didn't know they were going to switch plans."

"It's okay. I can wait until we eat." He rolled up the magazine he'd brought with him and tapped it against his leg.

Pastor Smith furrowed his brows. "Whatcha got there?"

Praying Johanna's father wouldn't ask any more questions, he unrolled it and showed him the cover. "Just a fishing magazine."

"I believe that one is Johanna's favorite."

Mike nodded. "I think you're right."

"I'm here."

A man's voice sounded from the other room. Pastor Smith pushed himself up to his feet. "There's Gavin. He's come for lunch as well."

Mike stood and followed the older man into the kitchen. Unsure what to say after the last time he'd seen Gavin, Mike cleared his throat and extended his hand.

Gavin smiled and grabbed it in a firm handshake. "It's nice to see you again, Mike. My dad's on some medicine, and he's doing much better."

Relief washed through Mike. Already nervous enough, he didn't need the added concern of eating with a guy who was frustrated with him.

They sat down at the table, and Pastor Smith said grace over their food. Mike wanted to dig into the fried frog legs, mashed potatoes, green beans, coleslaw, and corn bread. It all looked so good, and he put a spoonful of everything on his plate, but he only ate a few bites.

Mrs. Smith rested the fork on the side of her plate. "Mike, are you ill? You've hardly touched your food." She pointed to her husband. "Usually you eat more frog legs than Roger."

Mike took a small drink of his soft drink. "Actually, I do feel a bit queasy." There was no lie in what he said. The ring in his front pocket seemed to burn a hole in his leg, and he feared at any minute he would be sick from anxiety. He pulled at his shirt collar. And it was really hot in the dining room for some reason.

Johanna looked at him. "Mike, you do look pale."

Pastor Smith motioned out the window. "Maybe you need some fresh air, son."

Mike nodded. "Good idea." He placed his napkin beside his plate and excused himself.

He walked into the kitchen and heard Pastor Smith say, "Johanna, why don't you go and make sure he's okay?"

Mike grinned. His soon-to-be father-in-law was a smart man. Johanna walked up beside him and touched his cheek with the back of her hand. His cheek blazed at her touch, and he grabbed her hand in his. "Let's take a walk."

He walked back to the living room, grabbed the magazine, then guided her out the back door. They didn't talk as they headed up the hill to Johanna's favorite worship place. Once he reached the bench, he sat and patted the seat beside him for her to follow.

Johanna studied him. "You don't look so sick anymore."

"The fresh air cured me."

He opened the magazine to the last article he'd written. "Have you read John James's article this month yet?"

Johanna nodded. "I read it at the library on Wednesday." She pointed to the author's name. "Mike, I am telling you that man lives near us."

Mike bit back a laugh. "I haven't had a chance to read this month's issue." Which was technically true since he hadn't read the other articles yet. "What's it about?"

Johanna took the magazine out of his hand. "He talks about his favorite pond."

"Tell me about it."

"Okay. First, he talked about how when he sits on his favorite bench, the pond kind of looks like a jagged half moon." She lifted her hand and swiped it slowly in front of her. "Then he talks about how the thick green grass grows just beyond it with a large hill lifting up on his left and a small hill on his right."

She paused and looked down at the magazine. "Then he talks about..." She frowned and skimmed the page. "He talks about three pine trees that sit kind of off by themselves on the left." She glanced up; then her jaw dropped and she turned toward Mike. She pointed at the article. "John James is describing my pond. But that doesn't make—"

Mike wrinkled his nose. "Well, I would have bought some bushy gray eyebrows and a beard for you, but I just thought they'd be uncomfortable."

Johanna stared at him for a few moments; then she stood and swatted his leg then his arm with the rolled-up magazine. "Mike McCauley, you are John James?"

He lifted his hands in surrender. "I confess. I confess."

She smiled, and her eyes shone. "I can't believe you didn't tell me."

He patted the bench, and she sat down beside him again. "I haven't told anyone. You're the first to know." He shrugged. "Except my parents."

She peered down at the article then back at him. "You're my favorite writer."

His heart swelled. "I know, and you have no idea how happy that makes me."

She shook her hands, and a disgusted look distorted her face. "To think I've held hands with a grandpa."

Mike laughed and grabbed her hand in his. He kissed her knuckles. "And you're going to hold hands with me for a long time to come."

He started to reach for the ring box when his cell phone rang. To shut it off, he pulled it out of his back pocket and accidentally hit the TALK button. He barely recognized Drew's frantic voice. He lifted the phone to his ear. Drew screamed into the phone. "Mike! Mike!"

"I'm here, man. What's wrong?"

"It's Addy. She's gone into labor. They can't stop it. The baby's too early.

It's bad." Drew's voice cracked. "She's my sister, man."

"I'm coming." Mike grabbed Johanna's hand, and she stood. "Where is she?"

"On her way to the hospital. Hurry, Mike."

The phone went dead, and Mike held Johanna's hand while he raced down the hill. "Addy's in labor."

"It's too early, isn't it?"

Mike nodded. "I've got to get to the hospital."

"I'll go with you."

He looked at Johanna then wrapped his arms around her.

If she were the one in trouble. . . If it were their baby. . . He couldn't even think it. He whispered into her ear. "Thank you, Johanna."

They raced inside the house. Pastor Smith wore a smile that nearly split his face. Mike shook his head. "My friend's wife has gone into labor. It's too early."

"I'm going with him," Johanna said. "Pray for Addy and the baby."

They hopped in the truck and headed down the road. *God, this isn't how I planned this day. Have mercy on Addy and the baby.*

⌀

"How far along is she?" Johanna asked Gracie, the woman she'd just met.

Even though obviously fatigued, the woman had adorable short blond hair and deep eyes. Gracie cuddled her own fairly new baby against her chest. "Thirty weeks."

"Her water broke," added Melody, the woman who Johanna discovered had just married Drew. She pushed a long strand of dark-brown hair behind her ear. "They can't stop it."

Gracie shook her head then brushed a tear away from her eye. "I've got to call Mom and check on Wyatt Jr."

Swaying to keep the baby content, Gracie walked to the far wall of the hospital waiting room and pulled a cell phone out of her pocket.

"She has an eighteen-month-old at her mom's house."

Johanna turned toward Melody when she spoke. The tiny woman covered her face with her hand. "Drew is beside himself." She started to cry. "I've never seen him so scared. And Addy. . . And the baby. . . Nick."

Johanna pulled the woman into a hug.

Melody heaved as she said, "And both of their parents are gone on vacation. Together." She sniffed. "No one expected this to happen."

Johanna raked her fingers through Melody's hair. "We're going to pray for them. Lots of babies live when they're born at thirty weeks."

Melody shook her head. "Addy's baby was already small. They were monitoring him because he wasn't growing right. Or her. I don't even know if I have a niece or a nephew."

Gracie returned and wrapped her arms around Johanna and Melody. Johanna spied Mike and Wyatt to her right and motioned for them to come over. Wyatt wrapped his arms around Gracie and his baby. Johanna glanced at Mike. "Why don't we pray together?"

Melody sniffed and wiped the tears from her eyes with the back of her hand. "Johanna's right. We need to pray."

Johanna grabbed Melody's hand then took hold of Mike's. They all joined hands and bowed their heads.

"They kicked me out!"

Johanna looked up to see the man who had to be Addy's brother, Drew. Melody pulled away from Johanna's hand and wrapped her arms around her husband. He pulled her close to him. "My baby sister is in trouble, and they kicked me out."

Melody grabbed his hand and led him to the group. "Drew, we're going to pray together. It's the most powerful thing we can do."

"I can't pray right now." Drew's voice sounded panicked, and Johanna felt sure he wanted to run to the back and storm the delivery room.

"I'm going to pray," Mike commanded in a calm voice. "We all know God is bigger than this."

Peace swelled within her heart at Mike's words. She felt the collective calm that touched each of them. With every word of praise that Mike uttered, with every promise of God that Mike repeated, Johanna found herself basking in God's sovereignty and mercy.

"We ask you to save the little one Addy is delivering. The child is precious to us already. We know You are sovereign. We know Your will is best, but Jesus, we ask, we petition Your throne for mercy for this baby and for Addy."

Tears slipped down Johanna's cheeks at the urgency and honesty and pleading in Mike's voice. His words and tone were genuine, and a joy she couldn't explain even in her mind filled her to be petitioning her Father alongside this man.

He didn't stop praying. He quoted scriptures of peace and mercy. He reminded God, though He would never need reminding, that His Word promised where two or three were gathered, He would be there. And He was.

When Mike finally uttered an amen, the group sat down together in the waiting room. Mike sat beside her and held her hand. He squeezed it gently and whispered, "This is not how I planned to spend today." He kissed her knuckles, sending butterflies through her stomach and down her legs. "I'm glad you're here with me."

Johanna wouldn't have been anywhere else.

Time dragged by as they waited for an update. Hour toppled upon hour. Every once in a while, Drew grew anxious and asked the receptionist if she'd had any updates. The woman would assure him she hadn't; then Melody would wrap her arms around his waist in an attempt to keep him calm.

Finally, the emergency room door flew open, and Johanna recognized Nick from the library back in the spring. A tear slipped down his cheek, but it was the smile that overwhelmed his face. "We have a girl. Three pounds, five ounces. They expect her to be all right. And Addy is more wonderful than the day I married her."

Cheers rang through the waiting room. Drew raced to Nick and grabbed him in a bear hug. "Can I go back there?"

Nick shook his head. "Not yet. I'll let you know."

He appeared somewhat dejected, but he was still smiling. Drew hugged his wife. "We have a niece."

Mike wrapped his arm around Johanna's waist. She looked up at his face. His mouth was so close to hers. Only a whisper away. She only needed to tilt her head just a bit, and she could kiss him. She wanted to. Desperately, she wanted to.

A push came from behind Mike, deflecting the moment. Wyatt grinned at them. "Let's go get something to eat. We've been here for hours, and I'm starving."

Chapter 14

Nervous butterflies swarmed in Mike's gut for what seemed the millionth time since he'd awakened that morning. As he followed Johanna into the diner, he admitted the day had not gone as he had planned. Not at all.

He hadn't seen Lacy in quite some time, and it had been over three months since their failed date. He hoped she wouldn't still be angry with him. Or possibly that she wasn't working at dinnertime on a Saturday night.

He spied a dark-haired woman with her back to them. She didn't have to turn around. He knew it was Lacy.

"I've never been here before," Johanna said as she slid into the booth.

Wyatt moved into the inside of the booth on their side, while Gracie placed the baby's car seat in some wooden contraption designed to hold the whole thing.

"It's one of our favorite places to eat," Wyatt said. "Mike always orders meat loaf and mashed potatoes."

Mike scowled at his friend, and Wyatt laughed.

Gracie settled in beside Wyatt. She pointed to the menu. "Johanna, I always get the fried chicken. It's delicious."

The waitress walked up to their booth, and Mike blew out an audible sigh of relief when he saw the woman with long red hair whose name tag read SARAH. He'd be happy to take a "scraggly red hair" in his food today.

Johanna looked at him, her expression piqued with concern. "You okay?"

He wiped his hand across his face. "Just tired."

Sarah took their drink orders, but Johanna wanted to look at the menu a little longer before placing her order. Mike surveyed the room again. He hadn't seen Lacy since they'd first walked in. Maybe he'd been wrong, and the woman he'd seen wasn't her.

"What's the matter, Mike?"

Mike looked across the booth at his friend. Wyatt smirked, and Mike squinted at him. "Nothing's the matter, Wyatt."

Johanna looked up from the menu. "I think I'm going to try the chicken and dumplings."

Mike nodded. "Good choice."

Wyatt scoffed. "How would you know?"

Mike leaned toward Johanna. "He's right. I don't. But it sounds like a good choice."

Gracie and Johanna laughed, and Mike smirked at Wyatt.

Sarah came back with their soft drinks and took their orders. Greta started to fuss, and Gracie took her out of the car seat. Short blond hair stuck out all over the baby's head as if she'd stuck her finger in a light socket. She cooed and smiled at Gracie. The kid obviously wanted attention.

Mike noticed Johanna looked longingly at the little tyke. He had no doubt she would want a passel of kids. He hadn't had all that much experience with children, but he'd be willing to have as many as Johanna wanted, especially if they looked like her.

Gracie nodded to Johanna. "Would you like to hold her?"

Johanna perked up beside him. "You don't mind?"

"Of course not."

Wyatt moved the glasses out of the way while Gracie passed the baby over the table to Johanna. Mike watched as she nestled the girl close to her chest. Greta reached for her hair and cooed. Johanna traced her finger along the baby's cheek. "I'm so thankful Nick and Addy's baby is all right."

"Yes," they all agreed.

Mike couldn't take his eyes off Johanna with the baby. Everywhere he'd seen her with children she had taken to them naturally. And they'd always taken to her.

"Here's your food." Sarah stood beside them with a tray filled with their orders.

Mike inadvertently checked his food for any red hairs. He shook his head when he realized what he was doing. He'd have never done that if Lacy hadn't said what she had to him.

Once everyone received their plates, Wyatt said grace over their food. Johanna continued to hold Greta while she ate. He was impressed with how easy it seemed to be for her.

A shadow fell over him. He looked up and smiled, expecting to see Sarah returning to fill their glasses. It was Lacy.

"Hello, Wyatt. Mike." The dark-haired woman looked from one to the other. Disdain etched her features, and he knew this would not be a good visit. "I haven't seen you boys around here lately. You used to come in all the time."

Mike stiffened. His tongue stuck to the roof of his mouth. He'd done nothing wrong with Lacy. Nothing at all. But he had no idea what she would say or do.

Wyatt smiled up at her. "We've been busy." He pointed across the table to Johanna. Mike almost swallowed his tongue. What would Wyatt say to Lacy about Johanna? "As you can see, Gracie and I just had our second baby."

"I see that." Lacy smacked her chewing gum. "She's right pretty." She nudged Mike with her wrist. "How you doing?"

Mike forced his tongue to untwist. "Doing good."

This time she pointed to Johanna. "Who's your lady friend?"

Johanna's sweet, genuine, innocent, unknowing smile bowed her lips. "I'm Johanna Smith. It's nice to meet you."

Lacy nodded to her plate of food. "At least he bought you some dinner."

Johanna frowned and stiffened beside him. "What?"

She sneered at Mike. "You are paying for it, aren't you?"

Anger boiled within him. He knew she'd say something he didn't appreciate, but he hadn't imagined she'd say something that suggested he would be unkind to his date. He swallowed to keep from saying something he'd regret later. "Yes, I am. Thank you."

Lacy rolled her eyes and walked away.

"What was she talking about?" Johanna studied him. The confused expression that wrapped her face dug at his heart. He would explain everything to her on the way home.

Before he could respond, his cell phone rang. He pulled it out of his front pocket and read Nick's name on the screen. He pushed TALK. "Hey, Nick. Everything all right?"

He felt Wyatt, Gracie, and Johanna staring at him for any sign of trouble.

Nick still sounded elated. "Everything's great. I need you to do me a favor."

"Sure. Anything."

"Addy's water broke when she was making me rearrange the living room furniture. I've got just about all the furniture in the middle of the room."

"Okay."

"I wondered if you and Wyatt would go over there and put everything back for me. I can't get Drew to leave."

Drew's voice sounded in the distance. "Ain't no way I'm leaving my sister and my niece to go move furniture."

Mike laughed. "It's not a problem."

"Come on over to the hospital. I'll give you the keys to the house."

"Okay. See you after a while."

Mike hung up the phone and lifted his hands before the three of them attacked him at once for information. "Everything is fine. Nick just needs Wyatt and me to move some furniture at their house."

A collective sigh sounded around the booth.

"I'll take Johanna home then come back and get the keys and—"

Johanna frowned. "Mike, that's crazy. You don't need to drive to Hickory Hill then back. I'll just wait to go home until you're finished."

Mike shook his head. "It might be late, and I know your dad starts his early service at eight o'clock—"

Johanna cocked her head to the side. "I believe I've stayed up late before. I'll be fine."

Gracie interrupted their conversation. "Why don't you let me take her home?"

At the same time, Mike and Johanna said, "No."

"You don't need to do that," Johanna added.

Gracie put her napkin down in the middle of her plate. "I insist." She stood up and straightened her shirt. "Boys, you go pay for this, and I'll take Johanna home."

Johanna tried to decline again, but Gracie insisted.

Mike inwardly growled. Stubborn as a mule, Gracie would never back down until she got her way. But he needed to talk to Johanna. He needed to explain about Lacy. He peered into her eyes, noting the hurt that filled them. "I want to take you home," he whispered.

She averted her gaze. "It's okay. Thank you for dinner."

⁓⁓⁓

"Tell me your address. I'll put it in my GPS so you don't have to keep telling me where to turn."

Johanna told Gracie her address then buckled her seat belt.

Gracie winked at her. "Greta loves to ride in the car. Maybe she'll get good and tired and sleep well for me when I get home."

Johanna forced herself to smile. She didn't understand what had happened at the diner, but right now she simply wanted to go home and cry out to God.

"I love to drive through the country. It's so pretty." Gracie pointed out the windshield. "Look at those stars. Amazing."

Johanna nodded. Her mind kept replaying what the waitress had said. Obviously, Mike had dated the woman at some point, but it didn't make any sense to her that he would refuse to buy her dinner or pay for it or whatever she was talking about.

"I think I need to tell you about Lacy."

Johanna peered across the car at the woman she'd met only a few hours ago. "The waitress?"

"Yes. But I probably need to start at the beginning."

Johanna listened as Gracie told her about a no-women bet the four men had made several years ago, and how one by one they had all lost. She placed her finger on the side of her mouth. "Hmm. Except Mike. He's the winner. I guess that means you two get your wedding paid for."

"Oh, but, we're not—"

"Engaged?" Gracie raised her eyebrows and looked at her. "Honey, if Mike has anything to do with it, you will be."

Warmth traipsed up her neck at Gracie's words. She wanted him to ask her so badly. At least she thought she did. For a moment, earlier in the day, she'd thought he would ask her. But now, with what happened at the diner. . . She needed to know the whole story about the waitress. Surely, Mike was who she thought he was. He couldn't possibly have been fooling her family all this time.

Gracie popped her gum, and Johanna turned her attention back to the woman. Despite not knowing the woman very long, Johanna felt a natural drawing to her. Gracie seemed to be quite spirited, a real crackerjack, as her mother would say. But she also seemed as genuine as she was spirited.

She lifted her right hand off the wheel. "Now, let me tell you about Lacy. Mike had this crush on the girl forever. It was ridiculous. The man didn't know anything about her, but he had a crush on her just the same." Gracie reached over and patted Johanna's leg. "I know that probably hurts your feelings a bit, but I promise you the man is over the moon about you."

Johanna peered out the windshield. It did sting that Mike once had a crush on another woman. She remembered all the times she'd felt she should have experienced some sort of jealousy for Gavin, but she hadn't. She felt it now for Mike. The thought of Mike holding another woman's hand or looking at another woman the way he looked at her—it just made her sick to her stomach.

Gracie sneaked a quick peek back at the baby, who'd fallen asleep, then turned around and focused on the road. "So three years later Mike finally gets up the nerve to ask Lacy on a dinner date. They go, but he brings her back early, evidently without buying her dinner. It didn't work out."

Johanna frowned. "What happened?"

Gracie shrugged. "We don't really know. Mike won't say." Gracie turned down the air in the car. "Would you mind turning around and fixing Greta's head? It's kind of leaning over crooked."

Johanna turned around and folded a section of Greta's soft pink blanket. Gently, lifting the child's head, she tucked the blanket against the side of the car seat. Greta let out a contented sigh, and Johanna's heart melted. She turned back around. "Greta is absolutely precious."

"Especially when she's asleep." Gracie chuckled and swatted the air. "I'm just kidding. Thanks. But, back to Mike. You've known Mike a few months now. Have you ever heard him talk bad about anyone?"

Johanna thought a moment. "No, I haven't."

"That's just it. He won't talk about it. Just says they disagreed about faith. But he won't even tell us what he means by that." The GPS announced their arrival to her house, and Gracie pulled into the driveway. "Looks like we're here."

Johanna opened the door. "Thanks for bringing me home. It was really good to meet you." She paused. "And thanks for explaining things to me."

Gracie grabbed her hand before she got out. "Listen. Mike is a good man, and he is absolutely crazy about you. The fact that Mike McCauley won't talk about what happened during that date with Lacy speaks volumes about her, not him. Do you understand?"

Johanna smiled and nodded. "Yes. Thanks."

Once she stepped out of the car, the weight of the day bore down on her. Exhausted, she dragged her feet up the porch steps and into the house.

Her father met her at the door. "Are the baby and the mother okay?"

Johanna smacked her forehead with her hand. How could she have forgotten to call and update her family? "Daddy, I'm sorry I didn't call. Yes. The baby girl and her mother are fine. She'll be in NICU for a while, so we'll need to keep praying for her, but she's doing well."

"What's her name?" her mother asked.

"They haven't named her yet, but I think I'll go back to the hospital after church tomorrow and visit with Addy."

Her mother wrapped her arm around Johanna. "That sounds like a great idea, but you look exhausted. Go upstairs, get a warm bath, and then get in bed."

"Mama, that sounds like a wonderful plan."

Johanna made her way up the stairs. After starting her bath, she slipped into the warm waters and rested her head against the cool porcelain.

The waitress had surprised her. Her words had stung worse than any wasp sting she'd ever received. The fact that Mike once had a crush on another woman and for such a long time stabbed at her heart. Three years. She'd only known him three months.

God, Gracie says he is head over heels for me. But was he the same for the waitress? How can I know that what he feels for me, that what I feel for him is real? That it's from You?

God seemed especially quiet. Or maybe she was just tired and therefore not listening very well. She got out of the bath and slipped into her nightgown. Crawling into bed, she closed her eyes. She'd have to wait until tomorrow to figure it out.

Chapter 15

After taking one last long drink of her coffee, Johanna scooped up the present she'd bought for Nick and Addy's baby from the passenger's seat then walked into the hospital. She hadn't slept a moment the night before. Though she'd prayed God would allow her mind to rest, she continued to replay the concern and tension in the waiting room while Addy gave birth. Then her heart would swell anew with thanksgiving when Nick burst through the door with good news. Then Lacy's contemptuous expression and tone would push to the forefront of her mind, and she'd try to remember and believe all Gracie had said on the drive home.

But her mind was a tricky thing. It kept conjuring up images of Mike with Lacy on a date. She envisioned the woman's long brown hair cascading down one shoulder. Beyond the glasses, her sultry green eyes sparkled beneath long eyelashes. Looks of longing and adoration shone from Mike's gaze, and for a moment, his tongue dropped from his mouth like a dog that panted for water.

Get a grip, Johanna. Shaking her head, she blew out a breath at the dramatics of her thoughts. She pushed the elevator button. *Took that image a bit far, I think. Believe I'm feeling some good old-fashioned, green-eyed jealousy now.*

Though she'd wrestled with the fact that Mike had liked another woman, God reminded her over and again through the night that Mike had proven himself to be a man of God. She was reminded of Gracie's words of him not being willing to speak poorly of Lacy. Of Mike's prayer for Nick and Addy and their baby at the hospital. . . The way Johanna had seen Mike help his mother and his father at their house. The fact that he'd helped his friends at a moment's call. Even before Johanna knew it was Mike, the articles he'd written the past several years spoke of a love for God that could only come from Him.

She knew Mike to be a good man. A godly man. And she loved him.

The elevator door opened, and Johanna stepped onto the maternity floor—her favorite part of the hospital. She smiled at the teddy bears, lambs, sunshine, and balloon murals on the walls. After asking one of the nurses about Addy's location, she walked down the hall to the room.

Several voices pealed out from within the room. A wave of shyness washed over Johanna, and she gripped the present tighter. Yesterday she'd experienced such a deep concern for the woman she'd met only one other time that she simply had to see her again, to tell her how happy she was the baby had delivered safely.

Fearing Mike would be inside the room, and yet wanting him to be inside the room, Johanna willed her feet to move forward. Gingerly, she knocked on the doorjamb.

"Come on in," a voice boomed from inside. If she remembered correctly, it sounded like Drew.

Hesitantly, Johanna slipped inside the door. Seeing Addy in the bed, she ducked her chin and waved. "Hi. You may not remember me—"

Addy motioned her inside. "Of course, I remember you, Johanna. Please come on in."

Though her face was pale and her hair pulled back in a knot that stuck out at odd angles, Addy glowed like a woman who'd just been handed the whole world. Heat warmed Johanna's cheeks when she looked around the crowded room at Drew, Melody and Nick, and two women she'd never met before.

Addy motioned to her guests. "You know Nick, Drew, and Melody."

They nodded, and Johanna smiled back at them.

She pointed to the woman with short, sandy-blond hair. "This is my mother, Amanda." Then she pointed to the dark-haired woman. "And Nick's mother, Renee."

"It's nice to meet both of you."

Renee grabbed Johanna's hand. "Honey, we've just been dying to meet Mike's girl."

"Mom!" Nick groaned.

Amanda added, "She's every bit as pretty as Mike said."

"Mother!" Addy and Drew said at the same time.

Feeling dizzy from too much coffee and not enough food, Johanna prayed her knees would stay strong. She swallowed the embarrassment that welled in her throat then remembered the present crumbling beneath her death grip. She handed it to Addy. "I got the baby a present."

"You didn't have to do that."

"I wanted to."

Amanda patted Johanna's shoulder. "Renee and I are going to go check on our husbands. They went to get food over an hour ago."

Renee chuckled. "After driving straight through from Florida last night, we're starving."

Melody nudged Drew's arm. "Come on. We'll go, too. I'm hungry myself."

Drew frowned. "I'm fine."

Nick punched his arm. "Your sister is fine. I'm right here for her. She is my wife, you know." He turned to Johanna. "We can't get the guy to leave."

Melody grabbed his hand and pulled to try to get him up. "Let's let them be alone for a little while. We don't have to leave the hospital."

Reluctantly, Drew stood and followed his wife out of the room, leaving Nick, Addy, and Johanna alone. She took a step toward the door. "I'll let you two have some time alone."

"No, please." Addy motioned to the chair Drew had been sitting in. "Sit down. I'd like to visit a minute." She lifted up the package. "Besides, I'm dying to see what you brought."

Johanna wrung her hands together and sat down. This couple had occupied much of her thoughts and prayers in the last twenty-four hours, but actually sitting with them, she realized she really didn't know them at all.

Addy unwrapped the present and pulled out the pink-and-white sleeper outfit Johanna found at the department store. "Thank you so much." She laid the gift back in the box and handed it to Nick. "I remember you quite well from the library event."

Johanna nodded. "It was a good event. Having the two of you there made it a huge success. The children enjoyed the calf and the seed planting. I'm sure it was a first experience at petting a calf and planting a seed for many of them."

Nick lifted his right foot and rested it on his left knee. "I think you had them going reading that book as well. They watched you like they were watching a TV show."

Johanna grinned. Despite her normal bashfulness, when she read for children, something in her seemed to click, and her voice inflected with the events of the story.

"This may sound odd for me to say since this is only the second time we've met." Addy shifted in the bed. "But you're a godsend for Mike."

Johanna bit the inside of her lip. She already felt woozy from having not eaten breakfast. She didn't know how much more embarrassment she could take before she plastered the floor with her body.

"If that ain't the truth," Nick added. "I've never seen the man so happy. And he's the one who wanted a wife first."

"Nick!" Addy exclaimed.

Trying to change the subject, Johanna asked, "How's the baby?"

Nick smiled. "Perfect."

"Wonderful," Addy added.

"Have you picked out a name for her?"

Addy leaned forward. "Don't tell, but we're going with the name I picked out when I was fifteen."

Johanna furrowed her brows.

Nick huffed. "Yeah, the woman hounded me to marry her since she was no bigger than knee high to a grasshopper."

"Hey, now." Addy's eyebrows rose, and she glared at him.

He lifted his hands in surrender. "Okay. Okay. There's a little more to it than that."

Johanna chuckled at their antics. "So what is her name?"

Addy folded her hands in her lap. "Amanda Renee. After our mothers."

"When can you see her again?"

Addy peered at the door. Johanna turned and saw that a nurse had walked into the room.

"Looks like Nick and I can go right now." Slowly, Addy started to get up from the bed. Nick grabbed her hand to help her.

Johanna jumped out of her chair and headed for the door. "It was so good to talk with you both. I'm glad the baby is well."

Now standing, Addy shuffled around the bed. "She'll be in NICU for a little while, but she's doing well. Thanks for coming."

After saying their good-byes, Johanna walked out of the hospital and to her car. With her stomach queasy, she decided to head home. Her mind could think about Mike all it wanted, but her body needed some food.

<hr>

Mike had been waiting at the pond for well over two hours. He'd gone to the early service at Johanna's church, but Pastor Smith told him she'd felt so burdened for Nick and Addy that she'd visited them in the hospital instead.

Knowing Mike was anxious to talk to Johanna, the older man suggested he head to their house and wait for her there. Mike stood and paced in front of the bench. He looked at his watch. *Surely, she'll be here soon. I wanted to talk with her before everyone got back from church.*

He picked up the single red rose he'd bought for her, signifying she was his one love. He gazed up at the clear sky. *God, I pray she'll accept me.*

"Mike, what are you doing up here?"

He turned and saw Johanna making her way up the hill to the pond. Beautiful in a light green shirt that tied around the waist and white pants, she'd pulled back the sides of her hair in a clip of some kind. The breeze caught several wisps and blew them around her jaw. He spread his arms wide, still holding the rose in his hand. "I'm waiting for you."

She finished her trek then pulled away a strand of hair that stuck to her lip. "I saw your truck in the driveway, and—" She looked at the rose, and the color of her cheeks deepened. "Why are you waiting for me?"

"I need to talk to you." Mike stepped close to her. She peered up at him, and the expression of love shining from her eyes both humbled him and gave him courage. He caressed her cheek with the back of his hand. "I love you, Johanna."

"I know." She reached up and cupped her hand against his jaw. "I love you, too."

He couldn't resist. He lowered his head and gently touched his lips to hers. Releasing her, he started to lift his head, but she pulled him back to her, kissing him fully with passion and love. Unable to breathe and feeling too much emotion at one time, Mike stepped back. "Johanna, let me explain about Lacy."

She took a step closer to him. "I already know."

He stepped back. "Then I need to tell you about the bet."

She inched closer to him again. "Already know about that, too."

He cocked his head. "What else do you know?"

She pointed to his pocket. "I know there's a ring in that front pocket for me." She lifted her face and kissed his lips. "Am I right?"

His jaw dropped. "Johanna Smith!" He laid the back of his hand on her forehead. "Are you sick?"

She stomped her foot like a child. "Actually, I am a little queasy. I drank two cups of coffee and haven't had anything to eat yet because I was up all night thinking about Nick and Addy and their baby." She peered at him and stuck out her bottom lip. "And about you."

Mike let out a loud whoop. "Johanna, you are a hoot."

She wrinkled her nose at him as she pointed beneath her eyes. "Do these bags look funny to you?"

"I love the bags under your eyes." He touched her cheek. "And the dimple in your cheek. And your beautiful eyes." He placed a quick kiss on her mouth. "And your perfect lips." He raised one eyebrow as he stared at her. "So, you think I have something in my pocket?"

A full smile spread across her lips as she nodded. He reached into his pocket and pulled out the box. Opening it, she gasped at the small, delicate ring he'd picked out for her. She whispered, "It's beautiful."

Mike knelt down. He spread one hand toward the pond. "I wanted to ask you in your spot." He took her hand in his and peered into her eyes. "Johanna Smith, I love you. Will you be my wife?"

She nodded, and he jumped up, pulled her into his arms, and swung her around. Placing her back on her feet, he kissed her again. Releasing her, he searched her face. "How did you know?"

She brushed a strand of hair off her cheek. "You and Daddy were pretty obvious yesterday."

Mike laughed. "I thought we were being pretty sneaky."

Disbelief washed over Johanna's face.

He wrapped his arms around her. "I'm glad you bumped into me last spring."

She lifted up three fingers. "Took three times to get your attention."

"It will never take that long again."

Chapter 16

Johanna could hardly believe nine months had passed, and tomorrow she would be Mike's wife. True to their promise, Wyatt, Nick, and Drew had all been intricately involved in the planning of the ceremony, and they took care of all the bills. At first, her father had adamantly declined their offer, until they suggested he donate the money he'd have spent on the wedding to a couple at the church who felt called to foreign missions. Her father said he couldn't turn down an offer like that.

Her father had insisted he help Mike's parents pay and prepare the food for the rehearsal dinner. Johanna looked at the grandfather clock in the living room. The rehearsal had gone splendidly earlier in the day. Any minute Mike and his friends would arrive for dinner.

"Do I look okay?"

Johanna turned toward her now thirteen-year-old sister, Bethany, who was blossoming into a young woman. She wore a light blue shorts outfit with her long blond hair rolled in soft curls. She smiled, exposing the aqua bands put on her metal braces to match her bridesmaid dress. "You look lovely."

Amber flitted through the room. She held one silver sandal in the air. "I can't find my other shoe. Have you seen it?"

Johanna shook her head.

Bethany grabbed her hand and led her toward the door. "I think I saw it outside."

"Outside? Why would it be outside?"

Bethany shrugged. "You know Max likes your shiny shoes."

With a squeal, Amber rushed outside.

Johanna bit back a laugh. Pride swelled within her for her sister. Amber graduated from high school, earning a full music scholarship to a nearby small college. She'd even gotten an A in math.

The back door opened, and Johanna checked to see if it was Mike. Gavin peeked around the corner instead. "Hey."

She waved at her longtime friend. "Hi."

"Ready for tomorrow?"

"Definitely."

Amber walked in with two shiny silver shoes on her feet. She wrapped her arms around Gavin in a big hug. The silly grin that spread across his face made Johanna chuckle. His father continued to do well with the new medicine he'd started taking several months before. Amber already planned to spend much of her summer helping Gavin's mother care for her brood. Johanna knew Gavin wouldn't mind seeing Amber more often.

She made her way past them and looked out the kitchen window at her mom and dad grilling steaks, potatoes, and corn on the cob. It hadn't taken a lot of convincing when Johanna told Mike and their parents she simply wanted a cookout at her house for their wedding rehearsal dinner. Her mom and Mike's mom both had the reputation of being some of the best cooks in this part of the state.

Mike's truck pulled into the driveway, followed by his parents' car. Johanna ran outside to greet them.

"Where's your mother?" His mom lifted a pie from the backseat.

"My parents are around back, grilling."

She nodded for his dad to get the other dishes out of the backseat. "Come on. We need to help them get everything finished."

His dad winked and kissed Johanna's forehead then looked at his wife. "Whatever you say, dear."

As they walked away, Johanna smiled up at her fiancé. His sandy-brown locks were newly cut, and she reached up and touched the shorter hair. He growled as he kissed her lips. "One more day."

Another car sounded in the driveway, interrupting the moment. Johanna waved as Gracie and Wyatt pulled up in their minivan. She made her way to them and unbuckled two-and-a-half-year-old little Wyatt, while Gracie lifted out the barely toddling Greta.

Bethany ran up to Gracie. "You want me to take them to the backyard?"

Gracie sighed. "That would be wonderful."

Johanna watched as little Wyatt raced to the swing set her parents hadn't gotten rid of since she and her sisters were little. Greta was determined to walk, so Bethany had to hold her hand and move slowly behind the rambunctious Wyatt Jr.

Before Johanna could invite them inside, Drew and Melody pulled up in their Jeep. Nick, Addy, and their baby, Amanda, piled out of the backseat.

Johanna reached for the baby and clapped. "Come here, big girl."

The sweet cherub cackled and launched out of her mother's arms toward Johanna. Even though she was still a bit on the smaller side, Amanda continued to thrive and develop as she should.

The group meandered to the backyard and sat in lawn chairs beneath a large oak tree.

"Should be ready in about fifteen minutes," her mother called from beside the grill.

"Do you need any help?" Melody asked.

Mike's mother responded, "Nope. We're fine."

Johanna's heart warmed as she watched Mike's parents and her parents work together on the food. Mike's mother had come such a long way in the last several months. They'd even been attending her dad's church. Johanna knew God was healing her heart. Mike had given full credit to God for that. He insisted it was no coincidence that as his mother's love for Johanna blossomed, she remembered God's Word contained a promise—a promise of hope for the future. While it embarrassed Johanna whenever Mike praised God for bringing her into his mother's life, she was deeply grateful for the bond that had grown between her and the woman who would soon be her mother-in-law.

Johanna smiled at Mike and his friends. They sat in a line of sorts beside each other. By the expressions on their faces, she could see they were about to give each other a hard time about something.

Addy asked, "Are you all ready for tomorrow, Johanna?"

Johanna nodded. "I am. Hair at nine. Makeup at ten. Manicures and pedicures at eleven. A quick lunch then the wedding at two. I'm not going to have time to be nervous tomorrow."

"Have you seen the cake your mom made yet?" asked Melody. "It can't be any more beautiful than the one she made for Drew and me."

Johanna shook her head. "She's keeping it in the refrigerator in the garage. She won't let me see it."

Nick smacked at Mike's leg. "Are you ready for tomorrow, buddy?"

"Oh, yes." Mike grinned then wiggled his eyebrows at Johanna. She felt her cheeks flush.

"Really?" Nick crossed his arms in front of his chest. "You're ready for a woman to holler at you every morning for leaving stubbles in the sink when you shave?"

Addy squealed, "Nick Martin!"

Drew chimed in, "Or to grouch at you because you've forgotten to pick your socks up off the floor."

Melody cocked her head to one side. "Do you want me to show them right now that I can take you down?"

Wyatt howled. "And the two a.m. cravings for ice cream when she's seven months pregnant are killer."

Gracie smirked. "I know. And we're going to do it again."

The whole group gasped and looked from Gracie to Wyatt. Johanna sputtered, "Are you pregnant again?"

Gracie wrinkled her nose and pointed her thumb at Wyatt. "It's his fault."

A mischievous grin spread across Wyatt's lips. "I'll take credit for it."

They laughed, and her father called that the food was ready. After enjoying a delicious meal and nice fellowship, the crew loaded up and headed home. Johanna and Mike walked up to the pond and sat on the bench in silence as the sun set over the still waters.

Johanna rested her temple on Mike's shoulder. "This time tomorrow night we'll be husband and wife."

Mike wrapped his arm around her and pulled her closer to him. "I can hardly wait."

"I'm awestruck at God's blessing."

"As am I."

Johanna turned her face and kissed his jaw. "I love you, Mike."

Mike cleared his throat and stood. "I think we'd best be getting back to the house."

She stuck out her bottom lip. "What's wrong?"

He bent down and kissed her bottom lip then quickly stepped away from her. "You're entirely too cute, smell entirely too good, and I love you entirely too much. And you're not my wife until tomorrow."

Understanding filled her mind, and Johanna laughed. She stood up and grabbed his hand in hers. "Then let's head back to the house." As they walked down the hill, she leaned closer to him and whispered, "I can't wait for tomorrow either."

Epilogue

Two years later

Mike had never known his wife's true strength until she gripped his collar with her fist. "You've got to get me to the hospital right now."

"I know. I'm trying." Mike moved frantically through the house in search of the truck keys. He always put them on the key rack in the kitchen. Johanna had been the last one to drive the truck, and she never put them in the same place twice. *There is no way I'm going to mention that now.*

Out of sheer desperation, he opened the refrigerator. There they were, sitting on the butter. He shook his head. *I'm not even going to try to think about what weird concoction she was probably eating.* He yelled, "I got them."

"It's about time." She heaved from the other room. "I think I'm going to have this baby on the floor."

The last few months of Johanna's pregnancy had proved extremely interesting. Mike would argue with anyone that he had the sweetest, kindest wife in the world. She loved being his wife. She'd longed for children, and God blessed their prayers with this pregnancy. But he had no idea what happened to the woman he married when she reached her seventh month. His father promised him she would return to her senses soon.

He walked back into the living room and found Johanna gripping the back of a chair. She was leaned forward with her hand on the bottom of her stomach. "This is the worst pain in the world. It's like someone is stabbing me with a knife." She lifted up her face and gritted her teeth. "Feel this."

Mike touched her belly. It was hard as a basketball that had been inflated too much and was about to pop. And his wife, and he loved her with all his heart, she looked like she was about to pop.

When her breathing slowed and she took several long exhales, he wrapped his arm around her and hustled her out to the truck. He ran back in the house to get her purse and the baby bag. By the time he returned, she was gripping the door handle and groaning. Another contraction. He looked at his watch. It couldn't have been more than two minutes. They were coming fast.

Praying that God would give him grace for no red lights and no tractors or slow drivers in front of him, Mike pulled out of the driveway. He had turned onto the main road that led straight to the hospital when Johanna grabbed the door handle as well as his arm. He peeked at his wife. An expression of pure agony wrenched her face, and Mike begged God to ease the pain, even if just a little. Or at least to give her the strength to hang in there.

Two more contractions hit by the time he'd made the additional five-minute drive. Once there, he helped her out of the truck. She moved slow, and Mike wished he'd thought to get a wheelchair before he'd tried to get her out of the truck. Another contraction hit before they made it inside. He held her tight as she bent over and winced. Once inside, he blew out a slow breath. *Thank You, God, that we've made it to the hospital.*

He walked to the nurse at the front desk. He tried to remain calm, but he was slowly losing all capacity to do so each time he saw the extreme agony on Johanna's face. "My wife needs drugs. She's in a lot of pain, and I can't take it anymore." The woman harrumphed at him as she shoved a piece of paper across the desk.

Okay, that had not exactly come out in the best of ways. *God, I can't take it, though. She's dying, and I can't do anything to help her. It's even my fault, Lord. It's my fault.*

Another contraction kicked in, and Johanna doubled over again. Believing Johanna, the woman ran around the desk, grabbed a wheelchair from another room, and sat her in it. The nurse looked at him. "I've got to let the doctor know she's here. Hang tight for just a minute."

She started to walk away, but then she turned back and looked at him. "Are you okay? You look like you're about to be sick."

He motioned for her to go on. "I'm fine." He swallowed the knot in his throat and pulled at the collar of his T-shirt. He'd be fine as soon as someone did something to help Johanna's pain.

The emergency door opened behind them, and a familiar voice said, "Nurse! I need help. Nurse! Right now!"

Mike turned to see Drew helping a very full-term Melody through the door.

"Hurry!" He yelled again. Mike saw the look of panic in his friend's eyes. "Her water broke. Like ten minutes ago."

Melody muttered, "It's okay, Drew." She blew out a breath. "It's supposed to." She blew out another one. "It's going to be fine."

Drew's jaw dropped when he saw Mike. "What are you doing here?"

Mike pointed to his wife with his free hand. She held tight to his other, which was fine with him if it stopped some of her pain. "Johanna's in labor."

Drew pointed to Melody. "She is, too." He grabbed Mike's sleeve. "Man, this is awful. I can't take it. I can't do anything to help her."

Melody grabbed at Drew's hand. "Would you chill out?" She groaned, as a contraction must have hit her.

Johanna's grip on his hand tightened, as a contraction must have hit her as well. If the contraction didn't hurry up and subside, she was going to break every bone in his hand. Once again, he'd have never dreamed his sweet, angelic Johanna to be so strong.

The doors opened again, and Wyatt pushed in Gracie in a wheelchair. She smiled at Mike and Drew. "Time for baby number four." She grimaced for a moment with her hand on top of her belly then let out a slow breath. "Whew. That was a good one."

Mike wiped his brow with his free hand when Johanna finally loosened her tight grip. "You have got to be kidding me. If Addy goes into labor—"

"Already here," Melody muttered. "Called an hour ago."

Looking frantic, Drew leaned down and grabbed Melody's hand. "Don't talk, honey. Just concentrate on you and the baby. Everything is going to be fine."

Melody glared at him. "I am fine. You're the one freaking out."

"Oops." Johanna squeaked. "My water just broke."

Mike looked down at the liquid that ran down the front of the wheelchair. Tears rolled down Johanna's cheeks, and Mike couldn't decipher if she was scared, excited, happy, or simply still in so much pain it was leaking from her eyes. He motioned for the woman who'd gotten them a wheelchair. "Nurse! We've got to go."

The nurse shook her head and smiled. "It's baby night." She motioned for two other people to take Melody and Gracie, while she wheeled Johanna to the delivery room. "We've got us a full house."

As gingerly as possible, he helped Johanna out of the wheelchair. The nurse produced a gown of sorts. "Let's get her out of those clothes and into something more comfortable."

The woman worked with an efficiency Mike couldn't help but admire as she undressed and redressed his wife. He got the socks from the bag and did put those on for her, but it took him almost as long to do that as it took the nurse to change Johanna's clothes.

Johanna was calm as the nurse inserted her IV, checked her pulse, and felt her stomach. The woman looked at Mike. "Her contractions seem to be coming about every two minutes." She looked at Johanna. "I'm going to check to see where we are."

Again, Mike took Johanna's hand in his. She gripped it with the strength of a man, but Mike's heart melted when she looked up at him and tears streamed down her cheeks. "I'm scared," she whispered.

With his free hand, he brushed her hair away from her face. "You're doing so good, Johanna. I'm so proud of you."

She nodded, seemingly revived by his words. *Dear God, please let her be okay. Please let our baby come safely. Let the child be healthy. Keep me strong, too, Lord.*

The nurse pulled the curtain and checked Johanna. "Ten centimeters. She's ready." She turned to a woman standing in the doorway. "Go get the doctor in here." She patted the top of Johanna's leg. "Looks like you got here just in time, hon."

Things happened in a whirlwind after that with people coming and going and Johanna squeezing his hand as if she would never let go. He couldn't watch. He was too scared, too excited, too preoccupied with whispering words of encouragement in Johanna's ear.

A cry sounded through the room as the doctor lifted up the baby. His baby. Their baby. "It's a boy."

Tears swelled in his eyes, and he placed his forehead against Johanna's. "Good job, Johanna. You did so good."

The nurse wiped the baby off and placed him on Johanna's chest for just a moment. Mike kissed his wife. "I love you, Johanna." He kissed his son. "And I love you."

Mike cut the cord; then he picked up his son and walked him to the table where they would check to make sure he was fine.

After kissing Johanna once more, he walked to the waiting room to tell their family the news. With a happiness and joy he'd never known in all his life, he pushed open the doors and announced, "A baby boy. Seven pounds even."

His parents and hers squealed and ran up to hug him. "And he's beautiful."

"How's Johanna?" her father asked.

"She's perfect. She's wonderful. She's absolutely amazing."

Johanna's mother giggled. "But she's okay after the delivery, right?"

Mike laughed and nodded. "Yes."

He looked around the room and saw Nick's parents and Drew and Addy's parents, and Wyatt's and Gracie's. "Have you heard anything from any of them yet?"

"Not yet," Wyatt's father said. He grabbed Mike's hand in a firm shake. "But congratulations." For the next few minutes, he hugged the people who had been such an integral part of his life. He'd grown up with these people's sons, and they'd been like second parents to him. They'd seen him through thick and thin—teen years, farming, the death of his brother—everything he'd ever gone through and lived through. He was suddenly overwhelmed with thanksgiving that they would all be here at the same time.

As Mike turned to walk back to his wife and new son, Nick burst through the doors. He yelled, "A boy. Nine pounds, fifteen ounces."

His and Addy's families squealed.

Before they had time to even hug him, the door opened again. Wyatt called, "A boy. Six pounds, three ounces."

Mike laughed. It seemed too absurd for words that they were all having babies on the same day, and all boys.

Drew pushed through the doors, whooping like a wild man. "It's a boy." He high-fived his dad and lifted his mom in the air and twirled her around. "But we got us a surprise! Remember how Melody refused any ultrasounds after reading an article about. . ." Drew swatted the air. "Oh, I can't remember what it was about. Anyway, there were two of them in there. Two boys. Five pounds, six ounces, and six pounds, one ounce." He shook his head. "I knew she looked awful big for just one kid."

The men shook hands and congratulated each other. Five boys born on the same day. Drew sucked in his breath and hooked his fingers through his jeans' belt loops. "Yep. It's pretty cool that we all had boys on the same day." He shrugged. "Course, I don't see none of y'all having two babies at one time."

Wyatt huffed. "Whatever. I have four kids. Double what you got."

"Well, mine was the biggest," Nick added, pointing to his chest.

Mike crossed his arms in front of his chest. "Mine was born first."

Drew puffed out his chest. "Oh yeah, well, I bet you my sons. . ."